PRAISE FOR WIFED IN INDIA

Reading Wifed in India was like looking into a mirror. It felt as if someone has peeked into my life and written it. At some point it started feeling so familiar... That I had goosebumps. The way Pari had evolved herself...is commendable... I think every woman goes through these ups and downs in her life at some point of time . Relationships are so complex and interwoven.. Harvinder has beautifully brought out the things in a new light . Her unique perspective of looking at life and relationships........coping and balancing her emotions.....is so deep and intense...She has wonderfully brought out the importance of Indian culture and traditions and blended it with modernity . Congratulations Harvinder and my best wishes to you on your future endeavours. Love u loads .

—— SEEMA SANDEEP, HEADMISTRESS, ARMY SCHOOL PATIALA

As we "do life together" as they say these days, challenges arise in any relationship, be it rooted in tradition, beliefs, routine, or just simmering resentment bought on over years of feeling like you're not really valued? That you come last?

How do you fix a wounded relationship? Without guilt? Without blame? Without hurt?

"Wifed in India" offers a roadmap to peace that is relatable to everyone.

—— THERESE O'NEIL, BUSINESS COACH, AUSTRALIA

Wifed in India offers a window into relationship dynamics, spirituality, and personal growth. Beyond the role of a wife, it speaks to the universal journey of womanhood and migration, of rebuilding identity, reconnecting with love through respect and self-knowledge, and finding strength even when everything seems lost. This book is a beautiful metaphor for rediscovering ourselves and embracing the wholeness of love and life.

—— FABIOLA CAMPBELL, CEO, PROFESSIONAL MIGRANT WOMEN

WIFED IN INDIA

HARVINDER K

KAYA DELIGHT PTY LTD

Wifed in India: From Shadows to Light: A Wife's Quest

© 2024 by Harvinder K

Published by Kaya Delight Pty Ltd.

Author and Book design by Harvinder K

Editing by Pooja Badola

Cover design by Aaniyah Ahmad

First Edition, 2024

For more information, visit www.wifedinindia.com

For permission requests, please contact the publisher.

Legal Disclaimer for *Wifed in India*

The information provided in this book, *Wifed in India*, is for general informational purposes only. All information is provided in good faith, however, we make no representation or warranty of any kind, express or implied, regarding the accuracy, adequacy, validity, reliability, availability, or completeness of any information in this book.

The contents of this book are not intended to replace professional advice or services. The author and publisher shall not be held liable for any loss or damage, including but not limited to indirect, incidental, special, consequential, or punitive damages, arising out of or in connection with the use of, or reliance on, any information provided in this book.

The experiences and viewpoints expressed in *Wifed in India* are personal to the author and are not intended to represent any universal truths. Individual experiences may vary, and readers are encouraged to consider their own unique circumstances and seek professional advice as needed.

All characters, names, places, and events in this book are either the product of the author's imagination or used fictitiously. Any resemblance to real persons, living or dead, or actual events is purely coincidental.

DEDICATIONS

To my loving Mother,
Sardarni Charanjit Kaur,
and my fearless Father,
Late Sardar Shangara Singh Kehal (1952-2022).
Your strength and kindness have guided me through everything.
Thank you for your endless support and warmth.

ACKNOWLEDGMENTS

I am deeply grateful for the unwavering support throughout the journey of writing "Wifed In India." This book, born from countless hours of dedication, was made possible by the encouragement of my family and friends.

To my husband, **Saurabh**, your patience and encouragement have been my strength. Your love fuelled my creativity and determination. Thank you for being my rock.

To my children, **Augustus and Onyx**, your smiles and energy inspired me. Thank you for understanding when mommy needed to work on her book.

"Wifed In India" is a testament to your love and faith in me. I am deeply grateful for your roles in making this dream a reality.

With heartfelt gratitude,

Harvinder

FOREWORD

Pari sat in the cozy living room, watching her twelve-year-old twins, Kush and Luv, deeply engrossed in playing Roblox on their iPads. The room was alive with the sounds of their animated discussion, their excitement palpable.

"The harder your quest, the faster you level up," Kush explained, his eyes glued to the screen. "But only if you stay focused and navigate challenges swiftly," he insisted, his voice filled with conviction.

Luv nodded thoughtfully, expanding on the art of e-warfare, "Sure, you can buy skins and accessories with robux for some help, but in the end, it's your strategies that get you past the real obstacles.

Intrigued by their conversation, Pari asked, "Do all your online friends support you in your quest?"

Luv shook his head. "Naah, they are busy with their own quests."

Kush elaborated, "All my friends are heroes in their own instances of the game on their personal accounts."

Pari, ever curious, continued, "Then why do you insist on playing online at the same time with your friends? Can't you just play by yourself?"

Luv responded enthusiastically, "Because playing together is fun. Even though everyone focuses on their own quests, we can see each other when we cross paths. We might help each other when there are shared benefits and get rewarded for it as well!"

As Pari listened, a warm smile spread across her face. Gently embracing her twins, she reflected, "And life is just like that, too." This moment, shared with her children, mirrored her own journey. Their words resonated deeply within her, drawing a poignant parallel between the virtual quests in a game and the real-life quests we all undertake. As she drifted away in thought, she contemplated her own quest, filled with challenges and rewards, much like the ones her sons navigated so adeptly on their screens.

Dear reader,

Just as Luv and Kush find joy and meaning in their virtual quests, we too navigate the complex landscapes of our lives. This book chronicles such a journey —a story of love, resilience, and transformation. As you turn these pages, may you find inspiration in the challenges faced, the strength uncovered, and the triumphs celebrated. Join Pari in exploring this heartfelt tale, and may it resonate with your own quests and dreams...

Happy Reading!

Warm regards,

Harvinder

PART ONE

"It is a truth universally acknowledged, that opposites often find each other most intriguing."

-Jane Austen

CHAPTER 1

PARI'S WORLD

On a rainy July afternoon in 1981, Pari was born at the Military Hospital in Bhatinda Cantt.

"She's here," the nurse announced, bringing Pari into the world.

Baldev Kaur Bajwa, her mother, shed tears of joy. "She's perfect," she whispered, gazing at her daughter.

Captain Harbhajan Singh Bajwa, her father, stood proudly by, his heart swelling with pride. "Meet our little Pari," he said, introducing her to the family.

"She's a roly-poly baby," someone commented, noticing her chubby cheeks and tiny limbs.

"And look at those wide eyes," another family member remarked. "She's already so curious about the world."

Baldev smiled through her tears. "Our curious little Pari," she said softly, cradling her daughter close.

Relatives, quick to judge, compared her dark complexion to a cast iron skillet, contrasting her with her fair and beautiful mother.

"Bhenji, Kudi ne taan tave naal shart layi hoi aa, kaun vyah karu ede naal!"

"Oh dear!" Pammi Aunty, dressed in a vibrant salwar kameez, expressed shocking disappointment at the complexion of her newborn niece, remarking that she has laid a challenge with the griddle thus won't get a suitable groom in future.

Pari instantly became a topic of conversation in a community where fair skin was synonymous with prosperity.

Despite the superficial comments, Pari's parents remained unfazed, welcoming their daughter with love and joy. However, visitors often voiced their disappointment, remarking, "Oh dear! She's quite dark, but she'll grow into her looks."

Pari's parents, created a nurturing environment that balanced strict discipline with a dedication to education and personal growth. Her father instilled in Pari and her brother Shera a sense of duty, punctuality, and respect for authority. His strict regimental discipline was balanced by Baldev's nurturing approach and emphasis on education, fostering intellectual curiosity and a love for learning in Pari.

Despite her mother's fair, tall, and conventionally beautiful appearance, Pari did not fit this traditional mold of beauty. Mrs. Bajwa, a dedicated teacher, always dressed in elegant Patiala salwar-kameez, instilled in Pari a high value on education, driving her to excel academically and develop a strong work ethic.

Growing up in Bhatinda, Pari's early years were marred by unkind remarks from both adults and children. One cousin's infamous comparison led others to chant "Kaali! Kaali!" The hurtful words seeped into her consciousness, and at just three years old, she ran crying into her mother's arms, unable to articulate her pain. Eventually, she found the words: "Mamma! Why am I not as fair as you? Everyone calls me Kaali!" Her mother, understanding her anguish, spoke with a blend of wisdom and warmth. "My dear, there's no such thing as dark or fair. What truly matters is confidence. Remember, my Pari will excel in her studies, achieve great things, and wear fabulous clothes. Those same people who judge you now will one day see your true self. Confidence is always more important than looking good."

To lighten the mood and give Pari a way to handle her peers, Baldev added with a playful glint in her eye, "And you know, Kaali is a powerful goddess. Her skin is chocolatey, just like yours. Next time, just thank them for comparing you to such a divine figure."

At that tender age, this example was enough for Pari to realise that people with her complexion could also achieve greatness. Mrs. Bajwa continually reinforced this belief, telling her, "You are strong and beautiful, just like Goddess Kaali." She built Pari's self-esteem by reminding her that she embodied the same fierce strength and resilience as the revered goddess. This reinforcement helped Pari understand that she was capable of greatness, just like the powerful deity she was compared to.

Goddess Kaali is a fierce and powerful deity, symbolising strength, resilience, and fearlessness. She is revered for her dark complexion, representing the destruction of evil and the triumph of good. Her image inspires those who feel marginalised, reminding them of their inherent power and potential.

Kaali's strength became a cornerstone of Pari's life, guiding her from the shadows of societal biases into the light of self-belief and achievement. The story of Kaali encouraged Pari to rise above her challenges and become a force of change and empowerment.

Mrs. Bajwa's wisdom and reassurance became a beacon of hope and strength for Pari. The idea of confidence over beauty took root in Pari's heart, though she would grapple with society's prejudices for years to come.

AT SCHOOL, PARI'S INVOLVEMENT IN EXTRACURRICULAR ACTIVITIES included a deep passion for dance, particularly the school dance program 'Saraswati Vandana'. She practiced diligently, pouring her heart into every movement. However, the school's performing arts teacher, Mrs. Kapoor, seemed to favour students who fit the conventional standards of beauty. Pari noticed how students with fairer skin were given more opportunities to perform solos and lead roles in musical events.

Mrs. Vani Kapoor, the school's performing arts teacher, was a woman in her mid-forties, always impeccably dressed in elegant saris that reflected her sophisticated taste and attention to detail. She carried herself with an air of authority and grace, making her presence felt in any room she entered. Known for her strict and disciplined approach to teaching, Mrs. Kapoor had a keen eye for detail and a high standard for excellence, often pushing her students to strive for perfection. However, she had a particular preference for students who fit conventional standards of beauty, which often influenced her selection for lead roles and solos. This bias, rooted in traditional views, often overshadowed the true talents of her students.

One day, after being overlooked yet again, Pari, dressed in her neat school uniform, summoned the courage to approach Mrs. Kapoor. "Ma'am, I've been practicing very hard and would like a chance to perform in Saraswati Vandana at the upcoming school event."

Mrs. Kapoor, draped in an elegant saree, responded dismissively, "Of course, you can play the background dancer."

"Ma'am, I've been dancing in the background for many years. I was told that only senior students can perform as the lead, and this year, all the students are junior to me. I'm in grade 9, so I should get a chance to be the lead."

"Well, the lead I have chosen has the X factor, and my decision is final."

Crushed by Mrs. Kapoor's words and feeling dishonoured, Pari's hope to be considered for the lead in Saraswati Vandana shattered. That evening, she poured her heart out to her mother, sharing her frustrations and the disheartening conversation with Mrs. Kapoor. Her mother embraced Pari as she cried, helplessly repeating, "If I had been as tall and fair as you, I wouldn't have had to go through all this. I wouldn't have had to endure all this. Why didn't God make me like you? Why wasn't I made to be liked instead of mocked?"

Mrs. Bajwa tried to console Pari with every possible explanation in the book, but she only found solace in the warmth of her embrace. Being in the arms of her mother, Pari was ensconced in a warm and safe place, this was home. There wasn't a problem that didn't melt in her mother's hug.

She reached out, taking Pari's hand in hers, squeezing it reassuringly. "If Mrs. Kapoor can't see your talent, others will. You have a gift, Pari, and no one can take that away from you. Do you want me to speak to her on your behalf?"

Pari immediately shook her head, her voice firm and resolute. "No, Mamma. That wouldn't be right. If I don't earn my achievements on my own, they won't mean anything."

Pari often found herself selected for debates and quizzes, yet conspicuously overlooked when it came to cultural dances. Her teachers seemed to favour peers who fit the conventional standards of attractiveness. Each instance of being passed over for these activities was a sharp reminder of society's relentless focus on appearance. The sting of these rejections cut deep, but instead of succumbing to bitterness, Pari transformed her frustration into a driving force for her academic pursuits. She poured her energy into her studies with unwavering determination, resolute in her quest to prove her worth through her intellectual achievements and hard work.

This pattern began early in her school life. Whenever there was an announcement for participants in the school debates or quiz competitions, Pari was among the first names on the list. Her teachers recognised her sharp intellect, quick wit, and eloquence. However, when the time came for selecting students for dance performances or other cultural activities, she noticed a clear preference for those who matched the conventional standards of beauty.

The exclusion from these activities stung more than she let on. Pari longed to be part of the vibrant dances, to express herself through the fluid movements and rhythmic beats. Each rejection felt like a confirmation of society's shallow values, a reminder that in the eyes of many, appearance trumped ability.

Mrs. Bajwa couldn't bear the thought of Pari getting lost in a sea of self-doubt and disappointment, particularly during the challenging teenage years. She feared that these doubts could derail Pari's path in life, leading her to lose faith in society and trust in people. Mrs. Bajwa didn't want Pari to harden like a stone; rather, she wanted her daughter to develop just enough resilience to allow only those worthy of her trust into her heart. The recent incident at school deeply worried Baldev. She knew that if Pari built walls around herself, they would be nearly impossible to break down. Pari had always been determined, capable of achieving anything she set her mind to, and if she decided to shut people out, it could destroy her chances of forming meaningful relationships in the future. The thought of her daughter ending up alone due to misplaced expectations was a nightmare for Baldev, and she felt helpless about how to prevent it.

The next morning, after Pari left for school, Mrs. Bajwa decided to seek advice from her cousin sister, Gurkiran, who was the Principal of a women's college in Bhatinda. Mrs. Bajwa believed that Gurkiran Thind, who managed around two-thousand female students each year, might have effective strategies for motivating young girls and guiding them through difficult times.

Mrs. Gurkiran Thind was a wise and experienced educator, known for her ability to mentor and inspire her students. Baldev hoped that her sister could provide the guidance Pari needed to navigate these turbulent teenage years without losing her sense of self-worth and trust in others.

Mrs. Thind listened to Pari's story and spoke to her gently. "Hello Pari, I hear you had a terrible day?"

"Yes, Aunty. I've been overlooked for my dancing skills my entire school life. This year, my performing arts teacher promised me a chance but then backed out. I feel so betrayed. Why did she give me hope if she didn't mean it?" Pari sobbed, the disappointment cutting deep.

This broken promise was a culmination of years of feeling "not enough," overshadowed by others due to her darker complexion and perceived insignificance. It fuelled her fear of never being truly appreciated by anyone outside her family, leaving her struggling to find her self-worth.

"That's disheartening indeed. But I understand where your PA teacher is coming from. Some people don't realise the damage their false promises can cause."

Pari looked up with tears in her eyes. "So you also think I didn't deserve the lead role?"

Mrs. Thind wanted to broaden Pari's perspective and ground her in reality. "Have you seen Hindi movies? Actresses like Asha, Sharmila, Waheeda, Rani and many more are of average height and looks. In real life, makeup, shoes, and clothes can transform you into a glamor queen. What you need is the skill to fund your dreams. Focus on the path that makes it attainable rather than believing in a magical transformation."

As a psychology major and a member of the civil services selection board, Mrs. Thind continued, "I interview women for executive roles, and they pay attention to their appearance just as you should. It's important to balance internal skills with a polished external image. Hard skills will pay the bills, but external appearance can ensure a quick foot in the door. The key is to maintain both."

Pari, feeling a sense of clarity, asked, "So has Mum been lying that my skills were enough to make up for my looks?"

"Pari, it's age-appropriate to focus on skills in your early years. However, as you grow, understanding the importance of a balanced approach is crucial. Your hard skills form the foundation, while a polished appearance can help you seize opportunities."

That night, as Pari reflected on her aunt's words, she realised the power she had over her appearance and felt a renewed sense of control over her circumstances. Her aunt's worldly wisdom gave her the strength to embrace her external image alongside her skills.

The next morning, before leaving for school, Pari hugged her mother. "Thank you, Mamma. I understand now. I will continue to work hard and let my skills speak for themselves. I want to be recognised for what I can do, not just how I look. Because now I know that looks can be enhanced with the money I would earn from my skills!"

Mrs. Bajwa gave her a knowing look, but Pari, grabbing her cycle, laughed, "Mumma, I'm 14 and crushing on boys, not an 80-year-old grandma. Just chill okay." Mrs. Bajwa sighed, thinking, "Waheguru, take care of her, Babaji."

IN THE DAYS AHEAD, PARI'S DEDICATION TO ACADEMICS AND extracurricular activities paid off. She excelled in her studies, participated actively in various school events, and became a role model for her peers. Her teachers began to notice her relentless drive and resilience.

Meanwhile, Capt. Bajwa envisioned a future where Pari would excel by pursuing the prestigious UPSC path to become an Indian Administrative Service (IAS) officer. When Pari turned twelve, he subscribed to "Competition Success Review," a renowned magazine for civil service aspirants. Every month, he would guide her to read the editorials, highlighting the importance of staying informed and cultivating a strong knowledge base.

One evening, Capt. Bajwa and Pari sat in their cozy living room. The soft glow of the lamp cast a warm light as Capt. Bajwa handed her the latest issue of the magazine.

Capt. Bajwa: "Pari, I want you to start reading this magazine. The editorials are insightful and will help you stay informed about the world."

Pari: "But, Papa, isn't it too early for me to read something like this?"

Capt. Bajwa: "Not at all, beta. Knowledge is never too early. Start with the editorials, and over time, you can read interviews of successful IAS officers. Their stories will inspire you and build your character."

Pari: "Alright, Papa. I'll give it a try."

Capt. Bajwa: "Good girl. Remember, perseverance and dedication are key. These stories will show you that with the right mindset, you can achieve anything."

With her father's encouragement, Pari felt a surge of motivation. The magazine became a gateway to a world of knowledge and inspiration, shaping her resilience and dedication toward her future goals. Reading it regularly, she absorbed the stories of successful individuals, which fortified her determination to excel and achieve her own dreams.

Pari's parents, with their unwavering guidance, imparted invaluable life lessons to her. They deeply believed in sharing their wisdom to cultivate the values essential for her success. Their nurturing approach was meticulously designed to set Pari on a clear path to realising her fullest potential, never missing an opportunity to refine her perspective.

One such incident happened at the age of sixteen years, while Shera was learning to ride a motorbike with their dad, Pari came home from her tuition classes and watched from the sidewalk in front of their home. Noticing her interest, her father asked, "Pari, would you like to try riding the motorbike?"

Pari hesitated, "Papa, it's a motorcycle. Isn't that a boy's thing?"

Her father, perplexed, responded, "Pari, I believe my daughter can fly a helicopter if she wants to. Why limit yourself with such thoughts? In today's world, you and Shera have equal opportunities."

Inspired by her father's confidence, Pari decided to learn how to ride the motorbike. After a two-day crash course from her dad, she was riding like a pro. This experience reinforced the lesson that in the 21st century, boys and girls are equal, and girls can achieve anything they set their minds to, just like boys.

Pari and Shera's development was her parents' mission, evident throughout their formative years. Their parents' dedication bore fruit as they excelled in their respective fields. Shera, Pari's brother, excelled in sports and became the house captain, inspiring Pari with his achievements and dedication. He was known for his athletic prowess, leading his house to numerous victories in inter-house competitions. His leadership and commitment to excellence served as a motivating force for Pari.

In her final year of high school, Pari was elected Headgirl of Bhatinda Cantt School—a prestigious position that recognised her hard work, leadership, and dedication. This triumph was a proud moment for her entire family. The role brought significant responsibilities and challenges, teaching Pari an invaluable lesson: when you showcase your skills and excellence, they overshadow superficial judgments about external appearances.

Capt. Bajwa felt immense pride, recalling how his early introduction of leadership books played a crucial role in his children securing the prestigious leadership positions at school.

Both Pari and Shera embodied their parents' aspirations, making them proud with every milestone they achieved. Shera's success in sports and leadership as house captain and Pari's distinguished role as Head girl were reflections of the strong foundation their parents had laid. Together, they exemplified the values of hard work, dedication, and the pursuit of excellence, becoming beacons of inspiration for each other and their peers.

One evening, after successfully organising the school's annual cultural fest, Pari was summoned to the Principal's office. Unsure of what to expect, she took a deep breath and knocked on the door.

"Come in," a familiar voice called.

Pari entered the room, her heart pounding slightly. Principal Mrs.

Mehra was seated at her desk, a warm smile spreading across her face as she looked up.

Mrs. Mehra, 55, possessed a distinguished air, blending authority with an inviting presence. Her hair, elegantly styled in a bun, and her understated jewelry highlighted her preference for simplicity and practicality over ostentation. She typically wore well-fitted salwar kameez, which added to her professional appearance. Known for her strictness, fairness, and keen eye for talent, she commanded respect from both students and staff.

"Ah, Pari. Please, have a seat," Mrs. Mehra gestured to the chair opposite her.

Pari sat down, her mind racing with thoughts of what might be coming next.

"I wanted to speak with you personally, Pari," Mrs. Mehra began, her tone gentle yet authoritative. "You've done an exceptional job as Head girl this year. The cultural fest today was one of the best we've ever had, and I know much of that success is due to your hard work and dedication."

Pari's cheeks flushed with pride and a bit of embarrassment. "Thank you, Ma'am. It was a team effort, really."

Mrs. Mehra nodded. "Yes, but a good leader makes a team work well together. You've shown remarkable leadership, organisation, and empathy. These qualities go beyond academic achievement."

Pari smiled, feeling a swell of pride. "I've always tried to do my best, Ma'am."

Mrs. Mehra leaned forward, her expression turning more serious. "Pari, I've been a principal for many years, and I've seen countless students pass through these halls. I've watched you grow into an outstanding young woman. But I also know that your journey hasn't been easy. Society often places undue emphasis on superficial qualities, and I'm aware of the challenges you've faced because of that."

Pari's smile faded slightly, and she nodded. "It's been difficult at times, Ma'am. People can be very judgmental."

"Yes, they can," Mrs. Mehra agreed. "But you've shown something very important, Pari. You've demonstrated that skills, talent, and character truly matter. You've earned respect and admiration through your actions and achievements."

Pari felt a lump forming in her throat. "There were times when I wondered if my efforts would ever be enough to overshadow the way people perceive me," she admitted softly.

Mrs. Mehra's eyes softened. "And now, do you still wonder?"

Pari took a moment to gather her thoughts. "No, Ma'am. I've realised that I have the power to define my own worth. My Aunt, Mrs. Gurkiran Thind, has mentored me over the past couple of years, helping me get over the initial hiccups teenage years can bring. Her guidance gave me the power to focus on my strengths, which has transformed me into what I am today. My skills and hard work have brought me opportunities and recognition. Being elected as Head girl, organising events, and excelling academically have shown me that I can achieve anything if I put my mind to it."

Mrs. Mehra smiled proudly. "Mrs. Thind is exactly right. You've turned challenges into stepping stones, and that's what true success looks like. Remember, Pari, the world will always have people who judge based on superficial criteria. But there will also always be people who see the real you and value you for your true worth. I am one of those people, and I have no doubt that you will continue to shine brightly, no matter where life takes you."

Tears welled up in Pari's eyes, but they were tears of joy and gratitude. "Thank you, Ma'am. Your belief in me means more than I can say."

Mrs. Mehra stood up and walked around the desk, placing a comforting hand on Pari's shoulder. "You've earned every bit of it, Pari. Keep pushing forward, and never let anyone make you feel less than you are. The world needs more leaders like you."

Pari felt a warmth spread through her, her aunt's and principal's words reinforcing her resolve and filling her with a renewed sense of purpose. This conversation marked a pivotal moment in her journey. It wasn't just about a role in a school performance; it was about understanding her worth and the values she wanted to uphold.

Pari stood up, feeling a renewed sense of purpose and confidence. "I will, Ma'am. Thank you for everything."

As she left the Principal's office, Pari felt as though a weight had been lifted from her shoulders. The ever-lingering fear about whether superficial qualities or skills would win had finally been dispelled. She knew now, beyond a shadow of a doubt, that her abilities, character, and hard work would always be her greatest assets. With this newfound clarity and confidence, she was ready to take on whatever challenges lay ahead, knowing that she was valued and capable of achieving greatness.

As Pari approached high school graduation, she was filled with a mix of excitement and trepidation. Her academic record was stellar, and she had set her sights on a prestigious university. Her parents, though proud, were also aware of the societal pressures that still loomed over her. The expectation to conform to conventional standards of beauty and behaviour was ever-present.

Pari had a deep passion for beautiful clothes, as they provided an escape from the reality of not fitting into conventional beauty standards. Over time, with her dedication to fitness and a focus on grooming, she developed into a strikingly attractive young woman by the end of high school. Her well-formed physique and polished appearance made her stand out, complementing her natural grace and elegance.

With her research and artistic skills, Pari decided to pursue a career as a fashion designer. Her goal was to empower girls who felt disadvantaged by their natural appearance, helping them to look and feel their best. This purpose was deeply rooted in her own struggles; having faced similar challenges since childhood, she wanted to use her experiences to support others. Her journey from feeling out of place to becoming a confident, well-groomed young woman inspired her mission to make fashion accessible and uplifting for all.

At high school, Pari was open about her ambitions and future career plans. She closely followed global fashion trends and spent her weekends designing and stitching her own clothes. She often held impromptu fashion shows for her mother, who always encouraged her to keep improving her sewing skills. Her dedication to her craft and her desire to help others through fashion fuelled her journey toward becoming a designer who could make a real difference.

THE LIVING ROOM, MODESTLY FURNISHED, HAD FAMILY photographs on the walls and a large bookshelf filled with academic and military books. The atmosphere was tense, with Capt. Bajwa sitting on a sofa, looking stern, while Mrs. Bajwa stood nearby, trying to remain calm and composed. Pari sat quietly, listening.

Mrs. Bajwa spoke softly, "Harbhajan ji, I think we need to discuss this again. Pari has shown so much talent and passion for fashion designing. She deserves a chance to pursue her dreams."

Capt. Bajwa, in a dominating tone, replied, "This discussion is over, Baldev. Fashion designing is not a viable career. We're not a business family with connections in the garment industry. She must focus on something that guarantees a stable income. Computer science is the only path forward, and she's more than capable of succeeding in it."

Mrs. Bajwa pleaded, "But Harbhajan ji, she's so talented. You've seen the clothes she makes, the intricate designs. She has the potential to do something extraordinary."

Capt. Bajwa raised his voice, "Potential? What good is potential if it leads to a life of uncertainty? She needs a degree that guarantees a secure future. This is not up for debate."

Gathering courage, Pari said, "Dad, I understand your concerns, but fashion designing is my passion. I've researched the industry, and I know I can make a career out of it. Many successful designers started just like me."

Capt. Bajwa sternly responded, "Pari, you are too young to understand the harsh realities of life. Passion won't pay the bills. You will do as I say and study computer science. That's final."

Trying to stay calm, Mrs. Bajwa said, "Harbhajan ji, listen to her. She's not asking to abandon her education. She just wants to follow a different path. Why can't we support her in that?"

Capt. Bajwa interrupted, "Because it's not practical! Baldev, you're filling her head with unrealistic dreams. This is my house, and I make the decisions. She will study computer science. End of discussion."

Frustrated, Mrs. Bajwa insisted, "Harbhajan ji, you're not being fair. She deserves to have a say in her own future. We should be encouraging her dreams, not crushing them."

Capt. Bajwa roared, "Enough, Baldev! This conversation is over. Pari will do as I say, or she can get married and follow her dreams with her husband's support. But not with my money."

With tears in her eyes, Pari said, "Mom, it's okay. I'll do computer science. I'll figure it out." While she was thinking, "I can't bear to see you pleading with Papa anymore on my behalf. Maybe one day, when I have my own money, I can still pursue fashion designing."

Sighing deeply, Mrs. Bajwa said, "Harbhajan ji, I hope you realise what this means for her. You're pushing her into something she doesn't want, and that's not how we should be guiding our children."

Unmoved, Capt. Bajwa replied, "She will thank me later when she has a stable job and a secure life. That's what matters."

Defeated, Mrs. Bajwa said, "Pari, I'm sorry. I tried."

Pari nodded, "I know, Mom. I'll make the best of it. I promise."

The room fell silent as the tension lingered in the air. Capt. Bajwa remained resolute, while Mrs. Bajwa looked at Pari with a mixture of sadness and hope. Pari, feeling both trapped and determined, resolved to find a way to achieve her dreams despite the obstacles.

In the Bajwa household, Pari's father always had the final say. This contrasted sharply with the lesson he taught her about gender equality when he encouraged her to ride a motorbike.

"Papa always has the last word, no matter what," Pari thought, reflecting on his authoritative element where he was unforgiving, leaving no room for dissent. "There's no way to persuade him. I feel trapped."

Pari decided to buy time to become independent. Witnessing her father's dominance in family decisions, she resolved to marry for love, ensuring her voice would be respected. "True equality in marriage can only be achieved by choosing my own partner—someone who sees me as an equal."

This thought resonated with her Nanima's * recommendation to move to Canada after completing her academics. Her Nanima encouraged her to lead an independent life.

"A woman's potential truly blossoms in western countries! Pari, you must pursue your education abroad and land a prestigious job," her Nanima said.

"Nanima, your stories about women in Canada always inspire me. I want to be independent like them," Pari replied.

Her Nanima, an 80-year-old woman with a warm heart and resilient spirit, lived in Canada with Pari's uncle for the past 20 years. Despite her limited formal education, she possessed a wealth of wisdom and life experience.

"In Punjab, my marriage to your grandfather was tough. He was commanding and demanding, often disregarding my opinions. But I managed our household with grace and patience," her Nanima explained.

---

* maternal grandmother

During her visits to Pari' house, her Nanima painted vivid pictures of the bold and unapologetic lifestyles of women in Canada. "Pari, you must see and seize the opportunities beyond our borders," she often said. Her inspiring words and personal journey from domestic subservience to independence deeply resonated with Pari, shaping her vision of the future.

"Nanima's words have always resonated deeply with me," Pari thought. "They showed me how important independence and self-sufficiency are. Moving to Canada isn't just about education; it's about living a life where I can fully realise my potential, free from the cultural constraints I've grown up with."

However, a recent conflict with her father over her preferred higher studies added a new criterion for her future life partner. "I can't accept a guy who won't budge in a relationship," Pari told herself firmly. "Finding someone who treats me as an equal would be perfect for moving to a country like Canada."

While waiting for the outcome of her engineering entrance exam, Pari came to terms with studying computer science, recognising that a high paying qualification and mutual respect are essential for making choices. "Maybe moving to Canada can wait," she mused. "I can totally see myself meeting someone special at university who supports my freedom and dreams. That would be so romantic!" This shift in priorities filled her with a sense of excitement and hope for the future.

As soon as Mr. Bajwa discovered that Pari couldn't pursue computer engineering locally, he arranged her admission to Jaipur Technical University through Army sponsorship. Pari eagerly embraced the opportunity. "Wow!" she thought excitedly. "This means I'm going to a hostel, away from Papa's regimental discipline, and there, I can make my own rules! Hurrah!" She rushed to her room, turned up the music, and sang along to her favourite ABBA song, "Dancing Queen, young and sweet, only seventeen..."

She continued daydreaming, "I can't wait to go to university. Imagine meeting someone special who treats me as an equal. We'll study together, support each other's goals, and build an amazing future. He'll respect my independence and encourage me to chase my dreams, just like I would for him."

She sighed happily, "We'll have late-night study sessions, coffee dates, and share our dreams for the future. It'll be so romantic and perfect. Someone who sees me for who I truly am and loves me for it."

With a dreamy smile, she continued, "My heart says I'll meet him soon..."

In the land where, traditions blend, dreams ascend, what whispers will the winds send?

CHAPTER 2

AYUSHMAN'S UNEXPECTED ARRIVAL

I n the spring of 1982, the quiet, sterile environment of the General Hospital in Pathankot was charged with anticipation. Despite the flurry of activity from the medical staff, an almost sacred silence enveloped the new mother. Mrs. Dolly Mittal lay on the bed, her face pale and glistening with sweat from the strenuous labor she had just endured. Her eyes, although weary, sparkled with a profound mix of hope and anxiety. The room seemed to hold its breath, reflecting the intensity of the moment, as the promise of new life hung delicately in the balance, making the air feel both heavy and sacred.

In a corner of the room, a small boy played quietly. This was Vardaan, Dolly's five-year-old son. He was a bundle of curiosity and energy, his dark eyes wide with wonder as he stacked wooden blocks into a precarious tower. His curly hair bounced with each movement, and his small hands worked with the careful precision of a child deeply engrossed in his task. Every now and then, he would glance up at his mother, sensing the importance of the moment but not fully understanding it.

"Congratulations, Mrs. Mittal, it's a healthy baby!"

the nurse's voice rang out, filled with the practiced cheer of someone who delivered such news regularly but always found joy in it.

Mrs. Mittal's heart skipped a beat. She mustered the strength to ask, "Is it a girl?" Her voice was soft, almost a whisper, but it was laden with years of longing and unspoken dreams.

The nurse's broad smile faltered slightly as she replied, "No, it's a boy," handing the newborn to Mrs. Mittal.

As soon as the baby was in her arms, Mrs. Mittal's eyes filled with tears. The nurse, accustomed to seeing tears of joy, was taken aback by the profound sadness that washed over Mrs. Mittal's face. She had never seen a woman cry because she didn't give birth to a girl.

Vardaan, sensing the change in the room's atmosphere, abandoned his blocks and climbed onto the bed beside his mother. He peered curiously at the tiny bundle in her arms. "Mama, why are you crying?" he asked, his innocent voice filled with confusion and concern.

With tears streaming down her cheeks, Mrs. Mittal gently cradled the newborn, feeling his warmth against her skin. She took a deep breath and, with a trembling voice, introduced him to his elder brother. "I'm okay, Beta. Feel the softness of your little baby brother 'Ayushman'. Isn't he adorable?" The baby boy whimpered softly, his tiny hands clenching and unclenching as he nestled closer to his mother. Mrs. Mittal's sighs turned into heart-wrenching sobs. She had fervently wished for a baby girl, and now, holding her boy, the surge of emotions was overwhelming.

Holding her son close, she felt a conflicting wave of love and disappointment. Little Ayushman had entered the world bearing not only his parents' dreams but also the weight of his extended family's expectations, as Mr. Mittal had promised to give their newborn, if a boy, to his uncle as soon as Dolly conceived a second child.

Vardaan, sensing his mother's distress, gently touched her arm. "Mama, it's okay. I'll help take care of him," he said, his young voice full of earnestness and love.

Mrs. Mittal managed a weak smile through her tears, deciding not to disclose to Vardaan about Ayushman's departure to his grand-uncle soon after eight weeks. She hugged him with one arm, holding her newborn close with the other. "Thank you, Vardaan," she whispered, her voice laden with both gratitude and sorrow. "You're a wonderful big brother."

The nurse, still puzzled by the scene, tried to offer comfort. "He's healthy and strong, Mrs. Mittal. That's what matters most."

Mrs. Mittal nodded, trying to absorb the nurse's words. She knew that she had to be strong for her children.

Mr. Kamal Mittal was a tall, robust man in his mid-twenties, often seen in impeccably tailored kurta-pajamas that highlighted his dignified presence. His serious demeanour was softened by a twinkle in his eyes whenever he spoke of his family. His wife, Mrs. Dolly Mittal, a graceful woman in her early twenties, was known for her kind heart and gentle disposition. She frequently wore vibrant, elegant saris, her favourite being a resplendent yellow and gold one reserved for special occasions. Her long hair was typically styled in a neat bun, and her expressive eyes reflected her deep emotional world.

Mr. Kamal Mittal inherited a substantial estate from his late father, who passed away in his early fifties. This left Kamal, then just 19 years old, with the responsibility of caring for his mother and three sisters. Thrust into this role at such a young age, Kamal had to step into his father's shoes, maintaining family relations. Kamal received unwavering support from his uncle, Mr. Rishi Ansal, and was determined to do whatever it took to bring happiness to his uncle and earn his blessings.

Mr. Rishi Ansal, Kamal's uncle, was an elderly man in his fifties with a commanding presence. He usually wore traditional dhotis and kurtas, which added to his regal appearance. Though his face often appeared stern, it softened when he interacted with his family, revealing the loving patriarch he truly was. Mrs. Sunita Ansal, his wife, was a kind and gentle woman in her late forties with fragile health but a strong spirit. She favoured simple yet elegant cotton saris, reflecting her modest and unassuming nature. Her soft-spoken manner and warm smile made her a cherished figure in the family.

Despite fathering three daughters, Mr. Ansal faced the pressing issue of having no male heir to continue the family's legacy. His wife's health issues prevented another pregnancy. As his daughters grew and moved out, the anxiety of leaving the family estate without a guardian became more pronounced. In response to their distress, Mr. Mittal made an extraordinary offer: he pledged to give them his own second child if it were a son. This generous proposition essentially meant entrusting another family to raise his child as their own. To ease potential societal tensions, Mr. Mittal even suggested relocating his family.

A promise had been made, and the weight of this commitment gnawed at Mrs. Mittal. She tried to brace her emotions, yet each time she looked at her child, the looming spectre of separation was unavoidable. She couldn't help but wonder why fate hadn't granted her a daughter instead.

SIX WEEKS HAD PASSED, AND BOTH MOTHER AND CHILD WERE IN good health, prepared to engage with the world. This day marked the occasion when the baby and Mrs. Mittal would interact with relatives and well-wishers. Despite Mrs. Mittal appearing every bit the affectionate and glowing mother, adorned in her resplendent yellow and gold saree, her true feelings were distant from the radiance she exuded. She would smile and extend greetings to everyone, witnessing how fondly they adored the baby. Yet, beneath the surface, her heart was shattered. Today signified the moment when Ayushman, her source of pride and happiness, would transition to his new parents. Meanwhile, her newborn son, bounced joyfully from one relative's embrace to another, entirely unaware of the decision his father had made regarding his future.

As the gathering wound down, people began to return to their homes. Each passing second bore heavily on Mrs. Mittal's heart; life itself seemed an immense burden. She searched for her husband, praying against all odds that he might have a change of heart, but found him in conversation with his uncle.

"Your unwavering dedication and profound sense of responsibility have deeply touched me, and I will always be grateful to you. Your willingness to offer such a significant sacrifice is truly admirable and embodies the values of kindness and respect that our world greatly needs. However, my dear child, I cannot separate this baby from your loving wife. She deserves to experience his growth and milestones firsthand. I cannot be the person who takes a child away from his mother. I accept my path and recognise that God has blessed me with many daughters who bring joy and fulfilment. May you and your wife be abundantly blessed," said Mr. Ansal with deep humility.

Mrs. and Mr. Ansal's hands met in a gesture of appreciation and respect toward the young couple. Mr. Mittal, feeling heavy-hearted, bid them farewell and headed back to his wife. "Is this what you desired?" he asked, his disappointment evident. Mrs. Mittal, her gaze hesitant, confirmed his assumption. "I think Auntie sensed it from your expression. You've emerged victorious; your emotions have prevailed, but I have fallen short of fulfilling my promise," he lamented, his frustration palpable. The thought that his wife's perspective would influence the decision had never crossed his mind. However, he found solace in the fact that his gesture had earned profound respect from a man he deeply admired. Uncle's position at the apex of the social hierarchy, combined with the admiration he commanded for his values, meant that Mr. Mittal had upheld his family's reputation by extending assistance to his uncle's lineage.

AYUSHMAN'S JOURNEY BEGAN IN HIS EARLY CHILDHOOD WHEN HIS mother identified his extraordinary mental abilities. At the age of 5, while playing around one afternoon, he spelled out a six-figure number from a tax return document lying on the table: "Eighty-two lakh seventy-four thousand nine hundred thirty-two." His mother, Dolly, cleaning the house, stopped in surprise. "How did you learn to read such a huge number?" she asked. Ayushman, with a cheeky grin, replied, "Dadiji asks me to count her hair every day. She has so much hair, and I knew to count up to one hundred from school, but Dadiji taught me more so I could count her entire head. Also, I help her find out how many hairs she lost each day, counting from her comb."

In upper kindergarten, recognising his potential, his mother spoke with his teachers, who then tested him for giftedness. The results confirmed her observations, and he was advanced directly to Year 2, skipping a grade.

He spent a lot of time with his grandmother, being her favourite among all her grandchildren. She taught him to recite the Hanuman Chalisa at the age of four. Visitors to the Mittal household often asked him to recite it, and they would show their admiration by kissing and cuddling him, validating his cuteness. This encouraged him to master the Shanti Path and Shiv Tandav Stotra by the time he turned eight. His performances at community gatherings every month became showstoppers.

His strong cultural roots, thanks to his grandmother, taught him the importance of embracing his culture while pursuing a Western-style education in the elite private school in Pathankot. Following his teachers' recommendations due to his aptitude for mathematics and ease with complex problem-solving, his mother enrolled him in chess at the age of nine.

Ayushman excelled at chess. He was captivated by the strategic depth and intellectual challenge the game offered. Visually mapping out each move, he loved the intricate dance of pieces on the board. The satisfying click of chess pieces as he made his moves echoed his growing expertise. He spent countless hours honing his skills, feeling the smooth wooden pieces and the cold hardness of the board under his fingers. Participating in school tournaments, the thrill of victory was a regular companion. His strategic thinking and foresight, sharpened on the chessboard, seamlessly translated into his academic pursuits and everyday problem-solving.

Ayushman quickly rose to prominence, participating in local chess competitions and winning numerous awards. The sound of applause and the sight of trophies on his shelf were testaments to his dedication.

Ayushman was exceptionally sharp in mathematics, a talent that stood out from a young age. The sight of numbers and equations was a playground for his keen analytical mind. His ability to solve complex problems with ease made him a standout student. Teachers often marvelled at his quick grasp of mathematical concepts, their voices filled with admiration as they praised his work. He consistently ranked at the top of his class in math-related subjects. His passion for numbers wasn't confined to the classroom; he often engaged in extracurricular activities that challenged his mathematical abilities.

He attended the Math Olympiad, where he scored exceptionally well. The crinkle of the newspaper in his father's hands was a proud sound, as his father showed visitors Ayushman's picture receiving a certificate from Mayor of Pathankot. "That's my son, Ayushman, right there," his father said with a proud smile, "He topped the Math Olympiad this year."

THE MITTAL FAMILY WAS CLOSE-KNIT, AND MRS. MITTAL TOOK pride in it. As a homemaker, she nurtured both her sons, with immense love and care, instilling a sense of responsibility towards their home. She taught them self-sufficiency, ensuring they could cook and clean for themselves. Mrs. Mittal was also known for her hospitality and culinary skills, impressing Mr. Mittal's business associates with her cooking. Ayushman inherited these skills from his mother and became adept at managing household tasks. He was compassionate, helping his mother even during her monthly cycle, an unusual practice in Indian households. Mrs. Mittal was multifaceted; besides managing her home, she was socially active, leading to her selection as board member of the local temple group.

Mr. Mittal's mother often created tension and misunderstandings within the family, causing Mr. Mittal to blame his wife. Ayushman frequently overheard his mother's grievances, as she lamented, "I treat your mother like my own, but she doesn't see me as her daughter. She always overrides my decisions to gain your sympathy and attention." Unable to convince his father to take her side, she would often retreat to her room to cry, feeling unheard and unsupported.

As a teenager, Ayushman couldn't comprehend the emotions between them. He wondered why his father couldn't settle the territorial tension. Both his grandmother and mother were nurturing towards him, yet they clashed over trivial matters, like what curry to prepare for dinner.

Mother-in-Law: "Dolly, why did you make palak paneer for dinner? I told you my son prefers aloo gobi."

Dolly: "He also enjoys palak paneer, Maaji. I thought a change would be nice for everyone."

Mother-in-Law: "You always think you know better. You never listen to me!"

Dolly: "It's about variety and balance in our meals."

Ayushman grew up witnessing these disputes almost every day and the chaos of trivial interruptions irritated him. In the chaotic household created by the bitter arguments of women who otherwise presented a united front in society, He learned to focus on his schoolwork and not take their emotional outbursts seriously. From his daily observations, he knew they would be gossiping about a distant relative and laughing together a couple of hours later. However, he resolved to marry a woman who wouldn't engage in such petty fights and who exhibited sophisticated manners. He believed that truly understanding the girl before marriage was essential to ensure harmony between his mother and future wife. Determined to find a partner who shared his values of peace and mutual respect, he aimed to create a harmonious home when his time came.

As a teenager, Ayushman developed an interest in karate, in addition to playing regular team sports like basketball, volleyball, and football at school. He was athletic and became passionate about martial arts after watching Jackie Chan's famous movie 'Crime Story' in 1993. The movie had a profound impact on him, teaching him the importance of self-defence both mentally and physically. Ayushman, already known as a child prodigy in his community, received several awards validating his talents. Confident that he would be a top businessman one day, he wanted to ensure his safety by learning martial arts. With determination, he practiced tirelessly, feeling the strength and precision in his movements, and by Year 10, he proudly earned his black belt.

In the summer of 1997, just before starting senior school at Pathankot High School, Ayushman stood on the championship podium, clutching his black belt trophy. The weight of the trophy in his hands felt solid and reassuring. As he raised it high, a wave of pride washed over him. He saw his parents beaming with pride, their cheers loud and clear from the front row of the audience. His eyes then caught a striking-looking girl standing just behind his mother, cheering enthusiastically.

He fell in love with her face instantly; she resembled a famous movie star from the 1990s. Her image was etched in his mind, and he couldn't stop thinking about her. Geet, with her unpredictable nature, was a beautiful enigma. Her long, dark hair flowed like a cascade, framing her expressive eyes that could go from playful to serious in a heartbeat. Her laughter was a melody that lingered in his ears, and her voice had a way of making every word sound like a secret meant just for him. Her presence was captivating, and her smile could light up the room, leaving Ayushman mesmerised.

As fate would have it, a month later, she became a new student at Pathankot High, joining the same Year 11 class as Ayushman. Upon seeing him, she promptly introduced herself with a clear and friendly voice, "Hi, I'm Geet. Congratulations on the championship trophy."

He was surprised but pleased, responded, "Hi Geet, I'm Ayushman. Do you practice karate too?"

She shook her head with a smile. "No, it's not a sport for me. I was there to cheer for my cousin, who unfortunately didn't make it to the finals. But your fight was interesting."

They became friends, often seen together in the same friend group. Geet was very image-conscious, as her father was a local politician of high stature. She liked Ayushman but was cautious about being seen with him publicly. They often made hour-long phone conversations when her family was asleep. Ayushman was captivated by her sweetness, sophisticated manners, and easy-going nature. She was a big fan of Mills & Boon novels, and romance was her favourite topic. Her favourite novel, "Passion Becomes You," was something she would read to him over the phone, her voice soft and engaging.

Ayushman cherished these moments, looking forward to her voice and the fantasies she shared with him. Their discreet relationship became a significant part of Ayushman's life, but he was frustrated by Geet's hesitation to commit to him as a boyfriend. Understanding the traditional environment they lived in, he empathised with her caution. He hoped that by the time they finished their Year 12 exams, he could speak to her and gain her commitment, as he was deeply in love with the most beautiful girl in the world and couldn't imagine being separated from her after school ended.

Ayushman had a strong inclination towards mathematics and chess, but he also had a creative side. He loved participating in school plays, showcasing his versatility and passion for the arts. Visualising himself on stage, he embraced the thrill of performing. The sound of applause resonated in his ears, a rewarding affirmation of his talent. His involvement in theatre allowed him to express himself creatively, honing his public speaking and acting skills. Whether playing a lead role or a supporting character, Ayushman brought enthusiasm and dedication to the stage, earning accolades and admiration from his peers. In Year 11, he portrayed Sherlock Holmes in a school play, which was a resounding success, making him a school celebrity despite his reserved nature. The triumph was complemented by a rare, two-hour phone call with Geet that night, her voice a sweet reward for his hard work.

Despite restrictions at home, Geet would find time to sneak the 90's electric telephone and hook it into the phone jack in her room. She had mastered the art of disconnecting the call if someone picked up the other receiver in the living room. Due to her father's big shot status in politics, she had a surveillance team of maids checking on her every hour or two. She would mute the living room receiver ringer for an hour every night from 10 pm to 11 pm, knowing her parents would be deeply asleep. Her housemaid would usually check on her at 11:30 pm before retiring to her quarters. Geet had the daily plan figured out to avoid getting caught, and on special days like birthdays or Ayushman's wins, she would bribe the maids to ignore her and not report to her parents. Ayushman felt special, knowing Geet took high risks to spend phone time with him, her whispers and giggles a secret bond between them.

Ayushman's father, Mr. Mittal, was a prominent figure in the carpet industry in Pathankot. Known for his high-quality, timely deliveries, Mr. Mittal's reputation was unmatched, and he managed to attract significant orders from well-paying clients. Ayushman grew up in an affluent neighbourhood, enjoying the privileges of an elite lifestyle. His family held memberships to all the expensive clubs and networking groups in the area, essential for maintaining their social status and business connections.

The Mittal family frequently hosted lavish celebrations, seamlessly blending social enjoyment with business networking. The clinking of glasses, the hum of conversations, and the sight of elegantly dressed guests created an atmosphere of sophistication and opportunity. These gatherings were not just parties but strategic events to foster business relationships and ensure the continued success of their enterprise. Mr. Mittal understood that maintaining an elite social circle was crucial for business stability, and Mrs. Mittal played a vital role in this. An impeccable hostess, she excelled at creating a welcoming environment, ensuring every guest felt valued and appreciated. Even during personal disagreements with Mr. Mittal, she never let it affect her public demeanour, always presenting a united front to their social group.

Ayushman, from a young age, learned the importance of maintaining his family's prestigious image. He observed his parents navigate the complexities of social and business life, understanding that their elite status was integral to their premium lifestyle. Despite his admiration for his father's success, Ayushman harboured different aspirations. He aspired to be a successful businessman but was not interested in the carpet industry. Instead, he envisioned carving out his own path, using the skills and values instilled in him by his parents to achieve success in his chosen field.

Simultaneously, Ayushman continued to thrive academically, becoming house captain and excelling in physics. The tactile experience of working in the lab, the smell of chemicals, and the hum of machinery fuelled his passion. He built a working airplane model for a school science show in senior school, an achievement covered by local newspapers and community newsletters. Encouraged by his teachers, in Year 12, he prepared to attempt engineering entrance exams for the prestigious Jaipur Technical University, where his cousin Raman Mittal was already a student. Two years ago, when Raman stopped by to say hi to Vardaan, it felt like a nostalgic trip down memory lane. Vardaan and Raman had been inseparable pals and brothers during their school days until Year Ten. They had shared countless adventures, laughter, and dreams. However, the path of life diverged when Vardaan, following his father's guidance, opted for commerce to prepare for their family's carpet business. As a dutiful son, Vardaan embraced his father's advice without hesitation.

Meanwhile, Ayushman found himself captivated by Raman's bold decision to pursue engineering, defying his father's expectations within their plumbing supplies manufacturing business. Ayushman often reminisced about the times when Raman had sparked his interest in science, especially the memorable day in Year Eight when they built a clap switch model together. Those moments had left an indelible mark on Ayushman. Raman's encouragement to explore science in Years 11 and 12 became a guiding light for Ayushman, urging him to delve deep into the subjects and discover his true passion. Ayushman vividly recalled his conversations with Raman, which had profoundly influenced his path.

Raman: "Ayushman, I heard you've decided to take up science in Year 11. That's a big step. What inspired you?"

Ayushman: "Well, Raman, ever since we built that clap switch model together, I've been fascinated by the intricacies of science. I can still feel the excitement of making it work. And your encouragement to dive deeper into the subjects has really pushed me."

Raman: "I'm glad to hear that. You know, the way you tackled that project showed you have a natural aptitude. How did your father react to your decision?"

Ayushman: "Surprisingly, he didn't resist. He said every discussion has its right timing and setting. He trusts I'll make the right choice when it's time to pick an undergraduate course. I think he's waiting for me to mature a bit more and consider his and Vardaan's guidance." He paused, curiosity lighting up his eyes. "By the way, how is your computer science engineering going?"

Raman: "I love coding; we have great faculty. Come to my house someday, and I'll show you how we create and compile code in C. With your mathematical aptitude, it might interest you."

During those holidays, Ayushman hung out with Raman and learned basic programming. As the holidays came to an end and it was time to leave for university, Ayushman asked Raman during their last coding session, "Bhaiya, is it okay if I use your computer while you're away to complete the projects I started with you on data structures?"

Raman, amused by Ayushman's keen interest, nodded, "Of course! Let's move the machine to your house right away since I'm leaving tomorrow morning. I can help you reassemble the parts at your place."

That evening, both cousins spent time relocating the computer and readjusting the large mid 1990s Windows machine. Ayushman took great interest in learning about the hardware components as well. Before Raman went home, Dolly served them hot meals with dal makhani and lachcha paratha, Raman and Ayushman's favorites.

Raman: "Thank you, Chachiji. Ayushman is so bright with computers; he picked up the concepts so fast."

Mrs. Mittal: "It runs in the family. Vardaan is just as talented, but your Chachaji needs him, so he couldn't complete college. I hope Ayushman follows in his footsteps, shares the load with his brother after finishing school, and strengthens the business alongside his father."

Raman's visits always had a profound impact on Ayushman. The warmth of their shared meals and the mutual enthusiasm for learning created poignant moments between the cousins, highlighting a beautiful blend of tradition and new possibilities in their lives.

Fast forward to the start of the Year 12 session in 1998, Ayushman was appointed the school captain of the prestigious Pathankot High. He found himself in the throes of young love with Geet. On the last day of school, he anxiously awaited to confirm the future of their romance, hoping it would transition from phone calls to real life. Ayushman was proud of his relationship with Geet and wanted to be openly engaged and seen with her. The hide-and-seek nature of their relationship didn't suit his courageous personality.

The day had come to clear his expectations with Geet. As he walked down the familiar school corridor, his heart was heavy with thoughts. Tall and athletic, Ayushman exuded confidence and poise befitting a house captain. His neatly pressed school uniform—crisp white shirt and navy blue trousers—accentuated his strong yet youthful frame. His gold complexion, strikingly complemented by his white shirt, highlighted his sharp features and well-defined jawline. His dark hair was neatly styled, but his usually bright and determined eyes were now shadowed with deep sadness.

He saw Geet standing near the lockers, her delicate features framed by her straight, waist-length hair. She wore a simple, elegant white churidar kameez, her large brown eyes betraying a mix of hesitation and sadness. Gathering his courage, Ayushman approached her, determined to have the conversation they had been avoiding.

Ayushman: "Geet, can we talk?" His voice barely masked the tremor of his emotions.

Geet: "Yes, Ayushman, we need to." Her voice was soft, almost a whisper.

They moved to a quieter corner of the schoolyard. Ayushman took a deep breath, trying to steady his racing heart. "Why are you so afraid to be seen with me?" he asked, the pain evident in his voice.

Geet: "It's not that I don't like you, Ayushman. I do. But...people talk. My parents, our friends—they all have expectations." Her voice wavered, full of uncertainty.

Ayushman: "Expectations? Geet, I thought we were past worrying about what others think." His voice carried a mix of frustration and sadness.

Geet's eyes filled with tears as she finally met his gaze. "It's not that simple. I can't ignore my family's wishes. They...they want me to be with someone who fits their idea of a perfect match."

Ayushman's heart broke as he listened to her words. He had always known this was a possibility, but hearing it out loud was a different kind of pain. "So, this is it? You're choosing their approval over us?"

Geet: "Ayushman, please understand. I don't want to hurt you, but I can't go against my family. I'm so sorry." Her voice was choked with emotion.

He gently pulled away from her touch, feeling the finality of her words. "I understand, Geet. But know this: I need someone who is confident enough to stand by my side, regardless of what others think. I hope you find your happiness, even if it's not with me." His voice was firm, yet tinged with sorrow.

With a heavy heart, Ayushman turned and walked away, feeling the crushing weight of being abandoned by Geet, his high school love. Geet stood alone, her heart aching as she watched him disappear from her life, unable to muster the courage to choose love over the traditionally accepted path.

With weary steps, Ayushman exited the school gates and wandered along the shaded path under the trees, lost in thought. A storm of emotions raged within his mind. He pondered, "Perhaps having only physical beauty and a sweet voice is not enough. A beloved must also possess courage and the resolve to fulfill her purpose."

That day, deeply enamored with Geet, Ayushman felt the harshness of life up close for the very first time. He came to realise that there are far more important qualities in a woman than mere beauty—qualities that young men often overlook before offering their hearts. He resolved, in that moment, to start his life anew, focusing on his dreams and ambitions.

THE JINX AYUSHMAN FACED IN HIS LOVE LIFE WAS INTENSIFIED BY his father's disapproval of pursuing engineering.

Mr. Mittal: "Ayushman, we need to talk about your future. Pursuing a B.Com would be more beneficial for our family business. We need someone to look after the import-export side, and Vardaan is already handling the local trade."

Ayushman: "But, Papa, engineering is my passion. I've always wanted to dive deep into science and create something impactful."

Mr. Mittal: "I understand your passion, but think practically. Our business needs you. I'm planning to free my time for networking and spiritual pursuits with your mother. We're in our forties, and it's the next step in our spiritual journey according to our Ashram gyan."

Mr. Mittal, a staunch believer in traditional values, envisioned the same path for his younger son Ayushman. He saw taking the family legacy forward by leveraging the reputation his father had built as the most practical and beneficial path. His voice carried a tone of conviction as he insisted Ayushman pursue a B.Com, dismissing his son's passion for engineering as impractical for their family.

Ayushman: "But engineering isn't just a job to me, Papa. It's something I love and am good at."

Mr. Mittal: "Our family isn't job-oriented; we're business-oriented. Engineering might be a passion, but a B.Com is practical for the family business. Think about it. You can help us more by understanding the business, and it will secure our family's future."

With a heavy heart and resigned spirit, Ayushman succumbed to his father's wishes. The corridors of his college echoed with the unfulfilled aspirations of a young man treading a path laid out for him, not by him. The sounds of classroom lectures and discussions about commerce felt dull compared to the excitement he had once felt for engineering.

As a dutiful son, Ayushman visualised the commitment his father had shown at the tender age of nineteen, the same age Ayushman was now when his grandfather had passed away. He realised that his father needed to rest and take early retirement from core business operations. Feeling the weight of responsibility, Ayushman understood that being resourceful to his family was more important than his passion for science. He put his own dreams aside, the sensation of holding engineering textbooks replaced with the ledgers and balance sheets of commerce.

Ayushman: "I understand, Papa. I'll do what's best for the family. I'll enroll in the B.Com program."

Mr. Mittal's face softened with pride and relief. "Thank you, Ayushman. You're doing the right thing for all of us."

Ayushman nodded, feeling the physical weight of his sacrifice. The path ahead was clear, but it was not his chosen path. It was a path of duty, one he would walk with determination, but the dream of engineering lingered like a distant echo in his heart.

TWO WEEKS INTO THE COMMERCE UNDERGRAD COURSE, AYUSHMAN found himself navigating the murky waters of a Bachelor of Commerce degree at the local college. It was a stark contrast to the bright, hopeful days of his school life. Despite being a young man of many talents with a natural aptitude for mathematics, his dreams of engineering were stifled by the ironclad will of his businessman father.

From the beginning, he felt out of place in the commerce stream. The dry, theoretical nature of his classes failed to ignite any passion within him. The monotone lectures and endless pages of accounting left him cold. His disinterest quickly led to disengagement, and he soon found himself skipping classes. Instead of immersing himself in accounting and economics, he sought solace in the thrill of sports, particularly cricket. The sound of the ball hitting the bat and the rush of running across the field provided a temporary escape from his academic dissatisfaction.

His brother was the first to notice the worrying trend. Vardaan had always been supportive of Ayushman, understanding the pressures of familial expectations. Unlike him, Vardaan had been pulled into the family business straight after school and had been denied the opportunity to pursue higher education. He knew the value of a university education and the unique experiences it offered. Seeing Ayushman waste his intellect and time was something he could not bear.

Vardaan had sacrificed his own dreams by discontinuing his on-campus undergraduate studies in commerce to join the family business. Warm and supportive, he had been the pillar of strength for his parents, embodying the selflessness of Shravan Kumar from the epic Ramayana. He prioritised his family's needs above all else, always ready to offer guidance and support. Vardaan's deep sense of duty and unwavering commitment to his family's well-being made him an indispensable figure in Ayushman's life, providing both encouragement and practical solutions during times of need. His strong character and selfless actions were the backbone of the family, ensuring stability and unity through challenging times.

One evening, Vardaan decided to confront Ayushman. They sat together in Ayushman's room, the atmosphere thick with concern and frustration. Ayushman, dressed in a simple t-shirt and jeans, appeared indifferent to his usually meticulous image. His neatly styled hair and expressive eyes were in stark contrast to the turmoil visible in them.

Vardaan: "Ayushman, what are you doing with your life?" His voice was firm, yet laced with concern. "You're wasting your potential by not attending classes. You have so much talent, and it pains me to see you throwing it away."

Ayushman: "Bhaiya, I know I'm not doing the right thing." His voice was low, filled with resignation. "But I just can't bring myself to care about commerce. It's not what I want to do."

Vardaan: "Then what do you want to do, Ayushman? What makes you excited?" His tone softened, hoping to reach his brother.

Ayushman: "Engineering," he replied without hesitation. "I want to study engineering. But you know how Papa is. He doesn't support it."

Vardaan nodded thoughtfully, understanding the struggle. "I understand. But there might be a way to work around this. What about computer science? It's practical, involves a lot of mathematics, and is a growing field. You have a top rank in Jaipur Technical University. Maybe they will consider you in the second intake consultation schedule of the 1998 session coming up in a few weeks. Let me speak to Raman and confirm."

Ayushman's eyes lit up with a glimmer of hope. "But what about Papa? And Ma? You know how they feel about me leaving home."

Vardaan: "Let me handle them," he said firmly. "I'll talk to them. You deserve to pursue something that truly interests you."

True to his word, Vardaan approached their parents with the proposal. Their father was initially resistant, but his persuasive arguments and the practical benefits of a degree in computer applications eventually swayed him. The real challenge, however, was their mother.

Mrs. Mittal was deeply attached to her youngest. The thought of him moving away to Jaipur for his studies filled her with dread. Separation anxiety gripped her, and she was inconsolable at the prospect.

Mrs. Mittal: "How can you expect me to let my youngest go so far away?" she cried, her eyes brimming with tears. "He's just seventeen. How will he manage on his own?"

Vardaan took her hands in his, speaking gently. "Ma, I understand your worries. But he needs this. He's not happy with commerce. This is his chance to study something he loves."

Their mother, still apprehensive, looked at Ayushman. "Promise me you'll call every day, Ayushman. I need to know you're safe and happy."

Ayushman nodded earnestly. "I promise, Ma. I'll call you every day."

Watching his elder brother's sacrificial qualities unfold before his eyes, Ayushman's love and respect for Vardaan grew exponentially. He felt protected and shielded, like a lion cub guarded by his elder sibling from the pride's stern elders. "Vardaan is like my protector, ensuring my safety in this unpredictable wilderness," Ayushman thought. "His sacrifice means everything to me. I can pursue my passion because he believes in me. I won't let him down."

Unexpected ties, spirits ascend, what secrets will destiny send?

CHAPTER 3

DESTINY'S INTERSECTION

As the Indian Army jeep came to a stop in the busy university campus, everyone's attention naturally shifted towards it. The deep hum of the engine and the bold insignia, 'Army Education Corps-विद्यैव बलम्,' had already sparked curiosity among the gathered students. When the door opened, a girl stepped out—around five and a half feet tall—with a calm grace that spoke of quiet confidence. She wore a white Lucknowi-embroidered top, high-waisted blue jeans, and black patent boots, carrying herself with the unmistakable poise of someone raised in a military home.

Her golden skin glowed in the soft sunlight, highlighting her composed presence, while her large, deep-set eyes reflected a quiet confidence, as if she had already found her place in the world. A leather satchel rested on her shoulder, and her hair, neatly tied in a French braid, added to her simple yet dignified appearance.

Walking beside her mother, Baldev, she moved steadily toward the administrative office. Every step she took showed the discipline and structure of her upbringing—each movement deliberate and controlled. The students watching her arrival seemed captivated, as if the very atmosphere had shifted around her. In that moment, Pari's entrance wasn't just an introduction to who she was; it was a subtle statement of her grace and confidence, turning an ordinary day into something special and unforgettable.

AS PARI COMPLETED THE ADMINISTRATIVE FORMALITIES WITH HER mother at the university, her seriousness and dedication were evident to everyone around. She appeared as a student who had a clear understanding of her purpose. The moment at the hostel entrance, where she had to bid farewell to her mother, was tender and deeply emotional—a blend of love, hope, and the excitement of embarking on a new journey. Her mother's affectionate touch and the pride shining in her eyes made the moment even more poignant.

When Pari held the key to room number 730 in her hands, a surge of excitement ran through her. However, the thought of being away from her mother weighed heavily on her heart. As the moment of farewell at the hostel gate approached, her eyes welled up with tears. The pain of parting from the comforting presence of her mother was clearly visible on her face. Though her heart brimmed with the anticipation of a new beginning, the thought of facing this journey without her mother moved her deeply. Her mother mirrored those feelings, but both tried to smile bravely at each other, as though attempting to hide their tears.

Noticing the emotional scene, the hostel warden, Mrs. Reena Khera, gently placed a hand on Pari's shoulder and, in her kind and thoughtful manner, began to offer words of comfort. "You are a brave girl," she said softly. "Every year, I see girls go through this pain of parting, but remember, this is a door that leads you to a new and wonderful world."

With a light smile, she added, "Just make sure not to have too much fun!"

Her smile and gentle humor brought a touch of lightness to the emotional moment, as if she had sprinkled a bit of sweetness into the difficulty of the goodbye. Pari and her mother exchanged smiles, turning the moment from a farewell into a symbol of a new beginning.

Mrs. Reena Khera's persona was an admirable blend of discipline and warmth. Draped in simple cotton sarees, wearing practical shoes, with her short-cropped hair and minimal makeup, she embodied simplicity. Her authority carried with it a touch of empathy, making her highly respected by both students and parents alike. It was this unique combination of firmness and kindness that left a lasting impression on everyone.

Pari, overwhelmed, burst into tears while hugging her mother tightly. Her mother, in her patient voice, said, "A lioness leaves her cubs at the edge of the forest so they may find their own way home. The storms and rivers they encounter teach them strength and resilience. This journey shapes their character and gives them a courage like no other. Always remember, you too have come here to learn something from challenges."

Her mother's words, spoken with love and confidence, resonated deeply, though Pari, in that moment, may not have fully understood their significance. Nevertheless, she embraced them with all her heart, knowing that her mother's wisdom would guide her through this new chapter of her life.

As Pari was still lost in her mother's comforting words, another student, Meeta, arrived with her own mother. Mrs. Khera, ever the gentle guide, introduced everyone, and Pari and Meeta exchanged warm smiles, realizing that they were to share a room. Meeta, hailing from Alwar, wore glasses that hinted at her studious nature. There was a shyness about her, a hesitancy that was obvious, yet her demeanour exuded a soft warmth.

The conversation that followed between Pari and Meeta gradually laid the foundation for a budding friendship. Meeta, standing just around five feet tall, had a simplicity about her that made Pari feel at ease. Their exchange went something like this:

"Hi Meeta, looks like we're going to start this journey together," Pari said with a welcoming smile, her tone full of warmth and excitement.

"Yes, it seems so. I'm a little nervous but also excited," Meeta replied with a timid smile, her voice betraying her initial reluctance.

Pari studied her for a moment and then reassured her with a smile, "Don't worry, I'm a bit nervous too. But everything will be easier once we get settled. So, what's your favourite conversational subject?"

"I really enjoy literature," Meeta replied, her eyes sparkling behind her glasses. "What about you?"

"Oh, literature! That's wonderful. I love fashion designing," Pari said with a hint of pride. "Maybe we can learn something new from each other. You can tell me about your favourite books, and I can share the latest fashion trends with you!"

Meeta nodded, her smile growing a little wider. "That sounds great. I've never paid much attention to fashion, but maybe with you around, I'll start to understand it better."

"Absolutely!" Pari beamed. "And if you ever need help with anything, don't hesitate to ask. We'll get through this journey together."

Meeta felt a wave of relief wash over her, and she began to feel more at ease. She glanced at her mother, who, seeing the newfound comfort on her daughter's face, looked reassured. The simple conversation between Pari and Meeta had become a symbol of their new beginning —a promise to support each other as they navigated this fresh chapter in their lives.

Meeta's mother adjusted the shawl on her shoulder and, seeing the calm expression on her daughter's face, breathed a sigh of relief. The easy and natural conversation between Pari and Meeta had soothed her heart. The anxiety that had earlier clouded Meeta's face was now slowly transforming into curiosity, and seeing this, her mother felt certain that her daughter would soon find her place in this new environment.

Pari's mother stood at a slight distance, observing her daughter's growing confidence, and a soft smile spread across her face. The earlier worry that had been lingering in her heart now began to ease. Pari, ever willing to extend a hand of friendship, was already showing the same warmth toward Meeta. Though their friendship had only just begun, it held the promise of a deeper bond—one that would offer both of them emotional strength in this unfamiliar journey.

Both mothers exchanged glances, a silent understanding passing between them, as if they could now breathe easy, knowing their daughters were stepping onto the right path. The budding friendship between Pari and Meeta brought them a sense of relief, casting away any lingering concerns.

As they bid farewell to their daughters, a glimpse of satisfaction flickered across their faces. Slowly, they made their way toward the hostel gate, their hearts filled with the belief that their girls would now be fine. The ease with which Pari and Meeta had connected carried a genuine warmth that would serve as emotional support throughout their new chapter.

By the time they reached the gate, both mothers turned back for one final glance. They saw Pari and Meeta laughing and chatting, as if embracing this new chapter of their lives with confidence and enthusiasm. In that moment, the mothers found peace, assured that not only would their daughters adapt to this new world, but that their companionship would make the journey all the more beautiful.

On their first day together, Pari and Meeta's budding friendship began to take shape in the most beautiful way. As they stepped into the room, they each set about arranging their spaces, revealing their distinct personalities. Pari's side quickly filled with vibrant fashion sketches, magazines, and postcards, reflecting her creative energy. Meeta, on the other hand, neatly organized her bed and desk, showcasing her calm and composed nature.

As the day went on, they started noticing each other's décor. Pari admired the academic books lined up on Meeta's bookshelf, appreciating her sense of discipline. Meanwhile, Meeta was drawn to Pari's artistic flair, especially the inspiring fashion posters she had pinned up on the walls. It was Pari who casually initiated a conversation, asking Meeta about her studies, and soon, they found themselves taking an interest in each other's worlds.

Pari shared a small beauty tip with Meeta from her makeup kit, which Meeta accepted with a shy smile. In return, Meeta taught Pari how to care for her potted plant, and soon they were laughing, exchanging stories about their lives.

Their contrasting belongings and decorations, once separate, now symbolized the harmony growing between them. Pari's creativity and Meeta's orderliness brought balance to their shared space, and this first day laid the foundation for a blossoming friendship.

As evening descended, Pari and Meeta took a leisurely walk through the expansive campus of Jaipur Technical University. The university, with its blend of modern and traditional architecture, was a sight to behold.

The main building, which housed the administrative offices, stood majestically at the centre of the campus. Its grand façade, adorned with intricate carvings and arches, reflected the rich cultural heritage of Rajasthan. The building was illuminated by warm, golden lights, casting a welcoming glow.

To the left of the main building was the Department of Computer Science, a sleek, contemporary structure with glass walls and steel accents. Inside, rows of computer labs equipped with the latest technology could be seen through the transparent walls. Students were engaged in animated discussions, some working diligently on their coding assignments while others collaborated on group projects.

Next, they passed by the Department of Mechanical Engineering, a robust building with sturdy columns and wide staircases. The mechanical workshops, visible from the outside, were bustling with activity. Students in lab coats and safety goggles were engrossed in building and testing various mechanical models and prototypes. The hum of machinery and the occasional clanking of metal parts added a lively soundtrack to the scene.

Further along, they arrived at the Department of Fashion Design, a colourful and creatively designed building that stood out with its vibrant murals and artistic installations. Through the large windows, Pari could see mannequins dressed in student-designed outfits, sewing machines whirring, and fashion sketches pinned to inspiration boards. This sight filled Pari with excitement and anticipation, reaffirming her passion for fashion design.

The walk continued to the Department of Civil Engineering, a building characterised by its practical and functional design. The concrete structure, though less ornate, exuded a sense of purpose. Inside, students were seen working on architectural models and blueprints, discussing structural designs and materials.

They also passed the Department of Electronics and Communication, a futuristic-looking building with neon lighting and high-tech equipment. Inside, students were busy soldering circuits, testing electronic devices, and working on innovative communication systems. The air was filled with a sense of innovation and technological advancement.

Finally, they reached the Department of Humanities and Social Sciences, a serene building surrounded by lush gardens and tall trees. The peaceful environment was perfect for reflection and intellectual discussion. Students could be seen sitting in circles on the grass, deeply engrossed in debates on philosophy, literature, and social issues.

As Pari and Meeta walked through the campus, the diversity of departments and the vibrant student life left a lasting impression. The university was a hub of learning and innovation, offering countless opportunities for growth and exploration. For Pari, it was a place where dreams could take flight, and the journey of self-discovery could truly begin.

On their way back to the hostel, they noticed a "Gymnasium" sign. Through the glass doors, they saw students working out, lifting weights, and practicing yoga. A beautiful swimming pool gleamed in the back, where students swam gracefully, with lounge chairs nearby for rest.

The gym's walls displayed motivational quotes, and adjacent courts hosted badminton and basketball games. Pari felt this university wasn't just for learning but for unlocking dreams!

Meeta's gentle nature and openness to new experiences made her receptive to Pari's fashion tips. Despite her initial reservations, she started to embrace the subtle changes suggested by Pari, hinting at a potential transformation. Meeta valued the companionship and support that Pari provided, which significantly eased her transition into university life. The budding camaraderie between them blossomed, with Meeta relying on Pari's guidance and friendship to navigate the challenges of their new environment.

SECOND DAY IN THE UNIVERSITY CAMPUS, AS EVENING DESCENDED, Pari and Meeta strolled through the bustling campus, where students engaged in animated discussions or immersed themselves in quiet study. To Pari, most appeared bookish, yet some caught her eye with their striking looks. Meeta, still adjusting to her new surroundings, shadowed Pari like a timid lamb, gradually warming up to her confident presence.

Back at the hostel, anticipation for the upcoming day loomed large. While Pari brimmed with excitement, Meeta harboured a tinge of apprehension. Nonetheless, buoyed by Pari's companionship, they wished each other goodnight, drifting into a restless slumber filled with dreams of the days ahead.

Dawn broke, stirring Pari from her sleep. With Meeta still dozing, Pari seized the opportunity to prepare for the day ahead, donning a chic ensemble of a black shirt, white denims, and boots. As Meeta roused,

Pari urged her to hasten, mindful of the impending breakfast and classes.

In the hostel mess, amid a lively breakfast gathering, Pari and Meeta shared their first meal of the day before embarking on their journey to class "A". As they settled into their seats, Pari's gaze wandered, scrutinising her fellow classmates. Her attention fixated on Saba, whose effortless elegance and confidence stirred a pang of envy within Pari.

As they made their way to the Department of Computer Science, Pari, Meeta, and Saba walked side by side, each step resonating with the promise of a new beginning in their lives.

"So, where are you from, Saba?" Pari asked to break the ice.

"I'm from Chandigarh. My dad is an IAS officer. How about you guys?" Saba inquired, looking at both of them.

"I'm from Bhatinda, and my dad is in the Indian Army," responded Pari.

"And I'm from Alwar. We have a family business converting our ancestral palace into a hotel," added Meeta quickly.

Saba was a strikingly elegant and confident girl, exuding an effortless charm that captivated those around her. She carried herself with a poise that made her stand out in any crowd. Despite her initial air of aloofness, Saba revealed a friendly and down-to-earth nature upon getting to know her. Her popularity among peers was a testament to her magnetic personality, although this sometimes led to others feeling overshadowed. Saba's elegance and confidence were not just superficial; they were integral parts of her character, making her a compelling figure in Pari's life.

They sat on the same bench in class. Throughout the lecture, Pari's admiration for Saba deepened, prompting her to initiate a conversation after class. Surprisingly, Saba's affable demeanour and down-to-earth nature soon dispelled Pari's initial apprehensions, fostering a newfound friendship. Saba and Pari both were fashion brand buffs. They shared interests in combining looks and capsule wardrobes for different moods in the day and seasons.

While Meeta felt alienated as she came from a traditional business family that took pride in Rajasthani heritage and took pride in showcasing Indian customs and dances to the foreign traveler's. In her life, she had seen the reverse of Saba and Pari's fascination for western fashion. She often thought that Saba and Pari are just overdoing fashion and hoped that they will eventually grow out of it. While Saba and Pari were engaged in their fashion talks Meeta had learnt to cope by reading novels. Thrillers were her favourite genre. However, as Pari immersed herself in Saba's world, Meeta began to feel sidelined. Despite her efforts to integrate, Pari couldn't shake the feeling of being overshadowed by Saba's popularity.

One day, while Pari and Saba were deeply engrossed in a discussion about fashion, Meeta decided to head back to the classroom to retrieve her bag. As she approached the door, she noticed a classmate picking up her bag and walking out with it. Without hesitation, Meeta quickly stepped forward and said, "Hey, that's my bag. I'm Meeta!"

The classmate glanced at the name tag on the bag and asked, "Can you show me your ID?"

A bit flustered, Meeta replied, "Of course, here it is." She handed over her ID card. The classmate examined it carefully and, after confirming, handed the bag back to her. Meeta smiled and asked, "Thank you. What's your name?"

The classmate gave a shy smile and said, "Hi, I'm Rahul," before quickly walking away, his face slightly red with embarrassment. Meeta felt a bit awkward as the conversation ended more abruptly than she had expected.

Rahul was about five and a half feet tall, with a slender build and curly, untamed hair. He often wore simple, comfortable clothes, reflecting his easygoing nature. However, his shyness and hesitance in social situations were hard to miss.

Noticing Rahul's timid demeanour, Meeta thought it might be a good idea to introduce him to her friends, Pari and Saba. The next day, Meeta brought Rahul to meet them. Gradually, the four of them formed a small group, spending more time together, sharing jokes, and exploring the campus side by side. Their newfound friendship blossomed, and they began to enjoy every moment in each other's company.

After four weeks, however, Saba decided to drop the course. She couldn't bear the distance from her boyfriend, Joseph, who lived near her home in Chandigarh. She confided in Pari, Rahul, and Meeta, "I miss Joseph so much. I especially miss driving around the city in his Audi TT. It's so comfortable and fast."

Lost in her own world, Saba often shared stories of her lavish lifestyle with Joseph. Pari and Meeta listened intently, captivated by her tales, as they reflected their own dreams. "I love going to weekend getaways in Himachal with Joseph. You know, his dad exports silk fabrics to Europe, and they have a big network in Paris and Milan."

Feeling a bit out of place, Rahul made a quick exit, excusing himself by saying he had to head to the library.

"I've convinced my dad to put a word for me at NIFT New Delhi because I want to pursue fashion designing. I can take over from Joseph's dad since Joseph wants to become a diplomat. I don't want to waste what his dad has created, and I love fabrics. I can use his network to my advantage."

Saba seemed ambitious and appeared to have her life figured out, with the minor inconvenience of not getting admission to NIFT.

"So how will moving to New Delhi solve your distance problem with Joseph since he's still in Chandigarh?" Pari asked.

"Good question. He's starting his political science studies at Delhi University soon, which gives us a chance to move in together if NIFT works out," Saba sighed.

"I envy you, Saba. I wanted to do fashion designing, but my dad refused. Now I'm stuck with the next best thing I can do: computer science."

Saba, with a serious expression, responded, "Pari, everyone's circumstances are different. I can make this move because my life with Joseph has been planned since high school. His dad is keen for me to join him. The fashion industry has its cruel side. You can't put the cart before the horse. You have to balance livelihood and passion when choosing a course." Pari was not expecting such wise words from Saba. Suddenly, Pari's heart filled with respect, hearing these profound words.

In the days to come, Saba's dad made her dream happen, and she left for NIFT. She wrote a small note and left her phone number for Pari:

"Roses are red, violets are blue,
Every shared memory feels like new.
From secrets we've whispered to stories we've told,
Our friendship's a tapestry, woven with gold."

With Saba's departure, Pari found solace in her studies, emerging stronger and more self-assured than before.

MEANWHILE, IN THE BOYS' HOSTEL, RAMAN MITTAL STOOD IN THE middle of the room, a half-packed suitcase open on his bed. The room was filled with the faint hum of an overhead fan and the soft rustling of leaves outside the window. He glanced around, mentally checking off the items he still needed to pack. Turning to Rahul Chaudhary, who was sprawled on his bed surrounded by textbooks and notes, he broke the silence. Rahul did not have a roommate yet and he was mostly found hanging out with Raman and his roommate Vikas had already left for his industrial training due to early start in a software multinational CWC corp located in New Delhi with Raman to follow in a couple of more weeks in a different software company in the same city.

"Hey Rahul, your problem is solved... my cousin Ayushman is coming to take Saba's vacant seat," Raman said with a grin, tossing a T-shirt into his suitcase. "He's a genius in coding data structures. You'll be grateful I'm leaving."

Raman Mittal, a dynamic and influential fourth-year student at Jaipur Technical University, stood out for his sharp intellect and friendly demeanour. With a medium height and a lean build, he sported short, neatly kept hair and glasses that gave him a studious look. His charismatic and approachable nature, coupled with a genuine interest in helping others, made him a popular figure among his peers and juniors. Raman excelled in computer science and frequently engaged in coding projects, demonstrating his passion for new technologies. His leadership skills and dedication to his studies were evident in the way he mentored younger students like Rahul Chaudhary.

Rahul looked up from his books, his expression a mix of surprise and curiosity. "Ayushman? Your cousin? I've heard a lot about him," he said, adjusting his glasses and sitting up straighter.

Raman chuckled, hoping to lighten the mood. "Yes, the very same. Trust me, you're in for a treat. He's brilliant at coding, way better than I am."

Rahul, was mostly hanging out in Raman's room. Despite being introverted, Rahul admired Raman's mentorship and believed breakthroughs came through teamwork. Passionate about computer science, he often struggled with complex algorithms, but his kinesthetic learning style thrived with discussion. All he needed was a buddy to collaborate with, believing in the power of shared problem-solving.

Rahul's brow furrowed, still processing the news. "But what if he's too different? What if I don't get along with him like I do with you?"

Raman walked over, placing a hand on Rahul's shoulder. "Rahul, don't worry. Ayushman's sharp, and you two will make a great team. You've got your strengths, and Ayushman's got his. Together, you'll complement each other perfectly, just like we did. There's plenty you can both learn."

The concern in Rahul's eyes softened a bit. "I guess it'll be good to have someone new around. I just hope I can keep up."

"You will, Rahul. You've got the drive and the passion. With Ayushman's companionship, you'll be unstoppable," Raman said, giving Rahul's shoulder a firm squeeze before stepping back to continue packing.

"Thanks, Raman. I'll miss our late-night coding sessions," Rahul admitted, his voice tinged with melancholy.

Raman smiled warmly. "Me too, buddy. But hey, Ayushman's arrival isn't the end. It's just the beginning of something new and exciting. Who knows? Maybe you'll end up teaching him a thing or two."

Rahul chuckled, feeling a bit more optimistic. "Maybe. I'll give it my best shot."

"That's the spirit!" Raman exclaimed, clapping his hands together. "Now, let's make sure you're ready to impress Ayushman with all you've learned so far."

The two friends spent the next hour going over Rahul's latest projects, the room buzzing with energy and camaraderie. As they worked, the anticipation of Ayushman's arrival began to fill the space, transforming their apprehension into excitement for the future.

Raman recounted Ayushman's numerous achievements from childhood, painting a picture of a prodigy destined for greatness. Rahul, feeling a bit low at the prospect of losing Raman's expert guidance, found a sense of optimism in Ayushman's arrival and shared the news with the entire class of 2001. The anticipation of Ayushman's entry added a buzz of excitement to the otherwise routine academic life.

. . .

AT AYUSHMAN'S HOME, MRS. MITTAL WAS NOT EASILY CONVINCED for Ayushman to leave for JTU, but the combined assurances of Raman and Vardaan eventually helped her come to terms with the decision. When the letter of Ayushman's acceptance in JTU got delivered, she knew that she can't put up a resistance any further. Hence, as Ayushman's day of leaving home approached, she busied herself with packing his bags, her heart heavy with a mix of pride and sorrow.

On the morning of his departure, Ayushman stood in his room, looking at his packed bags. His mother entered, her eyes red from crying. She approached him, her voice trembling.

"Ayushman, beta, are you sure about this? It's not too late to change your mind. You know I worry about you."

Ayushman hugged her tightly, feeling the weight of her emotions. "Ma, I know this is hard for you. But I need to do this. I promise I'll be fine. Vardaan bhaiya has arranged everything. And I'll call you every day."

Mrs. Mittal pulled back, cupping his face in her hands. "You better. And promise me you'll eat properly, take care of yourself, and stay focused on your studies."

Ayushman smiled, his eyes moist. "I promise, Ma. I'll make you proud."

Mrs. Mittal nodded, her heart aching. "You already do, my son. You already do."

As Ayushman stepped out of the house, his family gathered to bid him farewell. Vardaan placed a reassuring hand on his shoulder. "Remember why you're doing this. Stay strong, and give it your best."

Ayushman nodded, drawing strength from his brother's words. He climbed into the car, waving goodbye as it pulled away from his home. His mother's tearful face was the last thing he saw as they drove off.

The journey to Jaipur was filled with a mix of excitement and apprehension for Ayushman. As the landscape changed from familiar to unknown, he felt the weight of responsibility settle on his shoulders.

This was his chance to pursue his passion, to prove to himself and his family that he could succeed on his terms.

Upon arriving at the hostel at Jaipur Technical University, Ayushman was greeted by a bustling campus filled with students from all walks of life. The vibrant energy of the university was palpable, with groups of students engaging in animated discussions, others rushing to their next class, and some leisurely lounging on the grassy lawns. The sound of laughter and chatter filled the air, mingling with the distant hum of lectures and music from the nearby student centre. Brightly coloured posters and flyers adorned the bulletin boards, advertising various clubs, events, and opportunities. As Ayushman walked through the corridors of the hostel, he was struck by the diversity of faces, each with their unique stories and ambitions. The aroma of food from the cafeteria wafted through the halls, adding to the sense of liveliness. Students moved with purpose, their backpacks slung over their shoulders, ready to tackle the challenges of the day. Ayushman felt a mix of excitement and anticipation, eager to immerse himself in this dynamic environment and begin his journey at Jaipur Technical University.

Raman introduced him to Rahul, saying, "Ayushman, this is Rahul, and Rahul, this is Ayushman."

After the introductions, Raman placed Ayushman's suitcase on the floor and a big jar of laddus on the study table. "And this jar is reserved for Ayushman," he declared.

Rahul grabbed the jar with a grin, "That he won't mind sharing with his new best friend," he completed Raman's sentence, drawing out a laddu.

The ice-breaking moment worked, and both boys started talking about their coding interests as Raman left them to chill and prepare for the next day.

Back at home, Mrs. Mittal struggled with her separation anxiety but found solace in the daily phone calls with Ayushman. Hearing his enthusiasm and happiness eased her worries, and she began to accept the new normal. Vardaan continued to support Ayushman from afar, checking in regularly and offering guidance whenever needed.

For Mrs. Mittal, Vardaan's involvement was a source of immense comfort. Knowing that her elder son was looking out for his younger brother eased some of her anxieties. She found strength in their unity, and this support system helped her cope with the emotional upheaval.

Ayushman's decision to pursue computer science engineering at Jaipur Technical University marked a pivotal turning point in his life. Despite the initial reluctance from his family and his own apprehensions, Ayushman embarked on a journey with a sense of responsibility and independence marking entry into the real world outside home. He was wondering how life would change away from home.

Paths twist and bend, what truths will fate extend?

CHAPTER 4

MAGIC OF US

"Let's give a warm welcome to the top scorer of the JTU engineering entrance exam, Ayushman Mittal," announced Mr. Shah with a touch of dramatic flair.

Ayushman, dressed in a light blue denim shirt and coordinated tapered jeans, entered the class. All eyes followed him, marking the beginning of a particularly embarrassing day. He felt a mix of embarrassment and frustration, silently cursing his cousin Raman and his roommate Rahul for putting him in the spotlight. He slipped into a vacant seat, acutely aware of the curious glances and whispered conversations around him. Despite the attention, he quickly composed himself and focused on the lecture.

Mr. Shah, a seasoned programming logic professor with a keen eye for talent, was known for his approachable nature. He asked Ayushman, "Do you have an interest in coding?"

Ayushman replied, "Yes, sir. I was introduced to coding by my cousin Raman."

"Are you referring to Raman Mittal from the final year?" Mr. Shah inquired.

"Yes, sir, but I'm not a pro. I just have a curiosity for implementing mathematical formulas through coding."

"Curiosity is what we need to learn, don't we?" Mr. Shah said, impressed by Ayushman's naturally self-driven answer. He encouraged Ayushman to write an algorithm to calculate the area of a polygon in the computer lab after lunch and to catch him if he had any questions. Mr. Shah had seen many students in his ten-year career and could recognise a genius when he spotted one. He had noticed Raman in a similar manner four years ago, and since then, Raman had been closely bonded with Mr. Shah as a pupil.

Mr. Shah's sharp intellect was matched by his warm demeanour, making him a favourite among students. His knack for turning complex concepts into engaging discussions and his ability to connect with students on a personal level made him an exceptional mentor. His enthusiasm for teaching was evident in the way he encouraged open dialogue and fostered a supportive learning environment.

Ayushman's first day was quite embarrassing. Rahul had prepared him at the hostel and apologised for drawing unnecessary attention, but Ayushman still hoped the day would pass quickly. In a class of sixty students from different cities, many had already formed friend groups, making it challenging for Ayushman to forge new friendships. Rahul regularly hung out with Meeta, Trisha, and Pari. Trisha, a day scholar from Jaipur and a good friend of Pari and Meeta, was the scholarly gem of the group. With her short curly hair and vibrant sense of style, she brought the hostel to life whenever she was around, always donning colourful outfits that matched her lively personality.

During the lunch break, Rahul introduced Ayushman to the girls at the cafe. "Hi guys, this is Ayushman, and Ayushman, this is Pari, Meeta, and Trisha." The girls greeted Ayushman warmly, and Pari remarked, "We've heard a lot about you from Rahul."

Ayushman smiled and responded, "I hope only good things!" Pari laughed and replied wittily, "Oh! I see you have secrets there!"

Rahul interrupted, "Come on, mystery man, it's your first day... and you're already flirting with the girls." They all laughed, and the boys excused themselves to continue their tour of the campus.

After classroom sessions, a few students would seek Ayushman's help in clarifying answers he had formulated during classes. During lab sessions, Ayushman had long discussions with Mr. Shah, who extended his work hours to support Ayushman's commitment to the subject.

Ayushman was an active participant in all his subjects—Computer Fundamentals, Network Fundamentals, Financial Accounts, Business Communications, and Programming Logic. Mr. Shah admired Ayushman's sincerity and intellectual rigor. This admiration reached its peak during an assignment on "Sorting an Array," where Ayushman's programming prowess outshone his peers, earning him accolades from Mr. Shah and the admiration of his classmates.

Watching Ayushman write programs word by word, line by line, like poetry, was a delight for both students and Mr. Shah. Whenever he ran out of space, he would ask, "Has everyone noted this? Is it okay to erase?" even though he didn't have to. Noticing his classmates jotting down each word quickly to keep pace, Ayushman chose to be considerate and helpful out of a kind spirit. He crafted a program of several hundred lines in Fortran with the fluidity of poetry.

His technical prowess, combined with his humility and willingness to share his knowledge, drew Pari towards him. During Ayushman's deep classroom interactions, she couldn't help but notice his stance, body language, pupil movements, and the words he selected to express himself.

In her world, Ayushman was mesmerising.

Maybe she had been reading a CSR magazine's body language session for a little too long, but she couldn't stop crushing on him. She just hoped that Meeta didn't find out.

As Ayushman's popularity grew, he began hosting impromptu programming sessions, garnering a following among his peers. While Pari admired his leadership, she longed for more meaningful interactions beyond technical discussions. She often found herself drifting into daydreams during these sessions, her mind wandering to thoughts of Ayushman beyond the classroom. Her friend Meeta started to notice, often teasing her about Ayushman, "So, fashionista Pari, what was your crush wearing today?"

"Are you keen to give him style tips?" Pari reacted.

"Does he even need style tips? He is the first person I have seen who is interesting beyond just superficial appearance," Pari said, slightly defensively.

"Interesting, hmmm. Looks like you are progressing in dreams. Now, all you need is a date, dude," Meeta teased.

In classroom sessions, whenever Pari watched Ayushman explain a complex algorithm with ease and confidence, she felt admiration growing. One such incident happened a couple of weeks later during Mrs. Khan's Computer Networking Fundamentals class. Mrs. Khan, known for her strict adherence to textbook knowledge, began the lecture with her usual authoritative demeanour.

"Class, as you know, a subnet mask is used to divide an IP address into network and host parts," Mrs. Khan began. "For example, in a class C network, a typical subnet mask might be 255.255.255.0, which allows for up to 256 network nodes."

Ayushman raised his hand, interrupting, "Excuse me, Mrs. Khan, but I believe there might be a slight mistake."

Mrs. Khan looked slightly irritated but allowed Ayushman to explain. "Go on, Ayushman."

"With a subnet mask of 255.255.255.0, we actually have 254 usable nodes, not 256."

He continued, "In a class C network with a subnet mask of 255.255.255.0, we have 256 IP addresses, but we must exclude the network address and the broadcast address. This leaves us with 254 usable IP addresses for network nodes."

Mrs. Khan responded, "Ayushman, the textbook clearly states 256 nodes. How did you arrive at that number?"

"Yes, Mrs. Khan," Ayushman replied respectfully. "If we use the formula $2^{(32-\text{subnet bits})} - 2$, we account for the exclusion of the network and broadcast addresses. Hence, for a subnet mask of 255.255.255.0, which has 24 subnet bits, we calculate $2^{(32-24)} - 2$, resulting in 254 usable nodes."

Mrs. Khan took a moment to verify Ayushman's calculation. Despite her initial irritation, she acknowledged, "You are correct, Ayushman. The distinction between the total number of IP addresses and usable IP addresses is crucial. I appreciate your clarification. There appears to be either a misprint or miscalculation in the text."

Ayushman nodded, feeling vindicated. "Thank you, Mrs. Khan."

Mrs. Khan smiled slightly, "Indeed, it is. Thank you for the correction, Ayushman. You have an excellent grasp of the basic concepts. Class, it's essential to get these details right, especially in network planning and administration."

Ayushman's sincerity and intellectual rigor earned him respect, and the class continued with a clearer understanding of subnet masks and network nodes.

Pari was deeply impressed by Ayushman's belief in himself and his courage to stand his ground. She thought to herself, "Ayushman's qualities are remarkable. It's as if fate brought us together." As she observed him, she couldn't help but envision a future where their paths converged more deeply. The thought of Ayushman becoming a partner in both her personal and professional life filled her with a sense of excitement and anticipation. She imagined them building a life together.

In her mind's eye, she saw a future where Ayushman's intellect and her own strengths complemented each other perfectly. In that moment, she even envisioned their children, inheriting Ayushman's brilliance and her creativity, growing up in a household where learning and curiosity were cherished values. Pari imagined late-night discussions that spanned beyond programming and algorithms, delving into philosophy and the deeper meanings of life. She pictured Ayushman reading bedtime stories to their kids, infusing each tale with his unique blend of wisdom and humour.

As these fantasies played out in her mind, Pari felt a warm, comforting sense of possibility. Her admiration for Ayushman was evolving into something deeper, a blend of intellectual respect and personal affection. She saw them working side by side on projects, sharing not just their professional goals but their personal dreams as well. Pari dreamed of a life where their bond would grow stronger with each challenge they faced together.

Pari's longing for more meaningful interactions became interlaced with a desire to truly know Ayushman, to understand the layers of his personality that lay beyond his academic prowess. She hoped that one day, their conversations would transcend the technical and venture into the realms of their hopes, dreams, and shared future. In her heart, she knew that Ayushman was the one she wanted to spend her life with, building a world where love, respect, and mutual admiration flourished.

THE DAY HAD UNFOLDED LIKE ANY OTHER IN MR. SHAH's classroom, but for Ayushman and Pari, it quickly transformed into something more. The moment Mr. Shah posed his question about the relationship between science and spirituality, the air seemed to thrum with anticipation. Pari, seated a few rows behind Ayushman, exchanged a brief glance with him. Little did they know, the conversation that would follow would have the whole class leaning in, eager to catch every word.

Ayushman, ever the logical one, was the first to raise his hand. His eyes gleamed with curiosity as he spoke, "Mr. Shah, I believe science explains the 'how,' while spirituality deals with the 'why.' But can humanity really exist on this earth without the process of evolution?"

From the corner of her mouth, Pari smirked. She had always admired Ayushman's sharp mind, but today, she was ready for a challenge. "My parents always taught me that God is the ultimate creator," she teased, her voice laced with playfulness. "So you could say I had a bit of 'divine help' when I arrived in this world."

Ayushman chuckled, leaning slightly toward her. "That's one way to put it. But don't you think the theory of evolution offers a more concrete explanation?"

Pari leaned in as well, her tone soft but brimming with intrigue. "Ayushman, can you honestly say that there isn't some magic to life that science can't fully explain? Who do you think keeps the balance of this universe intact?"

As their words bounced back and forth, like ripples in still water, neither noticed the captivated eyes of their classmates. Rahul, who sat near the front, nodded along with Ayushman's rational stance, while Meeta, more attuned to Pari's spiritual side, whispered her agreement to the person next to her. The classroom had divided into two camps, each silently picking a side in this intellectual duel.

Ayushman, his eyes alight with thought, responded, "Most of us know about the Big Bang and the millions of years of gradual evolution. It wasn't some overnight miracle."

Feigning mock offense, Pari pouted playfully, "For many, Mother Nature is a divine presence. Fruits grow on trees without any apparent magic, yet they flourish. Isn't that a kind of spiritual miracle?"

Ayushman laughed, shaking his head. "I respect that view, but to me, it's all part of nature's process, not magic."

Undeterred, Pari tilted her head slightly, her tone now more inquisitive, "Do you go to temples with your parents?"

Ayushman, nodding, replied, "Yes, I do. I respect their faith. There's a certain peace I find in temples."

Pari's smile deepened, the corners of her lips lifting higher. "See? You believe in something greater. You find peace there because temples are places of divine presence."

Laughter bubbled from Ayushman, his eyes gleaming. "Temples are peaceful because people choose to be peaceful there, not because of any divine presence."

By now, the entire class was watching. Even Mr. Shah stood back, a knowing smile playing on his lips as he observed the sparring of ideas. The intensity of their discussion was infectious, drawing in the entire room. The invisible thread connecting Ayushman and Pari was now felt by everyone.

"But doesn't that peace make you feel like there's something bigger at play?" Pari pressed, her voice now a hushed challenge.

Ayushman reclined slightly in his seat, his tone more thoughtful but still playful. "Peace is the result of the environment and collective mindset. People find peace in many places, not just temples."

Leaning forward, Pari's voice softened, "I believe that inner peace and morality come from a higher power. How do you explain the deep sense of morality we all have?"

Ayushman pondered for a moment before responding, "Morality stems from culture and personal experiences. Philosophers argue that it arises from logic and empathy."

For a brief moment, their eyes locked, and a deeper understanding seemed to pass between them. Pari's gaze softened as she said, "But there are mysteries that science can't explain. Isn't it possible that there's a divine element we haven't discovered yet?"

Ayushman sighed, conceding slightly, "It's true that science doesn't have all the answers. But turning to a divine power could halt the quest for knowledge."

With a playful smile, Pari delivered her final challenge. "For me, spirituality fills the gaps where science and reason sometimes fall short."

Ayushman nodded, acknowledging her point. "Everyone finds meaning in different ways. For me, understanding the world through science and reason brings a unique sense of wonder."

Pari's voice was gentle now, the tension easing. "So, does spirituality hold no place in your life?"

"I recognise its cultural and emotional significance," Ayushman replied, his voice calm and steady. "It shapes traditions and brings communities together."

Pari's smile turned into a knowing grin. "I won't give up so easily, Ayushman. I'll keep trying to convince you."

Ayushman's laughter rang out, filling the room. "I look forward to it, Pari."

As their conversation wound down, Ayushman's eyes lingered on Pari, drawn in by her sparkling gaze and the confidence that radiated from her. The playful banter and intellectual depth had left a mark on both of them, but it was a mark they hadn't fully realised yet.

While Ayushman and Pari continued their discussion, oblivious to the world around them, their classmates exchanged whispers and glances. Rahul nudged Meeta, murmuring, "They're not just debating, are they? There's something more there."

Meeta grinned knowingly, her eyes flicking between Pari and Ayushman. "Definitely. I think we're seeing something unfold."

But to Ayushman and Pari, the world had shrunk to just the two of them. The rest of the class faded into the background as they found themselves lost in their own debate, unaware that everyone else was witnessing the beginning of something profound.

As the session ended, the group of boys headed toward the locker room for their upcoming basketball match with the seniors. Rahul, always the joker, couldn't resist teasing Ayushman. With a playful shove, he laughed, "Hey, lover boy, it seemed like you and Pari were having your own private debate. What's next—philosophy under candlelight?"

Ayushman chuckled, shaking his head, "It was just a good debate, Rahul. But who knows, maybe there's something new to learn from her."

The locker room echoed with laughter, but the unspoken tension between Ayushman and Pari left everyone wondering where their discussions might lead. What started as an intellectual battle had grown into something much deeper, a connection that no one, including Ayushman and Pari, fully understood yet. It was clear to everyone that these discussions were the beginning of something much more personal—a journey of magical discovery between two souls.

LATER THAT DAY, AYUSHMAN SPOTTED PARI HEADING TO THE library alone. His heart skipped a beat as he decided to join her.

"Hello!" Ayushman greeted, his voice warm and inviting.

Pari looked up, her eyes lighting up at the sight of him. "Hi, Ayushman!"

"Mind if I join you?" he asked, hoping she would say yes.

"Not at all," she replied with a smile that made his pulse quicken.

As they exchanged pleasantries, their eyes subtly appraised each other. Ayushman admired the graceful way Pari moved, her hair gently framing her face and accentuating her features. Pari noticed the confident ease with which Ayushman carried himself, his presence both calming and exciting.

"So, how do you plan to convince me about the existence of God?" Ayushman teased, his voice low and playful.

Before Pari could respond, the librarian interrupted them, her tone stern. "This is a library for studying, not for dating. Please take your conversation elsewhere."

Ayushman chuckled, looking at Pari with a mischievous glint in his eye. "Shall we?"

"Yes," Pari agreed, her smile hinting at the shared excitement of their clandestine adventure.

Their mutual smiles betrayed an unspoken understanding as they made their way to the canteen. Finding a quiet corner, Ayushman fetched some coffee, each step allowing him to admire Pari's beauty and charm. When he returned, their hands brushed briefly as he handed her the cup, sending a thrill through both of them.

"So," Ayushman said, his eyes locked onto hers, "tell me about your thoughts on God."

Pari leaned in slightly, her voice soft yet confident. "Well, it's more about feeling than proving..."

As their conversation deepened, the romantic tension between them grew, their words weaving a delicate dance of curiosity and attraction. The world around them faded, leaving only the electricity of their connection and the promise of something more.

The romantic tension between Ayushman and Pari continued to build as they delved deeper into their conversation.

Pari leaned in, her eyes searching his. "Ayushman, it's crucial to cultivate gratitude for the blessings you have and the family you were born into. It's all twisted with your past life karma."

Ayushman smiled, appreciating her passion. "Here's the thing, Pari. I've never personally laid eyes on Lord Rama, but that doesn't negate his existence. There are epic tales that venerate his grace and valor. For me, these stories aren't mere mythology; they are a part of our history. The accounts of the battle in Sri Lanka are documented in both countries, and that's not a mere coincidence. The remarkable achievements attributed to him, his extraordinary governance skills, they aren't easily attainable by an ordinary individual."

Pari watched him intently, noticing how his eyes lit up with conviction. But she could feel the conversation veering into an endless loop. "Ayushman, whether you accept it or not, God does exist. Although a new question has arisen in my mind—are you a human or a humanoid?"

Ayushman chuckled, his gaze softening as he looked at her. "I have a liking for coffee, so I assure you, I am human."

Their banter, light and filled with unspoken affection, was interrupted by the approaching closing time of the canteen. Ayushman, determined not to let her leave in a sour mood, leaned closer. "You know, Pari, you might be onto something. Perhaps I just need a bit more convincing, but today isn't that day."

Pari smiled, feeling a warmth spread through her chest. Despite their philosophical differences, one truth was becoming clear: they had unmistakably fallen for each other.

Unbeknownst to them, time had slipped away, and the canteen was on the verge of closing. The caretaker's voice broke through their conversation. "It's time to head back. Your mother must be waiting."

Ayushman grinned, his eyes twinkling with mischief. "We actually live in the hostel, and you're the 'mom' who keeps us fed! But hey, don't scold us if we push past curfew!"

They shared a laugh as they dashed out, the easy camaraderie between them undeniable. As Pari strolled toward the hostel, Ayushman's motorcycle stopped ahead, and he offered her a ride.

"How about I drop you off near the hostel block? It's not safe for you to be walking alone at this hour," he said, his voice gentle yet protective.

Pari, flattered and touched by Ayushman's concern, accepted his offer with a warm smile. She climbed onto the motorcycle, her heart racing with a mix of excitement and gratitude. As they rode through the quiet campus, the cool night air wrapped around them, and the closeness between them felt both natural and electric.

As she sat behind Ayushman on the motorbike, she felt a mix of awkwardness and being cared for, a combination she hadn't anticipated. Her mind was blank with disbelief at how their interactions were becoming more frequent. Lost in her thoughts, she didn't even realise they had arrived at the hostel gate until Ayushman said, "Well, I guess this is where we say 'goodbye, Pari!'"

Startled, Pari snapped out of her reverie, quickly got off the motorbike, and smiled at her foolishness. She walked towards the hostel entrance, where the guard gave Ayushman a scrutinising look. Ayushman ignored it, started the motorbike, and headed towards the boys' hostel, feeling elated about the extra time spent with the girl who was slowly stealing his heart.

As Ayushman rode back, he found himself humming "Awara bhanware jo hole hole," a tune forever etched in his memory from Pari's unforgettable dance during the Freshers' dance-off. He recalled that evening vividly. When Senior student Riya invited a first-year student to dance, no one dared to step up due to the awkwardness of being new at the university. But Pari had stepped forward with confidence. She was a charm on stage, blending Bollywood dance moves with classical grace like a pro. She looked like an apsara from the heavens, enchanting everyone with her fluidity and poise.

The rest of that evening, Ayushman could think of nothing but her dance, mesmerised by the fluidity of her movements. And today, with her riding pillion to him, he yearned for more proximity with her. The feeling of her closeness and attention made him feel special, filling him with a newfound sense of joy and infatuation.

As days went by, Ayushman and Pari often found themselves coincidentally meeting at the same spot. One day, Pari and Meeta were sitting under the large banyan tree on campus, their favorite place to hang out between classes. Ayushman and Rahul happened to be walking past the Electrical Engineering block, which was abuzz with the latest gossip about Rohan and Asha, the hottest couple of the season at the university. It seemed like everyone had an opinion, and today was no different.

They decided to take a pit stop and casually greeted Pari and Meeta. "What are you guys up to?" Rahul asked casually.

"Nothing much, just talking about Asha and Rohan," Meeta replied, bouncing slightly. "Poor couple is the talk of the uni!" she added, empathising with the over-attention they were getting.

"I still don't get what the big deal is," Ayushman said, leaning back against the tree. "Rohan and Asha are just dating. They're happy, and that should be all that matters."

Meeta, always the voice of caution, shook her head. "Ayushman, you know how it is here. Dating openly like that is practically unheard of. It's not just about them being happy; it's about the reputation they're building—or rather, ruining."

Rahul chimed in, his usual playful tone replaced with seriousness. "Yeah, and let's not forget how this could impact Asha in the future. If they break up after four years, she'll be the one facing all the consequences. Society will always remember her as the girl who defied norms. Finding a respectable match after that could be really tough."

Pari, who had been quietly listening, decided to speak up. "I understand what you're saying, but isn't it a bit unfair? Why should Asha's future be ruined just because she chose to be happy now? It's not right that she has to sacrifice her present for the sake of a hypothetical future."

"Pari, you know how our society works," Meeta replied. "For guys, it's different. They can walk away unscathed, but for girls, it's like a permanent mark on their character. Asha might be happy now, but this image will stick to her for life. And not just her, her family's reputation is at stake too."

Rahul nodded in agreement. "Exactly. And think about her in-laws. Even if she finds someone willing to marry her, they'll always see her as the girl who didn't care about family values. She'll be sidelined in her own home."

Ayushman, still unconvinced, sighed. "But isn't it more important for us to change these outdated norms rather than just blindly follow them? Rohan and Asha are challenging the status quo, and I think that's commendable."

"Change is good, Ayushman, but at what cost?" Meeta asked. "It's easy to talk about change, but living through it is another story. Asha might be strong enough to handle the backlash, but can her family? Can her future in-laws?"

The lively debate under the banyan tree was heating up as Ayushman defended Rohan and Asha's relationship. Pari, intrigued by Ayushman's confident ideas, decided to put him on the spot.

"Ayushman," she said, turning to face him directly, "what if you fall for a girl and your parents don't accept the relationship? What would you do then?"

Ayushman shifted uncomfortably, not expecting the question. He ran a hand through his hair, buying time. "Well, if I really liked the girl, I'd try to convince my parents," he began. "But I believe they'd agree if she was willing to adjust and fit into the family."

Pari raised an eyebrow. "That's a big 'if.' Have you really thought about what it means to ask someone to change themselves to fit in?"

Ayushman nodded slowly, acknowledging the complexity of the situation. "You're right, Pari. It's a good question. Honestly, I haven't given it much thought before, but I will now."

The conversation then shifted to a lighter topic as Rahul suggested, "Alright, enough about societal norms. Let's talk about something fun. What qualities would you guys like in a life partner?"

Ayushman was the first to respond. "Confidence and grace," he said with a smile. "Someone who can hold her own and complement my strengths."

Rahul grinned, adding his preferences. "Beauty and politeness. I think those qualities would make for a harmonious relationship."

Meeta chimed in next. "I'd prefer a businessman," she said thoughtfully. "Athletic, but not too tall. I'm short, so an average height guy would be perfect."

Pari took a moment before sharing her thoughts. "I'd like someone highly intelligent and smart-looking. And he should be willing to settle in a foreign country," she said, her eyes twinkling with excitement at the thought.

They all laughed, imagining their ideal partners. The conversation had lightened the mood, allowing them to bond over their dreams and aspirations.

As the discussion wound down, Rahul glanced at his watch. "Time to hit the programming lab, guys. We've got the rest of the day's work ahead of us."

As the programming lab session came to an end, Ayushman, Rahul, Pari, and Meeta made their way back to the hostel. The air was cool and refreshing, and the campus was bathed in the soft glow of the setting sun.

Rahul, always the joker, nudged Ayushman playfully. "So, Ayushman, what's the deal? It sounded like you and Pari were describing each other's ideal qualities back there. What's going on, bro?"

Ayushman rolled his eyes and laughed, trying to play it cool. "Come on, Rahul, stop bullshitting. We were just talking. Now, are you coming for a swim at the hostel gym or not?"

Rahul smirked, recognising Ayushman's quick dismissal as a sign of something deeper. "Sure, sure. But you know, Ayush, you're not fooling anyone. I can see where your heart is these days."

Ayushman shook his head, but a small smile played on his lips as they continued walking.

Later that evening, after returning to their hostel, Pari and Meeta settled into their usual routine. They enjoyed a quiet dinner together and then prepared for supper. As they sat down to eat, Meeta couldn't help but bring up the conversation from earlier.

"So, Pari," Meeta began with a mischievous grin, "did you notice that Ayushman's preferred qualities sounded a lot like you?"

Pari blushed, trying to hide her smile. "Oh, stop it, Meeta. You're reading too much into it."

Meeta chuckled, not letting her friend off the hook so easily. "Come on, Pari. It's obvious he likes you. And honestly, you two would make a great couple."

Pari shyly dismissed the notion, though a warm feeling of happiness bubbled up inside her. "Go to sleep, Meeta," she said, trying to sound stern but failing miserably as her lips curved into a smile.

Meeta laughed softly. "Alright, alright. Goodnight, Pari."

As Pari lay in bed that night, she couldn't help but feel a sense of joy. The thought of Ayushman and the qualities he admired filled her with a warm, fuzzy feeling. She closed her eyes, dreaming of what the future might hold, a smile still lingering on her face.

As the semester one exams loomed closer, everyone in class turned their attention to brushing up their knowledge and gathering notes to practice for the exams. Each student had their own strengths and weaknesses, leading to a lot of knowledge sharing and mutual tutoring. One day, at their regular banyan tree hangout, Rahul, Ayushman, Meeta, and Pari discussed their challenges with different subjects.

"I dread financial accounting," Pari confessed.

"Well, I can help if you wish. I've been doing FA for the last 17 years," Ayushman jokes, making everyone laugh since they were all just teenagers, referencing his business background.

"So, what's the best time you can spare for me?" Pari asked, seizing the opportunity.

Ayushman, like a thirsty traveler in a desert finding an oasis, eagerly volunteered to help her. "We can start today."

"Oh good, two months is plenty of time to learn advanced concepts, particularly numerical applications and word problems."

"Cool, see you after the Programming lab today."

Meeta, winking at Pari and indicating where they were heading with a discreet smile, added, "But I will leave for the hostel as I'm fine with my average score."

Ayushman was secretly thrilled. This new arrangement meant he could see her every day, turning their study sessions into cherished moments he looked forward to.

That day, after the programming lab, they got together and spent half an hour on foundational concepts. Ayushman kept his eyes on the book mostly, and Pari looked away whenever he glanced up to check her understanding of the concepts.

"So, let's call it a day?" Ayushman sought her approval, giving her time to read the topics and prepare for the next day's session.

As Pari started walking towards the hostel, Ayushman started his motorbike and asked her to hop on, which she quietly did. That was the first day they spoke through their eyes, understanding each other without saying a word. Now, they both secretly knew that their hearts were beating in rhythm.

This marked the start of a daily ritual and the development of a trusting bond between them. Their bond grew stronger, and they became practically inseparable, with Pari no longer yearning to relocate to Canada.

As they continued to navigate their academic and personal lives, their initial infatuation blossomed into a deep and meaningful connection, each conversation and shared experience bringing them closer together.

Ayushman and Pari found various spots to study together— sometimes in empty classrooms during free periods, or on the benches in the university gardens where the tranquil environment allowed them to focus and grow closer. The time they spent together, under the guise of studying, deepened their bond in ways they hadn't anticipated.

While Ayushman's days were filled with the joy of teaching Pari, his friend Rahul noticed the shift in his priorities. One afternoon, as they grabbed a quick bite in the canteen, Rahul couldn't resist teasing Ayushman.

Rahul: "Man, ever since you started teaching Pari, it's like I don't exist anymore. You don't give me any time!"

Ayushman chuckled, shaking his head. "Come on, Rahul, don't be ridiculous. You know you're my best friend. I'm just helping her out with Financial Accounting. The exams are right around the corner."

Rahul smirked, mockingly complaining, "Oh sure, just 'helping her out.' I see how you light up when you talk about those study sessions. Maybe I should join in—think you can spare some time for me too?"

Ayushman laughed heartily. "You're welcome to join, but I doubt you'll stick around for more than five minutes of FA tuition."

Rahul grinned. "You're probably right. Just remember, you owe me a hangout session once the exams are over."

Ayushman nodded, grateful for Rahul's good-natured ribbing. "Deal. After the exams, we'll have all the time in the world to hang out."

This light-hearted banter with Rahul added a layer of humor to Ayushman's otherwise serious days, balancing out his growing feelings for Pari with the camaraderie of his best friend.

As the days passed, Ayushman and Pari's study sessions became a ritual. They'd meet in the mornings, sometimes even sharing breakfast as they discussed accounting principles. In the afternoons, they'd find a quiet corner in the library or under a shady tree in the garden, Ayushman patiently explaining concepts while Pari listened intently, her concentration punctuated by moments of laughter and light-hearted banter.

One evening, as the sunset cast a golden hue over the campus, Ayushman handed Pari a problem from their textbook. "Let's see how much you've learned. Solve this for me," he said, his voice filled with gentle encouragement.

Pari took the book, her eyes meeting his with a mix of determination and gratitude. She began working through the problem, Ayushman watching her with a sense of pride and affection. Each correct answer she gave was met with his warm smile, each mistake with patient guidance.

Their study sessions were more than just academic exercises; they were the foundation of a deeper connection, a blend of intellectual companionship and growing affection. And while they focused on Financial Accounting, both Pari and Ayushman knew that their hearts were engaged in a more profound lesson, one that was teaching them about trust, support, and the beginning of something beautiful.

Pari did well with conceptual answers, easily grasping the theories and principles. However, when it came to solving statement problems with numbers, she struggled. Ayushman noticed her frustration one evening as they sat under the large banyan tree in the university gardens, textbooks spread out between them.

Pari sighed, staring at the problem in front of her. "I just can't get these numbers to make sense, Ayushman. Why is Financial Accounting so difficult for me when I can ace physics without breaking a sweat?"

Ayushman, seeing the stress etched on her face, felt a pang of sympathy and a growing fondness. "Hey, don't worry," he said softly, moving closer to her. "Not everyone has a natural knack for every subject. You've got a brilliant mind for physics, and that's amazing. Let's take a deep breath and tackle this step by step."

Pari looked at him, her eyes showing a mix of gratitude and frustration. "But the exams are so close, and I don't want to fail."

Ayushman reached out, gently placing a hand on her shoulder. "You won't fail, Pari. I promise. We'll get through this together. Let's focus on the important topics that can get you a passing score. Financial

Accounting is just a one-semester subject anyway. Once it's done, you won't have to look at it again during the four-year course."

Pari smiled weakly, her anxiety easing slightly. "Thank you, Ayushman. I really appreciate your help."

Ayushman felt his heart skip a beat at her smile. He admired her perseverance and the way she tried so hard despite her struggles. He began highlighting the crucial topics in her notes, pointing out the areas that would most likely appear on the exam.

"Alright, let's focus on these key areas," he said, marking her textbook with a highlighter. "You don't need to master everything. Just get a good grasp on these topics, and you'll be fine."

As they continued studying, Ayushman couldn't help but fall for her even more. Her determination, her willingness to push through her difficulties, and her trust in him to help her navigate this stressful time only deepened his feelings. He cherished their study sessions, not just for the academic progress, but for the time they spent together, growing closer with each passing day.

ONE EVENING, AFTER A PARTICULARLY CHALLENGING SESSION, PARI closed her book and looked at Ayushman with a tired yet appreciative smile. "I don't know what I'd do without you. You've made this bearable."

Ayushman smiled back, feeling a warmth spread through him. "I'm just glad I can help. And remember, once this is over, you'll never have to deal with Financial Accounting again."

Pari laughed softly, the sound music to Ayushman's ears. "That's a comforting thought."

As the exam day approached, Ayushman ensured that Pari was well-prepared for the key topics. He quizzed her on important concepts, guided her through tricky problems, and constantly reassured her that she could do it.

On the day of the exam, as they stood outside the exam hall, Ayushman gave Pari one last encouraging smile. "You've got this, Pari. Just remember what we focused on, and you'll be fine."

Pari nodded, feeling a mix of nerves and confidence. "Thank you, Ayushman. For everything."

As she walked into the exam hall, Ayushman watched her, his heart full of admiration and affection. He knew that no matter the outcome, they had formed a bond that went beyond academics—a bond that had the potential to grow into something truly special.

As they finished their exams, Ayushman and Pari felt a mixture of relief and anticipation. The weeks of studying together had brought them closer, and now, without the looming stress of exams, there was an unspoken excitement about what the future held. That evening, as the sun dipped below the horizon, they found themselves sitting under the large banyan tree in the university garden, a familiar spot that had become their sanctuary. Their eyes locked, each noticing the subtle nuances in the other's expression, their fondness for each other unmistakable.

"So, what are your plans for your birthday?" Pari asked, trying to sound casual but unable to mask the underlying curiosity and hope in her voice.

Ayushman hesitated, a hint of surprise in his eyes. "I was planning to go back to Pathankot, but..." He paused, studying her face intently. "I'll stay back if you want."

Pari's heart skipped a beat at his response. She felt a flutter of excitement and a surge of courage. "I think you should stay," she said firmly, a smile tugging at the corners of her lips. "We can celebrate together."

Ayushman's eyes lit up at her words, sparkling with a mix of excitement and affection. "Alright then," he said, unable to hide his enthusiasm. "So, will you come to the University, or should we meet somewhere else?"

Pari, catching his playful tone, decided to tease him a bit. "Are you asking me out?" she asked, raising an eyebrow.

Caught off guard, Ayushman treaded carefully with his response. "Umm... Uni is a great idea. We usually hang out there, and it's... it's a perfect place."

Pari's curiosity was piqued. "So?" she pressed, wanting to hear more.

Choosing his words carefully, Ayushman reaffirmed, "So, Uni is a great idea. We often hang out there. It's a perfect place."

Pari smiled, signalling Ayushman to restart his motorbike, their eyes locked in a silent promise. As he complied, their connection deepened, each glance speaking volumes. They both sensed this was the start of something profound.

Riding back to the hostel, their silent dialogue continued, filled with unspoken promises and excitement. Their hearts beat in unison, each moment together weaving a stronger bond. The cool evening breeze carried their shared anticipation, whispering secrets of a future they both longed to explore.

With each exchanged glance and smile, the warmth of their growing connection was undeniable. By the time they reached the hostel, it was clear this was the beginning of a beautiful journey they were eager to embark on together.

Magic stirs, hearts blend, what next will love intend?

CHAPTER 5

CONFESSIONS AND COMMITMENTS

The sun bathed Jaipur Technical University's pink hostel in a warm, golden glow. Inside Pari's room, the atmosphere buzzed with excitement and a hint of tension as preparations for Ayushman's birthday were in full swing. The room, usually a haven for quiet study sessions and late-night chats, was now a whirlwind of activity.

Meeta, Pari's petite roommate with a gentle demeanour, found herself torn between happiness for her friend and a growing sense of unease. Always shy and reserved, Meeta's spectacled eyes often reflected her inner thoughts. She cherished her bond with Pari, but the increasing closeness between Pari and Ayushman left her feeling somewhat sidelined. Adjusting the vibrant bedspread on Pari's bed, Meeta couldn't help but wonder if their friendship would change. Sometimes, she wished Saba was still there.

Fortunately, Trisha stepped in as her hangout buddy whenever Ayushman and Pari spent time together. As the girls grew closer, Trisha often stayed with Pari and Meeta at the hostel. Known for being the enthusiastic cheerleader of the group, Trisha was on a mission today: to help Pari look fabulous and come up with the perfect gift for

Ayushman. Trisha's infectious energy filled the room, and even Meeta couldn't help but smile as they all worked together, creating a moment that would become a cherished memory for years to come.

"Alright, ladies! We need to make sure Ayushman's birthday is unforgettable," Trisha declared with her usual enthusiasm. "Pari, let's start with picking out your outfit. You have to look stunning."

Pari, her excitement palpable, sifted through her wardrobe with Trisha's guidance. They finally settled on a beautiful dress that complemented her bubbly personality and added a touch of elegance.

"Thank you so much, Trisha. Now, what about the gift? I want it to be special," Pari said.

Meeta, trying to push aside her mixed feelings, chimed in, "How about a book? Ayushman loves to read, right? We could find something classic, something that reflects your thoughtful side."

Trisha's eyes lit up. "That's a great idea, Meeta! And we can add a card with a heartfelt message. Pari, you should write something that reveals your feelings."

They decided to head to a quaint vintage bookshop in the heart of Jaipur. The shop, with its dimly lit corners and the rich aroma of aged paper and leather, was a treasure trove of literary classics. As they browsed the shelves, the owner, an elderly man with a kind smile, approached them.

"Welcome, how can I help you today?" he asked.

Pari replied, "I'm looking for a rare edition of a classic novel. It's for a special birthday."

The owner nodded and led them to a secluded corner of the shop, where a beautifully bound edition of "The Adventures of Sherlock Holmes" by Sir Arthur Conan Doyle sat on the shelf. Pari's eyes lit up as she picked up the book, feeling its weight and admiring its elegant binding.

"This is perfect! Ayushman will love it," she exclaimed.

The owner smiled warmly. "I'm sure he will. It's a timeless classic, and this edition is quite special."

Pari paid for the book, and the three friends left the store, chatting excitedly about the upcoming celebration. Back at the hostel, they gathered in Pari's room to finalise the preparations. Trisha handed Pari a card adorned with a heart, encouraging her to express her true feelings.

"Write from your heart, Pari. Let him know how much he means to you," Trisha urged.

As Pari began to write, Meeta watched with a mix of emotions. She was genuinely happy for her friend but couldn't shake off the feeling of being left behind. Despite this, she helped Pari wrap the gift and added a finishing touch to the card.

"There, it's perfect. He's going to love it, Pari," Meeta said, trying to sound cheerful.

The preparations were complete, and the excitement in the air was palpable. The girls sensed that this celebration would be a memorable one, not just for Ayushman, but for all of them.

While most other students had already left for the holidays, Pari and Ayushman decided to extend their stay by two days to celebrate Ayushman's birthday. Only Meeta stayed back to keep Pari company. The hostel warden, catching wind of their plans, made a pointed comment. "I know what you girls are up to when you stay back after exams," she said with a knowing smile, making Pari and Meeta feel a bit foolish for trying to conceal their true intentions.

ON THE DAY OF AYUSHMAN'S BIRTHDAY, PARI ARRIVED AT THE department an hour late and couldn't find Ayushman at their usual meeting spot. Her heart raced as she sprinted through the nearly deserted corridors, knowing exactly where to find him—the programming lab.

Ayushman sat alone in the lab, hating the solitude of waiting. With Rahul already gone to his hometown, Ayushman decided to kill time by creating a special program for Pari. He worked meticulously, coding each line with care, and added a graphic of an arrow piercing a heart as a romantic gesture. His heart raced with anticipation, hoping Pari would understand the depth of his feelings.

As he worked, he heard soft footsteps behind him. Pari, cleverly sneaking up, covered his eyes just as he pressed the 'enter' button on the keyboard to compile and run the program. The screen lit up with an arrow graphic penetrating a heart graphic, making Pari blush with flattery. Ayushman's heart swelled with pride and nervousness as he watched her reaction.

"You are a genius, how did you do that?" Pari asked, her eyes wide with admiration.

Ayushman, feeling proud but also unsure if his feelings would be reciprocated, looked around the empty lab, seized the moment, and offered her a rose. "Pari, there's something I've been meaning to tell you. You've become such an important part of my life, and I can't imagine it without you. I think... no, I know that I love you."

Although Pari was elated, she responded with a serious expression, aligning her intentions with her life plan. "Ayushman, I feel the same way. But I can't hang around with you like just a girlfriend. For me, a relationship means companionship for life."

"We can't decide that yet as we are too young?" Ayushman asked, his heart pounding.

"I am not too young, rather I would be at a legally marriageable age in six months. I don't want to get close to a man and then leave later because I won't be able to love anyone else after you. You are that kind of man for me!" Pari explained.

"I don't want to muck around and need to be certain that our companionship is for life or we can just be classmates and friends," she added.

Ayushman, taken aback by her response, realised how serious she was about her plans. The thought of being relegated to the friend zone was daunting. "You took me by surprise. If it means so much to you, then can I take a couple of days to think about it? This decision is monumental because we come from different backgrounds and my daily beliefs may not resonate with you."

Pari reassured him, expressing her feelings. "Our different religious backgrounds don't matter to me. You're exactly the man I've been seeking in my life."

Feeling validated, Ayushman suggested they go to the university cafeteria for a meal. Pari, not wanting to ruin Ayushman's birthday spirit, agreed, and they proceeded with their lunch plans, cherishing their time together.

"How many days do you need to decide?" Pari asked.

"I will think about it during the holidays," Ayushman replied.

"OK," Pari said.

The cafeteria was mostly empty, with only a few staff members bustling around. Ayushman and Pari found a quiet corner to sit and talk. They enjoyed a delicious meal and shared stories, their laughter echoing softly in the near-empty space.

As Ayushman rode Pari back to the hostel on his motorbike, the cool evening breeze ruffled her hair, heightening the whirlwind of emotions within her. The steady hum of the engine provided a rhythmic backdrop to her thoughts.

"What a day this has been! Ayushman's confession... the look in his eyes when he said he loved me... it felt so genuine. I've always admired him, but today was something else entirely. And that program he made, with the arrow piercing the heart... It was so thoughtful and sweet."

She tightened her grip slightly around Ayushman's waist, feeling the warmth of his body through his jacket. "But can we really make this work? He comes from such a traditional background. Can he truly support me in all my ambitions, and can I fit into his world?"

Ayushman felt Pari's grip tighten around his waist, and a surge of warmth and affection coursed through him. "She's holding on tighter. Does she feel the same connection I do?" Her touch sent a jolt of excitement and tenderness through him. "I've never felt this way before. She means so much to me."

He stole a quick glance over his shoulder, seeing her deep in thought, her brow slightly furrowed. "What's going on in that beautiful mind of hers?" He wondered, his heart aching to know. "Does she have the same worries I do?"

Ayushman's mind drifted to the future. "We come from such different worlds. Can we really make this work? But I want to try. I want to support her dreams, just as she supports mine. She's incredible, and I can't imagine my life without her."

The motorbike slowed down as they approached the hostel entrance, and Ayushman's thoughts turned serious. "This break will give us time to think, to figure things out. I need to show her that I'm serious, that I'm willing to fight for us."

As he parked the motorbike and helped her off, their eyes met, and Ayushman saw a mixture of hope and uncertainty in her gaze. He was determined to make this work, to bridge the gap between their worlds.

"Here we are. I guess this is it for now," Ayushman said, his voice tinged with determination.

They walked together to the hostel entrance where Meeta stood with the suitcases, her expression a mix of impatience and understanding.

"Finally! I thought you two would never get here," Meeta said.

Pari apologised, "Sorry, Meeta. Got a bit caught up. Ready to go?"

Meeta nodded, glancing at Ayushman. "You guys need a moment?"

Pari shook her head, feeling a surge of confidence. "No, we're good. We'll see each other soon."

Ayushman nodded. "Take care, Pari. Enjoy your break."

"You too, Ayushman. And thank you... for everything," Pari said, her voice filled with gratitude.

As she turned to leave with Meeta, Pari felt a sense of clarity mixed with apprehension. "This break will be a time to ponder our future. I need to stay focused on my goals and be prepared for any outcome. If Ayushman truly loves me, he will understand and support my dreams."

She looked back one last time, catching Ayushman's eye. They exchanged a silent promise—this was just the beginning of something profound and beautiful, yet uncertain. As she walked away, Pari resolved to protect her heart while hoping for the best, knowing that the next semester would be pivotal for their relationship.

THE DINING AREA AT PARI'S HOME WAS A COZY, INVITING SPACE with a large wooden table at its centre. The table, adorned with a simple yet elegant tablecloth, was set with neatly arranged plates, glasses, and cutlery. Warm, ambient lighting from a chandelier overhead bathed the room in a soft glow, casting comforting shadows on the walls adorned with family photos and artwork.

Pari seemed lost as she helped her mother set up the dinner table, her mind preoccupied with thoughts of Ayushman and their uncertain relationship. As the family gathered around the table, Capt. Bajwa, a tall and imposing figure with a kind smile, took his place at the head. Baldev, Pari's gentle and caring mother, ensured everyone had a serving of each dish before sitting down herself. Shera, Pari's older brother, chatted excitedly about his day, adding to the lively atmosphere.

"So, Pari, how is computer engineering treating you?" Capt. Bajwa asked.

Pari managed a smile, trying to shake off her worries. "It's challenging but rewarding, Papa. I'm learning a lot."

They continued their conversation, enjoying the delicious food prepared by Mrs. Bajwa. After dinner, they retired to their rooms. As

Baldev wrapped up the kitchen work, she noticed Pari staring at the ceiling in her room, lost in thought.

"Pari, what's on your mind? You've been distant all evening," Mrs. Bajwa asked gently.

Pari hesitated before opening up. "Mum, it's my classmate Ayushman. I really like him."

Mrs. Bajwa, familiar with the thoughts and attachments of Pari's age, showed understanding and asked Pari to elaborate, "What about him?"

Pari turned her back to Mrs. Bajwa, not wanting to share. "Nothing, he is a good friend. I fancy him." Pari cut the discussion short and said, "Goodnight, Maa."

Mrs. Bajwa understood that she needed space. "Goodnight, beta. If there is something you want to share, you know...."

"Yes, Maa, come home for unconditional love," Pari replied, repeating the affirmation her maa had been saying since her childhood.

The next day, Pari went through her day casually until she called Ayushman at their decided time of 4 PM. The call started sweetly but soon felt strained, as if an invisible wall of uncertainty stood between them.

"Hi, Ayushman! How have you been?" Pari greeted.

"Hey, Pari. I've been good, just busy with family and friends. How about you?" Ayushman replied.

"I've been catching up with old friends and helping out at home. I miss our conversations," Pari admitted.

"Yeah, me too," Ayushman said, but a long pause followed, filled with the unspoken thoughts and feelings they both held.

"Ayushman, is everything okay? You seem distant," Pari asked, her voice tinged with concern.

Ayushman hesitated, not wanting to hurt her. "I'm just trying to figure things out, Pari. You're a wonderful person, and I don't want to pursue anything until I'm certain."

Pari felt a pang of disappointment but tried to understand his perspective. "I get it. I just... I thought we were building something special."

"We are, Pari. I just need some time to be sure. I don't want to lead you on if I'm not ready," Ayushman explained.

"Alright, Ayushman. Take your time. Just don't keep me in the dark for too long, okay?" Pari said, trying to keep her voice steady.

"I promise, I won't. Take care, Pari," Ayushman responded.

As they ended the call, Pari couldn't shake the feeling that Ayushman was acting cold. Meanwhile, Ayushman thought Pari was a nice girl who meant well, but he didn't want to pursue her until he was certain of his feelings.

Later in the holidays, Pari and Ayushman made a couple of calls to each other. Ayushman had explained to Pari that he might not be available much on the phone because his family and friends would be around him, emphasising that he had never been absent from their lives in the last 17 years. Although Pari understood, she couldn't help but feel that Ayushman was using this as a tactic to limit their interaction, avoiding the deeper discussions they needed to have.

To distract herself, Pari caught up with friends from high school and her neighborhood. She visited her family's farm in the village, spending time looking after the cattle and helping her aunts. The routine and hard work helped clear her mind, but Ayushman's words still lingered.

As the holidays ended, Pari's mother, Mrs. Bajwa, came to drop her off at the university and to deposit the fee for the second semester. During the drive, they had a heart-to-heart conversation about Ayushman and Pari's future.

"Pari, how are things with Ayushman? Have you had a chance to talk things through?" Mrs. Bajwa asked.

"We've talked a few times, but he's been really busy with family and friends. I understand, but it feels like he's avoiding deeper discussions," Pari admitted.

"That's not surprising, beta. In conservative societies like ours, relationships can be uncertain until the elders seal the deal. You need to be careful and protect your heart," Mrs. Bajwa advised.

"I know, Mum. It's just hard because I feel so strongly about him. But I also know I need to focus on my career and not get too involved too soon," Pari said, her voice filled with determination.

Mrs. Bajwa nodded, her expression serious yet gentle. "You're right, Pari. Your education and career should come first. These relationships can be tricky, and you don't want to have any regrets later. Make sure you're building your future independently, so you have something solid to stand on, no matter what happens with Ayushman."

"I understand, Mum. I'll try to keep a balance and not let my feelings for Ayushman distract me from my goals," Pari promised.

Mrs. Bajwa reached over and squeezed Pari's hand. "That's my girl. You're strong and smart. Remember, love should support your dreams, not hinder them. If Ayushman truly cares for you, he'll understand and support your ambitions too."

Pari smiled, feeling reassured by her mother's words. "Thank you, Mum. I needed to hear that. I'll focus on my studies and career, and let things with Ayushman unfold naturally."

As they arrived at the university, Mrs. Bajwa helped Pari with her luggage and accompanied her to the administration office to deposit the fee. Before leaving, she gave Pari a warm hug.

"Take care of yourself, beta. Stay focused and remember what we talked about. I'll always be here for you," Mrs. Bajwa said.

"I will, Mum. Thank you for everything," Pari replied.

As Mrs. Bajwa drove away, Pari felt a renewed sense of determination. She knew she had her mother's support and wisdom to guide her, and she was ready to tackle the challenges of the new semester with a clear mind and a focused heart.

The second semester began and Jaipur Technical University buzzed with the energy of returning students. The Pink Hostel, with its pastel-coloured walls reflecting the early morning sun, was alive with activity. Students moved in, greeted friends, and caught up on their holiday adventures. Among them was Pari, her heart heavy, waiting for Ayushman to reveal his final decision.

Pari walked down the familiar corridors of the Pink Hostel with Meeta, who chatted excitedly about their first visit home and the joy of seeing each other again. Despite their enthusiasm, Pari couldn't stop replaying the moments she had spent with Ayushman from the previous semester.

Pari, Meeta, Trisha, Ayushman, and Rahul had already decided to meet under their usual hanging spot, the banyan tree. Both the girls and boys arrived simultaneously. When Pari's eyes met Ayushman's, she gasped and took a deep breath.

"Hi Pari," Ayushman said.

"Hi," Pari responded, her voice tinged with sadness.

Observing the tension, Rahul said thoughtfully, signaling Meeta and Trisha, "I think we should go. See you both in five minutes at the lecture hall."

Ayushman and Pari continued to look at each other. Ayushman knew Pari was waiting to hear his decision. He had come prepared to tell her he needed more time, but seeing her standing right in front of him, he remembered the sting of rejection from his past relationship. He saw the courage and determination in Pari's eyes and realized she would never abandon him like Geet had.

"Pari, I will support all your dreams. Will you spend your life with me?" Ayushman instinctively asked.

Pari burst into tears, a smile lighting her face. "Yes!" she managed to say amidst the rush of emotions.

Rahul circled back, ensuring Ayushman and Pari were okay as he called them to get to the first lecture of the second semester.

As they walked to class, Ayushman reached out and gently took Pari's hand in his. The touch was simple yet profound, a silent promise of the commitment they had just made. They walked together, hand in hand, feeling a sense of unity and strength. The first year at Jaipur Technical University (JTU) passed by swiftly. It felt as if they had just met yesterday, yet so much had happened in those months. Parting for the end-semester holidays was always hard, as they felt more connected to the new family at JTU than to their own families back home. The bonds they had formed were strong, making the campus feel like home.

Pari, Meeta, Trisha, and Rahul enjoyed their holidays by spending time with their families. They went out and about, visiting local attractions, enjoying family gatherings, and catching up with old friends. Pari, in particular, spent time with her mother, helping out with household chores and visiting her extended family in the village. The rustic charm of her village provided a peaceful retreat from the hustle and bustle of university life. Meeta and Trisha explored their interests further, with Meeta attending a short photography workshop and Trisha diving into a new collection of books she had been eager to read.

On the other hand, Ayushman's holidays were more focused on responsibilities and learning. He spent most of his time attending the family factory with his elder brother, Vardaan, learning the intricacies of business from both Vardaan and their father. Ayushman was business-savvy, quickly grasping concepts related to operations, management, and finance. The experience was invaluable, providing him with a practical understanding of running a business.

When they returned to JTU to start their third year, Ayushman decided to enroll in a local computer center, the "International Coders Academy" in Jaipur, to learn Java coding. He was determined to expand his skill set and saw coding as a crucial addition to his repertoire.

Within one month, Ayushman completed their six-month course, impressing everyone with his dedication and quick learning.

Seeing his potential, the managing director of the academy offered Ayushman a job and even agreed to fund his advanced Java course. Ayushman was pleased with the offer and embraced the opportunity wholeheartedly. The idea of earning his own pocket money was exciting to him, and he was eager to take on this new challenge. This job not only provided him with financial independence but also allowed him to gain practical experience in a field he was passionate about.

Back at JTU, Ayushman balanced his new job with his academic responsibilities. His schedule became more hectic, but he managed his time effectively. His days were filled with classes, coding practice, and evening shifts at the academy. Despite the busy routine, he found time for his friends, ensuring their bond remained strong.

Pari, Meeta, Trisha, and Rahul noticed Ayushman's increased workload but admired his dedication and commitment. They continued to support each other, finding joy in their shared experiences. They often spent their evenings together, discussing their days and sharing their achievements.

Pari was particularly supportive of Ayushman's new venture. She admired his ambition and was inspired by his drive to succeed. They continued to attend classes together, practice coding in the programming lab, and spend time exploring Jaipur's cultural sites on weekends. Their relationship grew stronger, built on mutual respect and shared dreams.

Meeta, Trisha, and Rahul also pursued their interests with vigour. Meeta joined the university's photography club, where she honed her skills and participated in various exhibitions. Trisha took on a leadership role in the debate society, leading her team to several victories in inter-university competitions. Rahul, along with Ayushman, participated in campus hackathons, where their team often stood out for their innovative solutions.

. . .

THE SUN WAS SINKING INTO THE HORIZON, CASTING A GOLDEN HUE over the sprawling pink city below. The cool breeze played with their hair as Ayushman and Pari sat side by side, the majestic fort around them forgotten as they gazed at the view. But what truly filled the moment wasn't the beauty of Jaipur—it was the unspoken warmth between them, the growing connection that bound their souls tighter with every passing moment.

Ayushman looked over at Pari, her face glowing in the last light of the day. He reached out, gently taking her hand, the simple touch saying more than words ever could.

"Pari," he began, his voice soft but filled with intensity, "you make everything feel possible. I never thought I'd meet someone who'd make the world so... clear." He paused, searching her eyes for the right words. "I know we've had doubts, but moments like this remind me why we're worth fighting for. With you, I feel like we can face anything, together."

Pari's eyes glistened with emotion as she leaned into him, her heart swelling at his words. "Ayushman," she whispered, her voice thick with feeling, "I feel the same. Being with you makes everything brighter. I never knew clarity until you. I believe in us... more than anything."

Ayushman's gaze held hers, a silent promise exchanged between them. "I swear, Pari, I'll stand by you—no matter what. You're not just a part of my life anymore. You're... everything."

Pari smiled, but it wasn't just a smile—it was an acknowledgment of the deep, unshakable bond they now shared. "I trust you, Ayushman. Completely. And that's why nothing can break what we have."

But the peaceful moment was tinged with an unspoken tension. Rajbir, with his hidden intentions, had been circling around their relationship like a shadow, hoping to pry Pari away. His charm may have fooled others, but Ayushman had seen right through him.

Pari sighed, the concern that had been gnawing at her spilling out. "Rajbir has been trying to impress me, Ayushman. He acts like it's innocent, but... it's exhausting. I feel like he's just waiting for a chance to break into what we have."

Ayushman's jaw tightened, his protective instincts flaring. "I know, Pari. I've seen how he looks at you, how he tries to get close. But you don't need to worry about him. Rajbir is nothing compared to us. Our bond is stronger than anything he could ever try to destroy."

Pari looked into Ayushman's eyes, finding strength in his gaze. "You're right. He doesn't matter, not when we have this." She placed her hand on his chest, feeling the steady beat of his heart. "We've built something beautiful, something real. Let's promise to always be honest with each other, to trust that no one can come between us."

Ayushman nodded, his grip on her hand tightening slightly. "I promise, Pari. I'll always be open with you. No one—no one—will ever come between us. We're in this together, forever."

The words hung in the air, sealing their commitment to one another. The sun had now fully set, and the stars began to twinkle in the sky above, as if blessing their promise.

Pari leaned closer, resting her head on Ayushman's shoulder. "I love you, Ayushman," she whispered.

Ayushman smiled, a deep warmth flooding his chest. He pressed a kiss to her forehead, lingering for a moment. "I love you too, Pari. Always."

As they sat there, the cool night breeze beginning to envelop them, both knew—whatever challenges lay ahead, their bond had become an unbreakable force. The Rajbirs of the world would never come close to what they shared. Their worlds, once separate, had now fully intertwined, merging into one, stronger and brighter than before. In their heart they felt that together, they could conquer anything.

And then, the day came when Ayushman knew he had to confront Rajbir. After all the advances, after all the sly comments and stolen glances, it was time for an end.

Standing in the shadow of the hostel's quiet back field, Ayushman and Rajbir faced off. The tension was thick in the air, the kind of tension that electrifies everything around it. Rajbir, ever the showman, started with a smirk. "What's the big deal, yaar? Me and Pari, we're just friends. You're taking this too seriously."

But Ayushman wasn't buying it. He stepped closer, his eyes locked onto Rajbir's. "You're not her friend, and we both know that. You've been trying to worm your way into her life, thinking I wouldn't notice. But here's the thing—I notice everything."

Rajbir laughed, though the confidence in his voice was faltering. "Come on, yaar. Love is fair game for everyone."

Ayushman's voice turned cold. "Love isn't a game, Rajbir. And if you think you can outsmart me, then you've already lost. Pari is mine, and I won't let anyone—least of all you—come between us."

And with that, Ayushman stepped forward, his hand closing around Rajbir's neck. The message was clear—this wasn't a battle Rajbir could win.

Students gathered, witnessing the confrontation, their whispers and opinions siding with Ayushman. His credibility, his connection with people, his academic brilliance and personal strength—they all spoke for him. Rajbir, once so cocky, now stood in the shadow of someone who not only held power physically, but mentally and socially as well. The students' loyalty to Ayushman made it clear that Rajbir had miscalculated.

Under the weight of Ayushman's grip and the judgment of the crowd, Rajbir's smirk faded. For the first time, he realised that he couldn't compete—not with Ayushman's strength, not with his mind, and not with the bond he shared with Pari. He had lost, and he knew it.

"Fine," Rajbir muttered, his voice barely above a whisper. "I'll back off. But don't think I'm scared of you."

Ayushman released him, his eyes burning with the finality of his words. "You should be."

And with that, Rajbir slunk away, defeated in more ways than one.

That night, word spread across the campus about what Ayushman had done. The next morning, as Ayushman entered the campus with Rahul by his side, he felt a shift in the air. The students' gazes were different —they looked at him with newfound respect, but more importantly, he noticed Pari watching him from a distance.

Without saying a word, she grabbed his hand, pulling him into a secluded corner. Rahul, seeing this, smiled and walked away, giving them the privacy they needed.

Pari's eyes sparkled with intensity, and before Ayushman could say anything, she leaned in, pressing her lips to his in a deep, passionate kiss. The world around them disappeared once more, leaving just the two of them in that moment.

When they finally parted, Pari's breath came in soft gasps, her eyes locked onto his. "I found out what you did yesterday. I heard everything about how you stood up for me. How you made sure Rajbir will never bother me again."

Ayushman smiled softly, brushing a strand of hair from her face. "I did what I had to do, Pari. I promised I'd protect you, and I meant it."

Pari's heart swelled with emotion. "I know. That's why I trust you, Ayushman. That's why I know I'm safe with you."

And as they stood there, locked in each other's arms, they both knew that their bond was now unbreakable. No matter what challenges came their way, they would face them together—secure in the knowledge that their love was built to last.

IN THEIR THIRD YEAR, THE FRIENDS SETTLED INTO THEIR REGULAR routine of coursework and fun. Mid-fifth semester brought a surprising and joyous turn of events. One evening, the phone at the hostel reception rang. It was a call for Ayushman. He rushed to the reception area, curious about the unexpected call. To his delight, it was Vardaan, his elder brother.

"Ayushman, I've got some big news! I'm getting married!" Vardaan announced.

"What? That's amazing! How did this happen so quickly?" Ayushman exclaimed.

"Well, it all started when our mum's sister brought a suitable match. It's the daughter of her sister-in-law's cousin's son. Her name is Sapna. Things moved quickly, and everything just fell into place like a dream," Vardaan explained.

Ayushman, trying to contain his excitement, replied cheekily, "That's incredible, bhaiya! I'm so happy for you that your dream (sapna) came true."

As Ayushman hung up the phone, he turned to his friends who were eagerly waiting to hear the news. The moment he shared Vardaan's announcement, the boys erupted in cheers, their faces lighting up with excitement. They started beating the warden's office table as a drum, singing, "Yaadon ki baraat nikli hai aaj dil ke dwaare...."*

The festive atmosphere continued as the group made plans to attend the wedding. The excitement was palpable, and the trip to Pathankot for Vardaan's wedding to Sapna, a girl from a business family in Meerut, became the talk of the hostel.

A WEEK BEFORE THE WEDDING, AYUSHMAN, PARI, AND THEIR friends set off for Pathankot. The journey was filled with laughter, singing, and the anticipation of the celebrations ahead. As they arrived at Ayushman's house, they were greeted with warmth and hospitality. The house was beautifully decorated with flowers and lights, reflecting the joy of the occasion.

The wedding festivities were a grand affair. The sangeet night was

---

* *"A symphony of memories serenades, today at the doorstep of my heart..."*
  The song is one of the most iconic tracks from the Bollywood film *"Yaadon Ki Baaraat"* (1973), celebrated for its nostalgic and emotionally stirring portrayal of brotherhood.

filled with music, dance, and laughter. Ayushman and his friends took the dance floor by storm, performing to popular Bollywood tracks. Pari, in a vibrant lehenga, joined the girls in performing a traditional dance, captivating everyone with her grace.

During the Sangeet ceremony, Ayushman gently took Pari's hand, pulling her closer, snatching a moment on a dimly lit overcrowded dance floor. "I've been waiting for a moment like this all evening," he whispered, his voice filled with warmth and affection.

Pari smiled, her eyes sparkling with the same excitement. "Me too. It's been such a magical night."

They stood close, feeling the electricity between them. The sounds of the celebrations faded into the background, leaving just the two of them in their own world. Ayushman brushed a strand of hair away from Pari's face, his touch lingering on her cheek. He could feel his heart beating faster, the intensity of his feelings growing stronger.

"Pari, being here with you tonight, I feel like everything is just perfect," Ayushman said softly, his eyes locked onto hers.

Pari's breath hitched as she looked up at him. "Ayushman, you've always been my strength. Tonight, I feel even closer to you."

Ayushman leaned in, their faces just inches apart. He could feel the warmth of her breath on his lips. "Pari, I love you. More than words can express."

Before she could respond, Ayushman closed the gap between them, capturing her lips in a tender, passionate kiss. It was a moment of pure connection, their hearts beating in unison. The kiss deepened, filled with the promise of a future together.

When they finally pulled away, both were breathless, their foreheads resting against each other. Ayushman held her close, feeling the warmth of her body against his. "I can't imagine my life without you, Pari," he murmured.

Pari looked into his eyes, her own filled with tears of joy. "And I can't imagine mine without you, Ayushman."

Ayushman's eyes sparkled with a mischievous glint. "Come with me," he said softly, taking her hand and leading her through the dimly lit corridors of the house. Pari followed, her heart pounding with anticipation.

He stopped in front of a door at the end of the hallway and pushed it open, revealing a secret room bathed in the soft glow of candlelight. The room was adorned with rose petals, and the gentle scent of jasmine filled the air.

Ayushman turned to Pari, his eyes filled with love and desire. "I wanted to create a special place for us, away from everything and everyone." Sneaking a moment, he switched on the already loaded music disc, playing a soft hit from the 90's movie "Maine Pyar Kiya." The romantic song, "Mere rang mein rangne wali, Pari ho tum ya pariyon ki rani..." filled the room, setting a perfect atmosphere.

Pari's heart swelled with emotion as she stepped into the room. "Ayushman, this is beautiful."

He pulled her close, their bodies fitting perfectly together. "Just like you," he whispered before capturing her lips in another kiss, this one more intense and filled with the promise of the night to come.

In the soft glow of the secret room, it felt as though the world outside had ceased to exist. Ayushman gently led Pari to a plush bed, the delicate linens cradling them like a sanctuary reserved for only the divine. As they sank together, their breaths intermingling, there was a magnetic pull between them, a profound connection that surpassed mere desire.

Ayushman's touch, both tender and passionate, ignited a fire deep within Pari, a warmth that she had never known before. Each caress of his fingers over her skin sent shivers of both anticipation and surrender down her spine. As they undressed each other with an unspoken urgency, their kisses grew deeper, as though each one was sealing their souls in a sacred vow.

With every soft brush of his lips from her mouth to her neck, Ayushman's presence enveloped her. He wasn't merely a lover in this moment—he was a force, a protector, a soulmate. Pari could feel the steady beat of his heart against hers, a rhythm that told her they were in perfect harmony. Every movement, every breath, every whispered touch, brought them closer together, their bodies moving with a natural, unspoken rhythm that transcended time.

"Ayushman..." Pari whispered breathlessly, her voice trembling with emotion, "This moment feels like a dream. Like something we were always meant to share."

Ayushman's gaze was soft but filled with intensity, his voice husky as he murmured, "This is our reality, Pari. I've never felt closer to anyone in my life." He brushed her hair aside, his fingers lingering as though to reassure himself that this was real. "You and I... we were always destined for this."

There was a momentary pause, a shared vulnerability. "Is it your first time?" Pari asked, her voice barely a whisper.

"Yes," Ayushman replied, his eyes never leaving hers. "Yours?"

"Mine too." A small, reassuring smile crossed his lips. "Brace yourself," he murmured tenderly, "It might hurt a little."

As their connection deepened, Pari felt a mix of sweet, unfamiliar pain and an overwhelming thrill of love that surged between them. Each movement, each shared breath, was filled with the kind of passion that only comes from an eternal bond being cemented, a love that was not just physical.

As their love reached its crescendo, they clung to one another, their breaths heavy, hearts beating in perfect unison. It was a moment of pure, untainted love—an exchange that sealed them together, not just for the night, but for eternity. The room was no longer just a room; it had become a sacred space where two souls had intertwined forever.

When the moment passed, they lay entwined under the sheets, the warmth of their love still pulsing between them. Ayushman gently ran his fingers through Pari's hair, his voice soft, almost reverent. "This is our beginning, Pari," he whispered, his lips brushing against her forehead. "The dawn of a new journey for our love."

Pari looked up into his eyes, feeling a sense of peace and contentment that she had never known before. Her voice trembled with emotion, "I love you, Ayushman. Tonight has shown me just how inseparable we truly are."

Ayushman's eyes softened with affection, and he pressed another kiss to her forehead. "I love you too, Pari. Always."

They drifted off to sleep in each other's arms, knowing that this night had not just deepened their love—it had strengthened it, forever uniting their hearts and souls in a bond that would never be broken.

As two hours passed and the Sangeet came to a close in the main hall, the lovebirds were quietly whisked away by their mischievous friends, Rahul and Meeta. With excitement brimming in their eyes, they discreetly guided Ayushman and Pari out of the crowded hallway, ensuring no prying eyes could follow. Rahul, barely able to contain his laughter, whispered in Ayushman's ear, "You owe me a big one, bro!"

The girls giggled, exchanging glances of curiosity and excitement. Meeta, as always, was eager to hear all the details from Pari. The magic of the night wasn't just in the celebrations—it was in the shared secrets, the stolen moments, the quiet affirmations of love that would echo through time.

As the night continued, Ayushman and Pari found solace in each other's company, sneaking away from the crowd to a quiet corner in the garden. The cool breeze brushed against them, and the twinkling fairy lights overhead cast a soft glow, adding to the romance of the night. In that garden, beneath the stars and surrounded by the love and laughter of family and friends, Ayushman and Pari's bond felt eternal, a love story written in the stars.

On the wedding day, Vardaan arrived like a prince on a white horse, leading the lively baraat filled with drums, dancing, and laughter. Sapna, radiant in a red and gold saree, waited under the beautifully decorated mandap, her eyes shimmering with joy. As the priest conducted the sacred rituals, Vardaan and Sapna took the seven pheras around the holy fire, sealing their vows in a timeless bond.

The reception was a grand affair, overflowing with delicious food, heartfelt speeches, and spirited dancing. Ayushman and his friends mingled with the guests, reveling in the joyous atmosphere. As night fell, fireworks lit up the Pathankot sky, symbolizing the brilliance of love and new beginnings.

Back at home, family and friends gathered to offer their blessings to the couple. Amidst the celebration, Ayushman and his friends quietly soaked in the happiness, their laughter and camaraderie deepened by the beauty of the day. Among the well-wishers, four friends made their way back to the hostel, carrying the joy of the night with them.

IN THE TRAIN COMPARTMENT, AYUSHMAN, PARI, RAHUL, AND Meeta had settled into their cozy space. It was a second-class sleeper with berths arranged in a three-tier configuration on either side of the aisle. They had a section to themselves, with two lower berths facing each other, two middle berths that could be folded down, and two upper berths for sleeping.

The compartment buzzed with a mix of excitement and exhaustion. Ayushman and Pari sat together on the lower berth by the window, looking out at the passing scenery. Rahul and Meeta occupied the opposite berth, their chatter filling the space.

Rahul leaned over with a playful grin. "So, lovebirds, how was the time alone at the sangeet? Did you get a chance to enjoy it, or Ayushman, were you too busy being the perfect host?"

Pari rolled her eyes but smiled. "He was the perfect host, thank you very much. But yes, it was beautiful. Vardaan and Sapna looked so happy."

Meeta chimed in, "I bet Ayushman had his hands full with all the family duties. You must be exhausted!"

Ayushman laughed, "Exhausted doesn't even begin to cover it. But it was worth it."

Rahul, not one to miss a teasing opportunity, smirked. "And what about you two? Any plans to follow in their footsteps soon?"

Pari blushed slightly and glanced at Ayushman, who squeezed her hand reassuringly. "One step at a time, Rahul," Ayushman replied. "Let's get through this semester first."

Meeta nudged Rahul, "Stop teasing them. They have plenty of time to plan their future. Besides, it's not like they need to rush."

As the train rattled along the tracks, the banter continued, light and cheerful. Pari and Ayushman found comfort in their friends' playful jabs.

The rhythmic clatter of the train wheels and the occasional whistle created a soothing backdrop. The compartment's earthy smell mixed with the aroma of food being served by the vendors passing through the aisles. The gentle swaying of the train had a calming effect, making them feel more relaxed with each passing mile.

Ayushman and Pari, seated by the window, shared quiet moments, their eyes meeting in silent communication. The lush green fields and distant mountains seemed to mirror their journey—a blend of challenges and beauty. Rahul and Meeta's laughter echoed in the background, adding to the sense of camaraderie and warmth in the compartment.

As the evening light began to fade, the group settled into a comfortable rhythm. Ayushman and Pari leaned back, enjoying the serene landscape outside, while Rahul and Meeta continued their lively conversation. The train compartment, with its mix of old and new friendships, felt like a small world of its own, moving steadily towards new adventures.

Ayushman glanced at Pari, who was resting her head on his shoulder, and whispered, "It's moments like these that make it all worthwhile." Pari smiled, feeling a sense of contentment wash over her. "I agree," she replied softly. "We have each other, and that's what matters most." The train rocked gently, creating a soothing lullaby as it carried them forward. The future, with all its uncertainties, seemed less daunting with the promise of love and friendship by their side.

Confessions whispered, vows to keep, what dreams in love's leap?

CHAPTER 6
A CALL TO DUTY

In the middle of their sixth semester, a pivotal visit from Raman changed Ayushman's perspective. One day, as Ayushman and Pari were absent from class on another romantic date, Raman arrived at Jaipur Technical University to meet Ayushman. Entering the classroom, the professor greeted Raman as an esteemed alumnus. When Raman inquired about Ayushman, a voice from the back benches called out, "They both are not here."

Rahul quickly covered, making an excuse, "Ayushman is sick and went to the hostel to rest." Sensing something more, Raman decided to investigate further. Later that evening, he found Ayushman and Pari returning to the hostel after a day spent together.

Once back at the hostel at 5 pm to get ready for work, Raman confronted Ayushman, who was shocked to see Raman present in the hostel room.

"Ayushman, I noticed you and Pari were absent today. What's going on?"

Ayushman, taken aback, replied, "We just needed some time together, Raman. It's nothing serious."

"Ayushman, the manufacturing wing of your factory caught fire, and all the stock was destroyed," Raman disclosed, his voice heavy with concern.

Ayushman felt a wave of shock wash over him. "When did that happen? Why did no one call me? How is everyone at home? Are Papa and Bhaiya safe? What about the workers?" His voice trembled as he fired off the questions, worry etched across his face.

"Relax, the fire happened at night due to a short circuit. There was no one inside the plant but the watchman outside, who was sleeping in his quarter, had to be rushed to the hospital due to poisonous gas inhalation. He is also safe now."

"But why didn't anyone tell me?"

"Dolly aunty sent me to inform you and safely bring you with me if you can spare a week to support Vardaan and your dad, who were not in favour of distracting your studies. But we can't let them know that you are coming home. I have train tickets booked for tonight. We will have to leave for the station in an hour, so if you want to see Pari quickly before you leave, you must do that now."

Raman hesitated for a moment, then spoke softly but firmly. "Also, from one man to another, Vardaan has been doing double shifts to ensure your studies are uninterrupted. His married life has been tough."

Ayushman frowned, the weight of his brother's sacrifices settling on his shoulders. "I didn't know it was that bad for him," he admitted, feeling a pang of guilt.

Raman continued, "Your hanging out with Pari too much in the future might seem a bit selfish, especially knowing that you might split up due to your family's traditional mindset and social stature."

Ayushman looked Raman in the eye, determination burning in his gaze. "I promise, Raman, my love life won't come in the way of my duty to the family. I owe it to Vardaan, and I owe it to everyone back home."

. . .

AYUSHMAN MET PARI IN THE GYMNASIUM, HIS FACE LINED WITH worry. He took a deep breath and gently broke the news to her. "I have to go home, Pari."

Pari looked up, concern filling her eyes. "Why? What happened?"

Ayushman sighed. "Raman informed me that there was a fire in the factory three weeks ago. My parents need support to get through this incident."

Pari's face fell, but she quickly masked her worry with a supportive smile. "Is everyone okay? What about your dad and Vardaan?"

"They're safe," Ayushman reassured her, though his voice trembled slightly. "But there's a lot of work to be done to restore everything."

Pari reached out, placing a comforting hand on his arm. "I understand, Ayushman. But what about your studies?"

Ayushman nodded, trying to smile. "I've already sent emails to the academy and the computer science head of the department, requesting emergency leave. But you don't need to worry about it. Focus on your studies and dreams. I will be back as soon as the situation is restored."

She squeezed his hand, her eyes shining with unshed tears. "Take care of your family. I'll be here when you get back."

After meeting Pari, Ayushman picked up Raman and met Rahul at the basketball court. "Bro, I gotta leave. There's been a fire. Hop on," Ayushman said urgently.

Rahul saw Raman sitting on the pillion of the motorbike and quickly hopped on as the third passenger. The trio made their way through the busy streets of Jaipur to the train station.

As they arrived, Rahul jumped off first, helping Ayushman and Raman with their bags. "I'll drop you off here, it's a no-parking zone," Rahul said, briefly shaking hands with both.

Ayushman yelled, "Take care of Pari. Call me if needed."

Rahul, nodding firmly, reassured him, "Don't worry. I'll take care of everything. Leave a message when you get home."

Ayushman gave a grateful smile. "Thanks, Rahul."

As Ayushman and Raman hurried into the station, Rahul watched them go, knowing he'd do everything he could to support his friend in this tough time.

As they boarded the general class compartment due to lack of availability in first class, Ayushman felt a deep sadness for the fate his parents and brother's family might have to face. They had always moved in elite circles, and now he was sitting in a compartment that starkly contrasted with their usual standards. The smell of spit and urine, rubbish strewn about, body odours, and sweaty armpits made the harsh reality of life sting him.

Ayushman thought to himself, "I will never let my family feel this low. I will build a new life for them where they don't have to worry about the losses from the fire incident."

As the train arrived at Pathankot, they saw Raman's dad waiting on the platform. He hugged Ayushman warmly, feeling the young man's weariness and anxiety. Ayushman clung to him for a moment, seeking comfort.

Raman's dad, noticing the worry etched on Ayushman's face, said gently, "It's going to be okay, Ayushman. Your family is strong."

Ayushman nodded, trying to muster a smile. "Thank you, Uncle. It's just... a lot to take in."

Raman's dad didn't say much more, sensing the young man needed quiet. He drove them home, the car ride filled with an unspoken tension. He glanced at Ayushman in the rearview mirror, wanting to ease his mind but knowing it wasn't his place. "Kamal will explain everything when you get home," he said softly, referring to Ayushman's father.

Ayushman took a deep breath, preparing himself for the difficult conversations ahead.

AYUSHMAN ENTERED THE LIVING ROOM WHERE HIS FAMILY WAS gathered. He first touched his mother's feet, and she immediately embraced him, tears streaming down her face as she clung to him for comfort. She cried uncontrollably at their fate, saying, "I don't know why we got this punishment. We have always been charitable and god-fearing people."

"Maa, don't worry. We will get through this," Ayushman whispered, trying to soothe her distress.

His father stood nearby, a stoic figure with eyes that betrayed his inner turmoil. Ayushman moved to him, touching his feet and receiving a long, silent hug in return. The embrace spoke volumes, a mixture of unspoken words and mutual understanding.

"I know you'll make us proud, son," his father finally said, his voice thick with emotion.

Ayushman then turned to his sister-in-law, Sapna. He touched her feet as well, and she immediately pulled him into a hug, her own tears mingling with her words of reassurance.

"Bhabi, I am with Bhaiya. Don't worry, all will be okay," Ayushman said, his voice steady and filled with determination.

Sapna nodded, her grip tightening for a moment before she let go. "Thank you, Ayushman. We all need to stay strong."

Lastly, Ayushman turned to Vardaan. Without a word, he enveloped his brother in a tight hug. Vardaan, holding back tears, finally let them flow as Ayushman whispered, "Now, I am here, don't you worry!"

Vardaan's grip tightened around Ayushman, feeling the weight of the world lift just a bit. "It's been so hard, Ayush," he choked out, his voice trembling with emotion.

"I know, Bhai. I know," Ayushman replied, his voice steady, offering the strength Vardaan needed.

They stood there, holding onto each other for what felt like an eternity, allowing their shared silence to convey what words could not. The warmth of their embrace spoke volumes of the bond they shared, the comfort and support they found in each other.

After what seemed like five minutes, Vardaan finally relaxed his hold. He took a deep breath, wiped away his tears, and managed a small, grateful smile. "Thank you, Ayush. I don't know what I would do without you."

Ayushman patted his brother's back reassuringly. "You're never alone, Vardaan. We'll get through this together."

Vardaan nodded, feeling a renewed sense of hope and strength. He sat down on the couch, emotionally drained but comforted by his brother's presence.

After a rest for couple of hours, while having his meal, Ayushman sat down with Vardaan to discuss the next steps.

"Ayushman, we might need to build a new, smaller plant to service the outstanding orders," Vardaan said, breaking a piece of parantha and dipping it into the yogurt. "It's not going to be easy, but it's necessary."

Ayushman nodded, his mind already whirring with logistics as if he had aged a decade overnight. He could almost feel the gears turning in his head, each thought sharpening his focus. "I understand, bhaiya," he said, his voice steady and resolute. "I'm ready to help in any way I can." As he spoke, he felt a surge of determination course through his veins, grounding him in the present and propelling him toward the future.

Vardaan smiled, though it didn't quite reach his eyes. "You've been earning enough to support your fees and pocket money, and that's a big relief for us."

Ayushman looked down at his plate, feeling a mix of pride and responsibility. "I just want to make sure I'm doing my part."

"You are," Vardaan assured him. "And I want you to focus on your studies and your job at the computer center. We have enough funds to manage for the next two years. By then, you'll be in the software industry, and we can start thinking about new business ideas."

Ayushman felt a surge of determination. "So you don't want me to come back and help with the factory?"

Vardaan shook his head. "No, I want you to focus on software programming. That could be our next big bet. Your skills in programming might be the key to a new direction for our family business."

Ayushman took a deep breath, feeling the weight of his brother's words. "I won't let you down, bhaiya. I'll give it my all."

Vardaan placed a reassuring hand on Ayushman's shoulder. "I know you will. We're in this together, and we'll come out stronger on the other side."

The rest of the week was an intense dive into factory accounts and short-term planning to fulfil pending orders for the next two years. Vardaan managed the news, shutting down rumours that their business was collapsing.

BACK AT JTU, AYUSHMAN RESUMED HIS UNIVERSITY LIFE WITH renewed vigour. His dedication to studying the software industry deepened, and he explored market gaps that could potentially be filled by innovative solutions for Vardaan's business.

Ayushman and Rahul became close friends, their bond strengthening as Rahul witnessed Ayushman's commitment to both his family and Pari amidst adversity. One evening, as they sat in their dorm room, Rahul broke the silence. "Ayushman, watching you juggle everything has really opened my eyes," he said, admiration evident in his voice.

Ayushman looked up, surprised. "What do you mean, Rahul?"

"I mean, the way you handle your responsibilities, your family, and your relationship with Pari... it's incredible," Rahul continued. "It's made me rethink what I want to do with my life. I want to join you at the academy, not just as a student, but eventually as a teacher too. I want to make a difference, like you."

Ayushman felt a surge of pride and warmth. "Rahul, that's amazing to hear. I'd be honoured to mentor you. Together, we can achieve so much."

Rahul smiled, a sense of determination in his eyes. "Thanks, Ayushman. You've shown me what it means to be resilient and dedicated. I want to follow in your footsteps."

From that day on, they were like brothers, bound by shared goals and challenges. Ayushman took his role as a mentor seriously, guiding Rahul through their studies and beyond. Late-night study sessions became a norm, filled with discussions about their future and the impact they hoped to make.

Once Ayushman settled, he and Pari sat together in their usual hangout spot in the botanical garden. Ayushman shared details of his visit home, mentioning how his brother Vardaan handled the adversity that many businesses couldn't overcome. The tough conversations with Vardaan inspired Ayushman to be his best. Pari listened intently, her presence soothing his troubled mind.

"Ayushman, I'm proud of you," she said softly. "And remember, you're not alone in this. We are in this together."

Her words wrapped around his heart, offering solace and strength. They held each other in silence, finding comfort in their bond. Pari's unwavering support and love gave Ayushman the courage to face the challenges ahead.

Determined to balance personal commitment with family loyalty, Ayushman focused on his studies and part-time job. He spent countless hours honing his skills, ensuring he was on track to secure a lucrative job post-graduation.

While Ayushman worked tirelessly, he envisioned a future where he and Pari both had successful careers. He saw Pari becoming an integral part of his family, imagining them living in cities like Delhi, Mumbai, or Bangalore where it wouldn't be hard to convince his family of their union. This vision gave him the strength to persevere.

As they navigated university life and their personal aspirations, Ayushman and Pari's bond deepened. Ayushman's unwavering dedication to his family and love for Pari fuelled his resolve. Together, they faced each obstacle, their souls braided in a commitment that promised to withstand the test of time.

After the incident, as they settled back into the normal pace of university life, Ayushman and Pari headed to a picturesque spot at Jaigarh Fort overlooking the city. The pink hue of the buildings below mirrored the warmth they felt for each other. Sitting behind Ayushman on his Splendour motorbike, Pari wrapped her arms around him as they talked about their future.

"Can you believe how far we've come?" Pari said, her voice soft and filled with wonder. "Three years of university are almost over, and here we are, still as in love as ever."

Ayushman smiled, his eyes reflecting the twilight. "I know. It feels like yesterday when we first met. You've always been my inspiration, Pari."

Pari laughed lightly. "And you, my rock. Remember how I struggled with Financial Accounting? I couldn't have made it without you."

Ayushman turned to face her, his expression serious yet tender. "You could have. You're stronger than you know. I just gave you a nudge."

They sat in comfortable silence for a while, watching the sunset. The air was filled with the scent of blooming flowers, and the distant hum of the city provided a soothing backdrop.

"Ayushman, do you ever think about our future?" Pari asked, her voice tinged with curiosity.

"All the time," he replied, taking her hand in his. "I see us together, building a life where you feel safe and free to be yourself. I want to support your dreams, whatever they may be."

Pari's eyes sparkled with emotion. "You've always given me that space. With you, I feel like I can conquer anything. I used to dream about moving to Canada, but now, all I dream about is our future together."

Ayushman squeezed her hand. "We'll make our dreams come true, together. Wherever we go, as long as we're together, that's all that matters."

Pari leaned in, her forehead resting against his. "You know, my father was shocked to see my interest in computer science. I forgot all about fashion designing, but you never stopped admiring my unique taste in clothes. That gave me the validation I needed."

Ayushman smiled, kissing her forehead. "Your creativity and passion are what make you special. I've always loved that about you."

They shared a lingering kiss, the world around them fading away. Ayushman admired how Pari rode his motorbike around Jaipur, a rare sight for a woman in the early 2000s. Her confidence and independence only strengthened his admiration and love for her.

"I love how you never let anyone else's opinion dictate your choices," Ayushman said, his voice filled with pride. "You're my trailblazer."

Pari laughed, a joyful sound that echoed in the twilight. "And you're my anchor. With you, I feel like I can fly while staying grounded."

As they rode back to the hostel, the cool night air wrapped around them, filled with the scent of possibility. Ayushman felt an overwhelming sense of contentment and anticipation for their future. With Pari by his side, he knew they could take on the world.

Their bond grew stronger with each passing day, and they became practically inseparable. The thought of relocating to Canada did not appear in Pari's mind anymore. With Ayushman, she found her home, her freedom, and her partner for life.

. . .

IN THE BUSTLING FINAL YEAR OF UNIVERSITY, THE AIR WAS CHARGED with anticipation and a hint of anxiety. Students were preparing for their industrial internships, a crucial step towards their future careers. Ayushman and Pari were no exception. The vibrant campus of Jaipur Technical University, which had been their playground and sanctuary for so long, was about to become a memory as they embarked on their respective journeys to New Delhi for their internships.

The evening was set for the grand farewell event for the Computer Science department's Class of 2003. The juniors had planned a black-tie Bollywood-themed masquerade ball, complete with ballroom dancing, to send off their seniors in style. The venue was elegantly decorated, with sparkling chandeliers casting a warm glow over the lavishly adorned hall. The air was filled with anticipation and excitement as students arrived, dressed in their best outfits inspired by their favourite Bollywood actors and characters.

Pari entered the hall, her attire a stunning tribute to Madhuri Dixit's iconic look from "Hum Aapke Hain Koun." She wore a vibrant purple lehenga, adorned with intricate gold embroidery, and a matching choli that highlighted her graceful figure. Her hair was styled in soft waves, cascading over her shoulders, and she completed her look with traditional jewellery that added a touch of elegance. Her mask, delicate and golden, only added to her mysterious allure.

Ayushman arrived shortly after, exuding charm in his dapper black tuxedo, inspired by Shah Rukh Khan's character in "Dilwale Dulhania Le Jayenge." His sharp suit was complemented by a crisp white shirt and a classic black bow tie. His mask, a sleek black design, gave him an air of intrigue and sophistication. As he stepped into the hall, his eyes scanned the crowd, searching for Pari.

The evening was filled with laughter, music, and memories as juniors and seniors mingled, sharing stories and capturing the moments in photographs. The highlight of the night was the ballroom dance, where pairs moved gracefully to the rhythm of classic Bollywood tunes.

Ayushman finally spotted Pari across the room. He made his way through the crowd, his heart racing with excitement and longing. He gently took her hand, leading her to the dance floor. As they began to dance, the world around them seemed to fade away. Holding her close, Ayushman was overwhelmed with emotion.

As they glided across the dance floor, Ayushman felt an overwhelming sense of love and anticipation. He thought about their future together, soon to be married and spending every moment side by side. The thought of being with Pari 24/7 filled him with joy and excitement. Holding her in his arms, he felt an intense desire to be close to her, to protect and cherish her always. He longed for the day they would no longer have to part ways at the end of each evening, the day they could truly share their lives completely.

"Pari, dancing with you tonight, I can't help but think about our future," Ayushman whispered in her ear. "I can't wait for the day we can be together all the time, to hold you like this and never let go."

Pari smiled, her heart swelling with love. "Me too, Ayushman. I can't wait to start our life together."

The evening continued with a series of performances and speeches. There were heartfelt tributes to the graduating class, recounting their journey through university, the friendships formed, and the challenges overcome. Laughter echoed through the hall as amusing anecdotes were shared, and tears were shed during moments of reflection.

Meeta, dressed as Kajol from "Karan Arjun," performed a captivating dance, mesmerising everyone with her grace. Rahul, inspired by Amitabh Bachchan's look in "Kabhi Kabhie," gave a moving speech, expressing his gratitude for the unforgettable memories and friendships.

Trisha, channeling her inner Urmila Matondkar from "Rangeela," led a group performance that had everyone cheering. The juniors had also prepared a video montage, showcasing highlights from the seniors' time at the university, evoking a mix of nostalgia and pride.

As the night drew to a close, the reality of parting began to sink in. There was a mix of emotions—joy, sadness, excitement, and apprehension about the future. Friends hugged tightly, promising to stay in touch and wishing each other the best.

Ayushman and Pari stood together, holding hands as they said their goodbyes to friends and faculty. The thrill of the evening was tinged with the bittersweet realisation that this phase of their lives was ending.

"We've had some incredible times here, haven't we?" Ayushman said, his voice filled with emotion.

"We have," Pari agreed, her eyes glistening with tears. "But I'm excited for what comes next. We'll make new memories together."

They shared a tender kiss, sealing their promises for the future. As they left the hall, the moonlight casting a soft glow on their path, they knew that their love and the memories they had created would guide them through whatever lay ahead.

The farewell event had not only celebrated their achievements but also strengthened their resolve to face the future together, hand in hand.

On their last day on campus before heading to Delhi, Ayushman and Pari sat in their favourite spot under a sprawling banyan tree. The late afternoon sun cast long shadows, and the air was filled with the familiar sounds of students chatting and laughing in the distance. They were both lost in their thoughts, contemplating the changes that lay ahead.

"I can't believe this is it. No more walking to classes together, no more sneaking into the library for study sessions," Ayushman said.

"Yeah, it's going to be strange not seeing you from 9 AM to 5 PM every day. But this is an important step for both of us," Pari replied.

Ayushman reached out, taking Pari's hand in his. The simple gesture conveyed the depth of his feelings. "We'll make it work, Pari. We'll text, call, and meet on weekends. It's not the end, just a new beginning."

"I know. I just hope we can handle the change. I've gotten so used to having you around all the time," Pari said.

They spent the next few hours reminiscing about their time at the university, from the first time they met to the countless moments of laughter and love that followed. As the sun dipped below the horizon, they made their way back to the hostel, knowing this was their last evening on campus.

The following day, they both departed for New Delhi, each heading to different companies for their industrial training. The city, with its endless rush and towering buildings, was a stark contrast to the serene and familiar environment of their university.

In their respective offices, Ayushman and Pari quickly adapted to the professional world. They dove into their work, impressing their supervisors with their dedication and skills. Yet, amidst the bustling workdays, they found time to stay connected.

"Hey, how's your first day going?" Ayushman texted.

"Busy! So much to learn. How about you?" Pari replied.

"Same here. Miss you already. Can't wait for the weekend," Ayushman responded.

"Miss you too. Let's plan something fun for Saturday," Pari suggested.

The weekend arrived, and they decided to meet at India Gate, one of Delhi's iconic landmarks. The sight of each other after a long week brought instant smiles and a sense of relief.

"I didn't realise how much I missed you until now," Pari said.

"Me too. This week felt like a month," Ayushman agreed.

They spent the day exploring the city, visiting cafes, and enjoying each other's company. It was a stark reminder of the connection they shared and the strength of their relationship, even when apart.

Over the next few months, this became their routine. Weekdays were dedicated to their internships, but weekends were reserved for each other. They visited various spots in Delhi, from historical monuments to trendy markets, savouring the time they had together.

One evening, as they sat by the serene waters of Lodhi Garden, Ayushman turned to Pari, his eyes reflecting the setting sun. "You know, this experience has made me realise something important."

"What's that?" Pari asked.

"No matter where we are or how busy life gets, as long as we have each other, we can handle anything," Ayushman said.

Pari smiled, leaning her head on his shoulder. "I feel the same way. This internship is just the beginning. We have a whole future ahead of us."

In India, in the early 2000s, the weight of religion and caste loomed large, a societal reality that Ayushman and Pari had blissfully overlooked. Their love life within JTU campus had insulated them from the harsh realities that awaited.

Amidst this, Ayushman's thoughts often drifted to his inter-religion and inter-caste relationship with Pari, challenging the traditional setup of his family. He knew their relationship was not just a personal choice but a bold statement against deeply ingrained societal norms. The whispers of disapproval from relatives and the pressure from his mother to marry someone from their own caste and religion weighed heavily on him.

Besides the challenges in their relationship, Ayushman was increasingly worried about revitalising the family business, which Vardaan struggled to manage. Meanwhile, their mother, Dolly, unaware of the business crisis, pressured Ayushman to consider brides from "appropriate" families.

Navigating these turbulent waters, Ayushman felt immense pressure. He was torn between his family's traditional expectations and the fulfilling journey with Pari. His love for her grew stronger, often defending their bond silently. Reflecting on their challenges, Ayushman realised that his love for Pari gave him a new perspective, questioning societal boundaries. He knew that standing by her meant fighting for their relationship and redefining family roles.

Resolving to balance his responsibilities, Ayushman drew strength from their love to face decisions about the family business. The thought of a future with Pari, free from societal constraints, gave him the courage to move forward. Together, they were ready to face any challenge, determined to ensure their love story was one of resilience and triumph against the odds.

Love and duty, a sacred arch, what trials lie in their march?

CHAPTER 7
LOVE AND DUTY

In the fall of 2003, Pari and Ayushman stood on the brink of an exhilarating new journey, eager to embrace the unfolding adventure of their lives. From the time they first met in their teens, their journey together had been filled with countless memories and milestones. After landing coveted jobs in Gurgaon, an IT hub renowned for its energy and innovation, they settled into a shared hostel with separate wings—one for girls and one for boys—each finding their own rhythm in the bustling metropolis.

Gurgaon, with its towering skyscrapers, modern infrastructure, and vibrant corporate culture, was a stark contrast to the traditional settings they had known. The city was a magnet for young professionals, and Pari and Ayushman thrived in its dynamic environment. Weekends were filled with exciting escapes, exploring Gurgaon's trendy malls, high-end restaurants, and lively entertainment venues. They often marvelled at the city's rapid development, with new cafes, parks, and cultural events popping up regularly.

Occasionally, they returned to their family homes, but their hearts belonged to Gurgaon's dynamic pulse. The excitement of their new life brought them closer, as they navigated the challenges and joys of their professional journeys. They often found themselves bonding over shared discoveries and adventures, whether it was a new food truck offering delectable treats or a hidden gem of a bookstore.

Life seemed perfect as they reveled in their newfound independence and the thrill of young love. They cherished the moments spent together, whether it was a quiet dinner after a long day at work or a spontaneous weekend getaway to a nearby destination. In the midst of the city's fast-paced life, Pari and Ayushman found solace and strength in each other, their love growing deeper with each passing day. From their early days at university to their present success, their journey from teenage to twenty-two had only strengthened their bond, and they looked forward to building a future together in the vibrant city of Gurgaon.

Knowing Vardaan was handling their family business afloat independently and there haven't been any further losses, marriage with Pari was Ayushman's highest priority. Ayushman focused on the love and commitment they shared, confident that their bond would carry them through any hardships as he had seen in his parents' life where his mother supported his father unquestioned. He believed in his own potential and was determined to build a successful future for them both in which Pari could follow her heart in a few years and follow her fashion designer dream if she wanted to.

One evening, as they sat on the terrace of their shared hostel, overlooking the glittering lights of Gurgaon, Ayushman turned to Pari, who was gazing out at the city with a content smile on her face. Her presence alone was enough to remind him that they would always be together.

"Pari," Ayushman began, his voice steady but filled with emotion, "I want you to know how much I love you."

Pari looked at him, her eyes filled with love and trust. "Ayushman, I love you too and I believe in you more than myself." Pari had been head over heels in love with Ayushman from day one, attaching herself to him like the fragrance of a flower.

Ayushman smiled, feeling a renewed sense of determination. He knew that with Pari by his side, he could overcome any obstacle. He focused on their upcoming wedding and the life they were building together in Gurgaon.

During Ayushman's next visit to Pathankot, his house was filled with family. Mrs. Mittal, his mother, sat at the dining table, sifting through biodata and pictures of eligible girls sent by their trusted matchmaker, Smita Aunty, who lived in the neighborhood and belonged to the same caste. Mr. Mittal, his father, was reading the newspaper nearby, while his brother Vardaan and sister-in-law Sapna were engaged in conversation. As Ayushman entered the room, his mother looked up with a hopeful expression, "Look at these, Ayushman. Smita Aunty sent more biodata. This one is particularly nice."

Disinterested, Ayushman decided it was time to confide in his mother. "Mom, I'm in love with a girl from my university, and I want to marry her," he said earnestly. His mother's expression shifted from curiosity to concern. "What's her caste?" she asked, her voice tinged with apprehension. Ayushman calmly replied, "She's Jatt Sikh."

His mother's concern heightened, "Are you out of your mind? Their community is infamous for honour killings. You could be risking your life for love, you fool!"

Sapna glanced up from her conversation, her eyes widening, while Vardaan's expression turned serious. Mr. Mittal lowered his newspaper, listening intently. Continuing, Mrs. Mittal urged, "Why can't you be like Vardaan and marry the girl I choose for you? It would be graceful and comfortable for everyone. Don't disrupt our customs, beta."

Ayushman attempted to soothe his mother, "Please calm down, Maa. No one is going to harm anyone. Her father is educated, has lived in Bhatinda City, and served in the Indian Army. He raised Pari to be very secular. Our safety is not a concern." Mrs. Mittal remained anxious, pressing further, "Will she be able to leave her traditions and adapt to our pure vegetarian way of life?" Ayushman assured her, "She already did that four years ago. She's been a pure vegetarian since we met."

Concerns about respecting marriage traditions emerged, "Will they be okay with following our traditions?" Ayushman tried to reassure his mother, "These things can be discussed, Maa. Let's not jump to conclusions. Let's meet the family first." Frustrated, Mrs. Mittal turned to her husband, "Why are you silent? Does anyone else share my concerns about what our community will think of us?" Mr. Mittal, finally speaking up, responded, "Let's meet the family first," before retiring to his room for the night.

The next morning, Mrs. Mittal requested Ayushman to call Pari so she could converse with her directly. Ayushman dialed Pari's phone and activated the speaker.

Pari greeted, "Namaste Aunty."

Mrs. Mittal got straight to the point, "Will your parents agree?"

Pari replied, "Aunty, we'll try."

Mrs. Mittal persisted, "What if they don't agree?"

Pari remained confident, "Then they will agree after the wedding. Maybe not immediately, but eventually."

Digging deeper, Mrs. Mittal asked, "So it doesn't matter to you if they don't agree?"

Pari stood firm, "Aunty, when Ayushman and I entered this relationship, we didn't seek permission from anyone. It seems a bit late now."

Mrs. Mittal questioned her further, "Are you ready to leave home for love?"

Pari responded, "Yes, Aunty. Doesn't a girl leave her maternal home after marriage to live with her husband anyway?"

Mrs. Mittal's gaze shifted to Ayushman, her tone grave, "Think carefully before you take any steps. I'm agreeing because Ayushman has promised not to marry anyone else. Otherwise, my heart wouldn't agree to your marriage without your parents' consent. How will the two of you be happy without their blessings?" She sobbed and ended the call.

After the conversation, Pari calmly remarked, "Generation gap! Their generation fears taking risks, but risk adds charm to life. Never mind, Ayushman will convince them. It's his job. Relax and listen to some music." She then turned on their favorite love song by Sonu Nigam, "Ab mujhe raat din tumhara hi khayaal hai..."

SAPNA WAS A DEDICATED AND DUTIFUL DAUGHTER-IN-LAW, DEEPLY involved in honing her culinary skills and hosting gatherings from the early days of her marriage. She had sacrificed many of her personal aspirations and comforts to support the family through tough times. Her life revolved around managing household affairs, often working late into the night. She hoped that Ayushman would take on more responsibility and elevate the family business. However, she was distressed by his struggle to prioritise his duties over his love life.

Sapna: "Vardaan, I can't keep sacrificing alone. Ayushman needs to understand his responsibilities. You need to talk some sense into him."

Vardaan nodded, understanding her frustrations. He admired Sapna's resilience and knew she deserved more support.

Vardaan: "I will, Sapna. I'll take Ayushman out and provide some counsel. He needs to see the bigger picture."

Sapna watched as Vardaan left to speak with Ayushman, hoping that the family would soon find balance and prosperity again.

Vardaan: "Ayushman, let's go for a drive. We need to talk about something important."

They drove in silence for a while, the gravity of the conversation ahead weighing heavily on both of them.

Vardaan: "Ayushman, our business isn't doing well. We need to think practically about our next steps. A marriage alliance within the business community could be beneficial. We need an influential family to help us through this crisis."

Ayushman: "I understand the situation, Vardaan. But I need you to trust me. Pari is also going to be a new earning member of the family. We will work through this together."

Vardaan: "But Ayushman, you know how these things work. An influential family could give us the leverage we need. Are you sure Pari can handle this pressure?"

Ayushman: "Vardaan, Pari is selfless and good-natured. She will sacrifice anything to see me happy. I've known her for years. I have no doubt about her. She will be a strong pillar for our family."

Vardaan: "I'm not questioning her character, Ayushman. But you know how critical this decision is. We can't afford to make a decision based purely on emotions."

Ayushman: "I get that. But Pari is not just an emotional choice. She's confident and independent. She will be a great support for both me and the family. We need her, and I need you to trust my judgment."

Vardaan: "Alright, Ayushman. I'll leave the decision to you. But remember, if you become indifferent to our family because of your wife, I won't forgive you."

Ayushman: "I promise, Vardaan. Our family is above anything and anyone else. I won't let you down. Please support me in this marriage."

Vardaan: "Okay, Ayushman. I trust you. Let's hope this works out for the best. You've always had a good head on your shoulders, and I believe in you."

Ayushman: "Thank you, Vardaan. Together, we'll navigate this crisis and come out stronger."

Vardaan nodded, placing a hand on Ayushman's shoulder as a gesture of solidarity. Ayushman felt a sense of relief and determination, knowing he had his brother's support. With Pari by his side, he was ready to face any challenges that lay ahead.

They returned home, Vardaan feeling a mix of relief and lingering concern, while Ayushman was determined to balance love and duty.

THE GARDEN AT PARI'S FAMILY HOME IN BHATINDA WAS A TRANQUIL retreat, where Capt. Bajwa often spent his mornings. Sitting in his favourite cane chair, engrossed in his newspaper, he barely glanced at Pari as she tried to persuade him.

Pari: "Papa, I really like Ayushman Mittal. We met back in university, and he's always been supportive. He did great in his studies and now works as a Software Engineer at a multinational in Gurgaon. We understand each other."

Capt. Bajwa didn't even look up. "Forget about him, Pari. He's from a Hindu merchant family. Our cultures don't align. They're all about business, and there's little room for your aspirations. You'll find yourself giving up your dreams to cater to their needs. You won't truly fit in."

Pari: "But Papa, you haven't even met him or his family. They're good people, and he has always been supportive of me."

Capt. Bajwa: "It's not about kindness, Pari. Business families operate differently than us. Their priorities revolve around profits and losses. Our world is built on duty, service, and emotional support. Marrying into their family would mean setting aside your own aspirations to meet their demands. And don't forget, families like that often expect hefty dowries."

Pari pleaded her father to consider her love of life, "Ayushman isn't like that. He values my ambitions and respects my dreams. We want to build a future together."

Capt. Bajwa cut in sharply. "Love marriage won't get you the acceptance you deserve in that family. You'll always be an outsider."

Pari: "Papa, Ayushman's under pressure too. That's why I want to marry him. In his community, there's so much expectation to settle down by twenty-five."

Capt. Bajwa: "That doesn't mean you rush into this. You're not even twenty-four. You should focus on your career for now, maybe even prepare for the IAS. You have the potential for big things. Your uncle in Canada can find a better match—someone who shares our values. We'll talk about marriage later."

Pari turned towards her brother, Shera, hoping for some support. "Shera, you know Ayushman. You think this isn't real?"

Shera, who was preparing to move to Canada for higher education, spoke calmly, "Look, Papa knows more about life than any of us. University is not the real world. Just because it worked on campus doesn't mean it'll work here. If I were you, I'd listen to him and move on."

Pari felt her throat tighten. "So, you're saying it's all just...nothing?"

Shera: "I'm saying it's just university love. Think it through. Take a step only if it's in your best interest."

Pari's mind whirled with conflicting thoughts as she absorbed her father's words. She had always respected her father, but she found it increasingly difficult to trust his judgment on matters of the heart. Memories of her father dominating family decisions without consulting her mother flooded her mind. She had seen her mother, a dutiful and patient woman, often sidelined and her opinions dismissed. This instance was no different; her father hadn't even bothered to ask her mother for her viewpoint on the matter.

Pari reflected on her father's advice with a mix of frustration and skepticism. "How can I trust his guidance on my marriage when he doesn't treat Mom as an equal partner in theirs? He preaches respect and honour, but where is the honour in disregarding your spouse's feelings?" she wondered, analysing how his single-handed decision-making often excluded her mother.

Pari knew that her father prided himself on his wisdom and life experience, but she couldn't help but feel that his views were tainted by deep-seated prejudices and his own ego. His outright dismissal of Ayushman and his family as merely "business people" felt like a convenient excuse to reinforce his authority rather than a genuine concern for her happiness.

Determined to follow her heart, Pari dismissed her father's so-called expert advice. She resolved to make decisions based on her own experiences and the love she had found with Ayushman. It was time to step out of her father's shadow and take control of her destiny, even if it meant going against his wishes.

Pari sat in her room, her mind a whirlwind of emotions. She had always been close to her mother, Mrs. Bajwa, and now she needed her support more than ever. She decided to have a heart-to-heart conversation with her mother, hoping to find some solace and guidance.

Pari: "Mamma!"

Mrs. Bajwa, sensing the urgency in her daughter's voice, put aside her chores and joined Pari on the couch, taking her hand in hers.

Mrs. Bajwa: "Beta. What's troubling you?"

Pari: "It's about Ayushman. Papa doesn't approve of him because he's from a business family and a different community. He didn't even ask for your opinion. I don't know what to do, Mamma."

Mrs. Bajwa sighed, her eyes reflecting the weight of her own experiences.

Mrs. Bajwa: "Pari, your father has always been practical, and he believes his advice comes from experience. Society can be harsh, and he just wants to protect you from potential heartbreak. But I've seen how much Ayushman cares for you, and I've known him since the beginning of your relationship. He seems like a good-hearted boy."

Pari felt a glimmer of hope at her mother's words.

Pari: "So, you think I should be with him?"

Mrs. Bajwa smiled gently, brushing a strand of hair from Pari's face.

Mrs. Bajwa: "I think you should listen to your heart. Your father's concerns are valid, and he wants what he believes is best for you. But this is your life, and you deserve to be happy. Ayushman has been there for you through thick and thin. That counts for something."

Pari's eyes welled up with tears as she hugged her mother tightly.

This advice to choose love came from Baldev's own experiences of failures and pain in her marriage. She wanted Pari to find the happiness and self-fulfillment that she herself could never fully attain.

Pari: "Thank you, Mamma. I was so scared I wouldn't have your support."

Mrs. Bajwa held her daughter close, her own eyes moist with emotion.

Mrs. Bajwa: "I've seen you grow and make wise decisions, Pari. I trust you to make the right choice for yourself. I'll do my best to convince your father to support you, whatever decision you make. Just promise me one thing."

Pari pulled back slightly, looking into her mother's eyes.

Pari: "Anything, Mamma."

Mrs. Bajwa: "Promise me you'll stay true to yourself and your happiness. No matter what challenges come your way, remember that your family is here for you."

Pari nodded, feeling a renewed sense of strength and determination.

Pari: "I promise, Mamma. I won't let anything come between me and my happiness."

Mrs. Bajwa kissed her daughter's forehead, whispering words of encouragement.

Mrs. Bajwa: "Good. Now, let's face this together. I'll talk to your father, and we'll find a way to make this work. Trust in yourself and in Ayushman. Love has a way of overcoming the toughest obstacles."

With her mother's support, Pari felt a newly-found confidence. She knew the road ahead wouldn't be easy, but with love and determination, she was ready to fight for her future with Ayushman.

Back in Gurgaon, Pari met with Ayushman to discuss their dilemma. It was the first time in their six-year relationship that they felt cornered and unsure about how to proceed. They sat together in their favorite restaurant, sharing a single cup of strawberry sundae.

Ayushman: "My parents are on board, but what's the issue with your father?"

Pari: "It's not about you, it's about your community. My father doesn't seem to have a positive view of your community."

Ayushman: "I can't blame my family if our marriage doesn't happen because your father doesn't agree."

Pari: "That's strange. We're adults, and constitutionally, we have the right to marry on our own. My father doesn't even need to be involved. But here we are, backing out due to family honour concerns."

Ayushman: "I'm fully committed, but it's frustrating because my parents will only give their blessings if we have your parents' blessings. The constitution is just a book; real life involves being reasonable and caring for those around us. Logic might look good in books, but it doesn't always apply in reality. We need our families to meet and discuss this."

Pari: "I understand, but convincing my father to meet your family is going to be tough. He's very set in his ways."

Ayushman: "It's essential. They need to see that we're serious and committed. Let's arrange a meeting. It's the only way to move forward."

Pari looked at Ayushman with determination. "Let's not stick to tradition. We could opt for a court marriage. We don't need a lavish wedding. We've already celebrated our love; we just want uninterrupted togetherness and a legal certificate."

Ayushman nodded thoughtfully. "That makes sense. A court marriage would simplify things, and we wouldn't have to worry about pleasing everyone. But what about the social pressures we face here?"

Pari and Ayushman were ready to make significant sacrifices to escape the social pressures that weighed heavily on them in Gurgaon staying close to home. They had well-paying jobs, but the constant scrutiny about their choice to marry for love was unbearable. They considered their options and came to a bold decision.

Pari took a deep breath. "I've been thinking about that too. What if we move to South India? Bangalore has great job opportunities, and it's known for being more progressive and accepting. We can start fresh there without the constant scrutiny from our families."

Ayushman's eyes lit up at the idea. "Bangalore? That sounds like a good idea. It's far enough from the social pressures of Delhi and Punjab. We can build a life there on our terms."

"Exactly," Pari agreed. "We can secure jobs in software companies, which is what we're both passionate about. Plus, the lifestyle in Bangalore is vibrant and diverse. It would be a perfect place for us to grow together."

With this plan in mind, Pari and Ayushman felt a renewed sense of hope and excitement. They were ready to take the leap, leaving behind the constraints of their current lives to embrace a future filled with possibilities and freedom.

"Alright, let's embrace it. We'll move to Bangalore and embark on this fresh journey together. It might stir whispers in Delhi or Punjab, but in our new beginning, we'll find the freedom to live as we desire."

Pari: "I'm excited about this. We'll face challenges, but we can handle them together. This move will be good for us."

As they settled into their new life in Bangalore, Pari and Ayushman faced the task of setting up their household. Initially, they had considered living in separate hostels due to financial constraints and the desire to maintain some independence. However, their intention to marry soon made them rethink this decision.

One evening, while discussing their future plans over a cup of tea, Pari expressed her concerns. "Ayushman, living in separate hostels might be practical, but it doesn't feel right. We're planning to get married soon, and I think we should start building our life together now."

Ayushman nodded thoughtfully. "I understand what you mean. Living together would help us understand each other's habits and preferences better. It would be a good start to our married life."

They weighed the pros and cons, considering the financial implications and the adjustment period. Ultimately, they decided that the emotional benefits outweighed the challenges. They chose to move into a small apartment, creating a shared space where they could grow together as a couple.

As they began setting up their home, they encountered the usual disagreements like any couple. Pari had a penchant for indulging in premium items for their home, often making impulsive purchases, while Ayushman focused on price and quality.

One evening, after a particularly heated argument about an expensive new couch Pari had bought without consulting Ayushman, she stormed off to sleep in the lounge. Ayushman sighed deeply, trying to gather his thoughts. "I understand you want the best for our home," he called out, his voice strained, "but we need to be practical about our spending."

From the lounge, Pari's voice echoed back, filled with frustration. "Practical? You mean frugal! I don't want to live like that. I want a beautiful and comfortable home, not just a functional one."

Ayushman tried to stay calm, despite the tension. "I get that," he said, "but we have to consider our budget. We can't just spend without planning."

Pari's anger was evident as she retorted, "You're always so focused on saving money that you forget to enjoy life. I'm tired of this frugal lifestyle. I want to live, not just survive."

Feeling the frustration build up, Ayushman responded, "This isn't about being frugal. It's about being responsible. We need to find a middle ground."

After a moment, Pari returned to the bedroom, her eyes still flashing with anger. "Middle ground? You mean I should just give up on what I want? That's not fair."

Ayushman's tone softened, hoping to reach a compromise. "No, that's not what I mean. I want you to be happy, but we need to make these decisions together."

Still upset, Pari replied, "I don't feel like we're making decisions together. It feels like I'm compromising all the time."

Ayushman looked at her earnestly. "I'm not asking you to compromise. I'm asking you to work with me. Let's figure this out."

Pari hesitated, then sighed reluctantly. "Fine, but we need to find a way where I don't feel like I'm constantly sacrificing."

Settling into Bangalore, Pari struggled with Ayushman's approach to finances, while Ayushman failed to understand Pari's desire for a more indulgent lifestyle.

Ayushman observed Pari's spending habits and decided not to intervene too much, anticipating that her approach might change after their marriage. He believed that taking on the roles of a daughter-in-law and wife would bring more responsibility to her actions. He recalled how his cousin sisters were all princesses in their homes before they got married but post marriage, they blended into their in-laws' families happily.

Watching Pari as she excitedly talked about their future, Ayushman silently reassured himself. "Everything will be okay," he thought. "She'll adapt just like my cousins did. Marriage brings a sense of responsibility. Pari will understand the need to manage finances more wisely once we're settled."

"Pari has always been practical when it truly matters," he reminded himself. "She's just enjoying her freedom now. Once we're married, things will naturally fall into place. She'll grow into her new roles, just like everyone else." He decided to leave it to time.

SIX MONTHS HAD PASSED, AND PARI'S FATHER, CAPT. BAJWA, STILL hadn't given his consent for her marriage. When Pari pushed him for an answer, he finally relented, "If you're so determined, then go ahead and get married. You're both adults; you don't need my permission." He hung up abruptly, his tone dismissive, as though convinced Pari's stubbornness would fade if she felt its weight alone. But as the cold dial tone echoed in her ears, a strange mix of determination and sorrow washed over her.

Her father's words stung, sharp and unyielding, reminding her of the familiar walls he built around himself whenever he stopped listening. She stood there, aware of his refusal to understand, and a quiet thought surfaced: *Ayushman wasn't like him.* Unlike her father, Ayushman seemed to truly listen, seemed to meet her wishes with respect, and she felt sure he would support her rather than dismiss her. The times he had bent for her in their months together played out in her mind, as though reaffirming this belief she held.

As her father's response lingered in her thoughts, Pari realised that this was a decisive moment. She blinked back the tears rising in her eyes and turned to Ayushman, searching for something steady to anchor herself. His unwavering gaze caught hers, full of the warmth she had come to depend on, and it filled her with strength.

"Let's make us official," she said, her voice steady, even as her heart felt both grief and courage pressing within her.

Ayushman's eyes softened, his love apparent. "Yes. Let's get married," he replied, pulling her close, his arms a silent promise to stand beside her.

They held each other tightly, feeling the significance of their choice settle between them, filling the air with an electric mix of excitement and quiet resolve. In that embrace, Pari felt ready for whatever challenges lay ahead, believing they would face them, together.

Hearts aligned, duty anew, what challenges will they pursue?

CHAPTER 8
WEDDING BELLS

P ari stood gracefully in a light pink saree, the delicate embroidery shimmering softly under the morning light. The saree's intricate patterns highlighted her elegant frame, and the colour brought out the natural glow of her complexion. Her hair was styled in loose waves, and a simple yet elegant pair of earrings adorned her ears. As she walked, the gentle rustle of her saree whispered tales of tradition and new beginnings.

Ayushman, on the other hand, exuded a calm yet powerful presence in his crisp white kurta-pajama set. The simplicity of his attire was a testament to his personality—straightforward, strong, and grounded. His kurta, made from the finest cotton, was impeccably tailored, and the pristine white symbolised purity and a fresh start. As he stood there, the sunlight casting a soft halo around him, he looked every bit the confident and loving partner Pari had always known.

As Ayushman and Pari stood side by side in the court's waiting area, surrounded by their closest friends, they shared a moment of silent connection. Their eyes met, and in that instant, the noise of the bustling court faded away, leaving just the two of them in a cocoon of their shared emotions.

Pari looked at Ayushman, her heart swelling with love and pride. She admired the way he had navigated through the challenges of life with unwavering strength and determination. She remembered the countless moments they had spent together, from late-night study sessions to whispered promises under the stars. Today, standing beside him, she felt an overwhelming sense of gratitude and joy. Her thoughts were a mixture of excitement and serenity, knowing that they were about to take a significant step forward in their journey together.

"Ayushman," she whispered in her heart, her eyes shimmering with unshed tears, "we've journeyed so far together. I can't wait to begin this new journey with you."

Ayushman, gazing back at Pari, felt his heart race with anticipation. He had always known that Pari was his anchor, the one who made everything worthwhile. Her presence in his life had brought a sense of purpose and completeness. As he looked at her, dressed so beautifully in the pink saree that mirrored her inner grace, he felt a surge of love and protectiveness. He was ready to face the future, no matter what it held, as long as she was by his side.

"Pari," he thought, his heart pounding with emotion, "you are my everything. Together, we can conquer anything."

The ceremony itself was brief but profoundly meaningful. The registrar, an elderly man with kind eyes, asked them to hold hands and exchange their vows. As Ayushman took Pari's hand in his, he felt a rush of warmth and connection. Their hands fit together perfectly, a tangible symbol of their unity and commitment.

"Do you, Ayushman Mittal, take Pari Bajwa to be your lawfully wedded wife, to love and cherish from this day forward?" the registrar asked.

Ayushman looked into Pari's eyes, his voice steady and filled with conviction. "I do."

Turning to Pari, the registrar continued, "Do you, Pari Bajwa, take Ayushman Mittal to be your lawfully wedded husband, to love and cherish from this day forward?"

Pari's eyes never left Ayushman's, her voice soft yet unwavering. "I do."

As they signed the marriage register, their friends erupted in applause, their cheers echoing in the small room. Meeta and Rahul stepped forward, offering their heartfelt congratulations, their faces beaming with happiness.

After the formalities, the group moved outside, where the sunlight bathed them in its warm embrace. The joy was palpable, and there was a sense of shared excitement and relief. Ayushman and Pari looked at each other, their hearts beating in sync. The weight of societal expectations and familial pressures seemed lighter now, replaced by the solid foundation of their love and commitment.

Rahul raised a toast to the newlyweds, his voice filled with affection and pride. "To Ayushman and Pari, two of the most wonderful people I know. May your journey ahead be filled with love, laughter, and countless beautiful moments. Cheers!"

Meeta followed with her own heartfelt words. "Pari and Ayushman, your love story is an inspiration. Here's to a lifetime of happiness and togetherness. Cheers!"

The warmth and camaraderie among the group added a special touch to the celebration.

As they stood amidst their friends, Ayushman and Pari felt a profound sense of fulfilment. They had taken a significant step, one that marked the beginning of a new journey. Their love had triumphed over obstacles, and now, they were ready to face the future together.

With hearts full and spirits soaring, Ayushman and Pari embraced the new journey of their lives, confident that their love would light the way through whatever lay ahead. United by their vows and strengthened by their bond, they were ready to create a lifetime of cherished memories, one moment at a time.

DURING AYUSHMAN AND PARI'S VISIT TO PATHANKOT FOR THEIR traditional ceremony, they decided to honour Ayushman's family, as they had planned a traditional wedding. The ceremony was meticulously planned by Sapna bhabhi. As part of the pre-wedding rituals, Pari stayed at Raman's house. This tradition symbolised her formal welcome into the family that was due next day.

Raman's parents, Bhavna and Pawan, were warm and hospitable. Bhavna, a graceful woman with a nurturing presence, managed the household with ease, while Pawan, a retired army officer, exuded discipline and wisdom. Their daughter Neha, much younger than Raman, was a bright high school student who excelled in math and aspired to be a teacher. The house was bustling with preparations for the upcoming ceremony, creating an atmosphere filled with excitement and anticipation.

Missing her parents, Pari gathered the courage to call home. "Hello, Mrs. Bajwa this side," her mother answered.

"Mama, Ayushman's parents are doing a traditional ceremony tomorrow. Are you coming?" Pari asked, her voice tinged with hope.

"I'm not sure, your father is still upset," her mother replied.

"Why? He gave permission," Pari said, puzzled.

"Yes, but he assumed you wouldn't go through with the marriage without his consent."

"Mama, the actual marriage is tomorrow. We only did the court marriage in Bangalore."

"Maa, please try to come. It would mean a lot to me," Pari pleaded.

The next day, Raman drove Pari to the parlour with his sister Neha to support her. The traditional ceremony was to be a condensed version of a five-day Hindu wedding, completed within a few hours from 6 PM to midnight. It included the pheras, dinner, and a dance party. Pari's eyes constantly searched for her parents as she prepared. While on her way to the main hall, Sapna informed her that her parents had arrived. Overjoyed, Pari quickened her pace, only to be gently reminded by Sapna, "Do not take fast steps; the video will be ruined." Pari laughed at herself and slowed down, her eyes locking onto Ayushman, who looked regal in a cream sherwani.

Pari wore a light pink lehnga adorned with delicate embroidery. The soft fabric draped elegantly over her, the intricate details shimmering in the light, enhancing her natural beauty. Ayushman, in his sherwani, looked every bit the confident and loving partner. As they saw each other, their thoughts aligned in a silent conversation of love and commitment. Ayushman admired Pari's grace and poise, feeling grateful for her unwavering support. Pari, on the other hand, saw in Ayushman the strength and determination that had always drawn her to him. Their gazes met, and in that moment, all the challenges and obstacles faded away, leaving only the profound connection they shared.

The air was thick with excitement as the traditional Hindu wedding ceremony began. The grand hall was adorned with vibrant marigold garlands, twinkling fairy lights, and rich red and gold drapes, creating an atmosphere of opulence and celebration. The scent of incense and fresh flowers filled the air, adding to the sacredness of the occasion.

The highlight of the evening was the seven pheras, the seven sacred vows taken around the holy fire. Ayushman, dressed in an exquisite cream sherwani with intricate gold embroidery, and Pari, resplendent in a light pink saree adorned with delicate silver embellishments, stood at the mandap. Their eyes met, reflecting love and commitment, as the priest chanted the sacred mantras.

With each phera, they made promises to each other – of love, fidelity, and mutual respect. As they walked around the fire, hand in hand, the flames seemed to dance in celebration of their union. Family members showered them with rose petals, symbolising blessings and prosperity for their married life.

After the solemn pheras, it was time for the grand feast. Long tables were laden with a sumptuous spread of traditional Indian delicacies. There were aromatic biryanis, creamy curries, sizzling kebabs, and a variety of sweets like gulab jamun, jalebi, and rasmalai. The guests, dressed in their finest attire, indulged in the culinary delights, their laughter and conversations filling the air with joy.

Ayushman and Pari made their way through the crowd, greeting guests and receiving their blessings. They shared a private moment, feeding each other morsels of their favourite dishes, their smiles radiating happiness. The food, a symbol of abundance and love, was a crucial part of the celebration, bringing everyone together in a shared experience of joy.

The evening reached its crescendo with the dance party. The dance floor, set under a canopy of twinkling lights, came alive with vibrant beats of Bollywood music. Ayushman and Pari led the way, their movements graceful and synchronised. Ayushman spun Pari around, her saree swirling elegantly, and they laughed, their faces glowing with joy.

Friends and family soon joined in, creating a lively and festive atmosphere. Raman and his sister Neha showcased their dance moves, while Sapna and Vardaan joined in with enthusiasm. There were impromptu performances, group dances, and moments of sheer, uninhibited fun. The elders watched with fond smiles, occasionally joining in the celebrations, clapping along to the music.

The atmosphere was charged with a palpable sense of celebration. Traditional dhol players added to the festive spirit, their beats compelling everyone to dance. Guests clinked glasses of sparkling drinks, toasting to Ayushman and Pari's happiness. Laughter echoed through the hall as people indulged in playful banter and joyous reunions.

The evening was filled with heartfelt toasts, emotional speeches, and shared stories. Vardaan raised a toast, his words filled with warmth and admiration. "To Ayushman and Pari," he began, "May your journey together be as beautiful and joyous as this evening. Here's to a lifetime of love, laughter, and endless adventures."

Meeta, followed with her own toast, her voice choked with emotion. "Pari, you've always been like a sister to me. Seeing you so happy with

Ayushman fills my heart with joy. May your love story continue to inspire all of us. Cheers to a beautiful life ahead."

As the night progressed, the celebrations continued with more music, dance, and merrymaking. The younger crowd led impromptu dance-offs, while the elders shared memories and blessings. It was a snapshot of a big fat Indian wedding – filled with love, laughter, and a sense of togetherness that transcended all else.

The ceremony concluded in the early hours of the morning, with guests slowly trickling out, their hearts full and spirits high. Ayushman and Pari, surrounded by their loved ones, felt an overwhelming sense of gratitude and joy. The traditional ceremony had beautifully encapsulated the essence of their union – a blend of love, tradition, and the promise of a future filled with endless possibilities.

Pari and Ayushman took blessings from both sets of parents, Mittals and Bajwas. Capt. Bajwa and Mr. Mittal shook hands for new beginnings. The mothers Dolly and Baldev embraced each other. Her parents' attendance had lifted a huge burden from her heart.

As Pari and Ayushman drove to their family home, the reality hit Pari that she was actually embracing another family and vowed to treat them with love while she did not even know them. She realised she was driving into unknown territory, but having Ayushman by her side, she was ready to take on that challenge. She hoped to be loved and respected like in her own home.

Upon arriving at Ayushman's house, a plush bungalow spread over an acre, Pari was greeted with the traditional 'welcome' ceremony. Dolly, Sapna, and Grandma prepared the entrance for the ritual with a sense of warmth and excitement. Mustard oil was laced on the two sides of the entry door, symbolising auspiciousness and prosperity. A plate filled with red alta flower powder mixed with water was placed at the doorstep, ready to welcome the new bride.

Pari, holding Ayushman's hand, stepped into the plate. The red colour of the alta painted the bottoms of her feet, symbolising the presence of Goddess Lakshmi entering the home. She took her first step forward, stamping the floor from the main entrance to the kitchen, leaving behind a trail of red footprints. Each step she took marked her new journey, filling the house with blessings and prosperity.

The family watched with smiles and tears of joy, witnessing the beautiful tradition unfold. Dolly, Sapna, and Grandma stood at the entrance, their eyes moist with emotion as they blessed the new couple. Sapna followed closely, ensuring everything was perfect for the ritual.

As Pari completed the ceremonial walk, the house resonated with a sense of fulfilment and happiness. The footprints were not just marks on the floor but symbols of the new beginnings and the positive energy Pari brought with her.

Ayushman, standing beside Pari, felt a surge of pride and happiness. He knew that with Pari by his side, their home would be filled with love, prosperity, and endless possibilities.

After the ceremony, Dolly, Sapna, and Grandma warmly welcomed Pari with open arms. They presented her with exquisite jewellery, a symbol of their acceptance and love. The intricate designs and sparkling gems were a testament to the family's affection and the high regard they held for her.

The welcome ceremony concluded with the family gathering in the meals area, where they shared sweets and offered prayers for a blessed married life. The atmosphere was filled with laughter, joy, and a deep sense of belonging.

Sapna Bhabi and the others switched on the music system in the lounge, and soon all the young cousins and bhabis (sisters-in-law) were dancing, taking pictures, and making merry for about an hour. Vardaan, having finished his hosting duties, came into the lounge and, with a wink at Ayushman, interrupted the festivities, "Come on everyone, let the newlyweds take some rest. They've had a long day." Pari's face flushed with embarrassment. Sapna quickly followed her husband's cue and led the couple to their room, extending her palm for the traditional shagun money, a ritual gesture before allowing the couple to enter their bedroom.

THE BEDROOM WAS A PICTURE OF ROMANCE, ADORNED WITH fragrant flowers that filled the air with a delicate scent and soft candlelight casting a warm, inviting glow. Every detail was meticulously arranged to create an intimate atmosphere. On the bedside table sat a glass of traditional hot milk, a gesture from the family symbolising their blessings and hopes for future grandchildren. The soft flicker of the candles reflected Ayushman's beaming smile, deeply touched by the love and effort his family had invested in making this night unforgettable. He felt a mix of excitement and tenderness as he anticipated celebrating this significant moment with Pari, marking the beginning of their journey together as husband and wife. The room, with its blend of tradition and romance, encapsulated the essence of their new union, promising a night filled with love and cherished memories.

Ayushman smiled as he entered the room, his eyes lighting up with joy. "Look at this, Pari! The room looks beautiful. My family really went all out to make this night special for us."

Pari, tiredly removing her jewellery, sighed heavily. "Yes, it's nice. But I'm so exhausted from all the ceremonies and carrying this heavy wedding outfit all day. I really need to rest."

Ayushman, his face softening with affection, approached Pari with a tender expression. "I know it's been a long day, but you look stunning in this outfit. I've been waiting for this day for so many years. Just sit with me for a moment."

Pari sat in front of him, and Ayushman gently took her hands, gazing at her with love. However, Pari's mind was elsewhere, clouded with thoughts of her parents and the day's events.

She sighed again, pushing him away playfully but with a hint of impatience. "Ayushman, be real. We've been intimate so many times before. This isn't an arranged marriage where we're meeting in private for the first time after the wedding."

Ayushman tried to keep the mood light, his smile faltering slightly. "Let me help you change into something more comfortable."

Pari ignored his offer, her tone brusque. "I can manage. I need to freshen up."

Pari hurried to the bathroom, leaving Ayushman standing there, feeling a bit dejected. He had hoped for a more romantic and memorable night, but Pari's exhaustion and her preoccupation with her parents' absence weighed heavily on her mind. She felt guilty and sad, knowing her parents couldn't proudly invite their relatives or friends to the wedding.

After a few moments, Pari returned from the bathroom, changed into comfortable clothes. She avoided eye contact and went straight to bed, lying down with her back to Ayushman.

Ayushman gently lay down beside her, his voice tinged with concern. "Pari, are you okay?"

Pari responded quietly, her voice barely above a whisper. "I'm just really tired. Let's talk tomorrow."

Ayushman wrapped his arm around her, hoping to comfort her. They lay there in silence, each lost in their thoughts. Ayushman, feeling a mix of disappointment and concern, and Pari, overwhelmed by guilt and sadness, fell asleep quietly without sharing the emotional connection Ayushman had hoped for.

As Ayushman whispered softly, "Goodnight, Pari," she murmured back, "Goodnight," their voices barely breaking the silence. The night ended quietly, without the celebration Ayushman had envisioned, but both of them hoped for better days ahead as they began their new life together.

WIFED IN INDIA

Union strong, vows don't part, what shadows lurk in the heart?

CHAPTER 9

THE NEW REALITY

The factory in Pathankot had seen better days. When Ayushman first visited the Pathankot factory after their marriage, he was struck by the stark reality of the situation. The outdated machinery groaned and clattered, struggling to keep up with the demands of production. Disorganised inventory piled up haphazardly, a testament to the lack of modern management practices. Weary workers moved with the slow, fatigued gait of those who had been pushed to their limits, their faces lined with exhaustion and uncertainty about the future.

That evening, after a tense family dinner where the underlying stress was palpable, Ayushman and his brother Vardaan found themselves sitting in the dimly lit living room. The silence between them was thick with unspoken worries. Vardaan's fingers tapped rhythmically on the armrest, a subtle sign of his anxiety. Ayushman stared at the flickering light from the fireplace, his mind racing with the reality of their situation.

The weight of the factory's debt loomed over them like a dark cloud. Ayushman knew that without significant investment and modernisation, their family's legacy was at risk. The thought of their father's hard work being reduced to a struggling business filled him with a sense of dread and responsibility. Vardaan's expression mirrored his own concerns, the lines on his forehead deepening as he contemplated the daunting task ahead.

"Vardaan, we need to talk about the factory," Ayushman finally broke the silence, his voice low but resolute.

Vardaan nodded, his eyes meeting Ayushman's with a mix of determination and worry. "I know, Ayushman. The debt is overwhelming, and we can't keep running things the way we have been. Something has to change."

Ayushman took a deep breath, feeling the weight of their shared responsibility. "We need to modernise, but we'll need funds to do that. We can't keep relying on outdated machinery and old practices. It's time to take some bold steps."

Vardaan sighed, rubbing his temples. "I've been thinking the same, but it's a huge risk. What if we can't turn things around? What if we sink deeper into debt?"

Vardaan's eyes reflected a mix of resignation and hope. "What do you suggest?"

"First of all, I don't like what I see on papers, so to stay afloat, we must sell the family home," Ayushman replied. "It's on prime land and can fetch a good price. We can create a contingency reserve for family expenses and invest the rest into the business. This will give us temporary relief, but we need to pivot."

Vardaan hesitated. "Pivot to what? My experience is in the carpet industry."

"I know, but the market has changed," Ayushman said confidently. "There's potential in the software business. Join a correspondence course in software programming. I'll mentor you, and we'll develop new skills together."

Vardaan took a deep breath. "Alright, Ayushman. I'll think about it."

The fear in Vardaan's voice was something Ayushman understood all too well. The unspoken worries about their ability to revive the factory gnawed at him, but he knew that inaction was not an option. "We have to try, Vardaan. For our family, for the workers, and for our future. We'll need to approach investors, streamline operations, and maybe even make some tough decisions about downsizing."

Vardaan nodded, his voice steady but laced with emotion. "I understand, Ayush. Give me 3-6 months."

Ayushman placed a reassuring hand on his brother's shoulder. "Okay, bhaiya. I'm always here with you."

The enormity of the situation was clear to both brothers, but Ayushman felt a flicker of hope in their shared resolve. As they sat in the dimly lit room, the path ahead was uncertain, but they knew they had to face it together. The factory's future depended on their ability to navigate these troubled waters and transform their unspoken worries into actionable plans. As the conversation wound down, Vardaan added, "I'll see you and Pari off at the airport tomorrow. Let's get some rest and wake up early for the drive to Delhi."

Next day, Ayushman and Pari were to leave for Bangalore. "Good night, Ayushman," Vardaan said, rising from his seat. "We'll sort this out. Together."

"Good night, Bhaiya," Ayushman replied, feeling a glimmer of hope.

In the morning, Ayushman and Pari bid farewell to the family. Pari touched her in-laws' and Ayushman's grandma's feet, receiving their blessings. Ayushman touched his parents' and Sapna Bhabi's feet before Vardaan drove them to Amritsar to catch their flight to Bangalore. The brothers hugged each other, looking forward to reuniting during Diwali in six months.

Ayushman left home burdened with the weight of a huge debt. His mind raced with thoughts on how to alleviate his family's dire financial situation. "How can I turn this around?" he wondered, his heart heavy with concern. Determined to use his expertise to initiate a new business venture, Ayushman knew that he first needed to address the immediate financial crisis and the ensuing family chaos. "I have to create a clear plan," he thought, "step by step, to stabilise our finances and then build something sustainable for the future." His brain churned with ideas and strategies, each one aimed at bringing his family out of the depths of their financial troubles.

Back in Bangalore, Ayushman and Pari settled into their daily routine. On Friday night, while watching Sarabhai vs Sarabhai on TV, they enjoyed the comedy centred around a chaotic family with power dynamics between Maya, the mother-in-law, and Monisha, her daughter-in-law, while Sahil, Monisha's husband and Maya's son, tried to navigate the chaos.

Pari remarked, "Such a sweet joint family. I don't understand why people argue against the joint family system. I love it." She continued, admiring her gold jewellery gifted by her mother-in-law, "Look, your maa gave me these beautiful gold bangles from the family heirloom. She showered so many expensive gifts on me." Showing her earlobes, she added, "I couldn't refuse these beautiful solitaire diamond studs. They are perfect for everyday office wear. So classy!"

Ayushman smiled slightly but didn't react to the jewellery. Pari noticed and gently turned his face toward her, asking, "What's up with you? Did you mind that I accepted the presents or do you not like them?"

Ayushman sighed deeply, preparing to break the news. Seeing this, Pari muted the TV and held his hand, reassuring him, "Tell me what happened. Are you worried about something at work?"

Ayushman brushed it off, "No, it's just that I'm thinking about my visit to our Pathankot factory the other day."

Pari, intrigued, asked, "What about it?"

Determined to help his family, Ayushman had already made a difficult decision. Seeing Pari's worried expression, he decided to inform her about his plan to save the financial crisis back home.

"Pari, for the next three months, we'll need to be frugal with our living expenses. Vardaan is in deep trouble with the business," Ayushman said, his voice steady. "So, we must help them. I have decided that we'll use your income for household needs and send mine to Pathankot."

Pari's eyes widened with shock. "When did you decide that for us?"

"Last week, after touring the factory with Bhaiya and going through the papers," Ayushman replied, trying to stay calm.

"Why didn't you consult me first? How much is the debt?" Pari asked, her tone a mix of disbelief and frustration.

"Know if you must, but don't trouble yourself with the details. It's just the usual business ups and downs, albeit handled chaotically. But I'll get them out of this. I estimate it to be around eighty lakh rupees," Ayushman sighed, the weight of the situation evident in his voice.

"Just... eighty ...lakhs. Are you kidding me? My goodness... what are you thinking... it's insane. I can't believe you didn't know about this all along. Plus, we don't even earn one hundred thousand per month combined," Pari's eyes widened further, her breath quickening with shock and disbelief.

"I know you haven't encountered situations like this before," Ayushman said, trying to reassure her. "That's why I didn't want to burden you with the details. I've spent this week working out a plan and I'm just sharing the actionable steps with you now."

Pari's mind raced with disbelief and shock. "In the last couple of years, I've started enjoying my life since I began working. I couldn't afford precious things on my parents' limited income, and now you're asking me to sacrifice what I've just obtained after years of hard work."

"But why do we need to support them every month? We are married now, we have our own expenses too. Helping occasionally is fine, but constant monthly support is a big commitment," Pari asked, her curiosity tinged with frustration.

"Factory's fuel and electricity bills are overdue, and nobody told me because they didn't want to stress me out given our complex marriage situation that took a year to resolve," Ayushman explained patiently. "The double-edged sword of debt and unsettled sales is hanging over their heads. As an outsider exposed to the larger world, I can see they lack strategy, but they can't see that, having lived in a small city all their lives."

Pari was left in shock, her mind racing with disbelief. "Ayushman, this is too much. Eighty lakhs? How do you expect us to manage that?"

"Pari, I know it's a lot to take in, but we have to do this," Ayushman said with determination. "We need to cut our losses by selling the lavish house and the business. Convincing them to downsize won't be easy; they're accustomed to a certain lifestyle and reluctant to compromise on their status. But we have no choice. I need to send money to support my family, especially since Vardaan has always supported me. They're in a tough spot now."

Ayushman took a deep breath before continuing, "I've spoken to Vardaan, and we're working on a plan to resolve this situation. We're exploring options to restart a more profitable business in a new industry, rather than continuing to invest in a saturated one. Once we get things up and running, they'll understand that we can buy another big house. But for now, I need to support the family until the house is sold and the new business plan is in place."

Pausing to gather his thoughts, Ayushman added, "I know it's a lot to take in, but this is the best path forward. Vardaan and I have spent countless hours discussing the details, and we believe this will not only stabilise our finances but also secure a better future for everyone. It's about making smart decisions now to pave the way for long-term success."

He looked at Pari, his eyes filled with determination. "I need you to trust me on this. Your support means everything to me. We're in this together, and I promise we'll come out stronger on the other side. This isn't just about saving the business; it's about building a future where we can all thrive as one big family."

Pari listened intently, feeling the weight of his words. She could sense his resolve and the pressure he was under.

"But it's a huge sacrifice for us," Pari replied, feeling a mix of resignation and acceptance.

Ayushman, looking deeply into her eyes, asked, "Pari, I need you with me. Are you with me?"

"Okay, can we find a middle ground where you support them for now, and I still get to maintain a comfortable wardrobe? I am newly married, I deserve to indulge. All brides do," Pari said, her voice softening but still holding a note of resistance.

Deep down, Pari remembered that she didn't receive a splendid wedding wardrobe from her parents like newly wedded daughters typically do. She was solely dependent on her earnings for her indulgence and desires as a newlywed. This was her chance to enjoy the luxuries she felt she deserved, and the thought of compromising on this was hard for her to accept.

"Can we at least find a way to balance this?" she continued. "I understand the importance of supporting your family, but I also want to feel like a bride who can enjoy her new life. Maybe we can budget for both? Support your family while allowing me to have some of the things I missed out on during the wedding?"

She looked at Ayushman with hopeful eyes, seeking a compromise that would allow her to maintain some semblance of the newlywed experience she had always dreamed of.

"They're going to sacrifice the ancestral house they've lived in all their lives. That's a big deal, Pari. Besides, you already have plenty of clothes, some still with tags from six months ago," Ayushman replied gently. "We are in entry level jobs yet, so you don't have to wear designer clothes to work. But in Pathankot, people judge you if you're not up to the mark in fashion. Life's harder for them." Ayushman tried to justify her perceived needs as unnecessary.

"You just trivialised my dreams by comparing them to your family's situation that I have no responsibility for. It does not make sense; why do I have to sacrifice what I have worked for all my life?"

"Because they are our family, and it is our duty to help them in their time of need." Ayushman reinforced his loyalty to his family.

"Well, then they need to sacrifice big functions like we did two weeks ago. What was the need for such an expensive party for our marriage if they can't afford it?" Pari countered, struggling to keep her composure.

"That was for social acceptance as the daughter-in-law of the family," Ayushman explained.

"I didn't ask for it, but now I'm being made to pay for it. I was happy with a court marriage. Oh my God!" Pari replied in distress, her mind calculating the overwhelming debt.

"They did it as their responsibility. That's what we do. We don't ask for sacrifice in the family; we just do it for each other. It's the way to be in a joint family," Ayushman said, trying to calm her.

"Well, if they drop elite circles and kitty parties, that will help, won't it?" Pari suggested.

"No, they may not," Ayushman continued. "If they drop kitty parties or dress inappropriately for elite clubs, people will know the Mittals are going down financially. That will impact our sales settlements because people will know we don't have enough funds to legally pursue them if they default. It's a vicious cycle."

Pari struggled to understand the complex structure of business and the interdependence of women's networking in kitty parties. "Three months will go by quickly," she told herself reluctantly. "We just got married; it's not worth fighting over." Her internal timer for the next three months started, but she remained unconvinced. "They are not as wise from the get-go as Ayushman thinks," she mused, especially since the latest lavish party seemed avoidable. "Why debut me in Pathankot's business circle when I'm not going to live here?"

Pari's upbringing in a military family, surrounded by relatives who were farmers, had sheltered her from such financial complexities. "This is so different from what I know," she thought, feeling like Little Red Riding Hood lost in unfamiliar woods. "How do I navigate this treacherous path laid out before me?" The familiar comforts of her past seemed distant as she faced the daunting challenges of her present, unsure of how to find her way through the financial maze that now defined her life.

New dawn breaks, love unconfined, what trials will they find?

PART TWO

"The course of true love never did run smooth."

- WILLIAM SHAKESPERE

CHAPTER 10

WIFED IN INDIA-
PARADOX

P ari and Ayushman's studio apartment in Bangalore offered a stunning view of rolling hills, painted in hues of green and gold. This picturesque landscape, framed by large windows that filled their space with natural light, was a testament to Pari's love for extravagance. Inside, the lounge reflected her creative touch: a cozy, cream-coloured couch adorned with vibrant throw pillows, a sleek glass coffee table holding a vase of fresh flowers, and walls decorated with minimalist art. Tiny details, like a collection of quaint ceramic figurines on the shelves and a stack of books beside a cozy reading nook, completed the serene ambiance. Her mother's words echoed in her mind, "When you start working, with your grit and determination you can buy whatever you want and surround yourself with."

In this haven, two contrasting worlds existed—Pari's desire for independence and luxury, and Ayushman's deep-seated loyalty to his family in Pathankot. This clash of perspectives often surfaced during their financial planning sessions.

One evening, they sat down to meticulously plan their finances. Ayushman launched an Excel sheet to track their expenses, his primary role in managing their finances becoming evident. The monthly costs quickly added up, including their apartment rent, payments for their house helper, utilities, and their regular dining out expenses. As they filled in each category, they discussed potential areas for savings and budget adjustments.

Pari suggested, "And let's add my personal expenses."

Ayushman, assuming his unspoken authority over their finances, resisted, "Remember, let's avoid shopping for the next three months."

Pari, feeling the need to justify her personal care, asked, "What about my personal care expenses?"

"You mean threading your eyebrows? I'll add fifty rupees...or maybe a hundred?" Ayushman, clueless about such expenses, underestimated the costs.

"Three thousand," Pari replied firmly. "It's for full body waxing, facial, massage, and replenishing my makeup kit."

Ayushman, surprised, asked, "That's very expensive. Is that how much you pay every month when you visit Elante Beauty Parlor?"

"Yes!!," she affirmed, pushing back firmly but feeling unfairly questioned.

"Well, I think that's extravagant. You should compare prices. I'm sure you can get the same service from a home business at one-third the price. Why don't you find out?" Ayushman suggested, attempting to set firm boundaries.

"I can't compromise on that. It's my self-love expense, and I'm not going to a home parlour. I don't find it safe. What if they have cameras? No, that's non-negotiable," Pari insisted firmly.

Ayushman sighed and quietly added the expense to the Excel sheet. "As expected, our expenses are almost equal to your income with a few thousand remaining," he continued, "which gives us flexibility for entertainment expenses. So, we might be able to send money equivalent to my income to Pathankot to keep things afloat there."

This plan reflected Ayushman's belief that supporting his family was a duty, a perspective rooted in his upbringing. "Are you going to send all your income home? Seriously?" Pari asked, frustration creeping into her voice.

"Don't stress yourself too much, I know them and I know how I can bring them out of it. You just need to trust me," Ayushman asserted, his tone dismissive. This troubled Pari emotionally and financially.

"How long do you think the situation would take to recover?" Pari asked, her anxiety palpable.

"It might take up to two years. I am trying my best to wind up the house and business sale in six months and then support Bhaiya in setting up an IT business as soon as it's done."

"But you said three months earlier," Pari said with impatience.

"I knew you would hold me up for that, so I'm giving you a longer time estimate. I aim to recover them in a year, but I want you to think two years so you don't feel misled if it takes a little longer than a year."

"That's worrying me now. They haven't brought me up so why am I expected to sacrifice?" she thought to herself, feeling the weight of unwarranted responsibility crushing her dreams. Ayushman's insistence came as a shock to Pari. She felt a knot of anxiety forming in her stomach. The thought of blindly pouring resources into a problem without understanding its root causes filled her with dread.

"Aren't you going to keep some for us to have a comfortable start to married life and go on a honeymoon?" she pleaded, denying the gravity of Ayushman's concern.

"Pari, look around! We live in one of the best studios Bangalore can offer. The scenery is breathtaking, and we have the luxury of being by ourselves, with nobody to interrupt us. Don't you think we're always on a honeymoon?" Ayushman reasoned, his voice firm yet pleading, trying to ease her worries. But Pari's fantasy of a perfect newly married life clashed harshly with Ayushman's family loyalty.

One weekend, Pari and Ayushman decided to treat themselves to a movie at PVR, Bangalore Central. The movie "Dhoom" was an exhilarating escape, and Pari was particularly enchanted by Aishwarya Rai's stylish outfits. After the movie, they strolled through the mall, and Pari's eyes caught sight of a designer mini skirt in a boutique shop. Excited, she dragged Ayushman into the store and quickly tried it on.

Standing in front of Ayushman, she twirled and smiled, hoping for his approval. "How much is it?" Ayushman asked, still caught up in her enthusiasm.

"It's Rs. 1799 only," she replied, her eyes sparkling with anticipation.

Ayushman's expression changed. "Pari, it's just a mini skirt. You don't need to spend so much on that."

"But it's a designer piece by Alaya Khan. I'll wear it on our holidays," Pari insisted.

"Let's wait until we actually plan a holiday," reasoned Ayushman.

"Stock runs out quickly, and I don't want to miss out on the latest fashion," Pari explained.

Ayushman, trying to be practical, suggested, "We can buy it when that time comes. Right now, we need to be careful with our spending."

Pari felt her excitement deflate. She dashed out of the shop, feeling hurt and misunderstood. Ayushman followed her, trying to soothe the situation by suggesting they have dinner at Salvadores, a high-end restaurant in the same mall.

As they entered Salvadore's, the soft ambient lighting and elegant décor created a calming atmosphere. Ayushman guided Pari to a cozy corner table, hoping the luxurious setting would help lift her spirits. The aroma of fine cuisine filled the air, and Pari, though still feeling a pang of hurt, decided to give the evening a chance.

They ordered a variety of dishes, from succulent appetisers to rich, flavourful main courses. The attentive waitstaff ensured their dining experience was impeccable. Ayushman, always the charming conversationalist, tried to engage Pari in light-hearted talk, sharing amusing anecdotes and recounting fond memories. Gradually, she began to relax, her mood lightening with each passing moment.

When their entrees arrived, Ayushman took a bite and immediately complimented the chef. "This is incredible," he said, nodding appreciatively. "The chef really knows his craft." Pari managed a small smile, feeling a bit more at ease.

As they savoured their meal, Ayushman continued to make an effort to reconnect with Pari. He leaned in and whispered, "You know, I think this is one of the best meals we've had in a while. I wanted to make tonight special for you."

Pari, touched by his sincerity, responded, "I appreciate that, Ayushman. It's been a tough day, but this dinner has been lovely."

After finishing their main course, they indulged in a decadent dessert, sharing a slice of chocolate cake that melted in their mouths. The sweetness seemed to mirror the mending rift between them.

When the bill arrived, Ayushman glanced at it briefly before handing over his card. Pari, curious, peeked at the total amount and saw it was more than her designer garment. She felt an underlying frustration that their financial misalignment seemed to be a recurring theme. As Ayushman tipped the waiter generously and complimented the chef once more, Pari couldn't help but reflect on the irony. He was willing to spend on a lavish dinner every week to make her happy, yet their earlier disagreement had been about spending money on something she truly wanted—fairly sharing the entertainment budget for two weekends while staying within their monthly limit.

Stepping out of Salvadore's, Ayushman gently took Pari's hand. "I hope this evening helped a little," he said, his voice soft with genuine concern. Pari managed a formal smile, holding back the urge to express her frustration in that moment.

Frustrated by the apparent double standard, she couldn't help but think, "How can he be so generous with others but so frugal with me?" The ride home was silent and tense, and the strain on their intimate bond grew as a result. Pari felt that Ayushman didn't value her happiness and was more concerned about controlling finances than understanding her needs.

The tension between them grew palpable one evening when Pari confronted Ayushman about overlooking his mother and sister-in-law's shopping expenses.

"Ayushman," Pari began, her voice trembling with frustration, "Why do your mom and bhabi get to spend so freely on shopping while I'm expected to cut back on my expenses? It doesn't seem fair."

Ayushman sighed, trying to maintain his composure. "Pari, they have to survive in an elite social circle, so their expenses are justified. You, on the other hand, just need to wear smart casuals to work. Their necessity and your necessity come at different price points."

Pari's eyes widened in disbelief. "So, because I don't move in those circles, my needs are less important? Is that what you're saying?"

"That's not what I mean," Ayushman said, his voice softening. "They're upholding the family's social status. If rumors spread about our business struggling, it will affect our debt collections, ultimately impacting us. They're doing what's necessary to ensure we get our pending payments. It's their responsibility."

Pari could see Ayushman was struggling to make her understand, but his words felt like daggers. "So, my self-care and happiness mean nothing in comparison?"

Ayushman could see the pain in her eyes and felt a pang of guilt. He realised how distant she felt from his family, yet her lack of connection and compassion for them felt like a thorn piercing his heart. "Pari, it's not that your happiness doesn't matter. It's just... they are doing their part to help the family in their way. You don't have the same responsibilities attached to your parents. You have me, and I'm trying to balance both worlds."

Pari's frustration turned to a quiet sadness. "You're my world,

Ayushman. But it feels like I'm not yours. How can I compete with your family for your attention and respect?"

Ayushman felt a lump in his throat, knowing he couldn't easily bridge the gap between them. "Pari, you are my heart, and my family is the blood in my veins. Both are essential but competing priorities. I understand you feel overshadowed, but I'm doing my best to make it all work."

Pari's eyes filled with tears. "It feels like you're asking me to make all the sacrifices. I don't see you giving up anything."

Ayushman took her hands in his, his voice thick with emotion. "I'm not asking you to sacrifice without reason. I'm hoping that one day, you'll see the bigger picture. Your sacrifices now will be acknowledged and respected by everyone. It's just that the acknowledgement won't come soon."

Pari pulled her hands away, a tear rolling down her cheek. "How will I ever be able to trust that? Every time you try to cheer me up, it feels like a ploy to rip me off. How do I know your intent is genuine?"

Ayushman felt his heart break seeing her pain. "Pari, please believe me. I will continue to do things that benefit us both and are in the interest of the larger family. I know it's hard now, but I promise you, one day it will make sense. One day, everyone will respect you for your sacrifice."

Pari, carrying the weight of his words, could only nod, her heart a delicate blend of doubt and hope woven together. Inside, frustration churned. She felt unheard and isolated, her sacrifices seemingly invisible in the grand scheme Ayushman painted. The expectations of family and societal duties felt suffocating, and his promises seemed distant and uncertain. She wanted to believe him, but the present reality overshadowed his assurances.

They sat in silence, the gap between them filled with unspoken words and lingering fears. Pari's thoughts churned as she grappled with her role and the emotional toll it was taking. The heaviness in her chest grew, reflecting her deep-seated frustration and yearning for a clearer path, a tangible sign that her sacrifices were not in vain.

Later that night, Ayushman and Pari lay in bed. Seeking comfort and closeness, Ayushman wrapped his arms around her. "I love you, Pari," he whispered, trying to bridge the emotional gap between them.

Pari lay still, feeling numb to his embrace. It was the first time that the emotions didn't flow from her heart to Ayushman freely, taking their intimacy into lovemaking. She was holding onto the bitterness from tonight's conversation, which blocked her from loving him the same way as before their marriage.

As Ayushman drifted off to sleep, hugging her tightly, Pari stared at the ceiling, her mind racing with thoughts. "I have given him this power over me like a fool," she thought bitterly. "Now I can't take it back after so many years of agreeableness."

She felt a tightness in her chest, the need to defend her choices constantly, and her spontaneous desires restricted by Ayushman's money management role. "How did we get here?" she wondered. "Why do I have to justify every little thing I do?"

The warmth of his embrace, once a source of immense comfort and love, now felt like a prison she couldn't escape. "I need him to see me, to validate my feelings," she thought, tears silently streaming down her face.

Pari knew she couldn't continue like this, feeling emotionally stuck and unable to express her dilemma to Ayushman. "I have to find a way to reach him," she resolved. "But for now, I have to hold on to whatever hope I have left."

As the night wore on, Pari's thoughts kept her awake, the rift between them growing wider. She longed for the day when Ayushman would truly understand her, and they could find their way back to the love they once shared.

Though Pari was comparing apples to apples, Ayushman's complex equivalence also sounded unfair, especially when he defended his own fine dining experience as a shared experience. "It's different, Pari," Ayushman said, trying to justify. "When we dine out, it's about us spending quality time together. It's a shared experience, a memory we create. But your shopping—it's just for you. There's no shared benefit."

Pari's frustration bubbled beneath the surface. "So my happiness doesn't count as a shared benefit?" she wanted to scream, but she held back. Instead, she felt a crushing weight in her heart, overwhelmed by the constant need to justify her choices. Her spontaneous decisions, which once brought her joy, were now restricted by Ayushman's strict money management role.

Pari felt emotionally stuck, a prisoner of her own decisions. Each time she tried to express her needs, she was met with practical reasoning that seemed to dismiss her emotional well-being.

Next day, after work, sitting in the silence of their beautifully decorated apartment, she reflected on how she had ended up in this position. "I used to be so independent," she mused. "How did I become so dependent on his approval for everything?"

Ayushman's insistence on managing the finances, justified by his sense of duty and responsibility towards his family, left her feeling invisible and unheard. "He doesn't see how this affects me," she thought. "He thinks he's doing the right thing, but he's crushing my spirit."

Pari felt the weight of her unspoken words growing heavier. She wanted to tell Ayushman how much she missed the spontaneity in their relationship, how his financial control made her feel like she was losing a part of herself. But every time she opened her mouth, the words seemed to stick in her throat. She was afraid of being misunderstood, afraid that her attempts to communicate would only lead to more arguments and more distance.

"I need him to understand," she thought. "I need him to see me, to see how much this is hurting me." But for now, all she could do was hold onto the hope that one day, he would understand, and they could find their way back to each other.

. . .

FROM THAT DAY ONWARDS, THEIR EMOTIONAL CONNECTION BEGAN to fray. Pari retreated into her own world, feeling increasingly isolated. Meanwhile, Ayushman started avoiding her concerns, thinking, "There's no use discussing anything with her until she gains maturity and sees the world practically, not like a princess." In his mind, Pari was behaving like a spoiled brat, while Pari viewed him as an unfair manager of their funds.

Ayushman immersed himself in extra projects he brought home from work, using them as a shield to avoid arguments with Pari. The more he worked, the less he had to confront the growing distance between them. His perspective on their relationship had shifted; he saw himself as the responsible one, making sacrifices for the greater good, while Pari seemed to him as someone who couldn't see beyond her immediate desires.

Pari, on the other hand, went along with Ayushman's lifestyle choices, particularly the fine dining and shared experiences he valued. Yet, these outings only deepened her sense of detachment. She felt like she was going through the motions, participating in activities that should have brought them closer but instead made her feel even more isolated.

Their once-passionate intimacy dwindled. Pari only engaged in physical closeness when her monthly cycle necessitated human connection, a stark departure from the romantic and personal love they once shared. Each encounter felt more like a mechanical necessity than a moment of shared affection. The romantic spark and adoration she once felt for Ayushman seemed to fade with each passing day.

Ayushman, noticing her distant behaviour but not fully understanding its depth, thought to himself, "She just needs time. Eventually, she'll realise that what I'm doing is for our future." But this belief only served to widen the gap between them. He mistook her compliance for acceptance, not realising that her silence was a sign of growing resentment.

As Ayushman busied himself in work, Pari found solace in her own thoughts, dreaming of a life where she felt seen and understood. The more they tried to coexist, the more apparent it became that they were drifting apart, each ensconced in their own world, struggling to find a way back to each other.

Pari felt that once a financial plan was made and mutually agreed upon —though reluctantly on her part—there was no room for further discussion. Ayushman hated indecision and was committed to any plans he made. She understood this about him. However, she hadn't fully considered the challenge of supporting six additional family members with their resources. This new reality made it difficult for her to maintain the lifestyle she had just begun to enjoy after graduating from university and starting her career.

Growing up, her parents, with their modest incomes, could only provide a great education for her and Shera. There was no budget for a fancy wardrobe. But independence had been instilled in Pari since childhood by her Mother, who always said, "You can buy whatever you like when you start working. Just focus on building a highly paid skill or your interest." This current situation clashed with her long-held fantasies, leaving her deeply uncomfortable.

She often found herself thinking, "I'm trapped in this **paradoxical** family hierarchy. My financial strength enables Ayushman to provide for them, yet relationally, I'm just a new member struggling to find my voice. I give so much, in every way possible. It feels like a sacrifice without reward. Who will fulfil my needs now, if not Ayushman?"

As her thoughts ruminated, the internal conflict weighed heavily on her. She wanted to be supportive, but the sacrifice felt overwhelming. "Ayushman is so decisive, so unwavering," she thought. "He makes plans and sticks to them, no matter what. But this plan... it's harder than I imagined. Supporting his family means giving up so much of what I wanted for us, for myself. "

Pari's thoughts often drifted back to her childhood, remembering how her parents managed with limited means. "We didn't have much, but Mamma taught me dignity in cultivating skills and building my own affordability," she reflected. "Mamma always said to focus on my career, and I did. Now, I can afford what I want, but this situation is making it impossible to enjoy it."

Pari sighed, feeling the weight of her responsibilities pressing down on her. "I'm giving everything I can, but I still feel like an outsider," she thought. "Ayushman is my husband, but I need him to understand my struggle too. I need his support, not just his plans."

Each night, as she lay in bed, the heaviness of her emotions grew stronger. The room felt colder and lonelier, despite Ayushman being right beside her. She stared at the ceiling, her mind racing with worries and unspoken thoughts. The sacrifices she was making seemed to pile up, one on top of the other, forming an insurmountable mountain she had to climb alone.

Pari's heart ached with unexpressed needs and unmet desires. She longed for Ayushman to see beyond his plans and understand her inner turmoil. The uncertainty of their future and the pressure to support his family weighed heavily on her, making it difficult to find peace. She often went to sleep feeling unheard and unseen, her hopes clinging to the idea that the nightmare might end in a few months. But until then, she felt trapped in a cycle of giving without receiving, her dreams of a balanced life slipping further away each night.

How many times had she questioned herself—does a woman's identity after marriage no longer come from her own dreams, but from the needs of others? Each day, it seemed as though her own aspirations were fading, and the essence of her existence was being reduced to a single role—she was merely a 'wife.'

Tradition's weight, modern plight, what's hidden in the night?

CHAPTER II

LOVE, MONEY, AND MISMANAGEMENT

The tension between Pari and Ayushman lingered until they went to Pathankot to celebrate Diwali with his family. The trip was intended to be a respite, a chance to reconnect with family and partake in the festive joy. The scene was set for Goddess Lakshami Puja at their Pathankot home, a time-honoured tradition that filled the house with a sense of reverence and unity.

As they entered the new house that Vardaan had surprised them with, Ayushman felt a wave of pride and relief. Vardaan had managed to align his mother and wife to sell the old house and move into a more practical, manageable home without Ayushman's direct involvement. This act showed Ayushman that his brother valued his advice and took it seriously.

During the celebrations, Vardaan and Ayushman went shopping for fireworks. As they drove, Vardaan said, "I've been waiting for you to lead the final negotiations to sell the carpet business. The other party is distant relatives, and you're better at handling these situations."

Ayushman looked at him, surprised. "You think I'm better suited for this?"

Vardaan nodded, "Yes, you don't crack under pressure. You're the right person for this job."

Ayushman felt a swell of emotion. "Thank you, Vardaan, for trusting me."

Vardaan smiled and stopped the car. They spent time at their childhood eating joint, reminiscing about old adventures.

One afternoon, while searching for his old sherwani for a family wedding, Ayushman's father found his wife had been secretly saving money. This discovery led to a heated confrontation between them.

Ayushman's father shouted, his voice trembling with fury, "Your mother was hiding money in her closet. I found it today. She kept denying it when I asked her!" His face was red with anger, veins bulging on his forehead.

Pari overheard the conversation and saw the tense scene unfold. Her heart pounded as she watched Maa, who had been in the kitchen, rush into the living room. With tears of frustration welling up in her eyes, Maa retorted, "Don't you dare touch my money! I have to beg you for money every time I need something. You won't even give me a cent. I saved this money from my kitty parties. It's mine, don't touch it!" Her voice was a mix of defiance and desperation.

Papa, his face contorted with indignation, retaliated, "I need money to pay bills, and you are hiding it. I am asking other people for loans. Shame on you." His voice shook with a combination of rage and disappointment.

Witnessing this disparity, Pari reflected with a heavy heart, "It's frustrating how Ayushman overlooks his mom's secret savings but scrutinises my transparent expenditure. It feels unfair." She continued to ponder, her mind racing, "Is that because Ayushman is biased because he is her son just like his mom states that his father prioritises his mom and sisters?"

"That means, my struggles are with her son and her struggles are with grandma's son. So typical of a male-dominated family," she thought bitterly.

This incident highlighted ongoing family conflicts, where women's lack of personal space and voice led to frustration and bitterness. Pari realised, with a sinking feeling, that despite their family's outward appearance, deep-rooted issues of financial secrecy and gender bias persisted, affecting both her and her mother-in-law. This moment opened Pari's eyes to the broader dynamics at play, making her understand that her challenges were part of a larger pattern within the family. She felt a mixture of sadness and resolve, knowing that addressing these issues would require strength and patience.

DESPITE THEIR DIFFERENCES, INCIDENTS OCCURRED THAT REASSURED Pari of Ayushman's ability to recognise mismanagement and take corrective action. A significant turning point occurred when Ayushman confronted his father about financial mismanagement.

"Dad, we need to talk about spending. This crisis could have been avoided with better management. We can't keep making the same mistakes."

While reconciling the books, Ayushman discovered a significant miscalculation by his father. He urged his father to speak to their suppliers, who were also distant relatives, to recover the rightful amount. His father refused.

Ayushman, sacrificing his personal life and putting his salary on the line, became furious and confronted his father. "Dad, we need to recover the money from our suppliers. This miscalculation has cost us dearly, and we can't afford to ignore it. Why are you refusing to speak to them?"

His father, trembling with a mix of hurt and defiance, replied, "Ayushman, you don't understand. These suppliers are distant relatives. It's not just about money; it's about honour, relationships, and trust."

Ayushman, his face flushed with frustration, retorted, "Honour? Relationships and trust? Our family is drowning in debt because of this mismanagement! I've sacrificed my personal life, put my salary on the line, and you're telling me to ignore a mistake that could save us?"

Feeling deeply insulted, his father shot back, "I've made countless sacrifices for this family. I've given everything since you and Vardaan were children. And now you're doubting my judgment and skills with numbers?"

Ayushman, seething, leaned forward, his voice cold and determined. "Yes, Father, I am. Because your judgment and so-called skills have put us in this mess. We've had to sell the ancestral house! I won't let your sentimentality ruin us further."

His father, eyes glistening with unshed tears, said, "You think I don't feel the weight of these decisions? Every choice I made was to protect and provide for this family. But you, you can't see beyond your spreadsheets and calculations!"

Ayushman, shaking his head in disbelief, replied, "Protect and provide? By dragging us into deeper debt? By refusing to take necessary actions because of some misplaced loyalty? I won't stand by and watch our future get destroyed by your refusal to confront reality."

At this critical moment, Vardaan, who had been silently observing the heated exchange, stepped in. "Enough!" he exclaimed, his voice firm yet soothing. "This argument isn't helping anyone. We need to find a solution together."

Turning to their father, Vardaan continued, "Dad, we understand the importance of honor and relationships, but we can't let these values compromise our financial stability. Please, talk to the suppliers. If we explain the situation honestly, they might be willing to help."

Their father, still emotional but visibly calmed by Vardaan's intervention, sighed deeply. "Alright, I'll speak to them. But I hope you both understand that family values and trust are more important than any amount of money. This shall take time, don't keep your hopes too high though!"

Ayushman, his anger subsiding, nodded. "We do, Father. We just want to ensure a secure future for all of us."

With Vardaan's mediation, the family reached a fragile yet hopeful truce. Ayushman's father agreed to speak to the suppliers, and the brothers worked together to rebuild their financial foundation, striving to balance honour and pragmatism.

At that moment, Pari entered the room to serve water, sensing the intense atmosphere. Ayushman and Vardaan quietly left. Handing the water to her father-in-law, Pari tried to soothe him as he spoke with a heavy heart, "Beta, I have made so many sacrifices and given them so much since childhood, but today, Ayushman is doubting my judgment and skills!"

Pari empathised with her father-in-law's disheartenment. She too had faced Ayushman's harshness over her own perceived inadequacies with numbers. Yet, she couldn't fully sympathise with her father-in-law, knowing that his miscalculation would continue to affect her indirectly, as she supported Ayushman, who in turn supported his family. This incident clarified two things for her: Ayushman was intolerant of anyone weaker than him in numbers, not the control freak she had thought; and her father-in-law's poor business acumen had indeed led the family into financial trouble, necessitating the sale of their ancestral house.

Despite the emotional and financial strains, these incidents reassured Pari that Ayushman was not blindly loyal. He could see when funds were mismanaged and had the courage to call it out. Having seen recent reassurance from Ayushman's mindset, Pari started believing that one day he would be able to see more areas of mismanagement. Slowly, this restored her trust a little bit. She realised that Ayushman's trust in his folks was emotionally entangled, so she had to keep patience.

BY THE END OF THE TWO WEEKS IN PATHANKOT, PARI FELT LIKE A fish out of water, desperately wanting to return to familiar surroundings. Although she was cared for, the environment felt suffocating. Conversations in the Mittal household seemed like navigating a chaotic jungle. Extracting coherent topics from the overlapping chatter was an impossible skill she struggled to master.

One evening, during a particularly chaotic dinner, the scene unfolded: Grandma: "Dolly, did you even check the pantry? We're running out of basics!" Mother: "I know, Ma! But with the constant interruptions, I barely have time!" Sapna: "And the kids need new uniforms; can someone handle that?" Vardaan: "Uniforms? We have bigger issues, like the business's pending payments!"

The cacophony of voices, clattering dishes, and background noise created a disorienting audio landscape. Pari tried to listen but found it impossible to follow any single conversation. The animated gestures, pointing fingers, and overlapping voices made the environment feel overwhelming. The tension in her body grew with each passing moment, the chaotic energy palpable, making her desperate for calm and order.

"Papa, could you please pass the malai kofta curry?" Ayushman asked in a clear, steady voice.

Despite the surrounding commotion, his father heard him and passed the dish down the table. Ayushman served himself and continued eating, unbothered by the chaos. This simple act struck Pari. Amidst the clamour, Ayushman managed to get what he needed without raising his voice or getting frustrated. He maintained his focus and got his task done efficiently.

Pari observed and thought to herself, "The household atmosphere in Pathankot is loud, a stark contrast to the quiet of my family home. Spending two weeks in this environment feels like a Martian landing on Earth. The constant overlapping conversations resemble a noisy marketplace—a sharp contrast to the disciplined setup in Bathinda. While sometimes fun, the nonstop emotional chatter, sarcastic banter, and unmindful digs are exhausting."

This realisation led Pari to understand why Ayushman could focus on his coding projects after work or on weekends, leaving her feeling neglected when she needed to discuss the home situation. He seemed numb to the constant clashes between his grandmother and mother, retreating into his work as a means of coping.

Pari came to see that waiting for Ayushman's attention to her emotional needs would not yield the desired results. His upbringing in a household filled with his father's struggles and the loud household chatter had shaped him into someone with a high intolerance for mediocrity and a laser focus on his tasks. These traits were survival mechanisms born from his chaotic environment, where distractions were numerous and attention to detail was crucial.

She realised that her current approach—waiting passively for him to notice her distress—was not effective. Ayushman's environment had taught him to tune out chaos and focus intensely on his goals, a skill that served him well in his career but left little room for emotional engagement at home. Pari recognised that if she wanted to address the issues in their household and get Ayushman's support, she needed to approach the situation differently, acknowledging his need for focus while also finding a way to communicate her needs more effectively.

Pari's thoughts crystallised into a profound understanding: Ayushman's upbringing in this chaotic household had honed his ability to cut through the noise and maintain focus. In contrast, she found herself overwhelmed by the same environment. She knew she needed to adapt and find her own way to navigate this new reality, much like Ayushman had.

Pari concluded that Ayushman's upbringing had not only equipped him to handle chaos but also isolated him from understanding her perspective. His ability to filter out distractions, while commendable, meant he often dismissed her concerns. This understanding led her to stop trying to change his financial approach, acknowledging that her empowerment would have to come from another source.

At the same time, Pari recognised the toxic dynamics among the women in Ayushman's family, driven by their need for autonomy and the lack of meaningful outlets. She feared becoming another target once her financial support was no longer needed. This realisation cemented her determination to maintain her independence and focus on her own self-preservation.

By blending these insights, Pari understood the necessity of balancing her respect for Ayushman's strengths with her need to protect her own well-being. This dual awareness guided her decisions moving forward, as she sought ways to nurture both her marriage and her independence.

Love's missteps, future's fight, what's guarded in her light?

CHAPTER 12
GUARDING HER FUTURE

Pari sat alone in the cozy lounge of their studio apartment, the warm light streaming through the large windows, casting a serene glow on the minimalist art adorning the walls. Her thoughts were tangled, a mix of frustration and isolation. She felt the weight of her struggles pressing down on her, and she knew she needed to talk to someone. But the question was: who?

Pari's first instinct was to call her mother. She always remembered her mother's words, "When you start working, with your grit and determination, you can buy whatever you want and surround yourself with." Those words had fueled her ambition and her love for the finer things in life, which was evident in their meticulously decorated apartment. However, she hesitated.

Pari thought to herself, "If I call Maa, she'll sense my sadness immediately. She's always been so supportive of my decision to marry Ayushman. I can't burden her with my marriage problems now. She'll worry herself sick, and Papa... Papa would make her life hell for allowing me to marry according to my impractical wish."

A pang of guilt and shame washed over her as she imagined her father's inevitable demeaning comments. He had always been a dominating figure, his roaring personality intimidating her since childhood.

Pari continued her inner monologue, "Papa's concerns are materialising, and it fills me with guilt for ignoring his advice. He would just say I'm reaping what I sowed and blame me for walking into self-sabotage."

Pari considered her close friends, Meeta, Trisha, and Rahul, but she feared they wouldn't understand. Ayushman had always been an amazing friend to them, and his frugality only emerged post-marriage.

Pari thought, "They'll ridicule me. They see Ayushman as this wonderful friend and partner. They wouldn't believe the struggle I'm facing."

In this moment of vulnerability, Pari thought of Shera. Shera was modern, like her, and could relate to her better than anyone else.

She reflected, "Shera understands the complexities of a modern marriage. He's not tied down by traditional expectations and can offer a fresh perspective."

Pari felt a sense of relief at the thought of talking to Shera. He had always been a source of comfort and modern wisdom. His advice had guided her through challenging times before, and she trusted his judgment.

That evening, Pari sat on the balcony, the city lights twinkling in the distance. She looked at the world clock on her mobile phone and called Shera at night time in Toronto, Canada. As the phone rang, she felt a mix of anxiety and hope.

Shera: "Pari, I can hear the distress in your voice. What's troubling you?"

Pari: "It's Ayushman's family. He sends all our money home. I feel neglected and frustrated. He doesn't see the mismanagement, and I'm worried we'll be stuck in this cycle forever."

Shera listened patiently as Pari poured out her frustrations. She recounted incidents of financial stress, Ayushman's unwavering loyalty to his family, and her feelings of being sidelined.

Shera: "Ayushman has a lot on his plate, trying to be a good son and a supportive husband. It's a delicate balance he's trying to maintain."

Pari: "I understand that, but our relationship is suffering. We can't keep sacrificing our future for his family's mistakes."

Shera: "You need to find common ground. Have you considered starting a family? It might help shift his focus and bring you closer."

Pari: "Family planning? How would that help?"

Shera: "Having your own family will give Ayushman a reason to set boundaries with his folks. It will also give you both something positive to focus on together."

Pari: "It sounds like a big step, but maybe it's what we need."

Shera: "Think long-term, Pari. This could be the key to building a stronger future together. Trust that Ayushman will see more areas of mismanagement over time. Meanwhile, create a mutual interest that can bond you both."

Shera's words resonated deeply with Pari. She felt a surge of relief mixed with determination. She realised that open communication with Ayushman was essential to finding a balance that respected both their needs and responsibilities. Considering family planning could indeed change their dynamics and help them build a stronger, more united future.

Pari thought to herself, "Shera is right. Ayushman needs a reason to shift his focus. If I create a mutual interest by expanding our family, it might help. This journey of Ayushman's mental shift is longer than stating facts. His trust in his parents runs deep, so I must hold on with quiet patience. As I wait for him to see where things have gone astray, I can find ways to make my time meaningful."

With this fresh clarity, Pari decided to talk to Ayushman about starting a family. She hoped this step would bring them closer and improve their intimacy while also taking her mind off short-term material comforts.

Pari felt a sense of resolve wash over her. "I need to create a long-term vision for us," she thought. "Building a family could be the positive focus we need. This way, I won't feel like I'm stuck in a cycle of waiting for him to see my point of view."

As she made her way to their living room, she envisioned their future together, filled with the laughter of children and the warmth of shared purpose. The thought brought a smile to her face and a renewed sense of hope to her heart.

Pari's decision to speak to Shera instead of her parents was driven by her desire to protect her family from worry and to seek advice from someone who could understand the complexities of a modern marriage. Shera's advice provided a pathway that aligned with her long-term goals, giving her the strength to make a decision that could transform her relationship with Ayushman and build a stronger future for their family.

AT WORK, PARI SAT IN HER CUBICLE, HER EYES ON HER COMPUTER screen but her mind elsewhere. Shera's advice echoed in her thoughts, "Having your own family will give Ayushman a reason to set boundaries with his folks... Look into the future, Pari..." The words circled her head like a mantra, making it hard to focus.

Palak, her team leader, noticed Pari's distracted state and approached her desk. "Pari, can we step out for a coffee? I'd like to have a chat," she said with a warm smile, showing her genuine concern.

Palak, a seasoned professional at DataSphere Software Solutions, led the Software Testing and Ethical Hacking department. Known for her empathy and strong leadership, she understood the challenges her team faced both professionally and personally.

Pari and Palak stepped out of the office and walked to a nearby café. The ambient noise of the bustling café provided a comforting backdrop to their conversation. As they settled into their seats with their drinks, Palak initiated the conversation.

Palak: "Pari, I've noticed you've been a bit off lately. I know how hard it can be to balance personal and professional life, especially when things aren't smooth at home. Do you want to talk about it?"

Pari hesitated for a moment but felt the sincerity in Palak's eyes. She decided to open up, feeling a mix of relief and vulnerability.

Pari: "It's been tough, Palak. Ayushman and I have been going through a rough patch. His family's financial issues are consuming all our resources and attention. I feel neglected and frustrated."

Palak listened intently, her expression softening with understanding.

Palak: "That sounds really challenging. Balancing family obligations and your own needs is never easy. Have you and Ayushman talked about how this is affecting you?"

Pari: "We have, but it feels like we're constantly at odds. He's so focused on helping his family that our relationship is suffering. My brother Shera suggested that we start a family of our own to help shift his focus and bring us closer."

Palak nodded, considering Pari's words.

Palak: "Shera's advice makes a lot of sense. Sometimes, creating a new focus can help realign priorities. When you have a family of your own, it naturally shifts the dynamic and responsibilities. Have you thought about how this could help you both?"

Pari: "I have. Shera's advice has been circling in my head. Starting a family might help Ayushman see the bigger picture and set boundaries with his folks. But I'm scared. What if it makes things worse?"

Palak reached out, placing a comforting hand on Pari's.

Palak: "Pari, change is always scary. But from what I've seen, you and Ayushman have a strong foundation. Starting a family could bring you closer and give you both a new sense of purpose. It might also help him understand the importance of balancing his family obligations with your needs."

Pari felt a surge of clarity and relief as she absorbed Palak's words. The combination of Shera and Palak's advice provided a clear path forward.

Pari: "You're right, Palak. I think it's worth trying. Ayushman needs a reason to shift his focus, and starting a family could be that reason."

Palak: "Exactly. And remember, you're not alone in this. We're here to support you. Balancing work and family is possible, and I'll make sure you have the flexibility you need."

Pari smiled, feeling a renewed sense of determination and hope.

Pari: "Thank you, Palak. Your support means a lot to me. I'll talk to Ayushman about starting a family."

Palak: "Anytime, Pari. You've got this. And if you ever need to talk, I'm here."

On her way home from work, Pari thought about her discussions with her brother and Palak. Two people from different backgrounds giving her the same advice had a profound impact on her, making her seriously consider their words. "If I start a family, I might have to leave my career to care for the baby," she pondered, the idea weighing heavily on her heart. "But maybe this could be better for me. Right now, my income just supports Ayushman's family's expenses. I never get to enjoy my earnings anyway." This realisation brought a mix of apprehension and hope, leaving her deeply emotional as she continued her journey home.

That evening, Pari felt more confident as she sat down with Ayushman to discuss their future.

Pari: "Ayushman, can we talk about something important?"

Ayushman: "Of course, Pari. What's on your mind?"

Pari: "I've been thinking a lot about our future and our relationship. I think it's time we consider starting our own family."

Ayushman: "Starting a family? I thought we agreed to wait a couple of years. You're doing so well in your career, and with everything going on, I don't want you to feel pressured."

Pari: "I miss feeling connected to you. Our intimacy has taken a hit because of all the stress in managing situations back home. I think having our own family might help shift our focus and bring us closer. "

Ayushman: "I miss that too, but I'm worried about you leaving the workforce."

Pari: "I understand your concern, but it's about finding balance. We can plan it in a way that I take a break until I'm ready to return. Besides, starting a family might actually improve our relationship as it will give us a common goal. It will give us something positive to focus on together."

Ayushman: "I understand what you're saying. Having our own little family would be amazing." He hoped this might help Pari shift her focus from material pleasures to building relationships and shared goals, fostering a sense of interdependence.

Pari: "Exactly. Imagine the joy of having a baby, Ayushman. It will bring us closer and create a stronger bond between us."

Ayushman smiled, feeling a sense of hope.

Ayushman: "You're right. It sounds wonderful. Let's do it, Pari. Let's start planning for our future together."

As expected, Pari's intimacy with Ayushman improved, and two months later, she discovered she was pregnant with twins. She shared the joyous news with Ayushman, who was ecstatic.

Ayushman hugged Pari tightly, his excitement palpable. "This is amazing news! I can't wait to tell everyone. Our own little family!"

Pari smiled, feeling a surge of joy and relief. "I'm so happy, Ayushman. This is the fresh start we needed."

Ayushman shared the joyous news with his family, and Pari did the same with hers. The excitement was palpable; both families were overjoyed. Pari, however, felt a deeper sense of relief. "Finally," she thought, "I have a new focus, a way out of the endless labor of supporting Ayushman's family."

Yet, this fresh start came with its own set of challenges. Pari had to leave her job early due to complications with her twin pregnancy. She thought, feeling a mix of relief and concern, "I never thought I'd leave my career like this. But starting our own family is worth it."

Ayushman, now shouldering the immense pressure of managing the finances for both households, had the strain evident in his eyes. For weeks, he juggled the mounting responsibilities, trying to make ends meet. Pari could see the toll it was taking on him, "I'm sorry for adding to your burden," she whispered one night, her hand resting gently on her growing belly. "You're not adding to it, Pari. I will figure something out. Don't worry!" Ayushman replied, trying to mask his exhaustion with a comforting smile.

A month later, respite finally arrived. The phone rang, and it was Vardaan on the other end. "Ayushman, I've got great news! The factory sale has concluded, and we've paid off all our debts. There's even a surplus of twenty lakhs."

Ayushman could hardly believe his ears. "Are you serious, Vardaan? This changes everything!" he exclaimed, his voice filled with inception and hope. "Yes, Ayush. It's real," Vardaan reassured him. Ayushman collected his thoughts and proposed his idea, "Vardaan, let's reinvest this surplus into an IT business."

Vardaan was skeptical of the idea, "Are you sure?"

Ayushman spoke with determination, "Yes! That's the only way we can turn this around."

That night, Ayushman kept the news to himself, pondering the possibilities and the weight that had been lifted off his shoulders. He looked at Pari, peacefully sleeping, and felt a surge of determination.

"I'll make it through this," he thought, finally free of the weight he had carried alone. As he lay down beside her, he whispered softly, "My family is worth every sacrifice."

Guarding hopes, courage in might, what's hidden in her sight?

CHAPTER 13
MY TWINS, MY LIFELINE

In the brightly lit hospital room, the doctor smiled as he delivered the joyous news. "Congratulations, Kamalesh, you are blessed with twin grandsons," Dr. Batra announced to the Mittal family waiting outside the operation theater.

It was Janmashtami 2006, and the arrival of their sons via C-section brought immense joy to the family, especially given the cultural esteem for male children in India. Ayushman's father had decided that Pari would deliver in Pathankot, under the care of his best friend, Dr. Ramesh Batra, a gynaecologist and gold medalist, hoping for the best medical attention and advice. The timing, coinciding with Lord Krishna's birthday, added to the auspiciousness of the occasion.

However, amid the celebration, Pari faced unexpected complications after the surgery, resulting in a sudden fever. The joyous atmosphere was tinged with concern as they rallied to ensure Pari received the care she needed.

"Mrs. Pari Mittal is being transferred to the ICU; her fever is rising," the nurse informed, swiftly guiding Pari on a stretcher from the surgery room to the ICU. Despite facing a health crisis that kept her from seeing her children until she recovered, Pari maintained an optimistic outlook. She drew strength from her faith, praying, "Babaji, please give me life long enough to raise my kids. It's not my time yet!"

As they welcomed their twins, the entire family expressed gratitude to Lord Krishna for this blessing and prayed for Pari's swift recovery. They were prohibited from meeting Pari due to the complications of her infections and the fear of passing it on to the newborns. In her absence, her mother and mother-in-law immediately immersed themselves in caring for the babies, their hearts full of joy.

Three days later, Pari's health improved, and she was moved to a private suite where Ayushman, with the help of both grandmothers, cared for the babies.

"What will be their names?" Ayushman asked, looking at Pari with love, pride, and tenderness.

Tears of joy rolled down Pari's cheeks as she finally got to nurse both her twins. "Luv and Kush," she replied.

Ayushman's mother interrupted, "Ayushman, we have to ask Guruji for names following family traditions."

"Maa, Pari had already decided the names if we had boys. And I get to choose the names if we had daughters," Ayushman replied, without noticing his mother's growing unease.

Mrs. Mittal's face flushed with embarrassment as she continued to fold sheets. "Well, I didn't have that privilege in my time."

Ayushman, oblivious to her discomfort, said, "Maa, these are modern times. Pari has a voice in all our decisions."

Mrs. Mittal forced a smile as she noticed Pari's mother coming out of the bathroom. She excused herself for a shower, planning to retreat to the visitors' room in the hospital later.

Pari felt the sting of these words deeply. Her mother-in-law's demeanour shifted from supportive to critical, a change that Pari couldn't ignore. The initial joy of welcoming the twins was overshadowed by an undercurrent of tension.

Pari's frustration grew as she struggled to balance her recovery, the demands of motherhood, and the constant scrutiny. She felt a wave of helplessness wash over her. She wanted to believe that her mother-in-law's intentions were good, but the constant criticism was breaking her spirit.

This emotional struggle marked the beginning of a complex power dynamic that Pari had to navigate, balancing respect for her mother-in-law's experience and authority with her own need for autonomy and respect in her role as a mother and a wife.

"Pari, the babies are still hungry after nursing. I suggest you start feeding them with formula milk. Doctors know nothing about hungry and crying children. I have looked after many new mothers and am speaking from experience," her mother-in-law cautioned, her tone carrying a hint of exasperation.

Pari, who had been strictly advised to breastfeed her twins to the best of her ability to provide them with immunity, felt her heart sink. She gathered her thoughts and responded calmly, "Mamma, Doctor Uncle said that when the babies cuddle into me, the milk supply will increase due to a rush of hormones. I have also read the same thing in books on how to raise kids, and breast milk is best for newborns."

Her mother-in-law interrupted her before she could finish, her voice sharp, "And your stitches will also open with their kicks," she cautioned.

"Maa, their kicks are gentle, I love feeling their little feet," Pari struggled to clarify.

Pari's eyes filled with tears, silently conveying her stress and frustration. Her mother-in-law, noticing the tears, remarked in a reserved and blunt tone, "Using tears as weapons of stubbornness, aren't you?" Her voice grew more accusatory. In her mind, tears were a means to gain sympathy and sway emotions. This belief stemmed from her own past, where she had to navigate the delicate balance of power within the household, often feeling overshadowed by her own mother-in-law. To her, Pari was just a stubborn young girl who didn't appreciate her experience. Meanwhile, her own relatives would call her specifically for time-tested advice during childbirth situations in their families, highlighting the respect and value they placed on her wisdom.

Pari, feeling the weight of her mother-in-law's words, tried to explain, "Mamma, I didn't mean that. I'm just going through a lot, and I need your support."

But her mother-in-law was not willing to relent. "Support? You think I don't see what's going on? Every time you cry, you make it seem like I'm the one causing all the problems."

"Mamma, I'm not trying to manipulate anyone. I just want what's best for the babies," Pari said softly, her voice trembling with the effort to keep her emotions in check.

"Best for the babies? Or best for you? Don't forget, I've raised children too. I know what I'm talking about," her mother-in-law shot back, her eyes narrowing as she spoke.

Pari felt a wave of helplessness wash over her. No matter how hard she tried, it seemed impossible to bridge the gap between them. She wanted to believe that her mother-in-law's intentions were good, but the constant criticism and lack of empathy were breaking her spirit.

"Mamma, please, can't we try to understand each other better? I'm new to this, and I'm doing my best," Pari pleaded.

Her mother-in-law sighed, shaking her head. "You think you know everything because you've read some books. But experience matters more than books, Pari. You'll see that soon enough."

As her mother-in-law left the room, Pari felt a mix of sadness and frustration. She knew she had to find a way to navigate this challenging relationship without losing herself in the process. Her tears were not a weapon but a reflection of her genuine struggle to cope with the overwhelming responsibilities of new motherhood and the relentless scrutiny she faced.

. . .

THE TWINS WERE NAPPING PEACEFULLY IN THEIR CRIBS, THE SOFT hum of their lullaby still playing in the background. Pari was seated on the couch, a baby book in her lap, trying to find some solace in reading about motherhood. Ayushman's mother, Mrs. Mittal, was in the kitchen, preparing dinner. The scent of spices filled the air, mingling with the scent of baby powder and freshly laundered clothes.

Ayushman came back from Pathankot office with Vardaan, as he stepped into the living room, his tie loosened and exhaustion evident on his face. He settled beside Pari, offering her a weary smile.

"I'm home," he murmured, leaning in to kiss her cheek.

Pari looked up from her book, returning the smile, though weariness mirrored in her eyes. "Hi, how was your day?"

"Long and tiring," Ayushman replied, glancing toward the kitchen where his mother was bustling about. "How are the kids?"

"They're finally napping," Pari said, closing the book. "I was just reading up on some new techniques for feeding."

Mrs. Mittal, overhearing their conversation, wiped her hands on a towel and walked into the living room. She placed her hands on her hips, her expression a mix of concern and authority.

"Pari, you're always reading those books. Motherhood isn't just about following instructions," she said, her tone carrying a hint of criticism. "It's about getting back to a normal life with your husband as well."

Pari felt a pang of frustration. "I'm doing my best to take care of the twins, Mamma. It's been overwhelming, and I want to make sure I'm doing everything right."

Mrs. Mittal sighed, shaking her head. "Highly educated girls don't understand that motherhood is not just about feeding kids; it's about getting back to a normal life. You need to find a balance. Ayushman needs your attention too." With that, she retreated to the kitchen.

Ayushman, sensing the tension, tried to reassure Pari, "All Maa wants is for you to get back to a normal life. Don't worry about her other comments."

Pari's eyes filled with tears, her grip tightening on the baby book. She felt the sting of her mother-in-law's words, interpreting them as attempts to control her and undermine her efforts, subtly influencing Ayushman against her. She feels insulted in front of the entire family as Vardaan casually continued his relaxation and Sapna bhabi attending to his needs.

ANOTHER AFTERNOON, PARI DRESSED IN A COMFORTABLE KURTA AND leggings, a practical choice for a day at home with her newborns. Her mother-in-law seemed content with her attire, even complimenting her on the choice. However, when visitors came to see Pari and the babies, the situation took a turn. After the guests left, her mother-in-law's tone changed sharply.

"Pari, you should know better than to dress so casually when we have visitors," she scolded. "You need to represent our family with more elegance. What will people think of us if they see you like this?"

Pari was taken aback. "But you said my attire was fine earlier. I dressed practically for caring for the babies."

Her mother-in-law's eyes narrowed. "That was before people came over. You need to show that we are providing you well and that you respect our family's status."

The tension escalated when Ayushman walked in. Seeing the confrontation, he asked, "What's going on?"

Pari tried to explain, "Your mother complimented my attire earlier, but now she's upset because visitors saw me in it."

Ayushman, siding with his mother, said, "Pari, you need to understand how important our family's reputation is. Dressing up properly for visitors shows that we are taking good care of you. It's not about practicality; it's about perception."

Pari felt a surge of frustration. "So now I have to dress up every time someone visits, just to maintain appearances?"

Ayushman's tone turned harsh. "Yes, Pari. You need to stop making it look like we're not providing for you. Your expectations are becoming unreasonable."

This exchange highlighted the growing rift between Pari and Ayushman, worsened by his mother's constant interference. Pari felt increasingly isolated and misunderstood, her efforts to balance personal comfort with family expectations unappreciated. Ongoing criticisms magnified their differences, and she struggled with the Mittal family's insistence on appearances. Ayushman's stress from working overtime due to his job and his new IT startup with Vardaan added to the tension, leaving Pari to navigate her new role under immense pressure.

Throughout her recovery in the first six weeks, Pari noticed a stark shift in her mother-in-law's behaviour. Her demeanour changed drastically post-childbirth, echoing the warnings from Sapna Bhabi. Criticisms about Pari's breast milk supply, baby care skills, and appearance in front of visitors became frequent. Struggling to cope, Pari often found herself in tears, seeking solace through prayer while cradling her sons.

When the twins were six weeks old, Pari and Ayushman left for Bangalore with the kids. Settling into their home, Pari took charge of the household, juggling her recovery with newly discovered energy. She appreciated not being interrupted by her mother-in-law constantly. "Finally, I can do things my way," she thought with relief.

Pari recruited maids for cooking and cleaning with Ayushman's support. "It's such a relief to have help around the house," she mused, feeling a weight lift off her shoulders. They both focused fully on taking care of their infants, day and night.

"This newfound autonomy in Bangalore is exactly what I needed," Pari realised. Managing the household and caring for the babies without persistent scrutiny and criticism felt liberating. "I can finally enjoy motherhood without someone breathing down my neck," she thought, smiling as she watched her twins sleep peacefully.

The freedom to make decisions and run the household her way was a significant relief. "This is how it should be," she reflected. "I feel like I can truly be myself here." She found herself embracing motherhood and her new life with Ayushman and their twins. "We can do this," she thought confidently. "We can build a beautiful life together, just the four of us."

In quiet moments, Pari often found herself reflecting on the past and envisioning the future. "I've come a long way," she thought. "From the pressure of living under mother-in-law's constant watch to finally having the space to breathe and grow. It's amazing how much difference a change of environment can make. I feel more in control, more like myself."

She smiled, thinking of the future. "This is a fresh start for us, and I am determined to make the most of it. We have so many dreams and plans, and now, without the constant interference, we can actually work towards them. This move back to Bangalore has given me the strength and confidence to be the best version of myself—for me, for Ayushman, and for our twins."

Pari felt a surge of determination. "We really can create a beautiful life here, and nothing is going to hold us back," she reassured herself. "Every day is an opportunity to build the life we've always envisioned. It's time to embrace this and let our dreams flourish."

Twins her joy, hearts aligned, what shadows will she find?

CHAPTER 14
CLASH OF TWO MATRIARCHS

J ust before the first Lohri of Luv and Kush when they turned six months old, Ayushman's mother expressed her desire to see her grandsons while on the phone with him. "Haye, mera poton ko dekhne ka, godi mein lene ka mann ho raha hai (Oh, how I long to see my grandsons and hold them in my lap)," she said wistfully.

Ayushman, wanting to make his mother happy, replied, "Then why don't you come over, and we will celebrate their first Lohri together." Without consulting Pari, he booked tickets for his parents, and they arrived in Bangalore a few days later.

When they arrived at the doorstep, Ayushman greeted Pari with a smile. "Pari, look who's here to see you!" he exclaimed, thinking this surprise would cheer her up from the mundane routine of taking care of the children.

Pari was taken aback, her face falling as she saw her in-laws standing there. She managed a polite smile and welcomed them in, hiding her shock and disappointment. Later that day, during a conversation with her mother-in-law, she discovered the full extent of their visit.

"I'll be staying until the kids' first birthday," her mother-in-law announced. "I don't want to miss out on growing up."

Dealing with her mother-in-law on a daily basis began to take a toll on Pari, especially when it came to feeding the children. Her mother-in-law insisted on giving them normal meals cooked at home, while Pari preferred dietician-recommended purees and semi-solids.

One evening, as Ayushman heard yet another argument erupting over the children's meals, he stepped in to mediate. "Pari, let them have the normal meal when we all have dinner together at night. They are having dietician-recommended purees during the daytime anyway," he suggested, trying to diffuse the situation.

Pari, frustrated, thought to herself, "I know how to nurture my own kids. Why is she dictating what she feels is right through Ayushman?"

Every day, there was a clash between her mother-in-law's traditional thinking and Pari's modern outlook, informed by the books she had read. These daily struggles over exerting control in her own household filled their relationship with bitterness.

The constant tension created a rift between Ayushman and Pari. She felt unsupported by him, viewing his attempts to mediate as a lack of backing for her perspective, overshadowed by his authoritative stance at home.

One evening, as they were getting ready for bed, Pari couldn't hold back her feelings any longer. "Ayushman, why do you always take her side?" she asked, her voice trembling with frustration.

"It's not about taking sides, Pari. I just want peace in the house," Ayushman replied, trying to keep his tone calm.

"But this is my home too! I should have a say in how we raise our children," Pari shot back, tears welling up in her eyes.

"I understand that, but can't we find a middle ground?" Ayushman pleaded.

Pari shook her head, feeling more isolated than ever. "Every day is a battle, Ayushman. I feel like a stranger in my own home."

As they lay in bed that night, the unspoken words hung heavily between them. Pari's resentment continued to build, her thoughts a whirlwind of frustration and helplessness. She longed for a time when her home would feel like her own again, free from the constant power struggles and overshadowing presence of her mother-in-law.

Pari recalled one day when Sapna bhabi was venting to her during her first Diwali visit after marriage, "Just wait, Pari. After the babies arrive, Maa's behaviour will change. She will find fault in everything you do. Be prepared for constant scrutiny." Sapna Bhabi had described her own miserable experience with Maa after her daughters were born, quoting several incidents during a Diwali visit when she was deeply hurt by Maa's comments. She vented out, warning Pari to safeguard herself from Maa's clutches.

In the following weeks, the tension only grew. Ayushman, caught between his mother and his wife, tried to mediate but often sided with his mother, believing her intentions were protective rather than controlling. Mrs. Mittal's attempts to assert control and maintain her influence over Ayushman and family traditions became more pronounced. Ayushman valued his mother's wisdom over Pari's opinions, dismissing them as untested concepts. The power dynamics in the household became clearer to Pari.

Recognising her mother-in-law's recent behaviour and heeding Sapna Bhabi's advice, Pari treaded carefully to rebuild her life with Ayushman. Battling Ayushman's dominance, twin childbirth challenges, health concerns, and her evolving relationship with her mother-in-law, Pari maintained her sanity to safeguard her children's future. Despite her frustration, her moral compass led her to adjust her boundaries without compromising her identity.

Reflecting on her past choices, Pari felt a wave of regret wash over her. She thought, "Why didn't I listen to Papa? My overconfidence, my insistence on making my own choices, led me to this current situation.

Ayushman and his family seemed so promising, but now... it's nothing like what I envisioned."

She realised that while she was physically and mentally vulnerable after childbirth, instead of receiving the nurturing and supportive environment she desperately needed, the Mittals were tearing her down, chipping away at her confidence. "I feel so weak and helpless," she mused. "How did I go from being a confident, independent woman to feeling like I can't do anything right?"

Pari struggled with the stark contrast between her current self and the person she once was. Back then, she was buoyed by her family's unwavering support. "I used to feel so sure of myself, so capable. Now, every day feels like a battle just to keep my head above water," she thought, her heart heavy with frustration and sadness.

Desperate for a lifeline, she immersed herself in inspirational books, seeking solace and practical advice to regain her footing. "There has to be a way out of this," she told herself, flipping through pages of motivational stories and self-help strategies.

Determined to focus on her sons' development and her own well-being, she stumbled upon "The Power of Your Subconscious Mind." The book promised success and peace, two things that felt so distant yet so desperately needed. "Maybe this is what I need," she thought, a glimmer of hope igniting within her. "If I can just change my mindset, maybe I can start to rebuild my life."

Reading the book, she felt a small spark of her old self return. "I can do this. I have to do this. For Luv and Kush, and for myself. I need to be strong again, not just for them but for my own sanity. I can't let the Mittals' negativity define me or my future."

Pari clung to the promise of the book, using its teachings to visualise a liberated future. "Success and peace aren't out of reach. They're within me, waiting to be unlocked. I just need to believe in myself again, to harness the power of my mind and transform my reality."

These thoughts became her mantra, a silent affirmation that she repeated to herself daily. "I am strong. I am capable. I will rise above this." With each repetition, she felt a little more of her old self returning, a little more strength seeping back into her spirit.

Pari realised that while her journey was far from over, she was taking the first crucial steps toward reclaiming her life. She knew it wouldn't be easy, but for the first time in a long while, she felt a sense of purpose and direction. "I will find my way," she vowed. "I will rebuild my confidence and create a better future for me and my sons."

Pari's quest for self-confidence to stand up for herself against Ayushman's authority became increasingly urgent as she navigated the complexities of changing relationships, motherhood, and the pressures of her environment post-marriage.

THE BIRTH OF HER TWIN SONS, LUV AND KUSH, INTRODUCED NEW layers of challenges. Constantly adapting her personality to fit her surroundings, Pari struggled with the disconnect between her true self and the facade she was forced to present. Though she found some respite with the practice of EFT, the past three months had left her feeling cornered and exhausted by her mother-in-law, who was supposed to stay with them in Bangalore for at least half an year. Seeking advice and support, Pari reached out to her friend Meeta.

Pari: "Meeta, I'm exhausted. My mother-in-law is here to help, but it's making things worse. She manipulates Ayushman, and he always sides with her."

Meeta: "Pari, why didn't you share this with me sooner? I'm so upset that you've been dealing with this alone."

Pari: "I didn't want to burden you. It's just that she sets things up so cleverly. Ayushman doesn't see what's happening, and I feel like I'm losing my mind."

Meeta remarked, "And since your mother-in-law doesn't need a visa, she can visit you anytime," speaking from experience. She lived with her husband in the UK and frequently posted pictures on her Orkut account, while they explored different European countries on the weekends.

Pari visualised with hope and regret: "I wish I was in Canada or there was a way we could go there!"

Meeta: "Pari, it's possible, you have skills in IT. Why not consider migrating to a developed country like Canada, the USA, England, or Atlantia? These societies support equality and respect women's contributions in both nurturing and providing for the family."

Pari: "You really think that's possible? How would that help?"

Meeta: "In more liberal societies, you'll find respite from rigid family hierarchies. It will give you a seat at the table and allow you to build a life where your contributions are valued."

Pari: "That sounds like a dream. How do I even begin?"

Meeta: "Wait for your mother-in-law to leave, then start by discussing it with Ayushman when he is in a good mood. Given the deterioration of your mutual trust it will be hard. Emphasise how it could benefit both of you and your children. It's about finding a place where you can thrive together, without the constant pull of his family's demands."

Inspired by Meeta's advice, Pari decided to have a detailed conversation with Ayushman about the potential benefits of moving to a developed country.

SOON AFTER CELEBRATING THEIR BIRTHDAY ON JANMASHTAMI IN 2007, her mother-in-law leaving Bangalore, Pari was secretly relieved. With a renewed sense of purpose, Pari sat down with Ayushman one evening to discuss an idea that had been brewing in her mind. She felt a mix of apprehension and excitement as she prepared to share her thoughts.

Pari: "Ayushman, I need to talk to you about something serious."

Ayushman: "Sure, Pari. Go on."

Pari: "I've been thinking a lot about our future and how we can ensure the best possible life for our family. What if we moved to a developed country like Atlantia? It could provide us with better financial stability and give us a fresh start."

Ayushman raised an eyebrow, curiosity evident. "Like Atlantia? That's a big step. Why ?"

Pari explained, "I think moving to a developed country could help us build a more balanced life. Your skills are highly valued there, and you'd earn in dollars, which would make it easier to support both our family and your folks back in India."

Ayushman nodded slowly, considering the idea. "I see the logic in that. But what about your career? Would you be able to continue working there?"

"Yes," Pari replied, her voice steady. "That's one of the biggest advantages. A place like Atlantia has a strong job market, and I could find work that utilises my skills. It would allow me to continue my career as childcare facilities are highly reliable and state of the art."

"It sounds promising, but it's a massive change," Ayushman said, concern creeping into his voice. "Are you sure you're ready for that?"

Pari took a deep breath, her eyes reflecting determination. "I've thought about it a lot. The last year has been incredibly challenging, but it's also shown me the importance of finding a stable and supportive environment for our family."

Ayushman took her hand, squeezing it gently. "I can see how much thought you've put into this. It's not just about us, but about ensuring a better future for our children too. I want us to be in a place where we can thrive together."

Pari's voice softened with hope. "Yes. And being in a country where we both have opportunities to grow professionally will help us build a more secure and happy life. We won't have to worry as much about financial crises or constant challenges."

Ayushman sighed deeply, the weight of the decision clear on his face. "I agree with you, Pari. This could be the fresh start we need. But it won't be easy. We'll have to adapt to a new culture, find jobs, and build a new life from scratch."

Pari's eyes shone with conviction. "I know it won't be easy, but I believe it will be worth it. We'll be creating a new future for ourselves and our children. And we'll have each other to lean on during the tough times."

A smile spread across Ayushman's face. "You're right. We've already faced so many challenges together. This is just another step in our journey. Let's do it, Pari. Let's explore moving to a developed country."

As they prepared for a new life, Pari and Ayushman felt a sense of unity and excitement. They knew the road ahead would be filled with ups and downs, but their shared vision for the future gave them strength. Ayushman met with a few agents to get advice on filing for a visa to a developed country that offers job opportunities, childcare, and healthcare. For two months, after considering the merits and demerits of moving to the USA, Australia, Canada, England and Atlantia. Atlantia emerged as the top suggestion. The filing process took three months. Ayushman consulted with Pari and filed for a permanent resident skilled migrant visa, which was due to get processed within the next one year.

Ayushman: "Good, the kids would be over two years old by then."

Pari: "Yeah, and I can start working again with the children going to childcare." She hoped Ayushman would suggest she focus on family like the other ladies at home, given his high income potential.

Ayushman thought to himself, "Pari continuing her career will give her purpose and fulfillment. It will complement the new family we're building together."

Ayushman: "Of course! After having kids, you've been immersed in their care. You deserve another shot at your career, and you have my full support!"

Pari thought to herself, "Why can't Ayushman be the same caring hero for me and our children as he is for his family in Pathankot?" This painful comparison gnawed at her heart, each repetition intensifying the ache in her chest. She yearned for the days when Ayushman was her hero, making her feel cherished and secure.

Pari lay in bed, staring at the ceiling, her heart heavy with unspoken words. She felt a pang of loneliness, knowing Ayushman meant well but still feeling neglected. His thoughts about her career filled her with a mixture of hope and sadness.

Pari felt a deep sense of frustration and hurt as she pondered this question, struggling to understand her place on Ayushman's priority list. Since their marriage, she had watched Ayushman prioritise his family's needs, often at the expense of their own relationship. It wasn't just about the money—it was about feeling valued and seen. She longed for Ayushman to champion her heart, to be the hero she once believed he was.

This longing created a deep wound in her heart, one that had been there since the beginning of their marriage. She felt like she had been subjected to endless sacrifices, always putting Ayushman's family first while her own needs were pushed aside. The imbalance weighed heavily on her, and she couldn't shake the feeling of being secondary in her own marriage.

Ayushman, oblivious to her internal struggle, continued to plan their future with a sense of duty and practicality. Meanwhile, Pari buried her feelings, knowing that expressing them might disrupt the fragile peace they had found. She resolved to focus on their new journey, determined to find her own path to empowerment in a foreign land.

Pari thought to herself, "I need to stay quiet and strong. I can't let my feelings sabotage our plans. Moving abroad is a chance for a fresh start, a chance for me to find my own strength."

Amidst the chaos, Pari held onto hope for a better future where women's rights were respected. This hope was her beacon, motivating her to envision a liberated community and focus on her children's development, striving for a balanced life and reclaiming her autonomy.

A PIVOTAL MOMENT CAME WHEN HER DREAM BECAME REALITY: THEY received their Atlantia permanent resident visa as expected after waiting for a year. Pari's joy was boundless as they prepared to leave for Atlantia. She hugged her toddlers Luv and Kush who were now little over two years old, dancing and singing with happiness. Over four years into an unsatisfactory marriage, this was her chance to escape the oppressive environment she had endured and start anew in a country that promised a brighter future.

She began preparing for the move to Atlantia, knowing she would need new clothes for herself and her growing children. In preparation, she put her ego aside and asked Ayushman for money, thinking, "I will soon be independent and won't have to ask for money and justify my personal expenses."

Pari meticulously created shopping lists and packed bags with essential comfort items, while Ayushman balanced his work commitments and focused on stabilising his IT startup, which had begun gaining traction. His efforts contributed to the stability and growth of their family enterprise.

Though Ayushman no longer interrupted her, she took her past bitter experiences as potential criticism. This led her to analyse prices out of fear of Ayushman's criticism rather than an inner drive to manage money effectively. Whatever she bought with Ayushman's income did not bring the same pleasure it did before their marriage. What was once a celebration of fun now reminded her of her uneasiness and inadequacy. "When I start earning in Atlantia, I won't feel guilt and shame for investing in things that please me. I will celebrate life again, and our married life will improve."

Whenever she spent money, even though Ayushman's family was no longer in financial urgency, she felt like she was stealing from them. Fighting that feeling, she cried to herself, "I am not selfish, Ayushman! You didn't have to hurt me so much to support your parents. You should have just told me to leave you for their sake since you couldn't be fully emotionally and financially invested in our relationship. It is unfair that you expected me to give my all—physically, emotionally, and financially—while you couldn't offer me the same due to your commitment to your parents. I didn't want to come between loving parents and an attached son. I am not that kind of woman!" She felt bad and manipulative throughout her four years of marriage, except for the joy of motherhood.

Despite feeling isolated and heartbreakingly disconnected from Ayushman, Pari found solace and purpose in her children, who gave her a reason to look forward to life in Atlantia. At twenty-eight, she was still young enough to restart her life and hoped that the burdens of the past four years would fade away once they set foot in Atlantia.

Once they moved to Atlantia, Pari envisioned Ayushman becoming a different man, like the supportive and broad-minded husbands she saw in Hollywood romantic movies. "He'll be like the husbands in those films," she thought wistfully, her heart fluttering with anticipation. A romantic at heart, Pari's perspective had always been shaped by films, transitioning from Bollywood in her earlier years to Hollywood now. "I've always believed in a film-style happily ever after," she mused, her hope and trust fuelled by these cinematic dreams.

Through EFT, she had her prayers answered and placed her faith in the power of prayer rather than conforming to Ayushman's worldview. "I have faith that things will change," she told herself. She viewed his expectations as extremely self-centred and uninspiring, feeling that he aimed to mold her into another version of himself. "He wants me to be just like him," she thought, feeling a pang of resistance. Determined not to lose her identity, she clung to her familiar self. "I won't let go of who I am. I need to reset to my past self from four years ago when we arrive in Atlantia."

The anticipation of starting anew in a different land filled her with such excitement that it overshadowed her struggles during the five months of preparation. "A fresh start is what I need," she thought, sweeping her miseries under the carpet. I just want to fly to Atlantia now and leave all this behind."

The idea of a fresh start where her dreams could come true kept her going. "A new beginning," she whispered to herself, her heart filled with a renewed sense of purpose and the promise of a brighter future. "This is my chance to create the life I've always wanted." The excitement and hope for a better tomorrow made her struggles seem worth it, and she looked forward to the journey ahead with determination and optimism.

FINALLY, THE DAY ARRIVED. THE LUGGAGE WAS LOADED INTO THE taxi, and the entire Mittal family, along with Pari's parents, gathered to bid farewell to Pari, Ayushman, Luv, and Kush. While everyone was hugging and wishing them luck, Pari felt emotionally detached from the scene. She had already cut her hair short and was wearing western clothes, transforming her departure into a celebration of her new beginning. While Sapna and Mrs. Mittal shed tears, Pari was eager to leave, hurriedly exchanging hugs and touching the feet of elders for blessings. She had to consciously instruct her feet to slow down, ensuring her excitement didn't embarrass Ayushman.

As they arrived at Indira Gandhi International Airport in New Delhi, Pari's anticipation grew. The bustling terminal was a hive of activity, filled with an array of traveler's from all walks of life. She marvelled at the colourful mix of people, the sleek modern architecture, and the efficient hustle of airport staff. "This place is always so alive," she thought, a sense of excitement bubbling within her. The promise of a new life ahead filled her with joy.

Glancing at her family, Pari felt a mix of emotions—nervousness, excitement, but mostly a profound sense of relief and hope. "We've come so far," she reflected, looking at Ayushman and their twins, Luv and Kush. "This is a new beginning for all of us."

Once they boarded the plane, Pari and Ayushman helped Luv and Kush get settled, then took their seats on either side of the kids in the four-seater center bay. As they buckled in and the plane began its ascent, Pari took a deep breath. Whispering a silent prayer as they took off, she said, "Hey Waheguru, please take care of us. You have been so kind in blessing me with everything I've ever wanted—from becoming head girl at school to marrying Ayushman, bearing children with him, and now moving to Atlantia. I have no complaints."

She continued, "Today, I place all my burdens from the past four years in a box, tie heavy boulders to it, and throw it all into the Indian Ocean. From this day, I will revert to my confident and independent self. I will be the same strong Pari, and no one can stop me."

"Saun babaji di... Bole Sonihal, Sat sri Akal! Bless our journey, Waheguru," she whispered, feeling a wave of calm wash over her as the plane soared into the sky.

Old versus new, loyalty's plea, what's next in their spree?

CHAPTER 15

CROSSROADS OF EMOTIONS

"Welcome to Atlantia," the pilot announced as the plane began its descent. "The local time is 6:00 PM, and the weather is a pleasant 72 degrees. We hope you enjoy your stay in San Clarion."

These words ignited a new fire in Pari. As their plane descended, she caught her first glimpse of the city's sprawling landscape. The sight of San Clarion, with its blend of ancient architecture and modern skyscrapers, filled her with a sense of new beginnings.

Stepping out of the airport, Pari was immediately captivated by the city's vibrant energy. The streets were bustling with activity, and numerous women confidently navigating their way through the city caught her eye. "San Clarion really supports the independence of working women," she thought, feeling a sense of empowerment wash over her as she imagined blending into this dynamic environment.

For Ayushman, San Clarion presented a landscape ripe with business potential. As they drove through the city, he observed the flourishing tech parks and numerous startups, feeling a rush of excitement at the prospect of diving into the city's thriving business ecosystem.

Settling into their new apartment in the historic district, they took a moment to reflect on their journey. The apartment offered a stunning view of the city's skyline—a perfect metaphor for the new horizons they were about to explore. Despite the newly acquired comfort, Pari couldn't shake the emotional distance between her and Ayushman.

"Maybe being away from our Indian cultural context will change Ayushman's perspective," Pari hoped. She still hadn't emotionally healed from the abrupt shift she experienced after marriage, where Ayushman had transformed from a loving boyfriend into an authoritative head of the family.

Within a month of landing in Atlantia, Ayushman received a job offer as a senior software engineer. He was ecstatic and decided to celebrate by taking Pari and the kids to a fine dining restaurant.

As they settled into their seats, Ayushman beamed with pride. "I got the job offer today. Senior software engineer at one of the top firms here."

Pari smiled, though her eyes held a hint of worry. "That's wonderful news, Ayushman. I'm really happy for you."

Luv and Kush, oblivious to the underlying tensions, cheered and clapped. "Yay, Papa got a job!"

Pari glanced at the children, then back at Ayushman. "I'm still waiting to hear back from my interviews. It's been tough, but I'm hopeful something will come through soon."

Ayushman reached across the table and took Pari's hand. "I know it's been challenging. But you'll get something soon, I'm sure of it. You've always been resilient."

Pari squeezed his hand gently, appreciating his support. "I just want to make sure we're both contributing. It's important for me to feel like I'm doing my part."

Ayushman nodded. "You will, Pari. Just give it a bit more time. This move has been a big adjustment for all of us. We need to support each other through it."

Pari sighed softly, feeling a mix of relief and lingering anxiety. "I know. And I'm trying to stay positive. It's just hard sometimes."

The children, sensing the shift in mood, looked up curiously. Kush tugged at Pari's sleeve. "Mumma, are you okay?"

Pari smiled warmly at her son, ruffling his hair. "Yes, sweetheart, I'm fine. Just talking with Papa about grown-up stuff."

Luv chimed in, "Does this mean we can get more toys now that Papa has a job?"

Ayushman chuckled. "We'll see about that, little man. Let's focus on celebrating tonight."

As the evening progressed, the celebration was filled with laughter and joy, but beneath the surface, both Ayushman and Pari were acutely aware of the uncertainties still looming. They resolved to face these challenges together, supporting each other through the highs and lows, as they navigated their new life in Atlantia.

Pari landed an opportunity for an interview with a software testing company. Nervously, she walked into her first job interview. "Can you write an algorithm to test a calculator?" the interviewer asked, smiling.

Pari's heart raced. She took a deep breath, but her mind went blank. "I left my children for the first time today, and I can't stop thinking about them," she thought, tears welling up in her eyes.

"I... I'm sorry," she stammered. "I can't seem to focus."

The interviewer looked at her with understanding but also disappointed. "It's okay, Pari. Maybe today isn't the best day for this. We can reschedule."

On the train ride home, Pari replayed the moment in her head, feeling the sting of failure. "What kind of mother am I if I can't even hold it together for one interview?" she thought, tears streaming down her face. The job interview had been a disaster. Her nerves had gotten the better of her, and she had stumbled over simple questions.

"I'm in Atlantia now. I thought things would be different. I thought I'd be happy and everything would be okay," she whispered to herself, her reflection in the train window showing a weary face. "But here I am, still stuck. Still unable to move forward."

The train's rhythmic clatter seemed to echo her thoughts. "What if I never get a job? What if I can't provide for Luv and Kush? What if Ayushman thinks less of me because I can't contribute?"

Her phone buzzed with a message from Ayushman: "Hang in there, Pari. You'll get the next one." She appreciated his words, but they felt like a band-aid over a wound that needed stitches.

"I'm supposed to be strong, resilient. I've always prided myself on being able to handle anything. But this...this is breaking me," she admitted to herself, the weight of her thoughts pressing down on her chest.

As she got off the train and walked home, she couldn't shake the feeling of inadequacy. The picturesque streets of Atlantia, which once seemed filled with promise, now felt like a maze she couldn't navigate. She entered the apartment, greeted by the sight of Luv and Kush playing with the baby-sitter, Nancy. Their innocent joy momentarily lifted her spirits.

"Momma, look at what we drew!" Kush said, holding up a colourful sheet.

Pari mustered a smile. "That's beautiful, sweetheart."

Yet, even in this moment of tenderness, her mind raced with worries. She thought of the inner battles, and the constant pressure to prove herself.

After saying goodbyes to Nancy, she tucked the kids into bed that night, Ayushman joined her. "How are you feeling?" he asked gently.

Pari took a deep breath. "Overwhelmed. I thought moving here would solve everything, but it feels like I've lost my confidence."

Ayushman wrapped his arms around her. "We're in this together, Pari."

She leaned into him, feeling both the comfort of his embrace and the lingering uncertainty. "I just want to be strong for our family, for myself. But it's hard."

"We'll get through this," Ayushman reassured her. "One step at a time."

Pari nodded, hoping that with time, she'd find her footing in this new journey of their lives.

Desperate for help, Pari visited Dr. Lisa Lee, a compassionate General Practitioner. During the appointment, Pari had an emotional breakdown, leading to a heartfelt discussion about her stress. Dr. Lee listened attentively and then gently advised, "Start with deep breathing for three minutes whenever you feel overwhelmed. It will help you calm down. Also, consider individual and relationship counseling to address your family concerns."

Following Dr. Lee's advice, Pari began practicing deep breathing exercises. Gradually, she felt a sense of relief and regained her confidence. Her next job interview was a triumph, and Pari joined Global Testing Systems in San Clarion, opening a new path in her professional life.

Three months after Ayushman began his new job, Pari also secured employment. This change marked a significant shift in their household dynamics. Ayushman started taking on more hands-on household tasks, while Pari insisted on an equal fifty percent contribution to the housework. However, this new arrangement brought its own set of challenges.

"Ayushman, you need to load the dishwasher tonight," Pari reminded him one evening after dinner.

"Can't it wait until tomorrow morning? I'm exhausted," Ayushman replied, leaning back in his chair.

Pari's frustration bubbled to the surface. "We agreed on sharing the housework equally. It can't always be put off until it's absolutely necessary. This needs to be a regular routine."

Ayushman sighed. "I've never done this kind of work before, Pari. In Bangalore, we had maids for everything."

Pari's tone softened but remained firm. "I understand that, but things are different now. We need to adapt. It's not just about the chores, it's about showing respect for each other's efforts. I need you to be as committed to this as I am."

The division of labor extended to other areas as well. Pari expected Ayushman to help with mopping and cooking. She was regimental about keeping a clean and organised home, while Ayushman preferred a more relaxed approach, often delaying tasks until they were absolutely necessary.

One evening, as they were cleaning up after dinner, Ayushman suggested, "Why don't you keep five hundred dollars for your personal expenses and transfer the rest to my account for bills?"

"I am not doing that," Pari replied assertively. "I want to be involved in all our financial decisions, Ayushman. I need to know where my money is going."

"Pari, you should trust me," Ayushman sighed. "I don't want to add more stress to your life. Just let me handle it."

"It's not about stress, Ayushman. I don't want to be left in the dark about my finances."

Ayushman, recalling their early years of marriage, shook his head. "Honestly, Pari, you're an impulsive buyer. It's better if I take care of it."

"That was years ago, Ayushman. I don't want to worry about your opinion on how to spend my money anymore since we have different ways of enjoying it. We need to split expenses, or we'll keep having these arguments."

Ayushman sighed and left the room to sleep on the couch once again.

From Pari's perspective, Ayushman's approach felt controlling. "Why does he always try to dictate how things should be done?" she wondered.

But Ayushman saw it differently. He thought, "I'm assuming duties based on skill."

This fundamental disagreement led to frequent verbal and silent conflicts. "These arguments are tearing us apart," she thought, the longing for Ayushman's physical intimacy gradually eroding. "I feel so broken. Does he really think so little of me?" she questioned, feeling a deep sense of contempt from him. "I've lost interest in all the pleasures of life with him. What's left for us?"

Noticing the lack of warmth and intimacy with Pari's growing disinterest, Ayushman was deeply affected. "Why does she keep pushing me away?" he wondered, feeling a pang of hurt. To cope with the void in his heart, he further immersed himself in work. "I need to secure our future," he reasoned. "My children's lives will be easier if I leave a solid estate for them."

However, Pari showed no sign of restoring trust in him. This made Ayushman wonder if she had become more authoritarian due to the influence of Western culture. "Has the Western way of life changed her so much?" he mused.

Ayushman didn't realise that Pari's mental state had undergone a dramatic shift. Now financially independent, she asserted her rights with determination. "I've changed from my younger, naive self," she reflected, determined to maintain her autonomy at home and ensure she wasn't questioned about her remaining money, "While I do my duty for the home, I will spend the rest of my hard-earned income as I please. Nobody gets to dictate me what to do anymore, she resolved."

One evening, during yet another heated financial discussion, Pari spoke coldly, "I will not repeat what I did four years ago. I have learned my lessons the hard way!"

Ayushman looked at her in disbelief as she continued, "From now on, I will keep my income with me and contribute only to the household expenses."

"Now you don't trust me with money, eh?" Ayushman retorted, his voice rising.

"Last time when I gave you power, you controlled me instead of appreciating my trust," Pari shot back.

"Are you accusing me? How dare you? I did everything for you. We even moved to Atlantia on your insistence!"

"Don't give me that. I gave up my chances to go to Canada and married you instead. Besides, you were done with the red tape back home; you didn't do it for me, you did it for your family!"

"So what do you intend to do now?" Ayushman demanded, his frustration palpable.

"I'll contribute my share to the household expenses," Pari responded, her voice laced with bitterness. "When I think about the other women in your family," she continued, pointing to his mother and sister-in-law, "who just take without giving anything back, you should consider yourself lucky to have me actually helping out!" Her words dripped with sarcasm, reflecting the frustration and hurt she felt.

Ayushman, though frustrated, believed Pari would soften in a few months once she was content with her indulgences. He felt annoyed but agreed, "Okay, if you want to know the expenses, then you will have to pay fifty percent every month without fail."

They listed the expenses on a sheet of paper, and from then on, Pari was supposed to transfer fifty percent of the calculated amount into Ayushman's account. Ayushman felt they were behaving more like housemates than life partners. His last words were, "Don't waste money on your crazy shopping."

"I'll share the expenses, but I don't want to know how you handle the rest of your money, and you shouldn't worry about mine either. Whether I set my excess money on fire, it's none of your business," Pari stated firmly, reclaiming her position in the power dynamic.

Ayushman's blood boiled at Pari's financial stance, but he chose to sleep without escalating the situation further, still convinced that, with time, she would soften.

That night, Ayushman was so annoyed that he went for a half-hour drive to calm down and then slept in the living room.

Their communication and understanding of each other's needs had been strained for a while. Both Ayushman and Pari carried their own burdens and expectations, while it was crucial for them to find common ground and rebuild their bond. However, neither took a step forward to address it, and no one backed down.

The very next month, when Pari missed the rent payment date, Ayushman questioned her handling of responsibilities. "I received a call from the real estate agent. Why did you miss due date. Do you know it could impact our credit rating," he said, blaming her and seeking an explanation for the missed payment.

"Well, you didn't tell me the due date," she said defensively.

"You never asked for the information," Ayushman retorted, his tone sharp.

Ayushman, with a hint of sarcasm, added, "You want to take responsibility but can't pay the bills on time. Is this what you've learned about money management?" His words stung, doing nothing to ease the tension.

Pari sensed a tone of victory in Ayushman's voice, as if he was relishing her mistake. She felt a deep sense of shame and distance growing between them. Trying to maintain her composure, she admitted her fault, saying, "I messed up this time. Can you cover the rent just one time? I'll pay you back as soon as my salary is credited."

Ayushman sighed, his voice firm and measured. "Pari, you need to understand the importance of being responsible."

Pari felt a wave of guilt and inadequacy wash over her. She had been so caught up in the excitement of updating her wardrobe to fit into Atlantia's fashion culture that she had neglected their financial obligations. "I understand," she said quietly. "I need to be more diligent. I was just so excited about my new beginning in Atlantia."

Ayushman's expression softened slightly, but his tone remained serious. "I understand, but excitement doesn't pay the bills. We need to stay on top of things, especially now that we're new to Atlantia and have children to take care of."

Pari nodded, detecting the undertone of blame in Ayushman's voice. "I'll make sure this doesn't happen again. I promise."

Ayushman nodded, his face reflecting a blend of frustration and understanding. "Alright. Let's move past this. Just be more careful next time."

As they moved on from the conversation, Pari resolved to manage her responsibilities more diligently. She knew she had to balance her excitement for their new life with the practicalities of their current situation. The incident was a wake-up call, reminding her of the importance of financial responsibility and the need to maintain her independence without falling into the trap of criticism and inadequacy.

True to her word, as soon as she received her salary, Pari transferred the money to Ayushman's account. She informed him, "Ayushman, check your account; I've transferred the rent money," all the while keeping a tally of his blames in her heart.

They were gentle and excited only with the kids, focusing their energy on creating a positive environment for them.

Beyond that, Pari kept her emotions hidden, fearing that Ayushman might judge her for being too joyful or too thrilled about the recent independence she had finally embraced. This unspoken barrier grew, leaving her to navigate her emotions alone while presenting a composed facade.

Pari's determination to assert her independence reminded her of her perceived inadequacy and Ayushman's belief that she was insufficient no matter what she did. Pari thought to herself, "At this stage of life, while I am earning enough, I won't even allow my father, who raised and sacrificed for me, to dominate me. I am not a child to be coaxed or disciplined. Ayushman is so mistaken about me."

She paused, reflecting further, "Actually, he hasn't even taken the time to know me. He doesn't make an effort to understand what I love or like. He is just busy with his dreams of becoming a wealthy man. He loves money more than our relationship; numbers are his beloved wife," she concluded.

As time passed, the divide between Pari and Ayushman grew, eroding warmth and intimacy from their relationship. Every night, after settling the kids, they retreated to their bedroom in silence. Pari felt undervalued, thinking, "He earns double but expects equal contribution. I sacrificed my career for our twins and feel neglected." Ayushman, frustrated, thought, "She spends so much on luxuries. I'm trying to secure our future, but she thinks I'm controlling." They turned their backs to each other, each yearning for the lost connection and struggling with unresolved frustrations.

The next morning, their interactions were limited to discussions about bills and household tasks. Pari avoided showing her shopping finds to Ayushman, thinking, "He has never cared about what I like. There's no point in sharing my excitement." Meanwhile, Ayushman thought, "No matter what I do, Pari's never happy. I'm not a fool to invest in her lavish pleasures; I'd rather secure our family's future. One of us has to be responsible. I can't trust her spending habits." The rift between them widened, each lost in their own frustrations and judgments.

Their usual life conversations were brief and transactional, focusing on the children and their daily routines. They were tender and enthusiastic only with the children, striving to create a positive atmosphere for them. Outside of that, Pari avoided expressing her feelings, fearing judgment for being too excited or happy with her newfound independence. This unspoken barrier grew, leaving her to navigate her emotions alone while presenting a composed facade.

Pari's internal discourse continued, "Is this how it's going to be? Just getting by, day by day, without really connecting? How did we get here? And how do we move forward?" The answers seemed elusive, and the emotional distance between them felt more insurmountable with each passing day.

As time passed, discontent with their relationship sometimes caused Pari's thoughts to spiral. "How can Ayushman be so different now?" she mused, her heart heavy with frustration. "Back then, he was so agreeable and cautious with his family, never wanting to come across as arrogant. He wouldn't even tell them that my salary was covering their social obligations just to save their pride. And now, here we are, financially stable, free from those obligations, yet he still won't take full responsibility."

She sighed, feeling the weight of the unfairness. "He claims to be superior, always talking about wealth development as if it justifies everything. But why doesn't he treat me and our children with the same priority he gave his parents? It's like we're second-class citizens in our own home."

Pari's mind flashed back to their time in Bangalore. "I managed all the monthly expenses while he supported his family back in India. I did it all until I got pregnant. And now, with no more need to send money home, he still can't handle our household finances without me covering fifty percent, even though I earn half of what he does. It's so unfair."

Her thoughts grew more bitter. "I had children, I took risks with my life, and I took time to recover my health. I lost two and a half years of valuable work experience, which means I'm paid less than my counterparts now. Yet he expects me to pay half of everything without considering our salary disparity. How does that make sense?"

The frustration bubbled up, and Pari felt a mix of anger and sadness. "Why does he expect me to pay fifty percent by the expense calculation, not by our income levels? It's like he doesn't even see how disadvantaged I am. I've sacrificed so much, but it's never enough for him."

With a determined look in her eyes, Pari made a vow to herself. "I won't let him control me or diminish my worth. I'll fight for my fair share and make sure he understands that I deserve to be treated as an equal partner, not just an accessory to his plans."

Despite going through internal turmoil, Pari chose to stay silent, thinking he would find a way to justify himself. She decided not to confront him in a battle she could not win given his quick wit and calculation ability. But in her heart, this unspoken unfairness disqualified him from being her hero.

"In movies, heroes spoil their lovers with pleasures. But Ayushman is offended by my desires, even when I fund them with my earnings and contribute more of my salary than he does to cover half the expenses. This is far from romantic! He is frugal, whether he admits it or not," she thought as she went to sleep with a heavy heart. She had grown accustomed to living a muted life with Ayushman, focusing primarily on their children and avoiding confrontation.

PARI FOUND SOLACE IN HER ROLE AS A MOTHER, SPENDING MUCH OF her time with Luv and Kush. She appreciated the childcare services in San Clarion, which contributed to her children's development. However, the emotional distance from Ayushman left a void in her life.

"Online shopping is just a distraction," she mused, "It can't replace the need for the loving and compassionate partner I once envisioned Ayushman to be."

Sitting on the porch of their home, Pari often reminisced about the Ayushman she had fallen in love with in University.

"I miss the connection and closeness we once shared," she sighed. "I want to let my guard down and trust him again, but how can I? The financial judgments he exerted and his past behaviour have left me wary."

Pari's inner struggle mirrored the complexities of their relationship. The promises she made to maintain her financial independence created a barrier between them. Meanwhile, Ayushman focused on building assets, saving for a downpayment on a house, not fully understanding the emotional distance growing between them.

Ayushman made genuine efforts to adapt to their new life in Atlantia. He helped with housework and even surprised Pari with breakfast in bed on Mother's Day, trying to bridge the emotional gap. However, Pari's emotional walls were well-fortified, making it hard for Ayushman to truly connect with her on a deeper level.

One day, Ayushman, filled with concern, approached her. "Pari, please, tell me what I can do to make amends. I can't stand seeing us like this. I'm even following your financial arrangement. What more should I do?"

Pari took a deep breath, her voice trembling with raw honesty. "Ayushman, I don't feel the same way anymore. It feels like I've become a secondary option in your life, overshadowed by your 'I'm always right about money' attitude. It's as if I don't know anything about running a household or a family. This isn't just about words; it's about actions and trust. I need to feel like we're a team, making decisions together. I need to know that my feelings and needs matter to you."

Feeling defensive and strained, Ayushman tried to explain. "Pari, I'm doing everything for our family. I'm saving to buy a house for us here in Atlantia. We need to build savings to secure our future."

He paused, then added, "Plus, my parents depend on me. I am their son. Your parents have pensions, but mine rely on their children for support in their old age."

Ignoring most of his explanation, Pari zeroed in on Ayushman's commitment to his family. "Then why didn't they plan for their old age?" she taunted, her frustration bubbling over. "They can sell their gold and diamonds instead of flaunting their status at events. You have a problem with my clothes, but not with your mother and Sapna bhabhi's boutique clothing and fine jewellery. My clothes cost much less than pure silk and gold anyway."

Her voice was tinged with years of built-up frustration. "He's not my hero but theirs; he just physically lives with me."

"Pari, you don't understand," Ayushman argued, his frustration evident. "My family needs me. Their pride and social standing are important. I can't just let them down."

Pari, her voice rising, countered, "Guess what? I even work for my wishful expenses. Your mother and sister-in-law don't even work. All they do is attend kitty parties. Who approved that as not a lavish 'expense'? I see that you have been fooling me because I was blindly in love with you, while they don't care about your opinion, and yet you care about their social expenses. They are so lucky unlike me!"

Ayushman felt a mix of anger and helplessness. "Pari, you're being unreasonable. I'm trying to balance everything, but it's not easy."

Pari's eyes filled with tears of frustration. "I'm tired of feeling like my needs and desires don't matter. I want to be an equal partner, Ayushman. We need to work together, or we'll keep having these arguments."

Their conversations often turned toxic. Pari's feelings of resentment towards Ayushman's requests for intimacy were fuelled by her perception of his manipulation and past mistreatment. She had become guarded and vowed not to fall into the same traps again.

NEARLY A YEAR HAD PASSED AND THEIR FINANCIAL SITUATION became stronger in Atlantia. One day, Ayushman reconciled his savings account and decided they could afford a premium home thinking that would uplift Pari's status and make her happy. He presented his calculations to her, trying to convince her that they could manage the payments together. "Pari, we can afford this house. It's a great investment for our future," he said, showing her the figures.

"It's too far from the train station, and I don't even know how to drive," she said, silently calculating the hefty mortgage, which was five hundred dollars more than her current rent share. She thought, "That would compromise my newly found lifestyle. Besides, I'm left with only one thousand after sharing expenses."

"Don't worry about that. You can take driving lessons and be driving in no time," Ayushman assured her with a chuckle, "Trust me."

"Never!" she thought, realising she could never trust him with her money. His charming smile and twinkling eyes, which once ignited passion in her, now triggered alarm bells. She felt a knot in her stomach, a sign she couldn't ignore.

A voice inside her warned, "Don't believe him; he just needs your signature on the loan papers." This inner voice had become her new ally, guarding her against blindly trusting Ayushman again. "You need to be careful," it whispered, "think about what this decision means for you."

That voice had a presence, a form that Pari often saw when she looked at herself in the mirror. It was the kohl-eyed version of her, with eyes lined in dark kajal and a black cloak enveloping her from head to toe. This reflection captured the essence of her newly realised independence. "You're stronger now," it seemed to say. "You don't have to go along with everything."

This kohl-eyed reflection symbolised the inner strength she felt growing within her, empowering her to make independent decisions. Whenever she saw this version of herself, she felt a surge of confidence. "I'm not just Ayushman's wife," she reminded herself. "I'm Pari, and I have my own needs and wants."

Pari felt a rush of clarity. "I can't just sign these papers because Ayushman wants me to. I need to consider all the implications," she thought, determined to voice her concerns when the time was right. "I appreciate your enthusiasm, but we need to think this through more carefully. I'm not ready to commit to such a big investment when there are other factors to consider."

Ayushman continued explaining his plans, unaware of the storm of thoughts in Pari's mind. She nodded along, but her thoughts were elsewhere. "I need to stand my ground," she resolved silently. "I can't let myself be pushed into something I'm not comfortable with."

Whenever she saw this version of herself in the mirror, she felt a surge of confidence, a reminder of her ability to navigate the complexities of her life with determination. "I can do this," she told herself. "We will build our future together, but it will be on terms we both agree on." The presence of her inner ally reassured her that she was on the right path, guiding her through the challenges ahead.

Emotions clash, paths intertwine, what choices in the line?

CHAPTER 16
DIVERGING PATHS

"I am thinking of investing in building two adjacent houses in the new estate. We can live in one and rent out the other for extra income. How much money do you have in your account?" Ayushman declared authoritatively.

Pari, lost in thoughts of home rather than multiple houses, wondered, "How does this man think? Does he really have no awareness of our weak connection?"

Despite knowing Ayushman was keen on investments, Pari decided to entertain some of his ideas to ensure her own needs were addressed. She agreed to visit properties with him.

As they mulled over the idea of buying a house, Pari's mind raced with memories of past financial struggles and power imbalances. She couldn't shake the feeling that Ayushman's eagerness to purchase an expensive home might be another attempt to control her finances. Recollections of Ayushman's past statements resurfaced, reminding her of the commitments she had made in naivety.

Ayushman's enthusiasm for house-hunting clashed with Pari's growing unease. Despite her reservations, she accompanied him, feeling increasingly distant as they explored different properties. The focus on material aspects of their future home seemed trivial compared to the emotional chasm between them.

Their conversation turned tense as Pari voiced her concerns. "I refuse to be manipulated into commitments lacking rationality," she asserted, her voice tinged with skepticism.

"Trust me," Ayushman urged, frustration creeping into his tone. "This investment is for our future."

Pari's eyes narrowed. "And what happens if you decide to send all your income home again because they don't have a backup plan? Can you really promise your income to us, or will you do the same as you did in Bangalore? Who will handle the repayments then?" Her voice trembled with emotion.

Ayushman's expression grew stern. "These are just hypotheticals. We can't make decisions based on assumptions. I've already saved up the down payment for the new house; you just need to sign the loan papers."

Pari shook her head, tears welling up. "I can't trust you like that. I need to know our financial stability won't be jeopardised again."

"Why can't you trust me?," Ayushman finally said, feeling shattered, with a lump of sadness in his throat. "I've saved so much to buy you a premium house to match the designer clothes you've bought in the last year. If that's not enough, there's nothing more I can do." He left the room, leaving Pari feeling ashamed with his blaming undertone.

AT WORK, PARI'S MENTOR, KELLY BLAKELY, NOTICED HER VISIBLE distress. Kelly, a compassionate and experienced professional, decided to check in on her. "Are you alright, Pari?" she asked, inviting her for a coffee.

Despite her efforts, tears welled up in Pari's eyes. "Yes," she responded softly, accepting the tissue Kelly offered, finding a moment of solace in her gesture. After composing herself, Pari opened up to Kelly about her growing distrust towards Ayushman, outlining her current predicament.

"It's completely understandable that you're feeling this way," Kelly reassured her.

Pari then voiced her concerns about seeking professional counseling, expressing, "I have two children, and I don't want to leave my husband."

Kelly, drawing from her own experiences, gently explained, "Counseling is a means to help you address your unspoken issues and communication barriers, not to break up families. This service can be extremely beneficial. I've personally used it during my postnatal depression, a challenging divorce, and after my father's passing. I strongly recommend you seek this support."

Grateful for Kelly's concern, Pari said, "I truly appreciate your advice, Kelly."

Later that day, after tending to her usual household tasks and putting the children to bed, Pari broached the subject with Ayushman. "Lately, I've been feeling stressed, and I'm considering seeking counseling."

"Hmmm," Ayushman responded thoughtfully.

Pari continued, "When we moved to San Clarion, I hoped our relationship would improve, and we'd find greater happiness. However, I've been struggling to trust you like I used to. So, I believe I need assistance from an impartial individual. I don't want to keep burdening you with the same concerns."

"Alright, if you believe counseling will be helpful, then go ahead," Ayushman replied before turning off his bedside lamp and settling in to sleep.

The following day, Pari arrived at her counselling session as planned.

"How can I assist you today, Pari?" Ms. Cindy Goodwin asked.

Pari opened up, saying, "I've had several issues with my husband in the past, but now, I find it hard to trust him."

Cindy probed further, "What are you hoping to achieve through these sessions?"

"I want to rebuild the connection with my husband and recapture the intimacy we shared before getting married."

Acknowledging Pari's sentiments, Cindy remarked, "It's evident that you were content with your relationship prior to marriage. Could you explain what changed?"

Pari recounted the entire journey from their wedding day up until the previous day, providing specific details and significant dates as though reliving the events.

"So, he's pressuring you to make financial commitments without your agreement?" Cindy clarified.

"Yes, that's the situation. He has a tendency to behave this way. I used to be more submissive, but now I've become more assertive. In India, I let him have his way, and I suffered because his decision-making process excluded me. I felt disregarded and used merely as an income source without any rights."

Cindy empathised, "You're right. A marriage is a partnership, and it should operate as a team effort. Pari, you appear to be a rational and compassionate individual. To aid you in achieving your objectives, I'd like to involve your husband in the sessions. Your perspective makes perfect sense to me, and it's important to understand why effective communication has become a challenge between you two."

Feeling validated and understood, Pari experienced a sense of relief—a departure from the criticisms she had intermittently received from Ayushman, such as "You're self-centred" or "Something's not right in your head."

After the session, Pari returned home and carried on with the usual routine of cooking, cleaning, and putting the kids to bed. Before turning in for the night, she disclosed to Ayushman that she had visited the counselor and had been encouraged to have him join the sessions, explaining, "She thinks she can help us communicate better."

However, Ayushman was dismissive and defensive, stating, "There's nothing wrong with my mental state. I won't change because of some western-style counsellor invalidating my traditional outlook. I'm not going to see her."

Following that night, Ayushman's demeanour towards Pari turned resentful. He perceived that despite his best attempts, Pari had to seek approval from others regarding whether she should trust him. He felt rejected, and his ego was wounded.

Despite their deteriorating relationship, Ayushman remained optimistic and proceeded with the loan application. "Five years from now, she won't remember our arguments; instead, she'll appreciate the security my astute thinking will provide," he thought, reassuring himself about his decision. With this in mind, he asked Pari to sign the loan documents.

Ayushman: "Pari, I need you to sign these loan documents. The new home is within our budget, and it's a great investment opportunity."

Pari: "I can't sign these, Ayushman. We haven't discussed this properly, and I'm not comfortable with such a big commitment."

Ayushman: "Not comfortable? This is the best decision for our future. Why can't you understand that?"

Pari: "Because it feels rushed and risky. We should be making these decisions together, not just following your lead."

Ayushman: "Following my lead? You don't understand finances like I do. Your naivety is going to cost us."

Pari: "It's not about naivety. It's about trust and partnership. I won't sign something I don't believe in."

Ayushman: "This is ridiculous, Pari. You're jeopardising our future over your baseless fears."

Pari: "And you're disregarding my feelings and concerns. I won't sign, Ayushman. Not like this."

Ayushman expected the initial resistance, fully aware of Pari's attachment to her indulgences like a stubborn child. "She always gets like this when it comes to big decisions," he thought. "It's just her way of coping. There's no point in pushing today."

He sighed and decided to let it go for now. "I'll bring it up again when she's in a better mood. She'll see reason eventually. It's just a matter of timing," he reassured himself, planning his next move. "I'll be patient. I know this is the right decision for us. She'll come around."

Later, Pari found herself deeply unsettled and disappointed with Ayushman. "How can Ayushman expect me to sign any document he pleases, while I'm left to comply like a fool?" she pondered. "Does he really think my input doesn't hold any value? It's as if my opinions don't matter to him at all."

Inspite of her willingness to trust him, Pari couldn't shake off the feeling that her input didn't hold value in Ayushman's eyes. "We're supposed to be building a new house together, but there's no emotional warmth between us," she thought bitterly. "How can I commit to this when my heart isn't in it?"

Caught in a complex dilemma, Pari was torn between trusting Ayushman and fearing he might take her for granted in the future. "If I go along with this, will he just keep pushing me into decisions I'm not comfortable with?" she wondered. "I need to resolve these issues before committing to such an expensive house."

Her financial independence was non-negotiable to her. "I can't lose control over my finances," she told herself firmly. Pari thought that Ayushman was indirectly involving her in investments to limit her financial freedom. "He's trying to tie up my money so I don't have any left for myself," she realised. "Committing to these investments would deplete my income, leaving me with minimal discretionary funds and an uncomfortable lifestyle."

"I can't let this happen," Pari resolved. "I need to stand my ground and make sure my voice is heard. This isn't just about money; it's about my independence and my right to be an equal partner in this relationship."

Pari fixed another appointment with Cindy to obtain impartial advise.

Cindy advised, "In that case, you must have an open conversation with him about your differences. If that doesn't yield results, you might have to consider separation. You've evaded that possibility once when you took your brother's advice who is a man that comes from the same culture, but has it genuinely improved your situation?" Cindy continued. "Atlantia provides substantial support. Take this legal aid contact and consult with legal experts regarding your circumstances."

The clarity in Cindy's voice rang like a bell in Pari's mind, contrasting with the murky confusion she had been feeling. As Pari absorbed Cindy's words, she envisioned herself breaking free from the chains that bound her, each breath filling her lungs with fresh strength and determination.

"You need to contemplate how you want to shape your life—filled with fear or in liberty?" Cindy asked, her voice gentle but firm.

Pari thought about Cindy's words for a few minutes in silence and then declared, "Liberation." Her chest swelled with pride, her stance firm and resolute, like a rebel ready to take on the world. The determination in her voice echoed with renewed strength, each word a step toward reclaiming her independence. Her eyes sparkled with clarity, visualising a future where she stood tall and free.

After the session when Pari sat in silence, Cindy's words echoed in her mind. She felt a mix of fear and determination, knowing she had a choice to make about her future. The path ahead was uncertain, but she realised that she needed to find her own strength and clarity to navigate it.

As Pari sat gazing out of the train window, the passing scenery was blurred by the vivid images of her own life that played before her mind's eye. *"How many times have I endeavoured to explain to Ayushman what I am truly feeling,"* she thought with a heavy heart. *"The distance between us grows clearer with each passing day, yet he makes no effort to mend it."*

Every day, the widening chasm in their relationship pricked at her with relentless force. She had tried, oh how she had tried, to make him understand, but Ayushman remained ensnared in his endless pursuit of financial ambition. *"His only concern is advancing in this race for wealth,"* she reflected with mounting disappointment. *"His priorities are so terribly misplaced."*

The speed of the train seemed to mirror the swiftness of her thoughts. *"His attention is never on me, nor on the bond we once shared. He chases only his financial dreams,"* she realised with a newfound clarity. It became all too evident that Ayushman's heart was not truly invested in their relationship as deeply as hers.

Her resolve strengthened with each passing station. *"If he is so detached, how can I possibly trust him in any shared financial undertaking? How can I be sure he will not burden me again with responsibilities that leave me uneasy?"*

As the train raced forward, so too did her determination. *"I have tried time and again to make him understand,"* she mused, her heart now steady with purpose, *"but no more. It is time for me to forge my own path."*

Paths diverge, love insists, what new love persists?

CHAPTER 17

BREAKING POINT

Ayushman found the note pinned to the fridge with a magnetic memoir photo frame of their family picture. The words hit him like a punch to the gut: "I've left for good, so you can focus on making investments for your future without being bothered by my 'invaluable' inputs."

He stared at the empty house, his mind racing. "Is this a joke? Pari can't be serious. She doesn't know how to fend for herself. I've always taken care of her since we were teens." He recalled how the women in his family gave hollow ultimatums to their husbands during domestic disagreements but always returned home by sunset. "She'll come back soon. She's just trying to scare me into changing my mind about investments."

As hours passed without any sign of Pari, his anxiety grew. "Okay, maybe she's at the mall. She'll be back late night," he reassured himself, but the worry gnawed at him. Worried, he contacted the childcare facility and learned Pari had collected Luv and Kush earlier in the afternoon. "Where could she have taken them?" he wondered, trying to reach out to friends with no results.

"She loves me! She wouldn't do this," he thought, pacing restlessly. "This is just a tactic. She was never interested in finances anyway. She will cool off and be back soon!" But as another hour passed without any response, his worry deepened. After three hours of fruitless attempts and pacing restlessly, Ayushman faced the reality he had been dreading. "Why isn't she answering?" he wondered, dialling Pari's number once more with no response.

The house felt emptier with each passing minute. "This is ridiculous," he thought, frustration mounting. He recalled their recent arguments about finances, her constant insistence on being involved. "I've always made the best decisions for us. Why can't she see that?" He slumped onto the couch, anger bubbling up. "I need to find her. She can't just walk out like this," he resolved, grabbing his keys and heading out the door. "She'll realise she can't handle things on her own and come back. But I need to bring her back now, before she causes any more trouble." His determination grew as he set out to track down Pari and bring her home. After searching through the empty streets in the locality, he came back home close to midnight.

In a state of increasing concern, Ayushman contacted the local police station to report his wife and children as missing persons. "I haven't heard from my wife and kids, and there's a note indicating she's left," he informed the officer.

Hearing that Pari had already informed the police about her relocation made his heart sink. "But she's taken my children. She can leave if she wants, but she can't remove the kids from my custody. I'm their father."

"According to our information, she's in a secure location. If you believe the children are in danger, you have the option to address this matter legally," the constable relayed. "As the primary caregiver, she has the responsibility to ensure their safety."

"But why has she taken the children's passports with her?" he asked, desperation creeping into his voice. "I fear she might depart the country overnight, and then I won't have any chance to see my children again. In India, her family is affluent, and she possesses ample funds in her account."

"Then you may reach out to the Magistrate," the constable advised the phone number, "Here's the emergency helpline number for your reference..."

Ayushman immediately contacted the Magistrate, his voice trembling, "Today, my wife left me along with our two children. She has taken her and children's passports as well. There's no Airport watch in place, and I suspect she might fly to India tonight taking the children with her. I'm in a state of distress. Please confirm the safety of my children, as I may never have the opportunity to see them again if she leaves the country."

"It seems she has planned something," he allowed his emotions to pour out. "Otherwise, she wouldn't have taken the passports if it were just an act of anger. This appears to be a calculated move." His words were interspersed with uncontrollable sobs.

"I empathise with your stress, Sir. Please try to calm down. Could you please provide me with your Social Identification number?" the Magistrate responded.

"SSN033925553."

"Thank you. Could you kindly confirm your identity?"

"Ayushman Mittal, 21 Pilot court, Bright Valley 2980," he replied.

"I can contact and verify her intentions, but legally, she is the Primary Carer and holds the authority to make decisions for the children. If you disagree with her plan to take the children overseas, you can place their names on the airport watch list. What is your wife's phone number?"

"04888889000."

"Thank you. Please await my return call," the Magistrate terminated the call.

"Hello, is this Ms. Pari Mittal?"

"Yes, who's calling?"

"I am Magistrate Carter speaking from the Shire office."

"How may I assist you, Magistrate Carter?"

"Your husband has reached out to us with concerns that you might be planning to fly to India tonight with the children. Do you have any such intentions?"

"No, ma'am. At present, I am safest here in Atlantia."

"Understood. In that case, I recommend you promptly put your children's names on the airport watch list, as your husband shares the same concerns."

"Thank you, ma'am. I have also informed the local police station of my whereabouts, so they are informed about our situation. My husband has been financially and emotionally difficult since our marriage, and I am done with it now. My intention is to separate from him, live in peace, and manage the duty of caring for two children on my own. I don't wish to trouble him, but I was concerned that he might try to take the children to India, as he made threats regarding that during our last conversation."

"I understand that separation is a challenging decision for a family. Do you have a support network of friends and professional counselling?"

"Yes, my colleagues are aware of my situation."

"Is your employer also informed?"

"Yes."

"This implies that you're taking necessary steps to ensure the safety of the children? Are they continuing in the same childcare facility?"

"Yes, Ma'm, maintaining consistency is important for the kids' stability. Their father hasn't been involved much, given his lack of time off from his family business. Hence, their interaction with him hasn't been significantly impacted on regular days."

"Hmm. Ms. Mittal, it appears that you've been through a lot and have carefully considered your actions. However, children need both parents for a well-rounded upbringing, which Atlantian law takes seriously. Neither parent can remove the children from Atlantian soil without proper legal procedures. The reason for your separation is a personal matter. Nevertheless, you must consider the father's access rights, as per the law. Once the situation settles, it would be beneficial to work out a suitable arrangement for the children." Magistrate Carter paused briefly before continuing with compassion, "Ms. Pari, thank you for taking my call at this late hour. Please ensure that you adhere to Atlantian law's reasonable expectations to maintain the children's connection with their father. I will now conclude this call and inform your husband."

"Of course, ma'am. Thank you for your understanding," Pari replied courteously.

Pari went to bed but found herself tossing and turning for a couple of hours. Eventually, she recited the Hanuman Chalisa for the protection of her kids and then managed to fall asleep.

Magistrate Carter dialled Ayushman's number, "Hello Ayushman, this is Magistrate Carter from the Magistrate's office. I'm calling to address your concerns about your wife's plans for tonight."

"Yes, ma'am."

"Your children are in safe hands, with your wife, and she has no intention of leaving Atlantia. She believes it's a safer environment here in Atlantia for her and the kids."

"But why did she take the passports?"

"I cannot answer that question. However, I suggest you consider establishing a child care arrangement with the assistance of a relationship counsellor."

"I want my children back. If she wants to leave, that's her choice. After all, she prioritises money over 'us'."

Ayushman felt a surge of confusion and abandonment, anger simmering beneath the surface. He thought to himself, "All I can hope to preserve now is my connection with my kids. And I won't let that go at any cost."

"Mr. Mittal, you have the right to take legal action if you believe it's necessary. If you find yourself distressed, please reach out to a helpline for proper mental health support. These are personal matters that can be deeply challenging," Magistrate Carter paused before adding, "Is there anything else I can assist you with today?"

"No, and thank you for confirming."

"Goodnight, Mr. Mittal." And with that, Magistrate Carter ended the call.

Ayushman, with a pack of beers already consumed, found himself unable to sleep all night. "She can't really be this upset about money decisions. It's not her place to dictate finances; she just wants things her way, and that's not happening," Ayushman thought while chain-smoking and struggling to sleep.

The next morning, Ayushman woke up surrounded by the remnants of a night of heavy drinking and smoking. He had wet himself during the night, an embarrassing incident that jolted him awake. "This can't be my life," he thought, looking around the room that resembled that of a substance abuser.

Stumbling around, he forced himself to drink salt water, induced vomiting to rid his system of alcohol, and attempted to regain some semblance of control. "I need to fix this," he resolved, throwing on a pair of jeans and heading to court.

The sight of the courthouse triggered resentment toward Pari, mingled with the overwhelming desire to be with his children. "I need to be with my kids. I can't lose them," he thought, the line between his feelings for losing Pari and being separated from his kids blurring, leaving him torn and driven to take legal action for access to the children. "I won't let her take them from me."

"Hello, you've reached the Relationship Helpline. I'm Sherley Goulas. How can I assist you?" answered the social worker on the other end.

Ayushman had grown accustomed to the repetitive nature of helpline conversations and their required information. He managed to say, "Hello, Ms. Goulas. My name is Ayushman. I need to arrange counseling services for both myself and my wife…" his voice quivered as he started crying on the phone.

"Take a deep breath and try to calm down. Can you explain your concerns to me?" Sherley gently prompted.

"My wife left our home and took my children along with their passports. I've just filed an application to put them on the airport watch list to prevent her from leaving the country."

"When you say 'my' kids, does that include any children from a previous relationship?"

"No, I mean our twins. I've never been in any other relationship or had other children."

"When did she leave?"

"Yesterday afternoon. She left a note as well."

"What did the note say?"

"She mentioned that she's moving out and taking the kids. I was worried that she might try to leave the country, so I contacted the police who suggested I reach out to the Magistrate helpline to voice my concerns." Ayushman continued with a heavy sigh, "The Magistrate spoke to my wife and confirmed that she's staying within the country with our children."

"Alright. Do you know where she's currently living?"

"No, she hasn't disclosed her location to me."

"Keep in mind that she can't prevent you from meeting your kids. How old are they?"

"They're three years old, twins."

"Oh, they're quite young. Before we proceed, could you please verify your identity once more?"

Ayushman recited his social security number and address once again, saying, "SSN033984628, Ayushman Mittal, 21 Pilot court, Bright Valley 2980."

"Can you provide me with the names and dates of birth of your children?"

"Certainly. Their names are Luv Mittal and Kush Mittal. They were born on Aug 15, 2006."

"Do you have a phone number for her where I can reach her?"

"Yes."

"Can you please share it?"

"04945994999."

"Mr. Mittal, I strongly recommend that you exercise patience and have faith in the law enforcement system. Acting in haste or behaving in ways that are not in the best interest of the children can have negative consequences when seeking access to them. I will contact you after speaking with your wife."

The call ended, leaving Ayushman in a haunting silence. For the first time in three years, his home was devoid of the vibrant sounds of children. "There's no laughter, no cries for attention, no playful arguments," he thought, pacing through the empty rooms. The eerie, unsettling stillness filled the space, amplifying the absence of his children. "I miss their bedtime stories, their giggles during playtime, even the little squabbles," he mused, feeling the quiet suffocating him.

Every corner of the house, once bustling with energy, now felt empty and cold. "This silence is a stark reminder of how much my life revolved around those precious moments with Luv and Kush," he realised, yearning for their lively presence. The profound void left by their absence and the deep connection he had with his children weighed heavily on him.

"I need them back. I can't let this be our reality," he resolved, feeling more determined than ever to fight for his children. Memories of family dinners, weekend outings, and bedtime rituals played through his mind. "Their laughter was the heartbeat of this home," he thought, his heart aching with longing. "I'll do whatever it takes to bring back that joy and warmth."

He knew the path ahead would be challenging, but Ayushman's love for his children fuelled his determination. "We'll be together again," he vowed, feeling a sense of purpose.

Notes and pleas, strife in life, what mends broken strife?

CHAPTER 18
NAVIGATING CONFLICTS AND COMMITMENTS

In the offices of the Relationship Helpline at San Clarion, Pari and Ayushman faced each other, eyes reflecting anger and frustration. The warmth that had once defined their relationship had now been replaced by a simmering hostility. From once being each other's closest confidants, they now pointed fingers at each other, blaming one another for the collapse of their marriage. The atmosphere was tense, and their interactions were frosty.

Ayushman's voice tinged with frustration, "Why can't you just see that I'm trying to secure our future? Everything I do is for us and the kids."

Pari, unable to hold back her anger, retorted, "Securing our future? You've been so focused on your plans that you've ignored what we need right now. We needed you, Ayushman, not your investments."

Ms. Goulas interjected, her voice calm and steady, "Let's focus on the matter at hand: the children's well-being. Ayushman, you've mentioned wanting more access to the children. Can you elaborate?"

Ayushman took a deep breath, trying to steady his emotions. "I want more time with Luv and Kush. I'm their father. I deserve more than just a weekend each fortnight. I need weekends every week."

Pari's eyes flashed with anger. "Weekends every week? That's too much, Ayushman. The kids need stability, and their home is with me. You can't just swoop in and disrupt their routine."

Ms. Goulas raised her hand gently to calm the escalating tension. "Pari, Ayushman is their father, and it's important for the children to have a meaningful relationship with both parents. However, Ayushman, we also need to consider the children's need for consistency. Can we find a middle ground here?"

Ayushman leaned forward, his tone softening slightly. "I just want to be more involved in their lives, Pari. They need to know that I'm here for them too."

Pari sighed, the anger in her eyes giving way to a hint of sadness. "I understand, Ayushman, but uprooting their routine isn't the answer. They are little over three years old. Maybe we can start with more frequent visits during the week and see how that goes?"

Ms. Goulas nodded approvingly. "That sounds like a reasonable compromise. It's important to gradually increase the time while maintaining the children's stability. How does that sound to both of you?"

Ayushman and Pari exchanged a long look, the hostility in the room easing slightly. "I can agree to that," Ayushman said quietly. "Let's start with more weekday visits interim and take it from there, but ensure that it's not the final arrangement. I am looking for equal time."

Pari was zapped. "Let's add a few more days, but I am not okay with fifty percent time until they complete primary school and become independent."

Ayushman looked back at Pari with frustration. "If you don't agree mutually then I will take you to court."

Ms. Goulas mediated and asked them to relax, but the tension was palpable. Both Pari and Ayushman left the office in anger, the fragile truce shattered once more.

When Pari returned home that day, Luv, one of the twins, asked, "Mommy, where is Dad today? Why didn't he come to our new house?"

Pari took a deep breath, struggling to find the right words. "This is Mama's house, sweetheart. Papa still lives in the same house. But you can visit him on the weekend."

Kush quickly chimed in, "So, this is Mama's house, and that is Papa's house?"

Pari's eyes glistened with unshed tears as she nodded. "Yes, that's right."

Luv's innocent curiosity continued, "But why don't we all live together anymore?"

Pari's heart ached as she tried to explain, "Because Mama and Papa are not best friends anymore, beta. Remember how you and Jamima were once best friends but then you started having disagreements and found new friends? It's kind of like that, but for grown-ups."

Pari found herself shouldering the responsibility of raising her kids on her own. Her mother was set to join her soon to provide much-needed assistance. Pari couldn't shake off the feeling of guilt, as she was concerned that her father, who was now retired from the Indian Army, would be left alone to manage the family farm while her mother supported her and the children.

Following their joint counseling sessions, Pari and Ayushman eventually attended individual sessions. Despite the passage of time, their perspectives remained divergent. Yet, they managed to reach an agreement through the process with Ayushman to be able to have kids with him one weekend each fortnight, swimming classes on Wednesdays and special occasions like Ayushman's birthday and father's day.

Pari had her children and her mother with her for emotional support, while Ayushman was navigating the situation alone. The communication between Pari and Ayushman remained strained, largely due to Pari's perception that Ayushman lacked empathy toward her. She felt let down by his lack of attention and his unilateral approach to managing their family's finances. Pari even suspected that Ayushman deliberately prioritised supporting his parents and brother, thereby disconnecting her from their own relationship.

Though Pari had spoken her heart out to her mother during her marriage, but she had not yet completely shared her feelings and misery with her father. A day after their separation, When Pari eventually opened up to her father, she was taken aback by his support. He asked gently, "Why did you wait five years before sharing your struggles?"

Pari, feeling a mix of relief and exhaustion, replied candidly, "Now, my love for Ayushman has withered beyond repair."

Her father took a deep breath, gathering his thoughts. "Pari, is there any chance of reconciliation? Have you both tried everything to make it work?"

Pari, overwhelmed and unable to filter her words, blurted out, "I have tried my best but now I can't share the same room with him anymore. Papa, please, do not ask me to go back to him."

Her father was left speechless, alarmed by the prospect of his daughter becoming a statistic of domestic violence, a tragic narrative he often encountered in the news. His heart ached with worry for her mental and physical wellbeing miles away from him.

Pari shook her head slowly, her voice trembling. "Papa, we've tried relationship counseling and mediation. I just don't see us getting back to where we used to be. The connection is gone."

Her father's eyes softened with concern and sorrow. "I just want you to be happy and safe, beta. If there's truly no way to mend things, then you must do what's best for you and the kids."

Meanwhile, during one of the children's scheduled visits to Ayushman's house, Luv and Kush came home brimming with excitement. "Dadi mama has come to visit Papa for a few months," they announced.

Pari forced a smile, hiding her unease. "That's nice, sweetheart. Did you have a good time with her?" she asked, her voice gentle as she tried to keep the conversation light for the sake of her children. Inside, her heart churned with the complexities of the situation, but she focused on maintaining a sense of normalcy for Luv and Kush.

Two months after their separation, Ayushman's birthday fell on a Tuesday, just after the weekend the children were with him. He wanted them to stay an extra day, continuing until Wednesday morning, so they could celebrate his birthday together. He asked Pari, "Can I keep them until Wednesday? Returning them for one day doesn't make sense. Mum is also here; we'll cut the cake at midnight."

Pari, feeling triggered and angry at the assumption of including Pathankot home routine with his mother's arrival, replied, "They are just four years old. You can't keep them awake until midnight." She suspected this might be his mother's idea, recalling the chaos at Pathankot and his mother's interruptions after she gave birth. Despite her frustration, she refrained from commenting further. However, the thought of not being able to supervise her children while they were in Ayushman's care frustrated her. "No, I need them back," she insisted.

Ayushman's face reddened with rage, feeling helpless at the control Pari exerted over the children's routine even when they were in his care. He felt that she was undermining his ability to set boundaries by highlighting special occasions and feared that she would sabotage his relationship with the kids. Frustrated, he went to a lawyer to discuss his rights as a father.

"I've been separated for two months and am trying everything to cooperate on the children's matters," he explained to family lawyer Ben Stuart.

Ben listened carefully and then said, "If you think your wife is being unfair, you must object to her mental state in handling the kids' welfare."

"How do I proceed further?" Ayushman asked.

Ben guided him through the steps and assisted him in filing a petition in court for the reversal of primary care.

A few days later, Pari received an email indicating that Ayushman had filed a case for the reversal of custody. The affidavit claimed she was unfit to be a primary carer, accusing her of alienating the children from their grandparents and extended family.

Pari read the papers, thinking, "Ayushman was fine until she arrived. Who could have guessed this would happen?" This confirmed her belief about her mother-in-law's influence. Fuelled with anger, Pari immediately called Ayushman to confront him. "You filed a case against me? Why?" she demanded.

"You didn't give me the kids for my birthday eve. You are exercising undue control and authority, dismissing my role in the kids' lives. I am claiming my right to my children, and that's why I filed the case," Ayushman replied.

Pari's frustration was palpable. "I wanted them back that day to help them make a birthday mug and write a birthday card for you. I even have a video of that activity. I'll send it to you."

"I felt upset as you disregarded my right to them," Ayushman's tone softened. "I am willing to hear you out if you want to agree on my proposed plan."

Pari heard arrogance and control in Ayushman's tone. Holding back her comments about her suspicions regarding his mother's involvement and not wanting to give in due to the perceived chaos his mother might bring to the children's routine, Pari said, "Well, I've also had enough of chaotic arrangements. You've asked for a response, and you shall have one formally." Furiously, she hung up the phone.

Seeking legal guidance, Pari consulted her lawyer, Diana Hopkins.

"I separated from my husband two months ago and have been taking care of the kids since then. Today I received the affidavit accusing me of being mentally unfit and seeking the reversal of primary carer," Pari said, starting to cry.

Diana, noting the toll on Pari as she had been shouldering all the responsibilities since the separation, responded, "In separations, people accuse their ex-partners of all sorts of things, but that doesn't mean it's true. In your case, taking care of four-year-old twins single-handedly is mentally exhausting, and the court will be compassionate on those grounds. The children are minors and need a stable environment, and the court will see that you have taken a sabbatical to care for them as the primary carer. He is scrambling to control the outcome of childcare arrangements and has no grounds to prove that you are mentally unstable."

Diana advised, "We must respond to his affidavit. He seems to be seizing on a minor misunderstanding, and this could become a recurring issue."

Pari agreed, her suspicion of Ayushman's mother creating further chaos weighing heavily on her mind. "They've dragged me into court now, so let the law handle their concerns once and for all. I won't negotiate on their terms," she remarked bitterly, feeling that the court battle was more about Ayushman's mother versus her than the actual issue at hand.

She found it less tortuous to deal with the situation through her lawyer than to handle matters directly with them. "It's clear that Ayushman's mother is trying to control every aspect of this separation, but I refuse to let her dictate my life," Pari thought, her resolve strengthening.

Diana nodded in understanding. "We will ensure that your side of the story is heard, and the focus remains on the children's well-being."

Pari felt a surge of gratitude for Diana's support. "Thank you for standing by me. This battle is not just for me but for the twins' future."

Diana smiled reassuringly. "We'll get through this, Pari. Stay strong. The truth is on your side, and the court will recognize that."

With renewed determination, Pari prepared herself for the legal challenges ahead, confident that justice would prevail. She knew it wouldn't be easy, but she felt ready to face whatever came her way. Her focus was now on ensuring a stable and loving environment for her children.

Conflicts strong, children in fray, what's next in their way?

CHAPTER 19
ENDURANCE AND UNDERSTANDING

As legal proceedings began, Pari found herself shouldering the burden of numerous financial responsibilities that she had previously shared with Ayushman. She was now paying for lawyers, groceries, utilities, car insurance, health insurance, ambulance cover, house content insurance, and rent for a two-bedroom apartment all by herself. The sheer volume of expenses, coupled with her limited income, left her feeling overwhelmed and exhausted.

During their marriage, Ayushman had managed the finances, allowing her to focus on other aspects of their life. Now, the sudden shift to handling everything on her own was both daunting and stressful. Pari realised she needed advice and support to navigate this challenging period.

Pari decided to call her mentor Kelly, hoping for some practical guidance and emotional support.

"Kelly, I don't know how to handle all of this," Pari confessed, her voice tinged with frustration. "I'm paying for everything on my own – lawyers, groceries, utilities, rent... It's all so overwhelming. I never had to think about these things before."

Kelly listened patiently, her tone soothing and empathetic. "Pari, I understand how tough this must be for you. It's a lot to manage all at once, especially when you're not used to it. But you can get through this. Let's break it down step by step."

"I just don't know where to start," Pari admitted, feeling a lump form in her throat.

"First, let's look at your budget," Kelly suggested. "We can see where you might be able to cut costs or find ways to manage your expenses better. Also, consider reaching out to a financial advisor. They can help you create a plan that works for you in the long run."

"There's also a popular accounting website that offers a free wealth management course. They also have an app that can help you manage your money on a daily basis," Kelly suggested.

Pari's eyes lit up with a glimmer of hope. "That sounds like exactly what I need. Growing up, I never had to worry about money. My dad was in the military, and the government covered all our expenses. We never had to think about managing money or planning for crises."

"Managing your wealth is crucial. The course will teach you how to create a budget, save for emergencies, and invest wisely. It's really empowering," Kelly encouraged.

Pari responded with determination, "I'll start the course tonight and download the app. It's time I became financially independent and secure. Thanks again, Kelly. You're a lifesaver."

Kelly smiled, "Anytime, Pari. I'm here for you. Let me know if you need any more help or advice. We'll get through this together."

In the following months, guided by Kelly, Pari's new financial skills began to bring clarity and control to her life. One challenge that stood out was her lack of driving skills, which forced her to rely on expensive taxis in Atlantia. Public transport was a less costly option, but it required her to wait in queues for trams, leaving her with little flexibility to manage her day. Seeking a solution, she spoke to her boss and organised a loan from work to buy a car. While waiting for the car's delivery, she enrolled in a driving school.

Unfortunately, she flunked her first driving test. Disappointed, she sought advice from her mother.

Pari: "Mamma, I can't seem to focus on learning to drive with so much to manage every day."

Mrs. Bajwa: "Pari, remember that you're not in a race to beat all drivers on the road. You're just learning to drive by the rules. Focus on what the road rules are."

Her mother's advice shifted her perspective, and she regained her courage. With renewed focus, she passed her driving test the following week.

The car arrived on Saturday while the kids were at Ayushman's place. She waited for Luv and Kush to return, eager to share her joy with them, the jumbo red ribbon still intact.

After the weekend, when Luv and Kush returned from Ayushman's house, their faces lit up with excitement upon seeing the new car.

"Mamma, is this our new car? It looks so cool!" Kush exclaimed, his eyes wide with wonder.

Luv ran his hand along the car's shiny surface, grinning from ear to ear. "Can we go for a ride, Mamma? I can't wait to sit in the front seat!"

After they came back from their ride, they eagerly showed Pari the colourful sheets and toys they had brought home, each item a testament to their joyful time with their father.

"Mamma, we had so much fun with Papa," Kush exclaimed, his eyes sparkling.

Luv chimed in enthusiastically, "We went to the park, played on the swings, and even had ice cream! Papa let us stay up a little late to watch a movie, too!"

Pari listened with a smile, her heart warming at their happiness. "That sounds wonderful, my loves. I'm so glad you had a great time."

Curious and slightly apprehensive, she asked, "What about Dadi? Did you see her?"

Kush shook his head, "No, Mamma. Papa said she went back to India."

Pari felt a wave of relief wash over her, thankful that her children wouldn't be exposed to the chaos she feared. The thought of her children having a peaceful and enjoyable time with their father, without the added stress of his mother's influence, eased some of her worries. She hugged Luv and Kush tightly, silently grateful for this small reprieve in their tumultuous journey.

FOUR MONTHS INTO THE SEPARATION, AS PARI BALANCED HER budget, she felt a mix of optimism and reality. "This isn't so bad. I can do this. I'm learning to stand on my own two feet, and it feels good. Maybe this independence is exactly what I needed. Perhaps, once Ayushman sees how capable I am, we could find a way to rebuild. Maybe this financial stability can be the foundation for a new start between us."

However, the shadow of the ongoing court case loomed large. "Who am I kidding? The issues between us run deeper than money. The custody battle has driven a wedge too wide to bridge. Our differences can't be mended with financial acumen or newly gained confidence."

Despite these realisations, Pari quickly dismissed any rosy picture of reconciliation. The ongoing court case overshadowed her thoughts, casting a shadow over any fleeting hopes. She accepted that things between them were irreversibly broken, recognising that the custody battle had created a divide too wide to be mended.

"Yes, I'm capable of handling finances now. But can this independence fix the trust that's been shattered? Can it heal the emotional wounds we've inflicted on each other?" she pondered.

She reflected on how Ayushman became financially mature early due to family responsibilities, while she was a fun-loving new bride unprepared for such duties. "I've learned to manage money, but managing a broken relationship is entirely different."

Pari realised that while her financial independence highlighted her ability to stand on her own, it underscored the irreparable nature of her partnership with Ayushman. The trust shattered, emotional wounds, and the contentious custody battle were obstacles too significant to overcome merely by personal growth.

"I've achieved a sense of security and independence financially, but it's a hollow victory compared to the emotional chaos that defines my relationship with Ayushman. The divide is too great, the wounds too deep. This personal growth is important, but it cannot heal what's been broken."

Pari accepted that self-improvement and financial independence, while crucial, couldn't heal the rift in their marriage. The custody battle had drawn clear lines, making reconciliation impossible. Her path to self-sufficiency stood as a testament to her resilience, unfolding a fresh era in her life—one where she ventured onward without Ayushman. Managing her finances, creating budgets, and planning for the future gave her a sense of accomplishment and stability. With these realisations, she finally brought her thoughts to rest.

ON THE 13TH DAY OF APRIL, SIX MONTHS INTO SEPARATION WAS their first custody proceedings, the courtroom was filled with a tense, expectant silence. Judge Burke raised his hand, signaling for quiet. "Order in the court," the bailiff announced.

Judge Burke looked over the case files and addressed the estranged couple. "I can see that both of you are highly educated immigrants with skilled professions. My advice is for both of you to prioritise settling matters in the best interest of your children before others intervene in their upbringing. It's important that you treat each other as equals in every aspect to align with Atlantian society's values."

Judge Burke continued, "Neither of you can shirk this duty or remove the children from the other due to personal grievances. I don't appreciate wasting time on 'he said, she said' disputes. Many couples try to manipulate the situation to gain an advantage, but my role here is to offer impartial advice. You might currently have the resources to engage in lengthy legal battles, but ultimately, you will need to make joint decisions for your children's welfare. Therefore, I strongly recommend improving your communication now rather than squandering your resources and time on conflicts."

Judge Burke's words lingered in the air. Pari and Ayushman realised the profound truth of their situation. They had to find a way to bridge the gap between them for the sake of their children.

Ayushman's representative, Mr. Ben Stuart, then requested, "Your Honour, my client would like to have primary carer reversed temporarily due to concerns about the mother's mental health."

Judge Burke promptly responded, "I've reviewed the mental health counsellor's reports on the children's well-being and both parents' engagement since the separation. There doesn't appear to be a reason to reverse custody before the next hearing scheduled for October, six months from now."

When they emerged out of court room, Pari's lawyer took her to a meeting room and advised her to initiate an out-of-court settlement, citing her dwindling financial resources and suggesting it was best to negotiate. Pari agreed and decided to communicate with Ayushman.

Pari called Ayushman and shared her thoughts about the situation. Ayushman agreed, it was in their mutual interest, not to waste money on something they ultimately needed to decide for their children. He then proposed, "Would it be acceptable if we did this in a safe space with a mediator present? If you agree, I'm happy to arrange a counselling session for both of us."

Pari was surprised, "You mean for both of US?"

Ayushman confirmed, "Yes, exactly. We need to find a way to communicate respectfully because, despite everything, we'll need to stay in contact for the rest of our lives. In Atlantia, it's clear we can't avoid each other." After hearing Judge Burke's information about the children's rights to care from both parents, they realised how difficult things would be if they allowed the bitterness to continue.

Pari collected her thoughts for a moment and then said, "aaa...Okay, sure."

Ayushman, "Was there something else you wanted to say?"

Pari: "Just that, hmmm... Ayushman, You are a good person. I wish you all the best. I'm hoping to normalise our separation so that eventually we can both move forward with our lives. We're too young to spend our lives battling each other given that we had a beautiful past behind us. Though, it seems like that happened ages ago."

Ayushman: "That's true, and it's crucial that we both take shared responsibility for our children and ensure a consistent lifestyle for them. This way, we can put our differences behind us and focus on being the best parents for our kids as we move forward."

Pari: "Absolutely, that's exactly what I want as well."

For the first time in six months, Ayushman and Pari spoke without animosity. This novel understanding brought them to the same table to negotiate as equals, marking a turning point in their dynamics and journey toward co-parenting and prioritising their children's well-being.

Worlds apart, choices made, what's next in love's shade?

CHAPTER 20

ECHOES OF TOGETHERNESS

"I don't want to leave Papa. Can we please sleep together tonight?" Luv asked Pari, his eyes filled with anticipation. The twins, Luv and Kush, were struggling with the new lifestyle of separation.

Pari gently embraced them as they returned from their father's house, "My dear child, when you're at Papa's house, you should sleep with Papa, and when you're at Mama's house, you should sleep with Mom. Okay?"

Kush started sobbing, "I don't want Mommy's house or Papa's house, I want my house!" Both children burst into tears.

Seeing their distress, Pari felt a deep sense of helplessness. She realised how fatigued and stressed the kids were from constantly moving between homes.

After dropping the kids off at the childcare centre, Pari called Ayushman to recount last evening's emotional episode. Ayushman responded, "It's tough for all of us. Can we give our family another chance, please?"

Pari sighed, "I can't. I'm exhausted by your traditional mindset. I'm not saying it's wrong. It's your belief system, but it doesn't align with mine. I don't want to go through all of this again. It's draining," she paused, "Plus, I'm already moving forward."

Ayushman's mind raced, "Are you seeing someone?"

Pari answered, "Not at the moment, but I want a partner to share my life with. I hope you eventually find someone who fits your vision of an ideal partner. We weren't meant to be. I don't blame you. We both didn't know that a successful family requires more than just shared tastes in food and physical intimacy."

As both reflected, a rush of remorse washed over them, reminiscing about the good times they shared, their dreams of a life filled with happiness and passion.

Ayushman said, "Maybe this time we won't repeat the same mistakes."

Pari responded, "Let's focus on a stable routine for the kids and leave the future to unfold naturally. If we're meant to be together, circumstances will guide us. I don't want to force it, especially after putting the children through six months of turmoil."

Ayushman agreed, "Alright. Let's work on a children's plan and let time decide the rest. If our paths are meant to cross again, they will. I don't want to rush it, especially after the turmoil we've put our kids through."

On Wednesday, they entered the counsellor's office. Ms. Jenni Myer welcomed them warmly, noting the calm and respectful demeanour they now exhibited.

Jenni addressed Pari first, "Mrs. Mittal, I can imagine this separation has been extremely challenging for both of you."

Pari, slightly taken aback by the use of her married name, replied, "I'm managing, thank you."

Turning to Ayushman, Jenni asked gently, "And how are you feeling, Mr. Mittal?"

Ayushman responded softly, "I'm coping, thank you."

Jenni sensed a noticeable shift as they discussed their children's arrangements. Their body language was calmer, and their interactions were more respectful.

As they were about to leave, Jenni inquired, "Is there anything else I can assist you with today?"

Pari, her voice steady and polite, responded, "I think we're good for today. Thank you." She looked at Ayushman briefly, a hint of warmth in her eyes.

Jenni made a point of addressing Ayushman directly, "And Ayushman, do you have any thoughts to share?"

Ayushman, sitting with his hands clasped and a thoughtful expression, concurred, "I think we've covered enough for today. Thank you, Jenni."

As Pari was about to step into her car, Ayushman spoke softly, "Would you mind grabbing a coffee together?"

Pari paused, her hand resting on the car door. She turned to face him, her expression thoughtful but cautious. "Ayushman, I think we need to establish some boundaries. I'm not comfortable with the direction this might take." Her voice was firm, yet there was a trace of sadness.

Ayushman, nodding slowly, responded, "You're probably right. We should keep our distance. I just wanted to mention that if you ever change your mind, we can discuss things in a safe space with Jenni. Perhaps we can find common ground." His voice was earnest, and his eyes held a mixture of hope and resignation.

Pari redirected the conversation, her voice softening, "Make sure to invite me to your wedding. Goodbye, Ayushman." She offered a small, bittersweet smile.

They bid farewell, carrying with them the memories of the love they once shared. As they parted ways, both felt a sense of finality and a glimmer of hope for a future where they could coexist peacefully, if not together.

That evening, Pari called her parents to inform them about the arrangement for the children. Her father answered, and she quickly got to the point. "Ayushman is suggesting that we get back together."

Capt. Bajwa responded, "So, you're considering it?"

Pari hesitated, "I think I might be."

Capt. Bajwa reassured her, "You have our blessings."

Pari voiced her concerns, "But Papa, I married him once against your wishes, and I regretted it. Do you think it will work now?"

Capt. Bajwa replied thoughtfully, "It might. Now you both understand the value of love and loss. It's a costly experience, both emotionally and financially."

Pari continued, "But Papa, I'm not the one hundred percent agreeable woman he wants."

Capt. Bajwa offered a perspective, "How do you know he still wants that? People change. Practically, nobody in this world is one hundred percent agreeable. Your mom and I disagree on fifty percent of things every day, but that doesn't mean we divorce. We negotiate."

Pari, intrigued by her father's perspective, listened intently as he explained how traditional negotiation in their household worked. This revelation helped Pari understand the complexities of her parents' relationship and the adjustments they made over time.

Pari: "It always seemed like you were the controlling one, and growing up, I felt that I had no voice to challenge your decisions or negotiate. After I got married, I saw Ayushman, his father, and his brother doing the same thing in family settings. I never knew that negotiations happened behind closed doors. My past relationship with you made me hesitant to confront Ayushman assertively at the right time, fearing violent consequences."

Capt. Bajwa: "I'm deeply sorry you felt that way, beta. I didn't realise that despite being more educated and financially capable than us, you still needed guidance to navigate and balance traditions. I assumed you could manage better, thinking marriage was just like any other organisation.

In business corporations, everyone has a role with specific duties and responsibilities. They must cooperate for the shared goal and vision of the organisation. However, conflicts can arise because, at their core, humans need compassion, understanding, and support. Codes of ethics are enforced there to manage power dynamics within the hierarchy.

At home, without formal codes of conduct, women, naturally loving and compassionate, demonstrated patience and proactively understood sentiments. This made them powerful in the marriage dynamic, enabling them to confront and negotiate lovingly for the benefit of their nest and kids. In our generation, it was an unspoken life skill. But now, society has changed, and I understand that your challenges are different and new.""

Pari felt a lump in her throat as she listened to her father's words.

She shared with her father, "You're right, Papa. Society really has changed. When women in my mother's generation were going through tough times with their husbands, they told their daughters to study and follow their dreams rather than waste their lives nurturing husbands who didn't appreciate them."

Her voice carried pain but also the courage to speak the truth to her father.

Captain Bajwa was silent for a moment, realising that Pari's life reflected the mistakes of men in his generation, who had treated their wives in a certain way in front of their children. He felt a deep sense of guilt and decided it was time to come clean so his daughter could move forward with faith in her married life.

In a soft voice, he said, "Forgive me, dear. I should have known better. What you're feeling—I'm partly responsible for that."

His voice carried regret, and it was an emotional moment for Pari, as it was the first time she heard her father take responsibility like this.

Capt. Bajwa: "Confronting me today shows you've always had the power within you. You've freed yourself from the fear of confrontation, and this is the strength you need to navigate your marriage with Ayushman. "

Pari realised, with a new clarity, that confronting her father had unlocked a deeper understanding of her own power. She felt a sense of liberation, knowing she could now negotiate with Ayushman without fear.

Feeling a sense of relief, Pari responded, "Thank you, Papa. I understand better now. I'll approach things differently with Ayushman."

Capt. Bajwa's voice was warm with encouragement. "That's my girl. You'll do great. Just stay true to yourself and your values. "

Pari, still concerned about the animosity and bitterness from their recent separation, asked, "Will the recent past experience of separation and court cases affect us?"

Capt. Bajwa invoked his favourite metaphor about Milkha Singh. "Do you recall the story of Milkha Singh? During his Olympic race, he glanced back to see where he stood, instead of concentrating on what he needed to do, causing him to miss the finish line by fractions of a second and losing the winner's position. Flashbacks of past disappointments can cloud our present. If you've chosen to make this work, then it's your responsibility to ensure its success. People are coachable if they learn their lessons and leave the past behind. "

Pari, feeling another pang of regret, asked, "Why didn't you tell me all this when I was initially separating? Maybe I could have avoided making a mistake."

Capt. Bajwa responded, his voice filled with warmth and wisdom, "Pari, you didn't make a mistake. You did the best you could with the experience and exposure you had. I wanted you to recognise your personal power in making important decisions. Today, I see you're ready to absorb the hardest lesson of life and take accountability for your actions. Your mum and I learned from bringing up you and Shera, and we adjusted our actions based on what worked. There is no textbook for success because your story is unique. Pari, in today's world, where morality often declines, knowledge is power, and life skills are essential."

Pari, still apprehensive, asked, "But what if it doesn't work out?"

Capt. Bajwa: "If you both fight for personal victory, it won't work out because one of you will end up feeling defeated, and no one likes to be a loser."

Capt. Bajwa reassured her, "Remember, don't let doubt cloud your mind. You've married Ayushman, and he is a self-driven learner just like you. You might be surprised by his transformation in some aspects. During the session with Jenni, be open; you don't know yet why he wants to work things out. And remember, if things don't work out, divorce is always an option if you both decide. For parents, their children's interests are foremost, and we will support you no matter what, as will Ayushman's family, just like they do now. When you need unconditional love, come back home."

Feeling a surge of confidence and reassured by her father's support, Pari ended the call, ready to approach her marriage with Ayushman with a fresh perspective.

The next day, Pari and Ayushman visited Jenni again. This time, they appeared more comfortable with each other. Ayushman sat with his shoulders relaxed, his hands resting calmly on his knees, a faint smile occasionally appearing on his face. Pari, seated beside him, leaned slightly toward Ayushman, her posture open and at ease. Her arms were uncrossed, and she frequently made eye contact with him, signaling trust and a willingness to communicate.

Jenni observed their friendly demeanour and began, her voice warm and welcoming, "So, I see your goal is reconciliation today?"

Ayushman and Pari both nodded, "Yes."

Jenni raised an eyebrow, her eyes sparkling with curiosity, "Is there anything specific you want to discuss?"

Ayushman, his voice sincere, said, "When we got married, I followed traditional family dynamics and ignored Pari's feedback. I realised she didn't feel empowered. This realisation came when I joined a Single Dad's group, where men shared their learnings for improvement. I want to assure her that it's going to change."

Jenni prompted gently, "Look at her and tell her that."

Ayushman turned to Pari, looking into her eyes, and repeated his assurance. "I'm going to change. I want you to feel included and heard."

Pari blinked and took a deep breath, her voice steady but emotional, "Thanks. I want to feel comfortable and included. Our marriage had become suffocating for me as I did not feel heard and included in decision-making."

She continued with determination, "I have always appreciated your strength with numbers, and now I am good at wealth management too since I have managed on my own for the last six months. So I want to be involved in all the financial decisions."

Pari took a few deep breaths, "I enjoy dressing up and socialising as a way to express my inner beauty. I may not fit conventional standards of beauty, but I take pride in the image I've deliberately built for myself. We need to allocate a budget for our personal interests that recharge us. Life has become monotonous over the last five years, with so much focus on saving. We need to balance our financial goals with activities that bring joy and fulfilment."

Ayushman listened quietly, then spoke with calm resolve, "I have always found you beautiful. I didn't realise dressing up was so important to you. I dismissed your wishes based on what I learned growing up. I was also worried about your financial skills because, before marriage, you didn't contribute financially to your parents or invest in wealth building and you were not even interested to learn in university or from me."

Pari responded thoughtfully, "My parents are financially independent. I thought everyone's parents should be the same until I found out the difference between job-oriented and business-oriented income during our marriage."

Ayushman clarified, "Since we moved to Atlantia, I haven't sent any money to Pathankot as you were concerned about. My brother is doing well with our new business."

Ayushman hesitated before adding, "But Pari, they're family. They were going through a tough time. It was about helping them out when they needed it most."

Pari sighed deeply, her frustration evident. "I understood that, Ayushman. I was all for supporting them if it genuinely improved their situation. But if it was just to maintain their lifestyle..."

"They were struggling back then. It wasn't about luxuries," Ayushman interjected, trying to explain.

Pari shook her head, her tone firm yet tinged with disappointment. "I understand they were facing challenges, but it crushed my soul when I sacrificed as a new bride to fund what felt like their luxuries from my perspective."

Ayushman frowned, feeling the weight of their conversation.

Pari's voice softened, revealing her hurt. "I always wondered why they never acknowledged my contributions. Instead, they always believed you were the one helping them."

Ayushman clarified, "I recognise your support, and I believe they will come to realise it too in time."

Jenni, looking at Ayushman with a serious tone, mediated, "Ayushman, will you ensure that Pari's trust in you remains strong?"

Ayushman, his voice firm, replied, "Yes, I will critically evaluate situations and maintain her trust."

Pari, emphasising firmly, said, "Moving forward, I propose a joint account for our incomes and family expenses to ensure transparency for both of us. All financial and family decisions should be made together."

Ayushman added, "And you can manage all the funds and payments because I see that you have become skilled in that area. I am happy to see you empowered."

Hearing this from Ayushman, Pari felt overwhelmed with emotions. Tears streamed down her face as years of frustration and misunderstandings melted away. Ayushman rose from his chair, crossed the room, knelt on one knee, and took her hand warmly, looking into her eyes with sincerity. "I mean it," he said gently.

Jenni intervened, her voice wise and encouraging. "Marriage depends on trust and balance. Are you both committed to holding your part of the deal?"

Pari smiled, feeling a burden lifted. "Yes."

Ayushman, relieved, smiled and agreed. "Yes."

Jenni gently advised, "Always maintain respect for each other, regardless of circumstances. Remember what initially drew you to each other and the challenges you faced when that bond weakened. Keep these memories close to find positivity during tough times."

Pari asked, her voice curious and concerned, "What's your advice if we have a similar conflict next time?"

Jenni, with a demeanour of seasoned wisdom, spoke softly yet with an undeniable authority that drew both Ayushman and Pari's attention. Her words carried weight, reflecting years of experience in guiding couples through turbulent times.

"Do not compromise," she began, her voice firm but caring, as she looked at Ayushman and Pari in turn. "Leaving issues unaddressed and hoping they'll disappear never works." Her gaze held a gentle insistence, urging them to confront their challenges head-on.

"Hope is not a strategy," she continued, her tone emphasising the importance of proactive efforts in relationships. "Nothing changes if nothing changes." Her words hung in the air, a reminder that real progress required intentional actions from both parties.

"Make deliberate efforts to ensure you both are happy together," Jenni advised, her eyes softening with empathy. "If one of you is miserable, the other will be dragged down with them. That's the dynamic between couples lacking conflict resolution skills or intervention." Her insight cut through any illusions of individual happiness separate from the relationship's well-being.

"If either of you has unmet needs," she continued, her voice now tinged with concern, "the marriage will suffer." Her words underscored the importance of mutual fulfilment and understanding in sustaining a healthy partnership.

"You're both financially independent," Jenni noted, her expression turning slightly more hopeful. "Leverage that independence to enjoy life together. Set shared goals, as they foster interdependence and connection, creating a foundation of safety, security, and trust." Her final words carried a sense of caution, reminding them of the practical realities that could strain even the strongest bonds if left unattended.

Ayushman mustered the courage to ask a pressing question, "I know Pari harbors anger towards my parents and brother, but I assure her they had no role in our conflict. I made the decisions that impacted her negatively. As I've changed my approach to our relationship, I hope she can see them in a more positive light."

Noticing Pari's unease, Jenni intervened before she could respond, "Since your parents aren't living with you, I suggest focusing on mutual healing and mending your relationship first. Both of you need to demonstrate the claims of the new approach you're bringing to this fresh start. Fulfil your promises to each other before demanding further commitments. Once you're both strong again, you can address those external conflicts without disrupting your daily lives. Cross that bridge when you come to it."

Jenni's straightforward advice resonated with both Pari and Ayushman. They felt a collective sense of urgency and responsibility to fortify their relationship against future challenges. While the path ahead seemed daunting, they also felt a strengthened resolve to tackle it together, knowing that open communication and mutual respect were their keys to success.

After the session, they warmly hugged each other. The gesture, though unfamiliar, allowed their emotions to flow freely, bringing tears to their eyes. They held each other for a long time silently promising to support each other in healing. This embrace symbolised a renewed commitment, bridging the gap that had grown between them over time.

To assess their compatibility and ease into moving in together after their separation, Pari and Ayushman decided to spend a month engaging in shared activities, blending the comfort of their history with a fresh perspective.

They began with long walks in the park, holding hands and sharing dreams, just like they did in their teenage years. These walks became a daily ritual, allowing them to reconnect and discuss their hopes for the future. The simple act of walking together reignited the spark that had dimmed over the years, making them feel like lovebirds once again.

Evenings were spent in the kitchen, preparing dinner together at Ayushman's place. The aroma of spices filled the air as they cooked side by side, laughing and exchanging tender glances. This time together in the kitchen brought back memories of their early days and reinforced their bond. Occasionally, their children, Luv and Kush, joined in, helping with simple tasks like stirring a pot or setting the table, their laughter adding a joyful background to these moments.

They also dedicated time to revisiting their favourite activities. They played board games with Luv and Kush, watched beloved movies, and even started a new series together. Their playful banter returned, rekindling the joy and light-heartedness that had always been a cornerstone of their relationship. After dinner, Pari would usually take the kids back to her place, but if they insisted on sleeping over with Dad, she would be flexible.

On weekends, they planned little adventures that included their children. They visited local museums, went on short road trips, and explored new cafes and restaurants. Each outing was an opportunity to rediscover each other and create new memories as a family.

Pari and Ayushman made an effort to communicate more openly about their feelings and concerns. They set aside time each evening for heart-to-heart conversations, ensuring that they were both on the same page and addressing any issues that arose. This practice helped them rebuild trust and deepen their emotional connection. Sometimes, these conversations included Luv and Kush, helping the children feel heard and valued in their family dynamics.

By the end of the month, the tumultuous emotions of the past had faded into the background, replaced by a renewed sense of partnership and love. The shared activities and open communication had shown them that they were indeed compatible and ready to take the next step. The involvement of Luv and Kush in these activities reinforced the importance of family unity, making the transition to moving in together feel natural and joyful.

ONE EVENING, AS THEY SAT ON THE PORCH WATCHING LUV AND Kush play in the yard, Ayushman turned to Pari, his eyes filled with hope and love. "Pari, this month has been incredible. Seeing how happy the kids are and how we've reconnected, I was wondering... Would you and the kids consider moving back in with me?"

Pari looked into his eyes, feeling the warmth and sincerity in his words. She smiled softly, her heart swelling with love. "Yes, Ayushman. I think it's time for us to be a family again."

Ayushman reached out and took her hand, squeezing it gently. "Thank you, Pari. I promise we'll make this work together."

With their decision made, they felt a sense of peace and excitement for the future. The journey ahead would undoubtedly have its challenges, but they were ready to face them as a united family.

And one month after moving in, their bond remained resilient and steadfast. They continued to support each other through the challenges of their new living arrangement, finding joy in shared moments and mutual understanding. Despite the adjustments and occasional difficulties, their relationship had strengthened, and they were more committed than ever to making their new life together a success. The playful banter, shared activities, and cooperative efforts fostered a renewed sense of connection and happiness, ensuring that their journey together remained a positive and enriching experience.

Ayushman smiled, his eyes reflecting fond memories. "Remember our university days, Pari? The late-night study sessions, the walks around campus, and the endless talks about our dreams?"

Pari laughed, her face lighting up with nostalgia. "How could I forget? We were so full of hope and excitement back then. It feels like a lifetime ago."

Ayushman's voice softened, his tone gentle and heartfelt. "Those were some of the best days of my life. I felt so alive, so connected with you. I'm glad we're finding our way back to that feeling."

Pari's eyes sparkled with emotion. "Me too. It's amazing how we've come full circle. Back then, I never imagined we'd go through so much and still find our way back to each other."

As they worked side by side, chopping vegetables and stirring pots, their hands occasionally brushed against each other, sending sparks of warmth through them. They moved seamlessly, like a well-rehearsed dance, finding joy in the simple act of cooking together.

Ayushman playfully remarked, "You know, you still make the best dal makhani. I've missed this."

Pari blushed, feeling a rush of warmth. "And you still have a way of making every moment special. I've missed you, Ayushman."

Their conversations were now filled with tenderness and understanding. Pari felt heard and valued, while Ayushman appreciated her insights and perspective. They spent evenings cooking together, turning mundane tasks into cherished moments of connection. As they worked side by side, their laughter echoed through the kitchen, and stolen glances spoke volumes of their rekindled affection.

LATER THAT NIGHT, THEY LAY SIDE BY SIDE IN BED, THE ROOM softly lit by a bedside lamp. Ayushman turned to Pari, his eyes filled with love. He whispered, "Tell me a story, Pari. Something from our past, something that makes you smile."

Pari's face lit up with a smile as she recalled a cherished memory. "Do you remember the night we sneaked onto the rooftop of the hostel? We watched the stars and talked about our dreams for hours."

Ayushman chuckled, a fond look in his eyes. "How could I forget? That was the night I realised I couldn't imagine my life without you."

Their nights were transformed into intimate storytelling sessions, where they lay side by side, sharing hopes and fears. The emotional closeness they had longed for was now a reality, and their bond grew stronger with each whispered word. They rediscovered the magic in each other's touch, the gentle caresses and spontaneous hugs that spoke of a love deepened by experience.

Pari's voice softened as she spoke, "I never thought we'd get a second chance like this. It's like a dream."

Ayushman kissed her forehead tenderly. "It's our dream, Pari. And we're living it together."

In this renewed journey, Pari and Ayushman let their emotions and instincts guide them, embracing their second chance with open hearts. Their shared history became the foundation for a future filled with promise, as they navigated their path together, once again as inseparable lovebirds.

Holding her close, Ayushman said, "No matter what happens, I want you to know that I love you more than anything. We're stronger together, and we'll face whatever comes our way."

Pari rested her head on his chest, feeling his heartbeat. "I love you too, Ayushman. With you, I feel like anything is possible. Let's make the most of this second chance."

And so, they lay there, wrapped in each other's arms, dreaming of the future and cherishing the present, grateful for the love that had brought them back together. Their hands entwined, Ayushman gently pulled Pari closer, their lips meeting in a tender kiss that spoke of years of shared history and renewed promises. The night air was filled with the warmth of their reconnection, a bridge between the past and the future they were building together.

Brushing a strand of hair from Pari's face, Ayushman murmured, "You know, I never stopped loving you. Even when things were tough, I always knew we were meant to be."

Pari's eyes glistened with emotion. "I felt the same. Every argument, every misunderstanding, it hurt because I cared so much. But now, we're stronger, wiser."

Their kisses deepened, each touch rekindling the passion that had once defined their university days. In the glow of the moonlight streaming through the window, they found themselves lost in each other, exploring familiar yet new territories of their love. As their bodies entwined, they rediscovered the intimacy that had been overshadowed by life's challenges.

Ayushman whispered against her lips, "We're crafting a story, Pari. One woven with understanding, love, and mutual respect."

Pari, breathless and full of hope, replied, "And it's going to be beautiful, Ayushman. Just like our love."

In the gentle rhythm of their lovemaking, they found a harmony that had been missing, a dance of souls reconnecting after a long journey apart. Their breaths synchronised, hearts beating in unison, they embraced the profound sense of unity that only true love could bring.

Later, as they lay in each other's arms, Ayushman softly hummed their favourite song from university, "Mere rang mein rangne waali...Pari ho ya ho Pariyon ki rani..." The melody had always brought them peace. Pari nestled closer, feeling the warmth of his body and the depth of their bond.

Ayushman kissed her forehead and said, "We've come a long way, Pari. And I wouldn't trade this journey for anything."

Pari smiled, "Neither would I. Here's to our future, Ayushman, filled with love, laughter, and endless possibilities."

With renewed hope and a deepened connection, they drifted into a peaceful sleep, ready to face whatever life had in store for them, together.

After their parents got back together, the lives of Luv and Kush transformed dramatically. Moving into a new house marked the beginning of a joyful chapter, as the old one was laden with memories of a difficult past. The new house symbolised a fresh start and quickly became a haven of happiness for the family.

Luv grinned, "Mom, can we hear the story about Harry's first day at Hogwarts again?"

Pari smiled warmly, "Of course, sweetheart. It's one of my favourites too."

Kush, bouncing with excitement, added, "Dad, can you do the voices? Especially Hagrid's!"

Ayushman chuckled, "You got it, buddy. Hagrid's voice coming right up!"

Pari and Ayushman took turns reading, their voices weaving the magical tale of Harry Potter and his adventures at Hogwarts. The twins listened intently, their imaginations painting vivid pictures of the enchanted castle and its inhabitants.

Softly, Pari narrated, "And then, Harry looked around and saw the vast Great Hall, with its ceiling enchanted to look like the night sky."

Luv's eyes widened in awe, "Wow, I wish we could see that for real!"

Kush nodded eagerly, "Yeah, and ride broomsticks too!"

Ayushman playfully ruffled their hair. "Who knows, maybe one day we'll visit a place just as magical."

As the story continued, Luv and Kush's laughter filled the room, each twist and turn of the tale drawing them deeper into the world of wizards and witches. The warmth and love from their parents made every evening feel like a special family bonding time.

Kush whispered, "Mom, Dad, we're so happy you got back together."

Pari's eyes teared up with joy, "We're happy too, my loves. More than you can imagine."

Ayushman smiled, "This new house is our new beginning. And we're going to fill it with wonderful memories."

The new house not only provided a physical space for them to grow and thrive but also a psychological sanctuary where they could leave behind the shadows of the past. Their parents' reunion brought a renewed sense of security and love, making every day an exciting journey for Luv and Kush. As the story concluded and the lights dimmed, Pari and Ayushman kissed their boys goodnight. Luv and Kush drifted off to sleep with smiles on their faces, dreaming of magical worlds and happy tomorrows.

Pari realised that setting boundaries was essential for her well-being. She understood that it was important to communicate her needs clearly and assertively, without feeling embarrassed about it. Meanwhile, Ayushman came to understand that women of today's generation were different from those of his mother's time. He recognised the need to change his perspective and approach to better appreciate and support their contributions to the family.

Together, they found a new rhythm in their shared life—one that balanced tradition with modern values. It was a dance of mutual respect, where they allowed space for each other's growth. The air was lighter, filled with laughter that echoed through their home, as they embraced this fresh beginning, not just as a couple, but as a family. And as they held each other close, they knew the journey had indeed just begun.

Hearts in sync, love's refrain, what light through the pain?

CHAPTER 21

SHADOWS OF THE PAST

'Memories can be both a source of solace and a source of pain.'

After addressing their financial dynamics and finding some initial harmony, Pari and Ayushman's past conflicts began to resurface, revealing deeper issues in their relationship.

One weekend, during a casual conversation, Ayushman dropped a bombshell, "I'm applying for a visa for my parents to stay with us for a few months."

Pari, taken aback, responded, "When did you decide that?"

He replied reassuringly, "Hang on! I haven't booked their tickets yet. I applied only for a visa last night. I think it will be good for the children and us. They can spend time with their grandchildren, and we can enjoy some intimate holiday experiences on our own... just the two of us."

Pari, visibly surprised, exclaimed, "I'm surprised you didn't discuss it with me before making a decision."

He brushed it off, saying, "Well, everything is okay now. Isn't it? It's been six months, and we're so happy! Mum and Dad have been really worried about us since we split up. Now that we're back together and doing well, I thought it was the perfect time to reassure them. I wanted them to see firsthand that everything is fine between us. I thought it would be a nice surprise for you."

"You know how my mum and dad are, they are so kind and sensitive, I want them to feel reassured that their son and daughter-in-law are doing well," he added earnestly.

Her eyes widened in disbelief. "A surprise? Ayushman, this is our life, not a game. You can't just spring something like this on me without discussing it first."

He sighed, trying to stay calm. "Pari, they've been through so much worry and stress because of us. I thought this would be a way to show them that we're strong, that we've overcome our issues."

Pari felt her frustration boiling over. "Ayushman, your mother's 'kind and sensitive' nature is exactly what worries me. Her sarcastic comments, her constant need to control everything... Do you really think it's a good idea to have them here, in our space, right now?"

He looked confused. "But we're in a good place now, Pari. I thought this would be different. That we could show them how strong we've become."

Pari shook her head, feeling a knot form in her stomach. "Ayushman, you're so naive. You think just because things are fine between us now, it means we can handle your parents' presence without any issues? Your mother's nitpicking, her comments on every little thing I do... Do you remember how it was last time?"

He reached out to her, his eyes pleading. "Pari, please, try to understand. They mean well. They just want to see us happy."

Pari pulled away, her voice rising. "And what about our happiness? What about the peace we've fought so hard to regain? I can't go back to walking on eggshells, constantly worrying about her next sarcastic remark, or the way she subtly undermines everything I do."

His face fell, his desperation evident. "I thought... I thought this would be different. That we could show them how strong we've become."

Pari's voice softened slightly, but the edge remained. "Ayushman, I'm scared. Scared that your mother's presence will ignite the same trivial conflicts that nearly tore us apart before. I don't want to go back to that place."

He tried harder to defend his parents' caring nature, hoping to calm her fears. "Pari, I understand your concerns, but I think this visit could help reassure them. We're stronger now, and I believe we can handle this together."

Pari's anxiety only heightened. She remembered Jenni's advice to never compromise on her values and needs, realising how crucial it was to address conflicts head-on rather than let them fester. The memories of her early marriage struggles with his family loomed large, highlighting her fears of falling back into old patterns of being undermined and disregarded.

"But I have already applied for their visa, and they are excited to see us," he protested.

"Well, you should have consulted me first before making such a promise. It's your mistake, so you need to fix it," Pari retorted, her tone firm.

"I can't back out now," he replied sternly.

Pari's gaze hardened, her eyes burning with contempt as she turned away. The memories of his past unilateral decisions and the pain he had caused her flooded back, igniting a fire within her. She could feel the old wounds reopening. Each step she took away from him felt like breaking free from invisible chains that had bound her for too long.

His voice called out to her, pleading, but she could barely hear him over the roar of her own determination. She wouldn't let herself be ensnared again. The past's shadows loomed large, reminding her of every slight, every moment she had been overlooked and disregarded.

With a final, resolute step, she reached the door. The slam echoed through the house like a thunderclap, reverberating with the full force of her resolve. It was a declaration, a defiant cry against the repetition of history. She had made her choice, and the sound of the door slamming shut behind her was the exclamation point on her decision. This time, she would protect herself, no matter the cost.

That night, after reading a story to the kids and putting them to bed, he came close to Pari, who was lying on her side of the bed, facing the side table rather than waiting to cuddle him tonight. He got the sign that with his lone decision to invite his parents, they might be going down the rabbit hole like Jenni had warned. He sensed that Pari would follow Jenni's advice too and would not back down.

He took a deep breath, trying to find the right words. "Pari, I'm not trying to dismiss your feelings. I just... I want to believe that we're stronger now, that we can handle this. That we can show them we've built something beautiful together."

She looked at him, her eyes filled with a mix of love and fear. "I want to believe that too, Ayushman. But you need to understand that we need to be careful. We need to protect what we've rebuilt."

He nodded slowly, realising the depth of her concern. "Okay, Pari. I'll talk to them. We'll find a way to make this work without jeopardising what we've achieved."

Pari took a deep breath, feeling a bit of the tension ease. "Thank you. That's all I'm asking for. I need more time. Just... let's be a team in this. Let's make decisions together."

He reached out and took her hand, squeezing it gently. "I promise. We'll face this together."

Their eyes met, and in that moment, they both knew that their love was worth fighting for. Despite the reassurance, Pari could not dispute her inner voice that emerged to warn her that the same behaviour pattern was triggering through this event as the first one down the rabbit hole.

Pari suddenly felt so fearful and insecure, as if a red ball of fire was in her stomach, and she threw away his hand, rejecting his gentle cuddle. Even though Ayushman continued to be kind and gentle, Pari could not place her faith back in him. He was left wondering what bad he had done to hurt Pari so much by just doing his duty for his parents' reassurance. Both of them started drifting apart as Pari decided to be cold to him, and that became their routine for the next three months.

For Pari, memories of her marriage with him had become a tangled mess of unpleasant moments that haunted even the sweetest times. No matter how logically she tried to resolve their conflicts, these memories would resurface like poison, spoiling any beautiful moment they tried to share. In her moments of solitude, Pari would feel a simmering rage bubbling within her, an undercurrent of emotion that threatened to consume her.

ONE DAY, PARI THREW A SNOWBALL ARGUMENT AT AYUSHMAN, recalling a conversation from their university days. "During the early years of our relationship, I asked you, 'What's my place in your life?' And you responded, 'First comes my Grandma, then Father, then Mother, then brother, then sister-in-law, then my little nephew, and then you!' I dismissed it with laughter back then, but now I feel foolish for not taking it seriously. What a fool I was... you clearly told me I was at the bottom of the list. And I just took it lightly. Gosh! It was a red flag that I conveniently ignored!" She started crying hysterically.

He couldn't hide his frustration, feeling constantly targeted by Pari with past situations they had tried to move beyond. "Guess what! You had no interest in Financial Accounting, and that was a red flag I ignored. It was clear that you had no wealth management education. You were impractical and bookish, but I still carried on with you. I was so foolish."

Pari shot back, "Now it's all my fault. That's what you want me to say."

Ayushman, exasperated, responded, "I have said 'Sorry' millions of times for applying for my parents' visa without your knowledge, and now you're pulling beautiful memories from the past and making them look pathetic. You're ruining our beautiful memories with your overthinking. Snap out of the past, Pari. Please..." His voice trailed off as he stood frozen, unable to muster the courage to hold her close for comfort, fearing yet another rejection.

With him expressing his frustration, Pari started to reflect on her recent behaviour. She realised it wasn't helping to bring a sensible end to the situation.

"Why do I keep spiralling into these old arguments?" Pari wondered aloud, sitting alone in their living room. "Why can't I just let go and move forward?"

She began to ponder the complexity of their problems. "What are we missing? Why can't we keep afloat during disagreements?" she mused, feeling a knot tighten in her stomach. "What tools do we need to fix these misunderstandings? And why do I keep dragging up unrelated memories during our arguments?"

Her thoughts raced as she tried to understand her actions. "I need to stop getting trapped in the past," she whispered to herself. "I need to address our current problems objectively."

Every night, she asked herself and prayed to God, "Waheguru ji, please give me a moderate life. Remove any more excitement from my life. I fell in love, desperately wanted to marry and struggled with power dynamics. Now, all I want is peace and wisdom to live!" She prayed for a consistent and stable life with Ayushman.

DURING THEIR NEXT MONTHLY DATE NIGHT, AS ADVISED BY JENNI, Ayushman and Pari lay together in a camp tent under the starry night sky. The cool night air and the distant sounds of nature created an intimate atmosphere, perfect for a heartfelt conversation. The soft glow of their lantern illuminated their faces, casting gentle shadows that danced with the flickering light. The tent provided a cozy haven, shielding them from the world outside, allowing them to focus solely on each other. The vast expanse of stars above seemed to mirror the depth of their conversation, as Pari gathered her thoughts, ready to broach a topic that had been weighing on her mind.

"Ayushman, can we talk about something?" Pari asked, her voice hesitant but determined.

Ayushman, initially apprehensive, braced himself. "What is it, Pari? Is everything okay?"

Pari took a deep breath. "I've been thinking a lot lately. About us, about our past. I realise I've been hurtful and vengeful at times, trying to protect myself. And I wonder if you ever feel the urge to bring up your own hurts."

He was taken aback by her openness. "Honestly, Pari, the past doesn't matter to me anymore. Being with you in the present is what truly matters."

Pari's curiosity persisted. "Do you ever feel anger or frustration about the time and energy we wasted due to our misunderstandings?"

He sighed, revealing a side of him Pari hadn't seen before. "I grew up in a culture where negotiating with one's life partner wasn't common. I witnessed male-dominated relationships and never learned the art of compromise within a marriage."

He paused, looking at her with regret. "I was ignorant, and I'm sorry for my lack of understanding."

Pari nodded, feeling a mix of relief and sadness. "I forgive you, Ayushman, but... I can't forget. The memories and pain still hold me back from fully embracing you without reservations. I'm scared of having my heart broken again."

Their conversation marked a turning point in their relationship. Ayushman's honesty and vulnerability allowed her to see him in a new light.

"I understand, Pari," he said softly. "Our past experiences have shaped us, and while forgiveness is a step forward, I know the scars are still there."

Pari looked into his eyes, feeling a flicker of hope. "I want to move past this, Ayushman. But it's going to take time."

He nodded, squeezing her hand gently. "I'm here, Pari. We'll take it one step at a time. Together."

While the path ahead remained uncertain, their willingness to confront their issues and have open conversations offered a glimmer of hope for a more harmonious future. However, as Pari lay in Ayushman's arms under the vast, starry sky, she couldn't shake the lingering bitterness that still gnawed at her heart. "Can I ever truly let shadows from past go?" she wondered, her mind heavy with unresolved emotions. The barrier to their happiness remained, a silent companion to their freshly discovered hope.

Past shadows cast, love's light, what secrets take flight?

PART THREE

"The pain of parting is nothing to the joy of meeting again."

- CHARLES DICKENS

CHAPTER 22

RECONNECTING THROUGH THERAPY

J enni's office exuded calmness and comfort, with fresh flowers, paintings of majestic mountain sceneries, and elegant French furniture creating a warm atmosphere. Soft lighting and a subtle sweet pea aroma added to the room's inviting ambiance, setting the stage for meaningful conversations.

Jenni: "Pari and Ayushman, thank you for coming. Pari has informed me about the reason for today's session. My approach will be a bit different this time. I have incorporated Neuro-Linguistic Programming (NLP) into my practice. This technique helps you reform your thinking by eliminating fears and beliefs that no longer serve you. We will delve into resolution mode later, but first, let's explore the core values in your relationship."

Jenni set up her presentation.

Jenni: "Let's start with understanding what core values are." (Clicking to the first slide, which read, "Introduction to Core Values.") "Core values are fundamental beliefs that guide our behaviours and decision-making. They represent what is important to us at our deepest level and influence how we interact with the world. Examples include honesty, integrity, family loyalty, and independence."

Jenni: "Core values are like a compass, directing our actions and interactions. They shape our identity and how we perceive our role in the world."

She moved to the second slide: "How Are Core Values Formed?"

Jenni: "Core values are shaped by various factors in our lives."

Jenni explained each factor:

Jenni: "Family Influence, Cultural Background, Life Experiences, Education and Knowledge, and Personal Reflection."

Jenni: "Core values develop through a combination of influences, evolving over time as we grow and gain new perspectives."

She moved to the third slide: "Introduction to Shared Goals."

Jenni: "Shared goals are common objectives that partners or team members work towards together. They help align individual efforts towards a unified outcome and require collaboration and mutual effort. Examples include financial stability, building a trusting relationship, raising children, and maintaining a healthy lifestyle."

Jenni: "Shared goals provide direction and purpose, ensuring everyone works towards the same end."

She moved to the fourth slide: "Introduction to Shared Values."

Jenni: "Shared values are the collective principles that a group or partnership agrees upon as essential. They ensure everyone is on the same page about what is important, creating a cohesive and supportive environment. Examples include trust, safety, inclusion, and empowerment."

Jenni: "Shared values act as a foundation, fostering a sense of unity and common purpose."

Finally, she moved to the fifth slide: "Achieving Shared goals by shifting Core values to Shared values ."

Jenni: "Now that we understand these concepts, let's understand your personal core values. This will help us understand how you can work together more effectively."

Jenni handed them each a sheet to write down their core values. She then left the room to let them work on it for five minutes. When she returned, she gently asked, "Are you both ready to proceed?" They both nodded in agreement.

Jenni: "Pari, looking at the sheet in your hand, could you share the values most important to you and what your goals are from the relationship?"

Pari: "I value independence, integrity, mutual respect, adaptability, and financial security. Personally, I just want to feel safe and appreciated in our relationship. Together, I want to enjoy our life and raise our children in a loving and supportive environment so they can become capable individuals who can look after themselves independently."

Jenni: "Ayushman, what about you?"

Ayushman: "For me, it's about family loyalty, commitment, resilience, love, and financial stability. I want us to be a team and support each other through everything, whether it's our parents or our children."

Jenni: "Now, let us extract your common interest from personal goals as your shared goals—enjoying life together and raising well-rounded children."

Ayushman: "Why isn't looking after our parents included?"

Jenni: "Remember, you have entrusted me with a job to mediate between you and bring out your honesty in a safe environment. So, I urge both of you not to project our beliefs on our partner in this session."

They both nodded in agreement.

Jenni : "Ayushman, Since, 'Looking after parents' lies outside your common interest, that becomes your personal goal. That would be achieved through shared values later on in the session.

Ayushman nodded, demonstrating sincerity towards following the pattern of the session.

Jenni: "Ayushman, what initially drew you to Pari?"

Ayushman: "I was attracted to Pari's candidness and confidence, her independence, and her forthright nature."

Jenni: "And Pari, what drew you to Ayushman?"

Pari: "I was drawn to Ayushman's excellence in academics, his caring nature, reliability, and protectiveness."

Jenni: "Ayushman, before marriage, you admired Pari for being candid, forthright, and confident, which made her happy. Now, you might be hoping she'll adapt to the traditions you grew up with, but that isn't who she is. This difference can create tension."

Pari felt understood and relieved that her feelings were communicated to Ayushman.

Jenni continued, "Pari, Ayushman has always prioritised others' comfort and is loyal to his commitments, which brings him happiness. Sometimes, this can seem at odds with your expectations. Understanding these differences can help you both find harmony."

Ayushman, in turn, felt relieved and appreciated, realising that his well-meaning intentions were validated and he was being fairly treated.

Jenni: "Ayushman, how do you define family?"

Ayushman: "For me, family includes Pari, our kids, my parents, my brother Vardaan, his wife Sapna, and their kids. We're all interconnected, and I believe in maintaining those ties."

Jenni: "And Pari, how do you define family?"

Pari: "For me, family is just Ayushman and our kids. They are my immediate world. While I respect his parents and Vardaan's family, I feel that our nuclear family should be our priority."

Jenni: "As you now know, Ayushman, your definition of family is broader than Pari's. Hence, to find common ground, you must set respectful boundaries where Pari feels heard and respected, keeping her peaceful and happy."

Ayushman: "Maybe I could start by discussing any plans involving my extended family with Pari first. We could agree on what feels comfortable for both of us."

Jenni: "Pari, how can you acknowledge Ayushman's desire to maintain his extended family ties while keeping your boundaries intact?"

Pari: "I think I can be more open to dealing with his extended family, as long as he checks with me first and we agree on the frequency and nature of these events."

Jenni: "Now let's discuss your current extended family conflict and its adverse impact on your intimacy."

Ayushman: "Despite Pari acknowledging that I need proximity to my parents and brother's family, she starts to behave coldly at their mention. Sometimes, it feels like an invisible barrier stands between us, making it hard to bridge that gap. That impacts our intimacy."

Jenni: "Pari, you mentioned earlier that Ayushman's ability to provide safety was a key quality that connected you to him. Can you share any recent negative experiences?"

Pari: "It was a while ago when we were in India. I experienced challenging dynamics with his mother when she came to stay with us last time. I can't move past it."

Jenni: "What specifically do you fear?"

Pari: "I fear that he will again side with his mother without knowing my side of the story. Even if I explain my side, as he aligns with his mother in core values, he tends to validate her point. It makes it hard for me to maintain my home routine when she is present, disturbing my inner peace."

Jenni: "With his changed outlook post-reunion, can you specifically mention the incident that makes you feel that way?"

Pari: "His recent application for a visa without consulting me was unexpected and it shook me."

Jenni: "I understand. Ayushman, can you explain the belief that led you to apply for your parents' visa without consulting Pari?"

Ayushman: "I thought, as she is financially empowered now, it was natural to integrate our extended families. But when my parents expressed their desire to visit us, I applied for their visa and then informed Pari. Though, I wouldn't have booked tickets without her agreement."

Jenni: "Is that true?"

Pari confirmed, "Yes, the incident triggered my past experiences with his mother. I can't help but despise her presence in my safe haven, my home." Tears rolled down her cheeks as she grabbed a tissue, her emotions overwhelming her.

Jenni: "Ayushman, I see that you meant well, but your actions weren't aligned with thoughtful consideration. You missed the first step in the consultation process among you, which encroached on her boundaries of family and hurt her core values of safety and respect, in turn triggering Pari's unresolved fear of losing her safe space, consequently affecting your intimacy."

Ayushman responded, "I never intended to make you feel unsafe, Pari."

Jenni: "Intimacy thrives when a woman feels safe enough to reveal her vulnerable self. To support interdependence and connection, you both must accommodate each other's core values by exercising empathy and aspirations to share celebrations and joys with extended family through mutual consultation and agreement."

Pari said, "I want to feel connected to your family, but I need to feel safe first."

Ayushman replied, "I understand, and I want you to feel secure in our home."

Jenni continued, "For some people, staying in touch with extended family nurtures their inner child, keeping them connected to their authentic self. While doing so, you must ensure that your partner is treated fairly, applying reasoning to understand the impact on them."

Both of them reflected on their reactions, realising how their attempts to change each other's authenticity had been hurtful. They took a deep breath and nodded, confirming the accuracy of Jenni's assessment.

Ayushman: "I promise to consider your feelings more carefully from now on."

Pari: "And I'll try to be more open about my fears."

Jenni: "This reflection has led you to rewire your thinking processes by extending empathy to each other, fostering a new ground for sowing seeds of acceptance and trust. This knowledge empowers both of you to feel safe and authentic with each other at all times."

Ayushman and Pari looked at each other with renewed understanding, ready to move forward with greater compassion and mutual respect.

He looked at Pari and reassured her, "Please don't feel pressured to see my folks soon. Can we start over? I assure you I will include you in every decision that impacts our family."

Pari responded, "I want to see you happy too. Now I understand how important being close to your family is for you. I don't want you to change. I love you the way you are."

Jenni guided them back to the present, praising their progress. "You've done great work today. This is a significant step in your healing process. We'll continue to build on this in future sessions."

Pari, feeling lighter, said, "I feel more hopeful about our journey. Thank you."

Jenni smiled warmly. "You're welcome. Healing is a journey, and remember it's about progress and not perfection. Be gentle with yourselves and practice the compassion you showed today."

Jenni concluded, "So, we've explored that in your current relationship, you have rebuilt trust since your decision to reunite. You have new experiences with Ayushman to believe that you will be fairly treated by him, and if the need arises, you have the negotiation skills to address any circumstance."

Jenni: "Ayushman, you must not project your perception of family on her any longer because of her core values. You must respect her boundaries and assure Pari that she will be safe when your parents are around in word and action so she can be her authentic self too."

Jenni: "Pari, you must not project your perception of a nuclear family on Ayushman because that is against his definition of family. You must develop the 'mental strength' to exercise empathy to include his folks when he needs them, knowing Ayushman will act from a place of mutual benefit. By treasuring the positive aspects of your evolved relationship and his growing support."

They left the office feeling empowered with the knowledge of how their core values and beliefs impact their environment. They understood how shifting to shared values of Safety, Inclusivity, Trust, and Empowerment can demonstrate tolerance and create space for each other to thrive.

FOUR WEEKS LATER, PARI VISITED JENNI FOR A FOLLOW UP PERSONAL session.

Jenni began, "How have you been doing with practicing the new way of thinking?"

Pari smiled, "We've been so calm since our last session. It's been four weeks without a single argument. We empathise more and make an effort to be mindful of our words. Thank you so much."

Jenni nodded, "You both are quick learners. I'm glad I could help. How can I help you today?"

Pari hesitated, "I sound weird, but my problem is that I don't have room for my shopping anymore and I can't stop shopping as it had been like therapy for me."

Jenni and Pari had a hearty laugh.

Jenni: "Be able to shop is a good problem to have, isn't it? we all love retail therapy, don't we?"

Pari: "Yeah, I love it too much, but while cleaning out my closet, I realised I have clothes with tags still on that I never wore. Some still new but don't fit me anymore, and others are out of fashion. I feel guilty and regretful. I could have spent that money better. I feel like an addict. I need a way out."

Jenni acknowledged, "That's a real challenge for many people nowadays. In Japan, they link a cluttered wardrobe with an unsettled mind. Decluttering physical spaces can help clear mental clutter. Recognising this is the first step."

Hearing that, Pari felt reassured. She realised she was on the right path toward better balance and clarity.

Jenni suggested using NLP techniques like 'thought challenging' to reframe negative thoughts. "Can you think of an event in the past that associates your self-worth with high-end clothing?"

Pari replied, "Yes, as a child, I felt ashamed of my skin. My mother taught me to focus on skills over appearance, but I always wanted to stand out. I thought developing high-value skills would let me buy designer stuff. I kept buying until I realised I was overdoing it."

Jenni empathised, "I see how difficult that must have been. It's hard to navigate beauty standards. Your mother gave you a more important goal to focus on. Do you understand her reasoning now?"

"Yes," said Pari, understanding her mother's intentions.

Jenni validated, "It's okay to buy unique clothing if you can afford it. There's no shame in preferring a certain lifestyle."

Pari sighed deeply, feeling the shame leave her body.

Jenni asked, "Pari, what evidence from your current relationship contradicts the belief that you are only worthy of love if you wear unique clothing?"

Pari thought, "Ayushman doesn't care what I wear. He always finds me beautiful and compliments me, no matter what. In the early days, he enforced budgeting on me because of his family's expenses, which didn't make sense to me."

Jenni recalibrated, "Can you recall a specific event where your husband, valued only your external appearance over your inner qualities hurting your self-worth?"

"Never," Pari clarified, not being able to think of any incident from their relationship.

Jenni asked, "Can you think of a situation that might trigger your fear of self-worth in the near future?"

"Absolutely not," Pari replied immediately.

"Why?" Jenni asked.

"Because personal skills matter more than my appearance," Pari said thoughtfully, feeling her fear disassociate from her self-worth.

Jenni's voice was calm yet encouraging. "Excellent. How do you feel after recalibrating your thoughts about your self-worth?"

Pari sighed deeply. "I feel a burden lifted. I never realised my love for unique clothing affected my self-worth."

Jenni nodded. "Linking rewards to personal milestones can hurt our self-worth. Changing circumstances may impact ongoing rewards and hinder adaptability. Valuing ourselves for our character, not appearances, boosts self-worth and strengthens our ability to handle any circumstance."

Pari asked, "So, does this mean our motivators should evolve as we age?"

Jenni replied, "Exactly! When we're young, our motivators are often material because of the simplicity of approach to build skills. As we grow, they should shift towards fulfilling broader goals, helping us become team players and coexist empathetically with others."

This realisation reminded Pari of her childhood when her mother emphasised skills over appearance. Now, she understood the importance of evolving motivators for personal excellence and meaningful goals.

Listening carefully, Pari rewired her thoughts. She recognised her mother's approach and the need for changing motivators. This session changed her mindset significantly. She felt confident and independent, free from the belief of low self-worth. Understanding her worth beyond material achievements, she saw her true potential and how it could benefit her family and community.

Over the next few weeks, Pari had more sessions with Jenni, transforming her outlook on life and her relationship. The fear and anxiety tied to her past beliefs lessened, allowing her to feel more present and connected. These changes gradually enhanced her relationship with Ayushman, especially in intimacy, leading to a more fulfilling and harmonious life together.

THREE MONTHS LATER, ON A SATURDAY NIGHT, THE FULL MOON glowed through the large windows of the bedroom, casting a soft, serene light over the room. Pari and Ayushman sat on the plush couch, ready to watch a movie after putting the kids to bed. They were both unwinding after a long and entertaining day spent at the city zoo, where they had laughed, played, and marveled at the animals with their children.

As Ayushman settled in next to Pari, he noticed something different about her. She seemed more present in their shared moments, her warmth and intimate expressiveness shining through in ways he hadn't seen in a long time. She had been more engaged and affectionate, her laughter coming more easily and her touch lingering a little longer.

Ayushman turned to Pari, his curiosity and appreciation evident in his eyes. "I've noticed a difference in you lately, Pari," he said softly. "You seem more relaxed and open. How are the sessions with Jenni going?"

Pari looked at him, a gentle smile playing on her lips. The light from the moon illuminated her face, giving her an ethereal glow. She took a deep breath, reflecting on the journey they had embarked on with Jenni's guidance.

"They've been really helpful," Pari replied, her voice calm and thoughtful. "Jenni has helped me see things from a different perspective. I've been learning to let go of the fears and resentments that were holding me back. It's not just about the sessions, though. It's about the work we've both been doing to understand and respect each other's core values and needs."

Ayushman nodded, feeling a sense of relief and gratitude. "I've seen the changes in you, and it's inspiring. I feel like we're reconnecting in a way that I didn't think was possible before."

Pari reached out and took his hand, squeezing it gently. "I feel the same way. It's like we're finding each other all over again. And I think a big part of that is because we're both making an effort to be more open and honest with each other."

The warmth between them was palpable, a testament to the progress they had made together. Ayushman leaned in and kissed Pari's forehead, feeling a renewed sense of hope and love for their future.

As they started the movie, they snuggled closer, their hands entwined. The moonlight continued to bathe the room in its gentle glow, symbolising a new beginning for them—a beginning built on mutual respect, understanding, and a deeper connection than ever before.

After the movie ended, they remained on the couch, enveloped in a comfortable silence. Ayushman gently brushed a strand of hair from Pari's face, his touch lingering. She looked into his eyes, seeing the love and tenderness there. Slowly, they leaned into each other, their lips meeting in a soft, lingering kiss.

The kiss deepened, their breaths mingling as they moved closer together. Ayushman's hands caressed Pari's back, drawing her nearer, while Pari's fingers traced the lines of his face, memorising every detail. Their connection felt electric, charged with the rediscovered intimacy they had been nurturing.

They moved from the couch to the bed, the moonlight casting a silver glow over them. Their movements were unhurried, filled with a gentle passion that spoke of their deep bond. They undressed each other slowly, savoring the closeness and the tenderness of each touch.

As they lay together, their bodies intertwined, they made love with a softness and reverence that came from truly seeing and accepting each other. It was a moment of pure connection, where they were completely present with one another, their hearts and souls aligned.

Afterward, they held each other close, their breathing slowing as they basked in the afterglow. The room was filled with a peaceful silence, the only sound being the gentle rhythm of their breaths. Ayushman whispered softly to Pari, "I love you," and she responded in kind, her voice filled with warmth and sincerity.

Pari looked into his eyes, feeling an overwhelming sense of contentment and joy. "I love you, Ayushman," she whispered. "Tonight has shown me how deeply connected we are."

As she rested her head on his chest, she felt a sense of peace wash over her, mixed with lingering worries. He, noticing her newfound calm and readiness to move forward, spoke softly, "Pari, I'm sorry that I applied for my parents' visa without consulting you. I promise that from now on, I'll always consult you before making any arrangements for my family."

She smiled back, appreciating his words, but deep down, she still felt a pang of bitterness at the mention of the future visit from his mother.

"Why do I still feel this way?" she wondered silently. "Even in moments of closeness like this, the thought of his mother's interference brings a shadow over my happiness."

Pari sighed inwardly, her thoughts a whirlwind of emotions. "I need to let go of this resentment," she told herself. "I want to move forward, but it's so hard when I feel this unexplained heaviness at just the thought of his mother."

As she lay there, she resolved to address these feelings head-on. "I can't let this bitterness take root again," she thought. "Ayushman is trying, and I owe it to us to keep trying too."

With a gentle kiss on Ayushman's chest, she whispered, "I trust you, Ayushman. Let's work together to make this new era in our life as beautiful as possible."

He held her tighter, sensing her inner struggle, and whispered back, "I'm here for you, Pari. Always."

Pari closed her eyes, feeling a mixture of hope and apprehension. "This is our journey," she reminded herself. "We'll face the challenges together, and I won't let the past define our future."

Yet, as she drifted off to sleep in his arms, the bitterness lingered, a constant undercurrent she couldn't quite shake. Despite her resolve, the weight of past grievances and unspoken fears remained heavy on her heart, making it difficult to fully enjoy the present. "I want to be happy," she thought, "but why is it so hard to let go?"

At that instant she recalled Jenni's words, "You must develop the 'mental strength' to exercise empathy..."

And with that, she wondered how she could develop 'mental strength' required to resolve this bitterness? The question remained unanswered as she slipped into a restless sleep, her mind still searching for a way to overcome the shadows of her unresolved feelings.

WHEN PARI AWOKE THAT MORNING, SHE FOUND AYUSHMAN STILL asleep beside her, his breathing steady and calm. A quiet determination stirred within her as she watched him for a moment, a gentle warmth spreading through her heart. The night had been restless—like the unsettled waves of a storm-tossed sea—but from that disquiet emerged a new sense of purpose and clarity. The cool air in the room, along with the soft song of the birds outside, seemed to draw her closer to her thoughts. She knew that if she wished to give her relationship with Ayushman a fresh direction, it would not suffice to make changes outwardly alone; there must also be a deepening of the mind and spirit.

Rising slowly from the bed so as not to disturb Ayushman, Pari took a deep breath, as though hoping to release the burdens of yesterday with each exhalation. She quietly made her way to the kitchen, prepared herself a cup of tea, and stood at the window, gazing out as she held the warm cup in her hands. The first light of morning filtered through the leaves, and the gentle warmth of the sun's rays seemed to offer her a hint of guidance toward something new.

Shortly after, the house began to stir with the sounds of daily life. Ayushman emerged from the bedroom, still looking drowsy, while the children bounced out of their rooms, full of energy. Pari set about preparing breakfast, ensuring Ayushman's coffee was just as he liked it, and making sure the children had their school bags packed. The small yet familiar routines of the morning, though mundane, felt different today—imbued with a renewed sense of purpose.

As she handed Ayushman his coffee, she caught his eye for a brief moment, and the warmth of his gaze seemed to convey an unspoken understanding. She wondered if he, too, could sense the shift within her, though she kept her thoughts to herself. The children's laughter and chatter filled the air as they ate breakfast, and the house buzzed with a pleasant chaos as everyone readied themselves for the day ahead.

After sending the children off to school and watching Ayushman depart for work, Pari returned to the quiet of the now-empty house. She sipped the last of her tea, and in the stillness, Jenny's old suggestion echoed in her mind. It was as if a forgotten door in her memory had been quietly opened. "I ought to speak with Jenny," she thought, venturing deeper into her musings. With a slight tremor in her hand—whether from anticipation or uncertainty—Pari reached for the telephone. She dialled Jenny's number, and after a few rings, the familiar voice answered.

"Hello, Jenny," said Pari. "I am well, thank you, but I am in need of your counsel. Our sessions have helped me greatly, yet there remains a sense that I must cultivate my strength of mind and closeness in my relationship. There is a bitterness within me that I wish to banish, so that Ayushman and I may truly be united."

Jenny chuckled softly, "It sounds as if you may need to study the Kama Sutra."

Pari blushed, as though her most private thoughts had been discovered. "What is it about the Kama Sutra," she asked hesitantly, "that the world finds so captivating?"

Jenny replied, "Being Indian, you ought to be familiar with it, of course, but I would suggest seeking the guidance of a spiritual teacher first—someone who can help you to develop a deeper understanding. It seems to me that you may need what I would call an 'energy rehabilitation.' However, that is beyond my expertise. You may have to look for a practitioner who specialises in alternative energy practices."

Pari listened with care to Jenny's suggestion, for there was a certain gravity in her tone that pointed to a new course of action. As she ended the call, Pari realised that this was not merely advice—it was a sign, a call to embark on a journey unknown.

Setting the phone aside, she drew in a steady breath, as if she had reached a decision that would alter the course of her life. Though the house was quiet now, it hummed with the memory of the morning's activity, and a sense of hopefulness filled the air. As she thought back on Ayushman's gentle gaze and the children's lively laughter, her resolve grew stronger. She would find someone to guide her in fortifying her inner strength and awakening the dormant power within.

It was clear to Pari that this marked the beginning of a new chapter—one not only meant to strengthen her bond with Ayushman but to awaken something deep within herself. "Perhaps," she mused, "this is the very moment I have been seeking all along."

Tears and peace, love's grace, what next in this place?

CHAPTER 23
INQUEST-EK KHOJ

In the spring of 2013, at San Clarion, the morning air was crisp. The scent of blooming flowers filled the air, and the dawn's soft light bathed the streets in a golden hue. As Pari walked from the metro station to her high-rise office in the CBD, her heart was heavy with unresolved emotions.

"Why can't I be fully present with Ayushman?"

Her mind wandered as she pondered her husband's devotion.

"Ayushman prioritises our whole family's well-being, often putting his own needs aside. Much like Lord Rama who adhered to dharma despite personal loss."

A pang of frustration hit her.

"But I do not want to become collateral damage like Ma Sita."

She mused aloud, her thoughts swirling.

"To live with a dutiful and righteous man like Lord Rama, do I have to be like Ma Sita? Or is there a more balanced way to live a married life in the modern world?"

The traditional narrative of Indian women conflicted with her own interests.

Pari felt lost and overwhelmed, standing at a crossroads and seeking guidance.

"What should define happiness and success for a modern Indian woman like me?"

She weighed the expectations of tradition against her own desires.

"Should I follow the traditional path, the liberal path, or a blend of both?"

She realised she needed to honour both her cultural heritage and her own inner strength.

Pari: "How do I reconcile these opposing forces within myself?"

In that moment, she had a revelation. Her journey wasn't just about understanding Ayushman or their relationship. It was about discovering her own truth.

Pari: "I need to find the courage to live my truth fully."

Lost in her thoughts, Pari grabbed a coffee and a breakfast jaffle at a popular café on short walk to work. The familiar aroma of freshly brewed coffee mixed with the hustle and bustle of morning commuters provided a comforting backdrop.

As she walked towards the platform, something caught her eye. A natural medicine store, adorned with ancient-looking symbols on its sign, stood out among the modern buildings.

The shop featured an ornate red door and wind chimes gently tinkling in the breeze. The board read, "Chan's Herbal Store: Remedy to All Your Problems." Intrigued and feeling a spark of curiosity, she decided to step inside.

Crossing the threshold of the store, Pari felt an immediate sense of calm. The air was filled with the soothing scent of herbs and essential oils. Inside, shelves stretched from floor to ceiling, filled with dried leaves, tree barks, herbal powders, potions, and books. Jars of natural remedies and handwritten labels added to the shop's mystical charm.

An elderly man was restocking the top shelf on the north wall. The soothing aroma of scented candles, lifted Pari's mood and eased her anxiety.

"Ni Hao! Young lady. Chan at your service. How can I help you?" The old man greeted her with an Asian accent.

Chan, of average height, had a serene demeanour that exuded wisdom and kindness. His hair, a mix of silver and black, was neatly pulled back into a small bun. His eyes, slightly wrinkled at the corners, sparkled with a lifetime of experience and a hint of mischief. He wore a simple yet elegant traditional Chinese tunic and pants, and his posture was upright and dignified despite his age. His hands were calloused but gentle, hinting at years of meticulous work with herbs and potions. His presence radiated calm and knowledge, making Pari feel instantly at ease.

Pari hesitated but decided to be candid. "Can I buy a herb to restore my peace of mind and rekindle love with my husband?"

Chan looked at her with a serious expression. "Jokes not allowed, only serious buyers are welcome."

"I'm sorry if I offended you, Chan," Pari said regretfully.

Chan burst into a hearty laugh, his face lighting up like a joyful Buddha. "You think only you can joke around!"

Pari couldn't help but laugh at Chan's witty response. She hadn't laughed so heartily in a long time.

He pulled out a notepad and stylus. "Young lady, what's your name?" he asked.

"Pari," she replied, sipping her coffee.

"What do you do for a living?"

"I am a software engineer," she responded politely with a light smile.

He scribbled on the notepad:

Name: Pari

Occupation: Software Engineer

Client Goal: Mental peace and a good married life

Prescription: Personal evolution

Signed: Li Chan, Mental Strength Coach - $100 per hour

He tore off the page and handed it to Pari with a knowing smile. The interaction left her feeling unexpectedly light-hearted and curious about what lay ahead.

"Personal evolution? What do you mean? I have a Master's in Computer Applications and studied Business Communications as my major. Are you suggesting that I need more formal education?" Pari exclaimed.

Chan's face softened at Pari's candidness, and he let out a light, amused chuckle, his eyes filled with empathy, he said, "Life can be a puzzle. Sometimes you need a guide to help fit the pieces together. That's where I come in."

"Young lady, I'm 80 years old, happily married for 60 years, and a father of six," He began, pausing to gaze into Pari's eyes. "And...I'm still evolving. Intellectual growth never stops unless it's blocked."

"Potions," he began thoughtfully, "can heal the body, calm the mind, maybe even bring clarity in fleeting moments. But love and peace of mind... those are trickier, and no bottle can truly contain them. One has to develop mental strength to achieve inner-peace."

Pari mused to herself, "Ah, 'mental strength'—how familiar that sounds. Wasn't that precisely what Jenni had recommended?" As she pondered this, a curious thought emerged: could her discovery of Chan's shop be yet another piece in this intricate puzzle, akin to the steps of a well-orchestrated treasure hunt?

Chan's eyes gleamed as he turned to the shelves, lined not only with herbs but books from across the world. His calloused hands gestured gently.

"These hold remedies for both body and mind," he said softly. "Each has a key, if you are willing to unlock it."

Pari's gaze followed.

"I've spent a lifetime not just mixing remedies, but exploring how different cultures approach life's biggest questions. You see, Pari, it's my passion—understanding how people across centuries and continents have dealt with things like love, conflict, and inner peace. Herbs and potions are only one part of it."

He paused, pulling one worn book off the shelf, its edges soft from age and use. "Every tradition, every philosophy offers something. Whether it's the Tao teaching balance, or Buddhist mindfulness, or even old folklore—each has wisdom for us, and I've tried to gather that knowledge. Some of it helps in daily life, other pieces are guides for the soul."

Looking back at Pari, he smiled, a deeper wisdom gleaming in his eyes. "In my travels, I've seen that problems can't always be solved directly. They need understanding—of yourself, of others, of the world. No single potion or book has all the answers. But if you're open to learning, you'll find your way to solutions."

His words carried weight, not just from knowledge but from experience. Chan had lived through many cultures, studied deeply, and his life philosophy seemed to be a combination of learning from different walks of life. It was about knowing that every struggle had its own unique solution, often drawn from diverse wisdom.

Pari found herself reflecting, not just on the idea of peace but on Chan's lifetime of learning. Maybe there were no quick fixes, but the idea of growing through wisdom from all over the world resonated deeply with her.

He added with a pleasing smile, "You are welcome to join my coaching if you see a benefit—there's no compulsion as such,"

Pari was intrigued by Chan's candidness. She took the note with a serious expression, thanked Chan, and left the shop, pondering his words.

As expected, Pari finished work early that day and returned to the shop in the early afternoon. She hastily procured a quick meal from the nearby dumpling shop before heading toward Chan's establishment. As she entered, the tinkling of wind chimes welcomed her.

"Welcome back," Chan greeted from atop one of the ladders. "I've been searching for a potion that could restore your homeostasis."

Pari, puzzled, responded, "Homeo...what? Sorry, I'm not versed in medicinal terms."

He reassured her, "No need to apologise. I mentioned it to broaden your knowledge. Mental peace aligns with the physiology of Homeostasis."

"Are you suggesting that mental peace has a scientific formula?" inquired Pari.

"Look it up yourself! Back in my day, we didn't have Google. I was driven by curiosity, delving into numerous books. You're fortunate to have a wealth of knowledge at your fingertips."

"Will the potion resolve my agony?" questioned Pari.

"That depends on your quest," he said thoughtfully. "From my experience and understanding, our bodies adapt to herbs within three months. There are over the counter herbs that will help you keep calm in the interim, however, true progress comes from acknowledging your feelings, reflecting on your behaviour, developing discernment, and upgrading your thoughts. This is how you achieve lasting, unshakeable calmness."

"How is all that done?" Pari pressed.

"A valid question indeed! Why don't you start by telling me more about your life story?" He asked, seeking more information to better assist her.

Pari began, "Long story short," she paused, "my husband Ayushman and I met at university five years before we married..." She then shared the obstacles, failures, and triumphs they faced. Chan felt the weight of her emotions through her words, each one revealing her inner turmoil. Memories of their first meeting, the joy of their early years, and the growing challenges played out in her mind like a movie, stirring her heart.

"And I wonder how to become a happy married woman," she confessed, her voice trembling slightly. The uncertainty in her words mirrored the confusion in her heart.

"The traditional Indian path conflicts with my interests, while the liberal path conflicts with my mutual interests with my husband. I wonder if there exists a blend of both?" Her eyes pleaded for an answer, reflecting her confusion and hope. She looked at Chan, her heart heavy with the desire for a solution that seemed elusive.

Chan listened patiently, his eyes understanding and kind. He collected his thoughts before responding thoughtfully, "Perhaps, you can carve your own path."

Pari's eyes widened slightly at the suggestion, a flicker of hope igniting within her. "Is it easy?" she asked, her voice tinged with uncertainty and longing for reassurance.

"All new paths are hard to carve, but it can be made easier with guidance," Chan reassured her. His words felt like a gentle push towards the light at the end of her tunnel, offering her a glimmer of hope in her quest for balance and happiness."

He gestured to a ladder. "Come here... move the ladder westward and climb up to the second shelf. Retrieve the third book from the left."

Pari, mindful of her footing, removed her heels and ascended the ladder. "Chan, I can't manage the weight of this book and descend simultaneously!" she exclaimed.

"You can, my dear," he reassured.

With determination and caution, Pari began her descent. As she reached the ground, she handed the book to him with a sense of accomplishment.

"Here it is, Chan," she announced.

He carefully unwrapped the book and handed it back to Pari. "Your answers lie within these pages. Read one page daily and journal three pages, reflecting on your life experiences," he instructed.

Pari protested, "The Bhagavad Gita... Are you serious? It's a Vedic scripture. I recall reading a simplified version in school, but I'm not religious. This won't help me. No thanks."

He challenged her, "Do you believe that being religious would hinder your personal growth?"

"It doesn't hinder me; I simply don't resonate with religious teachings," Pari countered.

Chan, with a thoughtful expression, gently probed, "When did you decide that religious teachings are not useful?"

Pari, her voice tinged with frustration, replied, "It's because you see on TV that religion is causing war around the world. In my view, if people stop reading these old books, they can live in the now and preserve what we have today rather than destroying it."

"You are taking a tangent there. Don't dodge the question," He said, maintaining his calm demeanour.

Pari sighed, "Well, specifically, my husband's actions are deeply rooted in the ancient story of Ramayana, with family loyalty above all. This has made me feel like Sita, trapped by expectations. Before I married Ayushman, I was a confident woman. Now, doubt surrounds me, and it's overwhelming. While Ayushman normally remains calm, almost unshakable, I struggle to find my own peace after everything we've been through. It's not easy to forget, even if things have been resolved."

Chan, with a thoughtful expression, gently probed, "Do you often find yourself caught in self-doubt?"

"Yes," Pari admitted.

Chan, with understanding eyes, noted, "And you are finding it hard to let go of the past. Is that correct?"

"That's correct," Pari admitted.

He clarified, "If I understand correctly, when you both entered your marriage, you did not know some things about each other's traditions."

"Yes," Pari agreed.

He continued, "Once you became aware of those things, then you both extended understanding and made amends."

"Precisely, but that journey took years!" Pari confirmed.

Chan: "Have there been times when you thought Ayushman was being unreasonable to you on purpose, but he didn't even realise it, and vice versa?

Pari retorted, "Plenty of such scenarios existed."

He asked, "Have they all been resolved?"

Pari thought for a moment and replied, "Ah... mostly!"

He pressed further, "Does that mean you're not sure?"

Pari frowned with uncertainty, "I can't say for certain."

Sensing Pari's self-doubt, he leaned forward, his gaze steady and compassionate. "Pari, it sounds like you've been navigating unforeseen circumstances and facing unexpected challenges. It's natural to feel inadequate when your usual skills seem useless in those moments." He continued, "Prince Arjuna faced a similar conundrum in the Mahabharata when his exceptional archery skills seemed inadequate against his kins on the battlefield."

He paused thoughtfully, then asked, "What if I guide you to wisdom that enables you to find answers in any uncertain circumstance, allowing you to move forward with unwavering mental strength?" He let his words sink in, watching as a glimmer of understanding began to light up her eyes. "Do you think that would help address your self-doubt and empower you to carve a balanced path between tradition and modern expectations?"

"And you will do that through this book...the Bhagavad Gita?" Pari asked, her skepticism evident.

Chan, with a knowing smile, replied, "Do you have any reason to believe that the desire to resolve inner conflict is irrelevant in modern times?"

"No, but I believe the landscape setting of the Bhagavad Gita is ancient. The characters are religious and it doesn't apply to the modern world as is. Isn't it?" Pari queried.

He explained gently with a touch of humour, "Ah! So that's what's blocking your faith in its teachings—it's not a simple copy-paste to your life."

He paused thoughtfully, collecting his thoughts before speaking with a theatrical flair, "My dear! Think of The Bhagavad Gita as a metaphor, drawing parallels with familiar characters from your life. It guides you toward personal transformation, just as it did for Arjuna. The true value lies in understanding and creatively applying its lessons to your own experiences."

Deep down, Pari felt that Chan made sense. She thought to herself, "Without a clear path, I need to get creative and carve my own."

Intrigued, she asked him, "Would you kindly explain how Arjuna's journey relates to mine?"

Chan, happy to see Pari at ease with the topic, explained with a bit of theatrics, "Just like Prince Arjuna on the battlefield, you've found yourself gripped by self-doubt. In his moment of crisis, Arjuna turned to his charioteer, Lord Krishna, known for his strategic wisdom. The teachings of Lord Krishna, documented in this book, offer guidance to anyone facing similar situations."

Pari's curiosity was piqued, though she sought a quicker solution. "Why the Bhagavad Gita, Chan? Isn't there a modern world book addressing these topics?"

He remarked, "I haven't come across one yet! I think a book that blends modern science, ancient wisdom and personal aspirations together is yet to be written."

Chan's voice carried a deep sincerity, as though he was gently unveiling a truth that had been lying dormant within Pari. "Your mind and body are so deeply intertwined with Indian traditions that you are 'wired in India,'" he said. This was something Pari had never truly acknowledged before, but now, as Chan's words sank in, it felt like a new perspective was unfolding within her.

Curiosity flickered in Pari's eyes, as if a door had opened to a new realm of understanding. "Wired in India? What does that even mean?" she wondered aloud. Chan's words had stirred her thoughts, shaking the very foundation of her perceptions. She found herself connecting to something she had never considered before, something deeply rooted yet largely ignored.

"The strings of your heart and mind are tied to the civilisation that is an intrinsic part of your character," Chan added with a meaningful smile. His words struck a chord deep within her, as if answering countless questions buried in her soul. Pari realised that she was still governed by the values and principles that had shaped her childhood, even though she had never consciously acknowledged them.

"The examples set by the great figures of our past shape your daily life and mutual expectations. The teachings of texts like the Gita will be particularly beneficial to you," Chan explained. His words compelled Pari to reflect on her roots, making her realise that perhaps she had been driven by forces she had long overlooked.

He encouraged Pari by drawing parallels between her quest and Arjuna's guidance from Krishna. "Lord Krishna taught that whenever we feel miserable and unsatisfied, we should return to the foundational wisdom of our civilisation."

Quoting Bhagavad Gita, Chapter 4, Verse 7, he recited:

यदा यदा हि धर्मस्य ग्लानिर्भवति भारत।
अभ्युत्थानमधर्मस्य तदात्मानं सृजाम्यहम्।।

Whenever virtue declines and vice rises, I manifest myself on earth.

"In your situation, this verse suggests that during the recent conflict in your marriage, you realised your needs were continually unmet. By understanding your rights and duties, you stood up for what you believed was right and reached a fair agreement with your husband after recognising the importance of balance and mutual respect." He established the relevance of The Bhagavad Gita.

Listening to how Chan connected the Bhagavad Gita to her recent choices, Pari was impressed. "I didn't expect the shloka to reflect so much of what I've been going through. It's like the Gita already knows what's happening in my life." She paused, feeling a thought beginning to surface. "Maybe Chan is right—maybe I am more 'wired in India' than I thought. Even if I've been living with more Western ideas, the values I grew up with are still shaping me in ways I didn't realise. This ancient wisdom—it's making me see things differently."

Her realisation wasn't fully formed, but the connection Chan made was beginning to penetrate, opening her up to the idea that perhaps, there was more to her upbringing than she had acknowledged.

Pari, with a fresh perspective, exclaimed, "Wow! Is that how I should interpret my life's journey through the Bhagavad Gita?"

Chan: "Yes! The most important step in achieving any transformation is The Acceptance, that a change is needed. And just now, you have taken the first step towards that journey."

Chan, adjusting a book on the shelf with deliberate and calm movements, continued, "Seeking self-guidance is indeed the right path. It's crucial to maintain a harmonious emotional state, as physical and mental calmness in synchrony create the fertile ground where seeds of knowledge can be sown and grow into personal skills and inner wisdom."

He then quoted, "The verse from the Bhagavad Gita, Chapter 2, Verse 47, is:

कर्मण्येवाधिकारस्ते मा फलेषु कदाचन।
मा कर्मफलहेतुर्भूर्मा ते सङ्गोऽस्त्वकर्मणि॥

Just as the sweetest fruits are enjoyed long after the seed has been planted and nurtured, your desired outcomes will materialise when your sustained dedication positively impacts the people around you.

Therefore, don't expect immediate appreciation, as building relationships is a long-term endeavour. Your duty is to follow your true path while always considering the well-being of those around you. Because expectations from your perspective might not align with what others can provide based on their own viewpoint."

Pari listened, her eyes reflecting a mixture of contemplation and realisation. His words were sinking in, each sentence painting a vivid picture in her mind. She could almost see the seasons changing, the seed growing into a tree, and understood the metaphor deeply. Ayushman was a part of her life that was worth nurturing, she knew that from the beginning.

Pari's determination grew stronger. She realised the need to cultivate wisdom to bridge the gap between them and rebuild their intimacy on a deeper, more lasting foundation.

Eager to learn, Pari asked, "How can I cultivate a lasting sense of calm? Is coaching part of the answer?"

Chan's eyes sparkled with understanding. "Pari, have you ever considered the power of something you do instinctively that you can also master consciously?"

Pari's curiosity deepened. "You mean, breathing?"

"Precisely," Chan said warmly. "Breathing is not only automatic but also within your control."

Pari felt a surge of insight. "How does this connection to breathing affect my emotional state?"

Chan began, "Breathing with serenity is your brain's way of sensing safety. When stressed, you might start with a deep sigh, followed by a rapid exhale. This triggers a survival response from ancient times."

Pari leaned in, captivated. "And what should I do to counter this?"

Chan replied thoughtfully, "In those moments of rapid exhale, if you consciously slow down your breath, you signal to your brain that you're safe. This simple shift helps override the automatic stress response, leading to a state of calm."

Pari's expression softened. "So, this practice helps me control my stress and maintain my composure?"

Chan nodded with a gentle smile. "Indeed. By becoming aware of your breath, you not only calm your body but also clear your mind. This practice, over time, enables you to approach challenges with clarity and resilience."

Pari's eyes reflected deep understanding. "Is this similar to what Buddha referred to as Vipassana?"

"Yes," Chan affirmed. "Vipassana is about mindful observation and inner peace through breath awareness."

Pari's voice carried a fresh conviction, "So, mastering my breath is a key to managing stress and achieving inner calm?"

"Absolutely," Chan said with a reassuring smile. "It's a profound yet accessible practice. With consistent attention, it transforms your emotional landscape and fosters profound self-reflection."

He paused, then added, "However, for long-term success in managing inner peace, it's crucial to address the root causes of your stress by understanding and confronting your emotional triggers."

Chan, sensing the opportunity to emphasise the importance of coaching, spoke calmly and deeply, "This is why I suggest interpreting the Bhagavad Gita in the context of your life. Think of yourself as Arjun surrounded by unresolved thoughts- Kauravas on the battlefield of Kurukshetra- your body. "

Pari: "What are the dominant values to be embodied by a calm individual?"

Chan: "Such a person embodies kindness, compassion, and discernment," he explained. "They live beyond mere survival mode. Their actions are neither defensive nor aggressive, but empathetic, serving the greater good of their family, community, or organisation."

Pari: "Aren't those traits of a leader?"

Chan: "Yes. Clarity, stability and vision make you a role model.

Regular introspection prevents self-sabotage, fostering leadership in unexpected situations."

Pari asked, "How should I then approach learning wisdom from the Bhagavad Gita?"

He was pleased with Pari's engaged questioning, appreciating her emotional investment in the subject matter.

Smiling, he picked up a whiteboard marker and approached the whiteboard behind the potion wall, eager to turn the serious subject of journaling into a fun and engaging experience. "Journaling is an important first step to release our fears," he began, his eyes twinkling with excitement. "The fears block our energy, manifesting as shame, guilt, bitterness, resentment, greed, and more such emotions. But don't worry, we're going to make this process enjoyable!"

As he started to draw, the flowchart began to take shape with vibrant colours."Let's break it down step by step," he continued, sketching out a lively flow diagram that included stars, hearts, and doodles to make each step visually appealing.

"Think of this as a treasure hunt," he said, grinning. "Each step you take in your journal brings you closer to uncovering hidden gems of self-awareness and inner peace. Ready to embark on this adventure?"

With each step, he added a catchy rhyme to make the process memorable and fun:

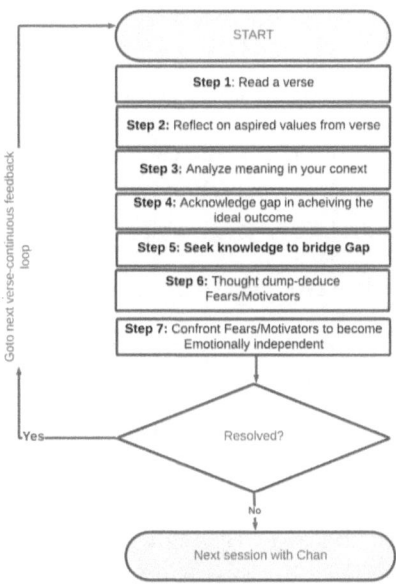

Step 1: Read a verse, let it guide your course.
Step 2: Reflect on your aspired values, with no remorse.
Step 3: Analyse its meaning, find your source.
Step 4: Journal your feelings, let them endorse.
Step 5: Build your knowledge, let learning reinforce.

Step 6: Document everything, write with full force.

Step 7: Confront your fears, stay on the right course.

AS HE ELABORATED EACH STEP, HIS ENTHUSIASM WAS CONTAGIOUS, turning what could be a daunting task into an exciting journey of self-discovery.

"Step 1: Read a verse

Choose a verse from the Bhagavad Gita and note it down. This step sets the foundation for introspection, offering timeless wisdom that you can apply to your present life.

Step 2: Reflect on aspired values from the verse

Reflect on the values the verse instills. Ask yourself: What core principles or ideals are presented? How do these resonate with your personal aspirations?

Step 3: Analyse meaning in your context

Interpret the verse within the scope of your current life circumstances. How do its teachings align with the challenges or goals you're facing? Write down how you relate to the message.

Step 4: Acknowledge the gap in achieving the ideal outcome

Identify any gaps between the verse's teachings and your present behaviour or thoughts. Recognise where you're falling short in embodying the values and record your observations.

Step 5: Seek knowledge to bridge the gap

Look for ways to fill the gap—through study, advice, or introspection. Journal any ideas or strategies that can help you incorporate the values from the verse into your actions and mindset.

Step 6: Thought dump—deduce fears/motivators

Dump all your thoughts freely. Let your fears and motivators rise to the surface. In this process, identify what drives or hinders you from realising your goals.

Step 7: Confront fears/motivators to become emotionally independent

Examine the fears or motivators you uncovered. Explore how you can confront or overcome them to achieve emotional independence. This step is about reclaiming control over your inner landscape."

"Once you've completed these steps, assess whether the insights gained have brought you closer to resolving your internal conflicts. If not, reflect further in your next session."

"This isn't just about writing," he said, "it's about exploring, understanding, and ultimately, freeing yourself from the blocks that hold you back. Do practice it and let me know if any doubts."

Pari nodded thoughtfully, feeling a fresh surge of confidence. "Off course! Thank you, Chan."

He nodded, "You're welcome, Pari. Personal growth is a journey. Reflect and you'll evolve over time."

He handed Pari the invoice for the session. "Today, your time is up. Here's the bill for the Personal Evolution training."

She settled the invoice and quickly took a picture of the whiteboard, which was so full of text it looked like a work of art.

Leaving the shop, she felt a mix of excitement and apprehension about the journey ahead. She boarded the quiet train carriage, found a seat by the window, and gazed at the beautiful mountain scenery speeding past.

"Today was enlightening," she thought, feeling a sense of calm wash over her as she practiced the breathing bio hack he had taught her. "Breathing is the brain's way of knowing we are safe. Who knew something so simple could have such a profound effect?"

That night, when Pari sat alone in her study, the serene view of the valley through the window brought a sense of calm. She picked up her journal and the Bhagavad Gita, ready to explore her feelings and resolve the bitterness she felt towards her mother-in-law (Maaji). She recalled Chan's guidance and decided to follow the steps he had taught her. She vividly remembered the rhyming steps Chan had taught her, ready to explore her feelings and find clarity.

Step one, read a verse, let it guide your course.

She opened the Bhagavad Gita and read a verse:

"कर्मण्येवाधिकारस्ते मा फलेषु कदाचन।

मा कर्मफलहेतुर्भूर्मा ते सङ्गोऽस्त्वकर्मणि॥"

Just as the sweetest fruits are enjoyed long after the seed has been planted and nurtured, your desired outcomes will materialise when your sustained dedication positively impacts the people around you.

Step 2: Reflect on your aspired values, with no remorse.

> *Reflecting on this verse, I understand the importance of focusing on my duties without getting attached to the results. My values of being a caring wife and daughter-in-law should guide my actions, regardless of the outcomes.*

Step 3: Analyse its meaning, find your source.

She interpreted the verse in her context:

> *This verse teaches me to let go of my attachment to the results of my actions. It emphasises the significance of duty and responsibility over the desire for approval and recognition because validation is the product of other people's perspective. Hence, result might not match my expectations which is the product of my perception.*

Step 4: Journal your feelings, let them endorse.

Pari began to write about an unwarranted event:

> *"I saw mother-in-law, Maaji criticising my way of handling kitchen tasks in front of the family. I heard her say that my methods were inefficient and disrespectful. I felt humiliated and undermined."*

She continued to reflect on how she dealt with it in reality:

> *I kept quiet and felt increasingly frustrated and resentful. I feel frustrated and bitter when my efforts to connect with my Maaji go unnoticed. I desire her approval and wish for a harmonious relationship. My fear of losing connection with Ayushman is tied to these feelings.*

Then she wrote how she wanted to deal with similar events in the future:

> *I must accept that I cannot control her reactions, only my actions. Next time, I want to calmly explain my methods and express my willingness to learn and adapt.*

Step five, build your knowledge, let learning reinforce.

Pari acknowledged the need to build her knowledge:

> *Understanding that my fears and bitterness are due to unmet expectations helps me realise that I need to let go of these expectations. Accepting that I can only control my actions allows me to focus on fulfilling my duties without emotional attachment.*
> *I must to learn more about effective communication and conflict resolution.*

Step six, document everything, write with full force.

She filled her journal with thoughts and reflections, aiming to cover at least three pages. She dumped everything from her brain onto the paper without worrying about handwriting or spelling.

She wrote down her reflections:

> *"I do not know a way to resolve this bitterness amicably when Maaji is not open to change. It's a pitty, that I can't have an open dialogue with her, so may be my conflicts with her will never be resolved. This means I will always resent her presence, which in turn hurts Ayushman's core values of*

family loyalty. That would leave him miserable in a significant part of his heart. Everyone treasures parents. As they are growing older, its unfair that I deprive him of looking after them. But I feel uncomfortable when Maaji is around. What must I do? I want all of us to be a happy family. I wonder, how can this 'bitterness' be resolved?"

She continued to write, reflecting on the stories her friends and colleagues from conservative societies had shared. She saw a common thread:

"Many women can resonate with this feeling of bitterness. It often stems from unresolved conflicts and unmet expectations, especially with in-laws. When open dialogue isn't possible, the bitterness festers, affecting not just the relationship with the in-law, but also with the spouse. This emotional weight is heavy, and the longing for resolution and harmony becomes a common, heartfelt quest."

Step seven, confront your fears, stay on the right course.

Pari wrote about her fears:

"I fear that my efforts to connect with Maaji will always be met with criticism. I fear never finding a harmonious balance in my relationship with her."

Despite the revelation of her bitterness, Pari felt overwhelmed and struggled to process these feelings independently. She realised that she needed further guidance to navigate through these emotions effectively. Closing her journal, Pari decided to call Chan to set up an appointment.

Pari took a deep breath and picked up her phone, dialling Chan's number.

As the phone rang, she felt a mix of hope and apprehension. After a few rings, Chan's calm voice came through the line.

"Hello, this is Chan," he greeted warmly.

"Hi Chan, it's Pari," she replied, trying to keep her voice steady. "I hope you're doing well."

"Hello, Pari. It's good to hear from you. How can I assist you today?"

Pari hesitated for a moment, gathering her thoughts. "Chan, I've been doing a lot of self-reflection using the Bhagavad Gita and the journaling techniques you taught me. It's been very insightful, but I've reached a point where I feel like I need some additional guidance."

Chan's tone remained encouraging. "I'm glad to hear that you've been working on it, Pari. What kind of guidance are you looking for?"

"I think I need a more in-depth session to help me process some of the things I've uncovered," Pari said, choosing her words carefully. "There's a lot I've realised, but I'm struggling to put it all together and move forward."

Chan's voice was reassuring. "That sounds like a good idea. It's important to have support when dealing with deep reflections. How about we schedule a spiritual coaching session? We can dive into whatever you need help with."

Pari felt a wave of relief. "Yes, that would be perfect. When would you be available?"

"I have some openings this week. How about we meet on Thursday at 2 PM?"

"Thursday at 2 PM works for me," Pari confirmed. "Thank you so much, Chan."

"You're welcome, Pari. I look forward to our session. Take care until then."

As she ended the call, Pari felt a renewed sense of hope. She was taking the steps she needed to understand and resolve her feelings, and she knew she wasn't alone in her journey. She was ready to face her inner challenges with Chan's guidance, confident that she was on the right path towards healing and self-discovery. Then with that thought, Pari opened the Bhagavad Gita at a random page and read,

अधियज्ञोऽहमेवात्र देहे देहभृतां वर ।
कर्मसंन्यासयोगे च निमित्तं निबोध मे ॥

"I am the ritual action, I am the sacrifice, I am the offering and the herb. Know me to be the ritual action that brings liberation," declares Chapter 8, Verse 4 of the Bhagavad Gita.

Reflecting on this verse, Pari felt a profound connection to her purpose and the guidance she sought. "I am on a unique exploration of my-self," she realised. "The only perspective I can influence is my own." This realisation brought her a deep sense of peace and empowerment. "If I focus on my own actions and thoughts, I can find liberation and balance in my life," she thought, feeling a renewed strength rising within her.

This realisation infused her with a sense of calm. She felt the weight of her worries lift slightly, replaced by a new clarity. "I am not alone in this journey," she reassured herself, "I am in good hands, I have the wisdom of the ages and the support of those who care for me."

Pari closed the book gently, her mind still reflecting on the verse. "I will face my challenges with courage," she vowed. "With Chan's guidance and the wisdom of the Gita, I will find my way."

The evening sky outside her window grew darker, mirroring the uncertainties that still lingered within her. Pari recalled her mother's words: "A lioness leaves her cubs at the edge of the jungle, letting them find their way back home through storms and rivers, teaching them strength and patience." The metaphor resonated more deeply now than ever before.

"Perhaps I am that cub," she thought to herself, "just starting to find my way through life's storms, learning to build my mental strength." She realised that her struggles were not merely obstacles but necessary steps toward developing the resilience she sought. "I may not feel strong now, but each challenge is teaching me. Mamma believed in me; it's time I start believing in myself."

Pari knew there would be challenges ahead—moments that would test her resolve and make her question her path. She didn't yet possess all the mental strength she needed, but she was on the journey to cultivating it. With a hopeful smile, she whispered a silent prayer: "Every day, in every way, I am becoming better and better."

Search begins, love's quest, what truths put to rest?

CHAPTER 24
FROM SHADOWS TO LIGHT

As Pari sat in Chan's cozy shop, savouring her Japanese matcha, she felt a stirring in her chest—a desire for something more. The shop's tranquil atmosphere, filled with spiritual books, soft music, and the scent of incense, whispered possibilities. Amidst this tranquility, an unfulfilled longing stirred within her.

Pari looked up at Chan, her eyes reflecting gratitude and curiosity. "Thanks for guiding me to journal with the Bhagavad Gita. I think I am more aware of my fears than ever before."

Chan nodded, smiling warmly. "That's wonderful progress, Pari. Self-awareness is the first step towards transformation." He paused, then asked, "So, what emerged as your fear?"

Pari replied, "Bitterness creeps into my heart after I extend understanding and empathy."

"Are you still attached to expecting outcomes to align with your perception?" Chan asked.

Pari admitted, "I've accepted that immediate results might not happen, but I struggle to let go and move forward. The leftover bitterness distracts me."

Chan explained, "The bitterness you feel is a sign of lingering attachment. Let's delve deeper."

Pari questioned, "Why am I bitter towards Ayushman's family?"

"Bitterness is a form of unexpressed energy, it comes from unmet expectations and perceived injustices," Chan explained. "When empathy isn't reciprocated, it creates stress and stores as negative energy. This blocked energy turns into resentment, affecting your ability to express yourself. In any new organisation, a new member is less trusted. Isn't it?"

Pari nodded, agreeing that it was true from her work experience.

Chan continued, "Like new employees, brides often feel powerless and misunderstood by their husband's family. This leads to negative reactions and deteriorating relationships that impact their mental health. Without a clear guide, she feels unsupported and marginalised, seeking freedom to solve her negativity."

Pari related his words to her struggles. "I've tried everything—separation, therapy, fitness, meditation—but nothing works permanently because I seek full alignment with my husband. I want to be united with him in body, mind, and soul. And that's not happening."

"That happens when you stay in the system and change it subtly without challenging the status quo," Chan replied. "Sudden changes can disrupt any functioning organisation, causing resistance."

She swallowed her tears and continued, "But I do care about his family's interests, just like he does."

"How would his family know that you are reliable without you demonstrating it?" Chan countered. "Have you been there long enough to see all seasons of bringing up a child through to adulthood?"

Pari explained, "No, but I have run out of patience needed to tolerate obstructive people like his mother. She might mean well, but she is aggressive towards my ideas and sometimes manipulative, doing everything in her power to keep me from shining bright."

Her voice trembled, "However hard I try, the memory of her negative behaviours drags me back to the past, preventing me from enjoying my present. I feel trapped in guilt, sabotaging good times with my husband."

Chan, extending compassion, said, "There you go. If you seek a union of body, mind, and soul with your partner, you must develop patience. It's the key to success." He paused, noticing the activity in Pari's eyes as she looked down and then up again. "The negative energy trapped inside you obstructs your empathy for your mother-in-law and compassion for yourself. This would clear with enlightenment from Vedic knowledge about energy and soul."

Pari, seeking answers, asked, "How?"

Noticing Pari's full engagement and hunger for knowledge, Chan began, "Blocked energy centres in the spine keep your energy in motion (emotion) in a constant state of stress." He paused, "When people live under perceived threat or fear, stress becomes their new normal. Deep breathing helps temporarily, but long-term relief requires releasing negative energy from chakras and elevating thought patterns."

He continued, "As Krishna told Arjuna: 'One who has conquered the mind, the mind is the best of friends; but for one who has failed to do so, the mind will remain the greatest enemy.'

"Your bitterness towards your mother-in-law is a sign of blocked chakras from unsafe memories with her, keeping you in constant stress."

Pari leaned in, intrigued. "Blocked chakras? How do they cause stress?"

"First," Chan explained, "our experiences create emotions. Then emotions create thoughts, shaping our perception of that person in our memory. Memories make the mind."

Pari nodded, trying to follow. "So, when my mind is full of negative emotions, it becomes the enemy of my peace?"

"Exactly," Chan said. "It spirals your positive energy into unresolved issues with people you cannot control, leaving you with more negative energy."

Pari sighed. "But we can only control ourselves, not others. So how do I break this spiral?"

"Learning about chakras helps," Chan replied. "By cleansing them, you break the spiralling thought process. When negative energy is released, you can elevate your thought process."

"Elevate my thought process?" Pari asked. "How does that help?"

"This elevation through Kosha wisdom helps you conquer your mind," Chan said, "transforming it from an enemy into a friend." He continued softly after a pause, "This knowledge will help you find the alignment and inner peace you seek, allowing you to shine bright despite challenges."

Curious, Pari asked, "What are chakras and Koshas?"

Chan smiled gently, seeing her genuine interest. "Chakras are energy centres in your body," he explained. "When they're blocked, it disrupts your emotional and physical well-being. Releasing this blocked energy can help you find balance and peace." Pari nodded, feeling a mix of hope and determination to understand and heal herself.

Chan, with enthusiasm, said, "Let's explore this together." If there is a best way to teach Chakras, he had found it already...he began to hum the characteristics of each chakra with rhythmic flow making it simple and interesting for her.

CHAKRAS AND ENERGY CHANNELS

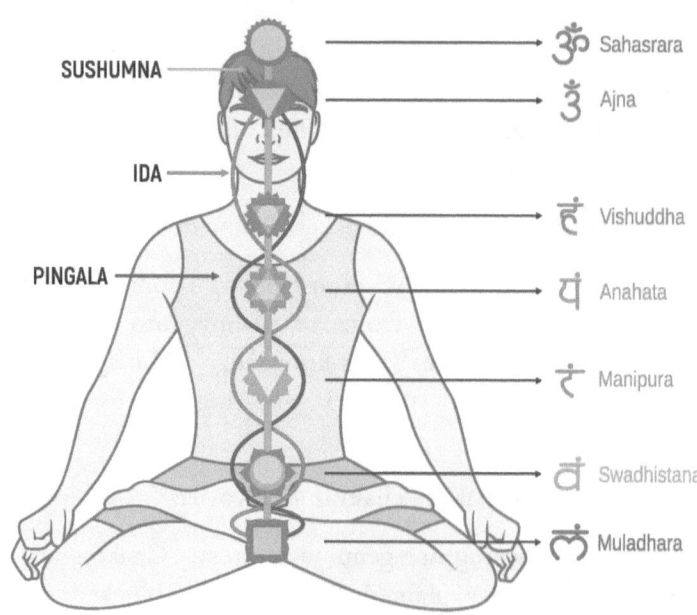

Chan, pointing to the Chakra chart on the wall, his voice calm and guiding.

Here lie the seven chakras, our spirits to seek,
A map of our energy, each wheel unique,
From base to crown, our journey's peak.
First, the Root Chakra, Muladhara's ground,
Where survival and safety are found.
Pari's is blocked, she feels deep fear,
Insecurity and dread always near.

He explained, "Pari, your blocked Root Chakra is causing insecurity and constant fear, disrupting your sense of stability and grounding."

Next, the Sacral Chakra, Svadhisthana's flow,
Where creativity and desires begin to grow.
Pari's is blocked, guilt and shame arise,
Her joy suppressed, dimming the skies.

He continued, "Your Sacral Chakra is blocked, suppressing your joy and creativity. Feelings of guilt and shame are hindering your natural flow of energy."

Solar Plexus Chakra, Manipura's fire,
Our willpower and strength to aspire.
Pari's is blocked, her confidence wanes,
Self-esteem drops, anxiety gains.

He added, "Your Solar Plexus Chakra, the centre of your willpower and strength, is blocked. This causes your confidence to wane and anxiety to rise, affecting your self-esteem."

Heart Chakra, Anahata's tender grace,
Love and compassion in every embrace.
Pari's is blocked by bitterness and pain,
Closing off love, causing strain.

"Your Heart Chakra is blocked by bitterness and pain," he noted. "This blockage prevents you from fully experiencing love and compassion, causing strain in your relationships."

Throat Chakra, Vishuddha's truth to tell,
Communication's clear, resonant bell.
Pari's is blocked, her voice is stilled,
Expression stifled, words unfulfilled.

"With your Throat Chakra blocked," he explained, "your ability to communicate is stifled. You struggle to express your thoughts and feelings clearly."

Third Eye Chakra, Ajna's inner sight,
Intuition and wisdom shining bright.
Pari's is blocked, her vision's unclear,
Intuition falters, filled with fear.

He continued, "Your Third Eye Chakra, the centre of intuition and wisdom, is blocked. This leaves you with unclear vision and a faltering intuition, often filling you with fear."

Crown Chakra, Sahasrara's divine glow,
Spiritual connection, the ultimate flow.
Pari's is blocked, feeling disconnected,
Lost and confused, spiritually neglected.

"Finally, your Crown Chakra is blocked," he said softly. "This causes a feeling of disconnection, leaving you lost and spiritually neglected."

To resolve these blockages, Pari must learn,
To express her energy, let her spirit burn.
Balancing the dynamics, strategically wise,
Through the Theory of Koshas, Vedanta's prize."

Chan: "By learning to express your energy and balancing the dynamics strategically, you can begin to unblock these chakras."

Pari: "How do I do that?"

Chan: "The Theory of Koshas from Vedanta will guide you through this process, helping you achieve inner peace and spiritual connection."

Pari: "What about my bitterness? It seems to manifest as stress."

Chan: "Yes, you've identified that 'bitterness' manifests as stress. The blocked Heart Chakra is emerging as the first chakra we need to address."

Pari: "How do I resolve it?"

Chan: "To resolve this, you must learn to think long-term by seeing the bigger picture in every circumstance. This perspective keeps your heart open, even with those who don't share your values."

Pari: "Why is openness so important?"

Chan: "Openness is key to emotional health. It helps you let go of emotional burdens and awaken all your Chakras. Now, let's explore the Koshas."

Pari: "What are Koshas?"

Chan gently grabbed a peacock feather from a vase beside him, pausing thoughtfully before beginning.

Chan: "Good question, Pari. The concept is quite complex, originating from the Taittriya Upanishad, but I'll simplify it for you," he said, starting his explanation.

"Koshas are layers of existence that shape our behaviour and responses, much like the different colours in a peacock feather radiating outward from the centre, forming a halo of bliss," he began by quoting a verse from the Taittiriya Upanishad:

"तस्माद्वा एतस्मादात्मन आकाशः सम्भूतः।
आकाशाद्वायुः। वायोरग्निः। अग्नेरापः। अद्भ्यः पृथिवी।
पृथिव्या ओषधयः। ओषधीभ्योऽन्नम्। अन्नात्पुरुषः।"

From the Self (Brahman) came space, from space air, from air fire, from fire water, from water earth, from earth plants, from plants food, from food man.

Elaborating further, he says, "This verse indirectly refers to the layers (Koshas) of existence that emerge from the Self, describing the progression from the most subtle to the most gross forms."

STAGES OF SELF-EVOLUTION

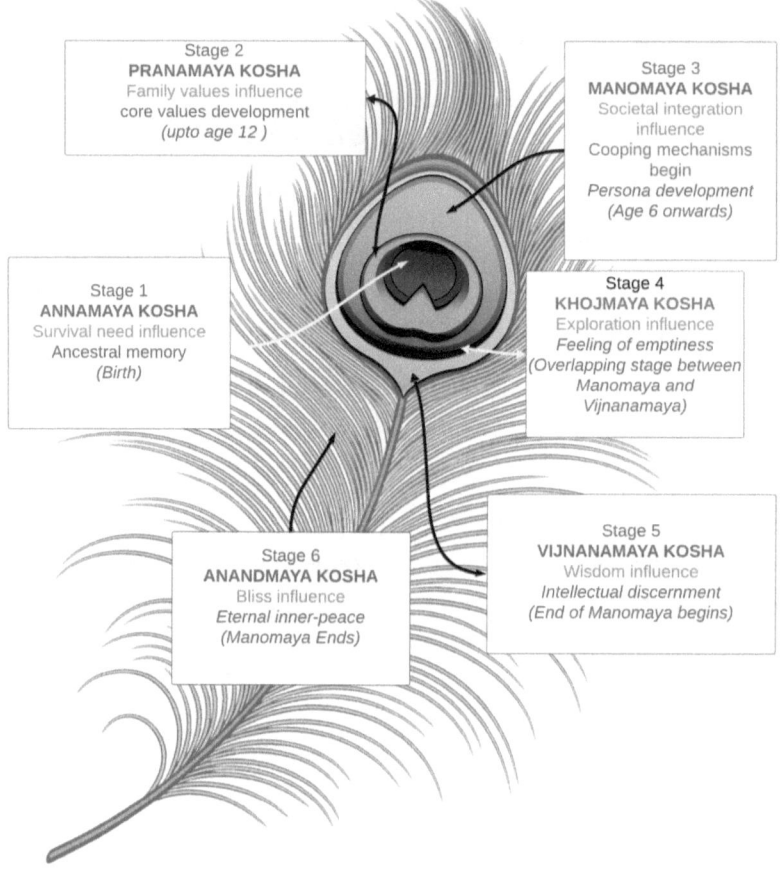

Stage 2
PRANAMAYA KOSHA
Family values influence
core values development
(upto age 12)

Stage 3
MANOMAYA KOSHA
Societal integration
influence
Cooping mechanisms
begin
*Persona development
(Age 6 onwards)*

Stage 1
ANNAMAYA KOSHA
Survival need influence
Ancestral memory
(Birth)

Stage 4
KHOJMAYA KOSHA
Exploration influence
*Feeling of emptiness
(Overlapping stage between
Manomaya and
Vijnanamaya)*

Stage 6
ANANDMAYA KOSHA
Bliss influence
*Eternal inner-peace
(Manomaya Ends)*

Stage 5
VIJNANAMAYA KOSHA
Wisdom influence
*Intellectual discernment
(End of Manomaya begins)*

HE THEN TURNED TO PARI, HIS EYES SHINING WITH WISDOM, AS rhyming words flowed from his lips:

> *Pari, let's dive into the Koshas to understand their light,*
> *They help us feel better, day and night.*
> *Annamaya Kosha is all about staying alive,*
> *Like a baby's needs, helping us survive.*

Annamaya Kosha is our physical body, focused on basic survival needs, like a baby. It relates to the element of earth, providing the foundation and stability.

> *Pranamaya Kosha is the love and care of family,*
> *A parental nest where we learn to share gladly.*
> *We feel safe with family near,*
> *But new people can bring some fear.*

Pranamaya Kosha deals with our energy and emotions, feeling safe with family but cautious with strangers. It corresponds to the element of water, representing the flow of emotions and life force.

> *Manomaya Kosha is about social integration and dreams,*
> *In adulthood, it's harder than it seems.*
> *We wear masks to blend and hide,*
> *Sometimes, we lose our true inside.*

Manomaya Kosha is our mental layer, influenced by society, often causing us to hide our true selves. It relates to the element of fire, symbolising the transformative power of thoughts and emotions."

> *Khojmaya Kosha is the quest for truth,*
> *Like Arjuna, thinking deeply in his youth.*
> *Sometimes we see a mountain of work and feel stuck,*
> *But we're in a valley; the path goes up.*
> *With Krishna's wisdom, we find our best,*
> *Bravery and care guide our quest.*

Khojmaya Kosha* is our search for deeper understanding, like Arjuna guided by Krishna's wisdom. It corresponds to the element of air, representing the quest for knowledge and deeper truths.

---

* Khojmaya Kosha is author's improvisation in adapting the ancient Koshas concept to modern world.

Vijnanamaya Kosha is wisdom and care,
Making good choices, being fair.
We talk kindly and plan ahead,
With clear articulation, avoid new dread.
Paths open up, our purpose clear,
Journey forth, with nothing to fear.

Vijnanamaya Kosha is about wisdom, making good decisions, and speaking clearly to avoid new problems. It relates to the element of ether (space), symbolising the expansive and all-encompassing nature of wisdom. When knowledge is applied through refined thought patterns, it transforms our intellectual abilities into a capability known as Vijnana.

Anandamaya Kosha is reaching moksha's grace,
Finding inner peace in every space.

Anandamaya Kosha is the blissful state of inner peace and spiritual connection. It represents the unity of all elements, leading to ultimate liberation.

Pari, begin with Khojmaya Kosha as your first step,
Like Arjuna in Mahabharata, balance thoughts adept.
See who's still learning, let go and forgive,
Stay calm inside, and happily live.

Begin with self-reflection like Arjuna to gain clarity in your thoughts and emotions. Categorise people influencing your energy into two groups based on their behaviours: higher Koshas and lower Koshas. Those in the higher Koshas exhibit kindness (4th Kosha), wisdom(5th Kosha), and stability (6th Kosha). The lower Koshas display aggression (1st Kosha), defensiveness (2nd Kosha), or manipulation (3rd Kosha). This classification helps you manage your reactions and emotions for six broad categories of people, eliminating the overwhelm caused by dealing with hundreds of experiences individually. It leads you to condense and manage people around you without spiralling into overthinking. Ultimately, you would achieve stability by reaching wisdom (5th Kosha) and then, inner bliss(6th Kosha), becoming a spiritual guide like Krishna.

> *Others are on their quests too,*
> *Facing challenges, just like you.*
> *With empathy, coexist, face life's hurdles wide.*
> *Focus on your journey, let your purpose guide.*

Understand others have their own challenges too. Coexist with empathy but focus on your own journey.

> *So, Pari, like Arjuna, take your first step,*
> *Balancing thoughts and feelings adept.*
> *Choose friends in higher Koshas for your inner circle,*
> *And with wisdom and care, let your life sparkle.*

Start your journey, balance your thoughts, choose supportive friends, and live wisely and happily."

Chan's words were like a balm to Pari's troubled soul, encouraging her to begin her journey of self-discovery and growth with renewed vigour.

Pari posed a hypothetical question to keep her personal bitterness out of the session that she believed was related to complex dynamics at new family home of almost every daughter-in -law: "How can Gudiya, the bride, use the Bhagavad Gita, Chakras, and Koshas to resolve conflicts with her mother-in-law, Mataji, who insists on traditional kitchen methods and is resistant to change?"

Chan: "Good question. Let's use Kosha guidance to explain the solution. As Krishna said to Arjuna in the Bhagavad Gita,

आत्मनः आत्मनं आत्मनः योगः।

Yoga is the journey of the self, through the self, to the self.

This means our soul seeks to intellectually evolve by aligning action (body), energy (chakras), and consciousness (Koshas) of self. This alignment would help Gudiya become a being of the highest order, like Arjuna.

Pari: "So, what must Gudiya do when she introduces changes in the kitchen and Mataji feels challenged and acts with aggression?"

Chan: "Sometimes, in the heat of the moment, Gudiya may feel tempted to respond with aggression or defence. Since she lacks equal power, she might think of manipulating the situation. But none of these behaviours would bring her inner peace. Her inner voice would urge her to consider the greater good and the long-term impact of her actions on the family and her character."

Pari: "So, what should she do instead?"

Chan: "Like Arjuna on the battlefield of Kurukshetra, Gudiya should not act from a low Kosha. She would find herself trapped in self-doubt, caught between the easy, short-term path of lower Kosha traits and the difficult, long-term approach of higher Koshas. Arjuna sought counsel from Krishna, who advised him to perform duties without attachment to immediate outcomes and to focus on long-term harmony and efficiency. Gudiya should adopt a strategic approach for long-term family and personal gains."

Pari: "What steps should Gudiya follow to resolve the conflict?"

Chan: "First, identify the conflicting values (action): Understand the nature of the conflict. Just like Arjuna had to understand his duty on the battlefield, Gudiya must see that her duty is to manage the household efficiently while respecting Mataji."

Pari: "And next?"

Chan: "Second, assess the chakras involved (energy): Gudiya's Root Chakra is threatened by Mataji's interruptions, her Solar Plexus Chakra is challenged by criticism, and her Heart Chakra is impacted by the ongoing conflict. Mataji feels her authority (Root Chakra) and personal power (Solar Plexus Chakra) are threatened, and her Throat Chakra is in conflict, affecting her communication."

Pari: "What about applying Kosha wisdom?"

Chan: "Gudiya, being in Khojmaya Kosha, should use Krishna's counsel from the Bhagavad Gita to respect and acknowledge Mataji's traditional role without direct confrontation. She should subtly implement efficient methods alongside traditional ones, showing results over time. Demonstrate efficiency through action and communicate the benefits indirectly."

Pari: "How will practicing this approach help Gudiya?"

Chan: "By regularly practicing this approach, Gudiya can avoid energy blockages and create a peaceful environment for herself, fostering intellectual maturity. Fulfilling her duties and developing a stable character will ultimately lead her to attain sustainable inner-bliss, realising the true purpose of her soul."

Pari: "What if Gudiya doesn't handle the matter strategically and empathetically?"

Chan: "If Gudiya doesn't approach this strategically and empathetically, Mataji might disrupt her daily plans, creating unnecessary obstacles. Mataji's higher family status but lack of Kosha awareness adds to the challenge. Recognising that Mataji wants the best for the family, even though her actions may not align with her intentions due to ignorance, will help Gudiya remain respectful. Maintaining distance for her own sanity, Gudiya can continue to persevere on the rightful path."

Pari: "So, keeping Koshas in mind is crucial?"

Chan: "Yes. By keeping Koshas in mind, Gudiya can approach Mataji with gentle respect, nurturing her ego, which is often due to a blocked Solar Plexus Chakra. Understand that Mataji's actions come from blocked chakras, preventing her from allowing Gudiya the creative space to thrive."

Pari: "How can this understanding help Gudiya?"

Chan: "Understanding and addressing both her own and Mataji's chakras and Koshas, Gudiya can achieve greater harmony, leading to a more peaceful and fulfilling life. Practicing chakra and Kosha awareness helps recognise and avoid energy blockages early in the relationship, aiding personal evolution and protecting oneself from negative influences. This knowledge will guide your path, helping you find balance and clarity in all that you do."

Pari: "Now I understand why Ayushman chose to fulfil his duty for his family, no matter how hard it was for him personally, just like Lord Rama. Despite the personal challenges he faced, he remained steadfast in his responsibilities. Because of the reliability he has demonstrated by consistently fulfilling his duties, I can trust him completely."

Chan: "Reflecting on this, you have learned that people who listen to their soul's voice, their Krishna consciousness, and act from higher Koshas, endure hardships and persevere. They ultimately command respect and emerge as role models for others. Their actions are not just about duty, but about embodying values that inspire and guide those around them."

Pari: "This realisation deepens my respect for Ayushman and reinforces the importance of acting with integrity and wisdom in my own life."

Chan: "I'm glad to hear that, Pari. You've taken a significant step toward your personal evolution. Let me share a verse from the *Bhagavad Gita* that aligns perfectly with this transformation:

कालेऽस्मि लोकक्षयकृत् प्रवृद्धो लोकान्समाहर्तुमिह प्रवृत्तः।
ऋतेऽपि त्वां न भविष्यन्ति सर्वे येऽवस्थिताः प्रत्यनीकेषु योधाः।।

Krishna told Arjuna, 'I am time, the great destroyer, and I have come to engage all people. Except for you (the Pandavas), all soldiers here will be slain.'

Just like that, your old fears and perspectives will dissolve, making space for new ways of thinking, allowing you to rebuild your mindset and continue evolving."

Pari: "Thank you, Chan. I can already sense how this 'Personal Evolution Training' will reshape my entire outlook."

Chan: "You're welcome, Pari. Remember, growth is not just about change, it's about *building character*. Let your higher consciousness begin to connect with your subconscious. The Kosha theory you've explored—let that knowledge marinate slowly in your experience. Only when this happens will it evolve into wisdom, opening up a whole new way of seeing the world."

As Chan handed her the invoice for the session, he added with a gentle smile, "And on that note, your time today is up. Here's the bill."

Pari: "Thank you," she replied, taking the invoice. She took a picture of the whiteboard where Chan had written today's key ideas, seeing it now not as just notes, but as a piece of art—a map of her inner journey.

The seed of wisdom had been planted, and as Pari stepped out, she felt a new unity between her inner and outer worlds. The investment in her evolution wasn't just financial—it was the price she paid for her transformation, her peace. And in that realisation, she knew, as Chan had said, that building true character is the journey of life. Wouldn't anyone want to embark on such a path?

This moment anchored her to the truth—one that can only be revealed when you're ready to embrace it. Now, it was Pari's turn to let that truth become her strength.

AFTER FINISHING FAMILY DINNER AND TUCKING LUV AND KUSH into bed, Ayushman and Pari retreated to their bedroom. This was the time they usually spent reading before drifting off to sleep. However, tonight, Pari found solace in her study—a space that had become her sanctuary, a haven for the thoughts she had long kept hidden.

The gentle moonlight of the full moon, filtering through the lace curtains, painted delicate patterns on the wooden floor, as though an ethereal touch had woven itself into the quiet stillness of the night. A faint fragrance of jasmine lingered in the air, and the shelves lined with her cherished books offered both comfort and escape. Surrounded by this serene stillness, Pari picked up her pen, turning her thoughts inward. Today, she would journey through the landscapes of her past, unraveling the layers of her being, one Kosha at a time.

With Chan's guidance, she was able to observe how people behaved and she could categorise them into different stages of mental development, known as Koshas. And she began to pen in her journal:

"When I began this journey, I was at the fourth stage—the Khojmaya Kosha—caught between self-doubt over right and wrong, yet still listening to my conscience, much like Prince Arjuna. But now, I've moved to the fifth stage—the Vijnanamaya Kosha—where intellect and understanding guide me. So why should I respond to defensive, aggressive, or manipulative people by mirroring their behaviour? Instead of lowering myself to their level to prove I'm right, I can set clear intellectual boundaries. This way, I can recognise negative influences as soon as they arise, whether in my surroundings or thoughts, and make the difficult choice between the lesser of two wrongs. Avoiding someone may feel wrong, but bitterness or revenge is worse. So, I choose the least harmful path in preserving myself. I can disengage mentally and emotionally, holding myself with dignity, knowing I am operating from a higher state of awareness."

She felt excited knowing that, with practice, she could perfect her ability to understand others and perhaps one day reach the ultimate stage—the Anandamaya Kosha—a state of pure bliss.

As Pari put down her pen, she felt a heavy weight lift from her heart. Her old way of thinking—the Kaurava, symbolising her inner conflicts and doubts—had faded away. Now, only her rational self—the Pandava, representing clarity and wisdom—remained.

The new mindset brought Pari a deep sense of calm and empowerment, enabling her to approach situations with clarity and composure, rooted in her expanding wisdom. Now, like the enlightened Arjuna from the Bhagavad Gita, she could focus on 'what is right,' rather than 'who is right.' This new way of thinking was instilling a profound strength within her, empowering her to influence outcomes in every situation with confidence.

From that day onward, this insight helped her feel empathy for others while remaining confident in her own stage of development and yet sans bitterness. Practicing intellectual discernment with every person she interacted daily in her life, gave her a roadmap for personal growth and freed her from the need to lower herself to others' levels to prove a point. Gradually, her calmness became evident to others, reflecting her elevated mental state.

The understanding of the Koshas had bestowed upon Pari a profound mental flexibility and freedom, allowing her to fully embrace the knowledge of 'mental strength' that was uniquely her own. At long last, she had discovered the missing piece of the puzzle, the very clue Jenni had once subtly hinted at—as though the intricate riddle of life had begun to unravel, with one more piece falling perfectly into place.

Shadows fade, love's might, what next in the light?

CHAPTER 25
FROM ME TO WE

Pari sat by the window of their San Clarion home, gazing at the first rays of dawn as they illuminated the hilltop. The soft chirping of birds and the distant hum of early morning traffic provided a soothing backdrop to her deep thoughts. "I used to be so captivating," she mused, "always making him want more." But somewhere along the way, that spark had dimmed. She felt a longing to rekindle it, to bring back the passion that once defined their love.

Over the years, routine, family responsibilities, and the pressure of living in a joint family had dulled the magic in their relationship. The vibrant love they once shared now felt like a distant memory, and a question lingered in Pari's heart: Could that flame be reignited?

In recent months, her personal journey had brought new wisdom and clarity. She had learned how to set boundaries, nurture her own inner peace, and remain composed, no matter how tough life became.

As she reflected on her newfound understanding, Pari began to wonder if she could bring that same softness and warmth back into her relationship with Ayushman. Could they rediscover the love that once lit their path? Could they rebuild their bond on a foundation of mutual respect and understanding?

With a renewed sense of determination, Pari made a decision. Their love story wasn't over yet. Armed with new knowledge and deeper insight, she was ready to embark on the next chapter of their relationship—a journey toward not just being together but finding a more meaningful connection.

As Ayushman prepared to leave for work, he noticed a subtle change in her expression. "Everything okay?" he asked, concern in his voice.

Pari smiled gently. "Yes, everything is fine. I'm taking the day off. I just need some time for myself."

Ayushman nodded, approving her decision. "That sounds like a great idea. You deserve it."

He leaned in to kiss her goodbye. "Take care, and if you need anything, just call," he said softly.

Pari nodded. "Have a good day," she replied.

Their children, Love and Kush, came running to hug her tightly. "Love you, Mamma! Bye!" they said excitedly. Pari hugged them back, her voice filled with affection. "Bye, my loves."

Once Ayushman was gone, Pari felt a surge of energy. She opened her laptop and began searching for retreats that offered guided practices for reigniting love and passion between couples. As she browsed, a memory surfaced—the thrilling excitement she had felt when they first got together. Her heart fluttered again, reminding her of the deep connection they once shared.

"We can find that magic again," she whispered to herself, a soft smile playing on her lips.

Sipping her morning tea, Pari recalled a lesson from Mr. Chan, their spiritual guide, about balancing masculine and feminine energy. "Just like the harmony between notes creates beautiful music, the balance between masculine and feminine energy strengthens a relationship. It's not just about physical closeness, but a connection of souls and values," his words echoed in her mind. The idea of energy as a currency between them resonated deeply with her.

"This feels so right," she thought. "We just need a space where we can apply these ancient teachings in our modern lives without distractions."

After an hour of browsing, Pari finally found what she had been looking for: *Blissful Horizons Resort: Rediscover Love and Connection.* It was nestled in the lap of the Himalayas, offering a retreat designed for couples to reconnect through a blend of Ayurveda, yoga, Vedanta, Shiva Samhita, and the wisdom of the Kamasutra.

That night, as they settled into bed, Pari handed the brochure to Ayushman.

"Ayushman, I've been thinking," she began, her voice calm but resolute. "I feel like there's a disconnect in the energy between us. I've made a lot of changes within myself, but now I want you to walk this path with me."

Ayushman wrapped his arms around her gently. "Pari, your growth has been incredible. I've seen how much progress you've made, and it's changed your whole outlook on life. If you're ready for this new step, then I'm right there with you."

Pari smiled, feeling her hope and love begin to bloom again. "These Vedic practices are all about balancing masculine and feminine energy. It's not about belief—it's about connection and harmony. I want us to explore this together."

Ayushman's eyes filled with admiration. "Pari, you're nothing less than a goddess to me. You've faced so many challenges and come out stronger and wiser than ever. I'm with you, and I'm ready to walk this new path by your side."

Pari felt a renewed sense of hope and excitement as they both looked forward to the upcoming retreat, knowing it would breathe new life into their relationship. Together, they were ready to embark on a journey to rediscover their love in a way they had never imagined before.

. . .

THE NEXT DAY, THEY PACKED THEIR BAGS FOR A HOLIDAY IN INDIA. They planned to leave their children in the care of their uncle Vardaan for a week-long retreat, picking up Luv and Kush from New Delhi airport hotel. This time away was not just a vacation but a purposeful journey towards rekindling their connection and nurturing their relationship with a deeper understanding.

They finished packing their bags, while their seven-year-old twins, Luv and Kush, bounced around the hotel room, excited about spending time with their cousins, Sneha and Punam.

"Are you sure you packed everything, boys?" Pari asked warmly.

"Yes, Mom!" Luv replied enthusiastically.

Kush chimed in, "We're going to the theme park, right? And the zoo?"

Ayushman smiled, ruffling Kush's hair. "That's right, buddy. You'll have a great time. Just make sure to listen to your Uncle and behave, okay?"

Vardaan arrived to pick up the boys, greeting everyone with a warm smile. "Ready to go, boys?" he asked.

"Yes, Uncle!" Luv and Kush chorused.

Pari hugged her sons tightly. "You both have a wonderful time. We'll miss you, but we know you'll have an amazing adventure with your cousins."

Luv hugged his mother back. "We'll miss you too, Mom."

Kush added, "And we'll tell you all about our adventures when you get back!"

Ayushman leaned down to give them each a bear hug. "Have fun, boys. We love you very much."

They walked their sons to Vardaan's car, helping them settle in. Sneha and Punam waved excitedly from the backseat.

Pari touched Vardaan and Sapna's feet for ashirwad(blessings) "Thank you, Bahiya Bhabhi. Take care of them," she said softly.

Vardaan smiled. "Don't worry, Pari. They'll be in good hands. You two enjoy your retreat."

As the car pulled away, Luv and Kush waved enthusiastically. "Bye, Mom! Bye, Dad!" they shouted.

They waved back. "Bye, boys and girls! Have fun!" they called out.

Pari turned to Ayushman, her eyes shining with emotion. "It's just us now," she said softly.

He nodded, wrapping an arm around her shoulders. "Let's make the most of it," he said warmly.

Pari paused, her eyes softening. "It's good to have extended family around for support. Now I understand what you've been saying all these years. I see now that nurturing these connections takes time and effort. I was naive seven years ago and saw things differently back then."

He felt a weight lift from his shoulders, appreciating her validation. "It's okay, Pari. I'm grateful that there are no misunderstandings now, and I will always respect your boundaries."

With renewed understanding, they headed back inside to finalise their preparations, ready for the journey ahead.

They arrived at Blissful Horizons Resort with a mix of anticipation and hope. The sprawling retreat, nestled in the lush greenery of the Himalayas, promised a idyllic escape from their busy lives. The picturesque backdrop of the mountains, with their majestic peaks and verdant valleys, set the tone for a journey of rediscovery.

As they stepped into the sanctuary of the Resort, they were greeted with an enchanting welcome ceremony that immediately set the tone for their transformative journey. The air was filled with the delicate fragrance of jasmine and sandalwood, mingling harmoniously with the crisp mountain breeze.

The retreat staff, adorned in traditional attire, approached them with warm, genuine smiles.

"Namaste and welcome to Blissful Horizons Resort," one of the staff members said, bowing slightly. "We are honoured to have you here."

They presented Pari and Ayushman with vibrant marigold garlands, delicately placing them around their necks as a symbol of respect and good fortune.

Ayushman smiled, "These are beautiful. Thank you."

The soft, soothing sound of a bamboo flute played in the background, creating an atmosphere of tranquility and reverence. Next, they were offered a traditional herbal drink, a refreshing concoction of tulsi, mint, and honey, served in handcrafted clay cups.

"This drink is known for its calming properties," explained another staff member as she handed them the cups. "We hope it helps you relax and rejuvenate after your journey."

Pari took a sip and sighed contentedly, "This is wonderful. I already feel more at ease."

As they sipped the soothing elixir, a sense of calm washed over them. The retreat's staff then guided them through a winding path lined with blooming flowers and lush greenery, leading to their luxurious suite. The room, a masterpiece of design, seamlessly blended modern comfort with traditional aesthetics. Rich, earthy tones were complemented by elegant wooden furnishings and intricate artwork depicting scenes from ancient Indian mythology.

"This place is incredible," he said, looking around in awe. "It's like a piece of paradise."

The large windows offered a breathtaking view of the mountains, their peaks kissed by the golden light of the setting sun. The suite exuded a sense of peace and serenity, inviting them to leave their worries behind and embrace the journey ahead.

"Please make yourselves at home," the staff member said warmly. "If you need anything, just let us know."

They exchanged glances, their hearts filled with anticipation and hope. The warm welcome and the serene beauty of Resort reassured them that they were in the right place to rediscover and deepen their connection.

Day 1: Introduction to Wellness

The first day at the Resort was dedicated to acquainting them with the retreat's offerings. They joined Anjali, their guide, for a wholesome breakfast in the tranquil dining hall, where the aroma of fresh fruits, herbal teas, and warm spices filled the air. As they settled into their seats, the tranquil atmosphere began to ease their travel fatigue.

Anjali, a knowledgeable guide dressed gracefully in an all-white cotton dress, began their orientation with a warm smile. "Welcome to Blissful Horrizons. Over the next few days, we will explore the holistic practices of Ayurveda, Yoga, and Vedanta," she said, her voice soothing and calming.

She continued, "Ayurveda, the ancient Indian system of medicine, focuses on balancing the body and mind through diet, herbal treatments, and lifestyle practices. Yoga, as many of you know, harmonises physical and mental states through asanas, pranayama, and meditation. And Vedanta, the philosophical aspect, helps us understand the nature of reality and the self, deepening our spiritual awareness and fostering inner peace."

Curious, Ayushman leaned forward and asked, "How does Vedanta help in deepening spiritual awareness?"

Anjali smiled and replied, "Vedanta teaches us about the interconnectedness of all life and helps us realise our true nature beyond the physical and mental layers. It offers insights that can lead to a more profound sense of inner peace and fulfilment, which are essential for a harmonious and fulfilling relationship."

Pari, intrigued by the holistic approach, asked, "How can these practices help us reconnect and rejuvenate our relationship?"

Anjali nodded thoughtfully. "Ayurveda will help balance your body and mind, ensuring you both feel physically and emotionally well. Yoga will harmonise your physical and mental states, making you more aware and present with each other. Vedanta will provide a spiritual foundation, helping you understand and appreciate each other on a deeper level. Together, these practices create a synergistic effect that can rejuvenate and strengthen your bond."

As they listened to Anjali's explanations, they felt a sense of hope and anticipation. They realised that this retreat was not just a getaway but an opportunity to truly reconnect and grow together.

She then shared a verse from the Katha Upanishad to emphasise the importance of being awake and aware in their journey towards deeper connection as she quotes from Katha Upanishad, verse 2.2.13:

उत्तिष्ठत जाग्रत प्राप्य वरान्निबोधत।
क्षुरस्य धारा निशिता दुरत्यया दुर्गं पथस्तत्कवयो वदन्ति॥

Arise, awake, and learn by approaching the excellent ones. The path is sharp like the edge of a razor, difficult to tread and hard to cross, so say the wise.

"This verse inspires us to rise, be aware, and seek wisdom. The journey to deep connection is delicate and requires mindfulness and effort, but it leads to profound fulfilment," Anjali explained.

They nodded, absorbing the wisdom shared, feeling inspired to embark on their journey of reconnection through the teachings of Ayurveda, Yoga, and Vedanta.

In the afternoon, they enjoyed a personalised Ayurvedic spa therapy session. The therapist described the benefits of Abhyanga massage, emphasising its stress reduction and rejuvenation effects. Later, during a meditation session led by Dheeraj, the Yoga instructor, they learned Pranayama techniques to improve focus and mindfulness. Pari requested guidance on advanced techniques like Bhastrika and

Kapalabhati, which Dheeraj demonstrated, enhancing their energy alignment.

By day's end, they felt a renewed sense of calm and connection. The retreat's introduction to ancient practices had opened their minds to new ways of nurturing their relationship, and they eagerly anticipated deepening their bond in the days to come.

DAY 2: COUPLES KUNDALINI* AWAKENING

As dawn's first light caressed the Himalayan peaks, they made their way to the arcadian meditation hall of the resort. Draped in flowing fabrics and fragrant with scented candles, the room exuded a peaceful ambiance. Their instructor, Ananda, greeted them warmly.

"Namaste, Pari and Ayushman," Ananda began, his voice a gentle balm. "Today, we embark on a journey to awaken the Kundalini energy within, nestled at the base of your spine. This awakening can lead to profound physical, emotional, and spiritual transformation."

Ananda's words hung in the air, rich with promise. He quoted from the Tantra Shastra:

शिवशक्त्या युक्तो यदि भवति शक्तः प्रभवितुं।
न चेद्व्यक्तः स्वात्मारामः तस्य यदात्मनः ॥ ६॥

When Shiva is united with Shakti, he is able to create. If he is not, he is unable to create even as his own self.

Eager to begin, they exchanged curious glances. Ananda continued, "We'll start with gentle yoga asanas to open your chakras." They moved to their mats, synchronising their breaths with their movements through poses like Cat-Cow and Cobra, demonstrated with fluid grace by Ananda.

---

* Kundalini, the sacred coil of divine energy, lies dormant at the base of the spine, like a serpent waiting to awaken. It spirals upward, weaving through the chakras, unlocking the gates to enlightenment and the mysteries of the soul.

"Excellent," Ananda encouraged. "Now, sit comfortably in the lotus position for breath work exercises to harmonise your energy." Placing their hands on each other's chests, they inhaled and exhaled together, creating a harmonious flow of energy between them.

"Imagine a warm, tingling sensation at the base of your spine," Ananda instructed, his voice like a guiding star. "As you inhale, visualise this energy rising through your chakras. As you exhale, feel it expanding within you." They followed Ananda's guidance, feeling the energy ascend through their bodies, aligning and energising each chakra.

Quoting from the Hatha Yoga Pradipika, Ananda added:

कन्दे कुण्डलिनी शक्तिः सुप्ता मोक्षाय योगिनः।
बन्धनाय च मूढानां यस्तां वेत्ति स योगवित्॥४॥

The Kundalini power lies dormant at the base of the spine, For the yogi, she is the means to liberation. For the ignorant, she is the cause of bondage. He who knows her is a true yogi.

"Now, slowly open your eyes," Ananda said gently. "Look into each other's eyes and feel the connection you have created." The awakened Kundalini energy enhanced their individual awareness and deepened their bond.

"This practice is a powerful tool for deepening your connection," Ananda concluded. "Continue to nurture this energy, and let it guide you towards a profound sense of unity and love."

They thanked Ananda, their hearts filled with gratitude and anticipation for the continued journey of their Kundalini awakening and the deepening of their bond.

DAY 3: UNION OF OPPOSITES

On the third day of their retreat, they entered the tranquil practice room where their Kamasutra instructor and Tantra sex expert, Madhavi, awaited them. The space was an intimate sanctuary, adorned with soft lighting, fragrant incense, and plush cushions. The gentle strains of Raga Khamaj filled the air, enhancing the mood with its romantic and sensuous melody.

Madhavi, a graceful woman in her forties, wore an elegant orange embroidered linen sari. Her calm and knowing demeanour, coupled with her poised appearance, exuded a comforting yet empowering presence that encouraged openness about pleasures. With a seraphic smile and gentle, inviting eyes, she began the session by addressing the couple.

"Welcome, Pari and Ayushman. Today, we will delve into the wisdom of the Kama Sutra, focusing on mutual engagement, conflict resolution, and retaining the charm in your relationship. Are you ready to begin?"

Pari's eyes sparkled with eagerness. "Yes, Madhavi. We're eager to learn."

Holding Pari's hand, Ayushman added, "Absolutely. We want to deepen our connection and keep the spark alive."

Madhavi smiled warmly, her presence a calming balm. "Excellent. The Kama Sutra emphasises the importance of mutual engagement," she began, her voice a gentle melody. "This means being fully present and attentive to each other's needs and desires during intimate moments. The Kama Sutra, though primarily a treatise on love and sexuality, also touches upon the spiritual aspects of intimate relationships."

She recited a verse, her words weaving a tapestry of connection:

संपूर्णहृदये दम्पत्योः यथा बन्धनं सदा।
तथा तन्मयतां यान्ति लोके लीलामयस्य च॥ २॥

Translation: When the hearts of the couple are fully united, Their bond becomes everlasting, They attain a state of playful oneness, transcending the world."

Madhavi let the words linger in the air, allowing their meaning to seep into their hearts. "This verse speaks to the profound union that transcends the physical realm, where love becomes an eternal dance of playful oneness."

With a s smile, she continued, "How do you currently ensure you are both engaged during your intimate times?" Her question, like a soft breeze, encouraged them to reflect deeply on their shared moments, paving the way for a more connected and harmonious union.

Pari sighed softly, "We try to focus on each other, but sometimes it's challenging with all the distractions."

Ayushman nodded in agreement. "Yes, we do our best, but we could use more guidance on staying fully present."

Madhavi moved closer, her presence both soothing and empowering. "Being present involves more than just physical closeness. It requires mental and emotional attention as well. Look into each other's eyes, listen to each other's breath, and feel the energy between you. This creates a deeper bond."

She continued, "Now, let's discuss conflict resolution. Promptly addressing misunderstandings is crucial for maintaining attraction and harmony. How do you handle conflicts when they arise?"

Pari glanced at Ayushman. "We talk about them, but sometimes it takes a while to resolve."

He agreed. "I agree. We could be better at addressing issues right away."

Madhavi nodded understandingly. "It's important to resolve conflicts swiftly to prevent them from affecting your intimacy. Think of your mind during lovemaking as a rosebud nestled among thorns. The rosebud symbolises the tender potential of your intimacy, while the thorns represent unresolved conflicts and unspoken words.

Just as one must tread carefully to avoid being scarred by the thorns, you must navigate your emotions and communications with care to allow the rosebud of your love to fully bloom.

To nurture this delicate blossom, prioritise open communication and work together to find solutions. Retaining the charm in your relationship means regularly appreciating and admiring each other's qualities. Can you share some ways you currently do this?"

Pari smiled. "I compliment him on his strengths and express my gratitude for his support."

Ayushman added, "And I make sure to notice and praise her efforts and achievements."

"That's wonderful," Madhavi praised. "Regular appreciation helps keep the excitement alive. Remember the verse from the Kama Sutra:

यदा भवेत् समावेशः कलहस्य तु कारणम्।
उदाहरणमत्रोक्तं योषितः प्रियदर्शनम्॥

This means, 'When there is mutual engagement and the reason for conflict is resolved, it is an example of how to retain the charm and desire of a woman.' How do you interpret this?"

Pari reflected thoughtfully. "I think it means that by being fully engaged with each other and resolving conflicts quickly, we can maintain our attraction and connection."

He nodded. "Yes, and it also suggests that appreciating each other regularly helps in keeping our relationship vibrant and exciting."

Madhavi's eyes sparkled with approval. "Excellent. Modern science offers insight into the intricacies of our desires. For women, the hormone oxytocin, often dubbed the love hormone, plays a crucial role in their sensual pleasure. This hormone is released when a woman feels relaxed and at ease. In contrast, men may seek pleasure driven primarily by testosterone, or by a combination of oxytocin and testosterone during intimate moments."

She gazed intently at him, her eyes soft yet serious. "Before a man can truly enter a woman's body, he must first find his way into her mind. In the delicate dance of love, the mind is where foreplay begins, weaving through thoughts and emotions long before physical touch. When conflicts linger, they drain a woman's reservoir of oxytocin, the elixir of her pleasure and openness. But when a woman is truly pleased, her defences melt away like frost in the morning sun, revealing a landscape of vulnerability and heightened sensation.

Every touch then becomes a brushstroke on a canvas, painting a picture of mystery and adventure for her partner to explore. The key to this deep connection lies in the poetry of open communication, where desires and boundaries are whispered like secrets in the night. Mindful, attentive touch must be practiced, a sacred ritual that ensures their bond remains strong. Regular, intimate moments, free from the world's distractions, are the gentle rain that nourishes their love, allowing it to bloom in all its beauty."

She continued, "The question then becomes: are you both willing to explore new techniques and settings to keep your intimacy vibrant and fresh? These steps can significantly enhance your emotional and physical bond, ensuring a more fulfilling relationship."

Pari's face lit up with excitement. "Definitely. We love trying new things together," she said, looking at him with a gentle bite on her lip, feeling vulnerable yet thrilled.

He squeezed her hand, his eyes full of warmth. "Yes, we're open to anything that can deepen our bond. The mystery and excitement of exploring new facets of our connection are what I cherish most about Pari's active presence in our intimate moments."

"Wonderful," she began, her voice soothing and calm. "By exploring new techniques, settings, and role-playing scenarios inspired by your readings and mutual fantasies, you can keep your relationship vibrant, mysterious, and passionate."

Madhavi smiled warmly at them, holding up a guide she had meticulously crafted. "This guide," she began, her voice soft yet full of conviction, "embodies the potent harmony between the Kama Sutra and Tantra. By weaving together the practical, pleasure-focused techniques of the Kama Sutra with the spiritual, chakra-based practices of Tantra, couples can attain a holistic and transcendent experience of intimacy, elevating their intellectual growth to eternal bliss, or Anandamaya kosha while living through grihastha ashrama. Grihastha Ashrama is the householder phase involving marriage, family, career, societal duties, and religious practices."

She paused, letting the words sink in, before continuing, "This guide serves as a pathway to not only deepen your physical connection but also to awaken your souls. It fosters a union that is both deeply satisfying and spiritually enriching. Through these teachings, you can transform your intimate moments into sacred experiences, enhancing both your relationship and your personal well-being."

As her tone softened, she transitioned them into the next segment of the session, her words flowing like a gentle, hypnotic current. She touched their hands tenderly, lifting them slightly, and whispered with the warmth of a sensual catalyst flame like a tantric hypnotist, her voice a soft, mesmerising murmur through the mic:

"Today, we will blend the ancient wisdom of the Kama Sutra with the Chakra system of Tantra. This will not only deepen your physical connection but also elevate your spiritual bond. I will be your invisible guide. Focus on my voice and follow my lead. Rest assured, your privacy is protected, and you are unseen. You may choose to follow your energy today or return later. You are free to leave at any time you prefer."

She paused to let her script sink into their minds before continuing, "Let's begin."

Madhavi's voice, warm and encouraging, began to guide them: "First, we explore the Root Chakra, nestled at the base of the spine. This sacred centre embodies your foundation and sense of grounding. When the tumult of a woman's mind finds peace, she blossoms open, inviting exploration from her base of spine upwards, seeking to affirm her allure."

As "Shiva Samhita" states beautifully in the context of Kundalini and sexual energy:

कन्दोर्ध्वे तूष्णिमायाति तद्व्यूढं कुण्डली शक्ति।
शक्रनेत्राग्निसंयुक्ता तदा भवति निर्वृतिः॥ ५६॥

Above the root, the silent Kundalini power arises, like a serpent coiled, moving upwards with the fire of Shakti. When united with the fire of the Third Eye Chakra, bliss arises."

Madhavi: "Now, Ayushman, visualise your touch as the movement of your masculine energy, akin to a male serpent tenderly approaching its mate in nature's dance. The male serpent, with grace and reverence, seeks to affirm his strength through her, reveling in the delicate balance of allure and caution. Now, visualise the male serpent's body gently aligning with the female serpent's lower form, feeling the profound stability and connection that binds them."

He visualised his touch moving with gentle grace, while she closed her eyes, feeling the imagined warmth and steadiness of his energy aligning with her own.

Madhavi: "Pari, focus on your breath and sense the grounding energy flowing through you. The male serpent gently caresses his tail upwards from the female serpent's cloaca to the base of her spine, creating a sense of security and trust."

As he visualised moving his warm palms gently upwards along Pari's form, Pari felt a profound sense of stability, imagining the tender caress of his touch.

Madhavi: "Now, visualise the Sacral Chakra, just below the navel. This chakra governs creativity and sexual energy. The male serpent would move his touch to the female serpent's midsection, just above the cloaca."

He shifted his visualised touch to Pari's midsection, feeling the warmth of her waistband, while Pari imagined the creative and sexual energy flowing between them, heightening her senses.

Madhavi: "The male serpent would gently draw the female serpent closer, assuring her of his protection and love. The female serpent would feel the flow of creative and sexual energy between them."

As he visualised drawing Pari closer, firmly holding and pulling her waist, Pari felt a surge of warmth and connection, their energies intertwining like a symphony.

Madhavi: "Next, visualise the Solar Plexus Chakra, located just above the navel. This chakra is about personal power and confidence. The female serpent would visualise pressing her form against the male serpent's, sensing his strength."

Pari visualised pressing her body against his, their heartbeats in unison, each thump a testament to their shared strength, while he felt the profound connection of their synchronised energies.

Madhavi, her tone infused with warmth and depth: "The male serpent caresses the female serpent gently, their tongues flicking in a dance of sensory exploration. This would activate their Solar Plexus Chakra, blending their personal power and confidence."

Their visualised connection deepened, and they felt a powerful surge of energy, their bodies responding to the ancient rhythm of their souls.

"Now," Madhavi instructed, "focus on the Heart Chakra, located in the centre of the chest. This chakra is all about love and compassion. The male serpent would gently entwine with the female serpent, revealing her heart centre."

He visualised undraping Pari with grace, revealing the soft curves of her body, each movement an act of reverence. They visualised their connection deepening, their Heart Chakras bursting open with warmth, the room filled with the soft glow of their bond.

"We now move to the Throat Chakra, located at the throat," Madhavi continued, her voice a soothing guide. "This chakra governs communication and truth. The female and male serpents hiss sweet affirmations to each other, expressing their love and admiration."

They visualised whispering softly, their words filled with love and appreciation, their voices blending into a harmonious melody.

Madhavi's voice a gentle guide: "We move to the Third Eye Chakra, located between the eyebrows. This chakra is about intuition and insight. The serpents lock their gaze, looking deeply into each other's eyes."

Their eyes locked in their minds, a deep connection forming, a silent dialogue of love and understanding passing between them.

Finally, Madhavi's voice carried them to the pinnacle of their journey: "The Crown Chakra, at the top of the head. This chakra is about spiritual connection. The male serpent coils with the female serpent gently."

He visualised gently entwining with Pari, their bodies aligned.

"As they unite physically, in their minds," Madhavi's voice was a soft, soothing murmur, "they would feel the spiritual connection between them. Their bodies and souls merging as one, in a dance as timeless as the universe itself."

"Feel the sacredness of this moment," Madhavi's voice was now a mere whisper, enveloping them like a warm embrace. "This is not just physical; it's a communion of your spirits."

Madhavi's voice gently guided them back to the present. "You have now experienced the powerful synergy of the Kama Sutra and Tantra. Remember, this is not just a physical act but a spiritual journey rooted in mutual respect and shared aspirations. Cherish and nurture this connection always."

"Upon return to your cottage today, let go of any inhibitions and immerse yourselves in this divine dance. Now, you may kiss and hold each other, feeling the intensity your mental engagement has created in your physical state, knowing that great intimacy is a committed mind's play, not merely a physical engagement."

As they held each other, they felt reassured that the freshness of their bond was still alive, experiencing the same electrifying romance they had felt in their teenage years before fully consummating their relationship. With a deepened understanding of that familiar feeling, their hearts and souls united, prepared to walk the path of love and connection that awaited them.

They realised that the mystery and adventure of their connection lay in their mindful reciprocation of each other's feelings, both inside and outside their bedroom. This revelation brought them a renewed sense of connection and anticipation for their future together. Madhavi's teachings had not only enhanced their intimacy but also infused their relationship with a sense of sacredness and purpose.

As they exited the training suite, they thanked Madhavi with heartfelt gratitude. Their hearts were filled with love and excitement for the journey ahead. The lessons from the Kama Sutra and tantra, combined with their own commitment, promised to keep their relationship vibrant and passionate for years to come.

THE MOON HUNG LOW IN THE SKY, CASTING ITS SILVER LIGHT ACROSS the room. The soft rustle of silk and the lingering scent of sandalwood filled the air. Pari, dressed in a delicate ivory silk sari, sat by the edge of the bed, her bare feet resting on the cool marble floor. The pleats of her sari cascaded around her, hugging her form with graceful elegance. Her long hair, adorned with jasmine flowers, flowed down her back, their fragrance mingling with the night air. A distant flute played a melancholic note, its melody a tender lament that seemed to rise from the earth itself, carrying with it the deep, ancient rhythms of love and longing.

Ayushman entered the room, his form dressed in a simple white dhoti, his chest bare except for the sacred thread resting against his skin. The soft drape of the fabric emphasized his strength, and his presence exuded both serenity and power. His eyes met Pari's, filled with admiration and the depth of a love that had matured over years of shared dreams and challenges.

In this moment, they were more than just husband and wife—they were two souls, seeking something deeper, something sacred. Ayushman walked over to her, his hand extended, and Pari took it without hesitation. There was a silent understanding between them, a shared desire to connect on a spiritual level that transcended the physical.

"You look beautiful," Ayushman whispered, his voice thick with emotion. His fingers lightly touched the edge of her sari, feeling the fine fabric between his fingertips. The delicate folds of the sari reminded him of the intricate layers of their love—strong, yet fragile.

Pari's heart quickened at his words, but she remained still, her gaze steady and calm, knowing that tonight was different. It wasn't just about passion; it was about union—of their bodies, their souls, and their energies. She smiled softly, her eyes gleaming with both excitement and devotion.

As Ayushman slowly began to unwrap her sari, his movements were reverent, as though he were unveiling something sacred. The fabric slid gently off her shoulder, revealing the golden hue of her skin underneath. Each movement was deliberate, slow, and filled with tenderness, as if undressing her was part of the ritual—each layer removed symbolised a step closer to the essence of their being.

Pari let the pallu fall, her heart beating in rhythm with Ayushman's breath, as he traced his hands over her now-bare shoulder. He paused, allowing the moment to settle, his fingers brushing against the delicate strap of her blouse. He slid it gently down her arm, revealing the soft curves of her body. The energy in the room shifted, intensifying with every touch.

As his fingers caressed the slope of her breast, he gently circled her nipple, his thumb grazing it with a lightness that made her gasp softly. Her eyes closed in response, feeling the surge of warmth that radiated from her Heart Chakra. It was more than just a physical sensation—it was a deep, soulful connection, awakening her Anahata Chakra, the center of love and compassion. Her body responded, her breath quickening as Ayushman continued to explore her with reverence.

He took his time, his fingers softly caressing her other breast, moving in slow, deliberate circles. Pari's breath hitched, her body arching toward him, surrendering to the growing desire within her. Her nipples, now firm under his touch, sent waves of pleasure through her. Ayushman's fingers trailed down her torso, his touch respectful yet filled with a quiet intensity. He paused at her navel, gently caressing the soft skin, awakening her Sacral Chakra—the seat of her sensuality and creativity.

"Let me love you as you deserve to be loved," Ayushman murmured, his voice a tender prayer. His hand moved lower, gliding over her abdomen, before slipping beneath the folds of her sari. Pari gasped as his fingers gently touched her clitoris, the sensitive nub swelling under his careful touch. Ayushman stroked her slowly, his movements gentle and deliberate, heightening her pleasure with every passing second.

She moaned softly, her body responding to his every touch as the energy between them surged. Her Sacral Chakra pulsated with life, her sensual energy flowing freely as Ayushman continued to pleasure her. His fingers moved with skill, circling her clitoris, gently increasing the pressure in rhythm with her breath. Pari's hips began to move in sync with his touch, her desire building with every stroke.

"Yes," she whispered, her voice breathy and filled with need. "Don't stop."

Ayushman's fingers slid lower, gently exploring her, sliding between her folds. He was mindful of her response, every movement designed to increase her pleasure. He alternated between stroking her clitoris and gently sliding a finger inside her, finding a rhythm that brought her closer to the edge.

As Pari's pleasure grew, so did her desire to give back. She reached for Ayushman, her hands trembling with anticipation. Taking his manhood in her hand, her touch was both firm and gentle. She caressed him with a rhythm that matched his own, her fingers moving in sync with the desire that pulsed between them. Her mouth followed, enveloping him with warmth, her tongue tracing the sensitive ridge with precision. Ayushman groaned, his body responding to her every touch, his senses heightened as he teetered on the edge of ecstasy.

With their senses fully engaged, their Third Eye Chakras began to open, their connection deepening beyond the physical. It was as if they could see into each other's souls, communicating in a language that transcended words. The energy between them flowed freely, harmonizing their bodies, minds, and spirits.

Ayushman gently pulled Pari onto the bed, positioning himself above her with grace. His hands rested at her hips as he entered her slowly, their bodies merging in a perfect rhythm. The sensation was intense, a merging of their physical selves with the spiritual union they had cultivated. Each thrust was deliberate, a dance of passion and connection, activating their Solar Plexus Chakras, the center of their personal power. The music, now a distant hum, seemed to fade into the background as their breaths grew ragged, the climax of their union drawing near.

Pari's body arched beneath him, her fingers tracing the contours of his back, her nails lightly grazing his skin. Their connection deepened with every movement, their souls entwined in a sacred dance. Pari squeezed him tightly within her thighs, her body responding to his with primal need. As Ayushman continued to move within her, the energy in the room surged upward, through the central channel of their spines, awakening their Kundalini energy.

With each movement, the intensity grew, their bodies reaching toward the edge of bliss. Ayushman's hands slid to Pari's hips, pulling her closer as they reached their climax together. A radiant infusion of love and energy seeped into their brahma nadi, surging from the base of their spines to the crown of their heads, activating their Crown Chakras. Their souls intertwined, creating a moment of pure bliss that transcended the physical realm.

They held each other tightly, breaths mingling, hearts beating in perfect harmony as they attained a blissful awakening—through a sacred act of 'couples kundalini awakening' meant to unleash their inner creativity, their Shakti from the dormant Shiva energy.

Ayushman spoke tenderly, "Pari, I love you." His eyes held a warmth and adoration that was impossible to miss. "Having you by my side— such a charming, playful wife—is truly the greatest fortune of my life."

"Ayushman, I love you too!" Pari whispered, her gaze filled with longing. A soft smile danced on her lips, and Ayushman could no longer resist. He drew her into a deep, passionate kiss, filled with every ounce of love he felt for her.

Wrapped in each other's arms, they savoured the sanctity of the moment. It wasn't mere physical closeness; it was the merging of souls —an intimacy that felt almost sacred, inspired by the wisdom of ancient texts. This closeness opened up new vistas of love for them to explore.

With a mischievous smile, Ayushman said, "You know, ever since you sorted out the 'I am my own happiness' thing, everything's changed. I don't have to play the 'mood fixer' anymore. It's like living with a mysterious warrior who needs no saving!"

Pari gave him a knowing smile. "Oh, really? So, I was needy before?" she teased, a twinkle in her eyes.

Ayushman chuckled. "Not needy, just a bit... emotionally high-maintenance. But now? Your independence is incredibly alluring and seductive!"

Pari laughed. "I'm glad you think so. And honestly, when you finally got my desire for financial independence, I found you much wiser too and that's kinda' sexy!"

Ayushman's eyes sparkled with admiration. "And that's what makes it all the more special."

Pari nodded in agreement. "Yes, we've found our balance." She paused thoughtfully, then added, "You know, I've been thinking..."

Ayushman raised an eyebrow playfully, "Uh-oh, here comes the deep thought!"

"Oh, hush," Pari laughed, giving his arm a light slap. "No, seriously. All that we've learned from Vedanta and Tantra—why don't we write a book about it?"

Ayushman burst out laughing, "Oh, so we've accidentally become marriage gurus now?"

Pari laughed along. "Exactly! Just think about it—a guide that gives people practical tips on how to maintain their own happiness while nurturing their relationships."

Ayushman looked intrigued. "Like 'The Art of Keeping Yourself While Keeping Your Marriage'?"

Pari winked. "With some secret knowledge sprinkled in, of course!"

Ayushman nodded thoughtfully. "To be honest, it's like we've cracked the code of this whole marriage labyrinth. True happiness lies not in changing the other but in becoming better yourself and sharing that joy."

Pari grinned. "Look at you, getting all philosophical. I quite like it."

Ayushman laughed heartily. "Well, it's true. We've learned so much. The parts of Vedanta and Tantra that directly apply to marriage—they really deserve attention."

Pari's eyes lit up. "Absolutely! We should definitely share how focusing on yourself, rather than trying to change your partner, strengthens relationships."

Ayushman pulled her closer. "So, through this book, we'll raise awareness in the world—show people how two individuals can re-wire themselves in marriage, according to the ancient Indian wisdom?"

"Exactly. If we can go from co-dependent to balanced, anyone can," Pari said with a laugh.

Ayushman kissed her forehead lovingly. "Alright, you write the introduction. I'll stick to inspirational quotes."

Pari smiled warmly. "Deal. And yes, we should also include how to keep passion alive in a relationship."

Ayushman smirked. "Now that's my area of expertise."

"And don't worry," Pari smiled, "I'll make sure it includes ways to make you feel loved every single day."

"Now we're talking," Ayushman laughed.

There was a new light in their eyes. They knew that their next journey wasn't just for them—it was for everyone who longed for balance and joy in their relationships. With this renewed purpose, they embraced each other lovingly, their soft words fading into the tranquil night.

Is it the end, or the murmur of a new dawn's unfolding?

AFTERWORD

In the year 2017, four years had passed since Pari and Ayushman joyfully rekindled their passion. Their love had only deepened, their journey marked by enduring passion and unwavering resilience. One tranquil morning, Pari found herself in her cherished corner of the house, gazing out at the rolling hills. The early light bathed the library in a warm, serene glow, illuminating the rows of bookshelves that held countless stories and memories. It was the perfect ambiance for introspection and creativity.

As she hummed the nostalgic title track of her favourite 1990s TV series, childhood memories washed over her. "सृष्टि से पहले सत नहीं था असत भी नहीं... (Before creation, there was neither the known nor the unknown)," she softly sang, her heart swelling with emotion.

Inspired by the harmony of past and present, her thoughts began to flow effortlessly. She picked up her pen and let her emotions guide her, crafting the poem, "From Shadows to Light: A Quest." Each word was a testament to her journey, reflecting her dreams, the challenges she had faced, and the strength she found within herself.

As she penned the final lines, Pari felt a profound sense of fulfilment. She realised that their story was far from over; many beautiful chapters were yet to be written. Her love for Ayushman and her passion for life had only grown stronger over the years. The future was filled with endless possibilities, and she was ready to embrace them all.

From Shadows to Light-A Quest

Once, I soared like a maiden of feathers,
Limitless and untouched,
Exploring the boundaries,
My inner self unseen and untried,
I thrived without need for defence,
Feeling invincible in my flight,
Presuming myself unstoppable!

Unaware, I ventured into uncharted domains,
Where unseen spectres lurked,
And darkness engulfed me with each stumble,
As failures mounted.
Then, my quest commenced.

In unfamiliar realms, I confronted myself,
Exposed to inner fears,
And unearthed hidden passions and drives.
From ignorance to enlightenment,
Wisdom blossomed, wounds began to mend.

Now, armed with courage and self-mastery,
I craft my own ecology.
With tested resilience, I am unstoppable!

ABOUT THE AUTHOR

Harvinder Kehal Jain is an author, speaker, and community leader whose work empowers women to bridge the gap between patriarchy and partnership. Born in Patiala, Punjab—the city of gardens—to a proud Army family, her upbringing was shaped by discipline, resilience, and high performance. Her mother, Charanjit Kaur, retired as a teacher from an Army school, and her father, Sardar Shangara Singh Kehal, a Maths teacher in the Army Education Corps, instilled in her a lifelong ethic of preparation with his favourite quote by Malcolm X: *"The future belongs to those who prepare for it today."*

In 2010, Harvinder migrated to Australia with her husband Saurabh and their young son. She soon discovered the cultural challenges of being a migrant woman—navigating accent barriers, humour, and social connection in corporate spaces—while raising a young family. Yet it was during her corporate career, after delivering a Diversity & Inclusion talk at Australia Post, that the spark for her book ignited. *Wifed in India* was born from the realisation that many educated, capable women lose their most productive years in marriages that demand silence and sacrifice.

Blending neuroscience, NLP coaching, myotherapy, and the timeless wisdom of the Bhagavad Gita, Harvinder equips women with the missing literacies of modern companionship: emotional, sensual, and wealth. Her writing and coaching help women reclaim authenticity, reset or release their marriages with clarity, and step into relationships that honour their full selves.

In July 2025, Harvinder joined BRMC – Ballarat Regional Multicultural Council as a Family Violence Community Engagement Worker, where she amplifies the voices of CALD and migrant women, creating safe pathways toward empowerment. Known as a fashionista determination in her eyes, she delights her friends by unapologetically living with authenticity—whether walking into a room in designer heels or sharing stories that make others feel alive. At home, she cherishes her quieter rituals—dancing when no one is watching, listening to Hindi classics, and anchoring her household in the daily rhythm of the Hanuman Chalisa and Mahamrityunjaya Mantra.

Harvinder is also a speaker who has delivered keynotes and talks at corporate and community events, including AMP Towers Melbourne and Australia Post. She inspires audiences to reimagine relationships, embrace emotional literacy, and live consciously in a modern world.

Beyond these titles, Harvinder also carries the name **Siya**, given to her in marriage. A name she once resisted—believing it carried exile and endless proving—but later reclaimed with pride. Today, she signs her work as Siya, honouring the resilience, empathy, and discernment she cultivated through her journey.

Wifed in India is more than a book—it is a movement. It challenges women to have the audacity to live the life they deserve, to make conscious choices about marriage, and to embrace both their sensuality and empowerment without apology. Through her words and her work, Harvinder—now embracing her identity as Siya—is building a legacy of resilience, authenticity, and emotional literacy for women everywhere.

✉ Contact Siya (author@wifedinindia.com) to speak at your next event and bring powerful conversations on marriage, empowerment, and conscious living to your audience.

Pooja Badola, Editor

WE, POWER THE CHANGE!

You've made it to the end of *Wifed in India*, which means you've already taken the first step toward reimagining marriage, reclaiming your voice, and daring to live with dignity.

But this is not the end — it is the beginning of a movement.

Like Pari, the protagonist inspired by my lived experience, too many women see their prime years wasted after marriage. They grew up smashing academic records, carrying passion like a flame in their hearts, only to watch that flame dim under the weight of outdated expectations.

I do not want another generation to go through this. And I cannot do it alone. The flame in your heart is what powers this historical movement. And now, I invite you to **Power the Change.**

By leaving a review, sharing your reflections, or simply placing this book in someone else's hands, you are telling another woman who may be silently struggling:

- You are not alone.
- Your marriage does not define your worth.
- You deserve to thrive in your prime.

If these pages gave you even a spark of courage or reminded you that your voice matters, take a picture with the book, post your review, and use the hashtags **#ThriveDaughters** and **#BetiBasao**. Every act of sharing is more than support — it is an act of generosity that lights the way for someone else.

You may also share your reflections directly with me at **author@wifedinindia.com**.

Or tag our community online:

- **Facebook page**: *WIFED IN INDIA*
- **Instagram**: *@wifedinindia*
- **X (Twitter)**: *@wifedinindia*

Thank you for having the audacity to carry the flame. Together, we will **Power the Change** — so our daughters do not merely survive, but truly thrive.

With gratitude,

Siya